Ba

These tiny b...
even the strongest man...

Three passionate novels!

In June 2006 Mills & Boon bring back
two of their classic collections, each
featuring three favourite romances
by our bestselling authors...

BABY LOVE

Marriage and Maternity
by Gill Sanderson
The Midwife's Secret
by Fiona McArthur
The Midwife Bride by Janet Ferguson

OUTBACK PROPOSALS

Outback Mistress
by Lindsay Armstrong
Outback Baby by Barbara Hannay
Wedding at Waverley Creek
by Jessica Hart

Baby Love

MARRIAGE AND MATERNITY
by
Gill Sanderson

THE MIDWIFE'S SECRET
by
Fiona McArthur

THE MIDWIFE BRIDE
by
Janet Ferguson

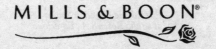

MILLS & BOON®

MILLS & BOON and MILLS & BOON with the Rose Device
are registered trademarks of the publisher.
Harlequin Mills & Boon Limited,
Eton House, 18-24 Paradise Road, Richmond, Surrey, TW9 1SR

BABY LOVE © by Harlequin Enterprises II B.V., 2006

Marriage and Maternity, The Midwife's Secret and The Midwife
Bride were first published in Great Britain by Harlequin Mills &
Boon Limited in separate, single volumes.

Marriage and Maternity © Gill Sanderson 2002
The Midwife's Secret © Fiona McArthur 2002
The Midwife Bride © Janet Ferguson 2002

ISBN 0 263 84963 5

05-0606

Printed and bound in Spain
by Litografia Rosés S.A., Barcelona

MARRIAGE AND MATERNITY

by

Gill Sanderson

Gill Sanderson, aka Roger Sanderson, started writing as a husband-and-wife team. At first Gill created the storyline, characters and background, asking Roger to help with the actual writing. But her job became more and more time-consuming and he took over all of the work. He loves it!

Roger has written many Medical Romance™ books for Mills & Boon®. Ideas come from three of his children – Helen is a midwife, Adam a health visitor, Mark a consultant oncologist. Weekdays are for work; weekends find Roger walking in the Lake District or Wales.

Don't miss Gill Sanderson's exciting new novel
A Nurse Worth Waiting For
out in July 2006 from Mills & Boon
Medical Romance™

For Kate Conlan, Marie Murray and Sheila Walsh – Three writers of Southport Writer's Circle who have helped me so much.

CHAPTER ONE

THE night shift hadn't started well for Sister Angel Thwaite.

There were five babies in the neonatal unit, enough to keep her reasonably busy. Then came a desperate phone message. 'Come along to Theatre, meet your consultant there. We've got an urgent Caesarean section. Baby an estimated thirty-four weeks.' Angel winced. This was going to be hard.

The full horror of the situation only revealed itself as she talked to Linda Patterson, the paediatric consultant.

'We've no idea who the mother is. She was in a car crash, brought into A and E. Someone noticed the contractions, put her on a monitor. Her waters broke, heart rate and oxygen saturation levels crashed and she turned blue. We think she might have had an amniotic embolism.'

Angel nodded. Amniotic embolisms were very rare, but when they happened they were nearly always fatal. Amniotic fluid was forced into the mother's bloodstream. The mother died shortly afterwards, and usually the baby died, too. 'How's the baby?'

'Well, she's still alive.'

They were in a recess to the side of the main operating theatre. Angel had checked the Resuscitaire, the machine they would use to do what they could for the baby once it was born. Until then all they could do was wait and watch the team round the main operating table.

There was something about the green-clad team's demeanour that told her that the news wasn't good.

Suddenly they were in business. A bloody, sticky child was brought over to them.

'Mother didn't make it,' a voice said. All attention was now on the baby. It might make it—if they were lucky.

The baby was almost motionless. Angel did an instant Apgar test, assessing colour, heart rate, muscle tone, breathing and stimulus response. The baby scored four out of ten, not good. She was floppy, blue, there was little respiratory effort. She had suffered severe birth asphyxia. Her dying mother had not been able to give her the oxygen she needed.

Quickly she was sucked out then intubated and ventilated, oxygen being pumped into her system. After a while there seemed to be a positive response. She was less blue.

'Let's get her back to the unit,' Linda said.

Once in the unit the baby was quickly weighed—all decisions about feeding, drugs and oxygen depended on her weight. Then she was put in an incubator, ventilated again and connected to the full monitoring system.

Angel didn't exactly enjoy the work. This little girl was fighting for her life, you couldn't enjoy that. But technology and scientific knowledge were helping the fight, and Angel felt proud that she was helping, too.

Now heartbeat, blood pressure, temperature, respiration levels and oxygen saturation were all being monitored. Linda slid in an UAC line—an umbilical access catheter—through the umbilicus and then the baby was X-rayed to ensure that the tube to her lungs and the line were in place. She was written up for antibiotics and morphine.

'We really ought to have a signature for permission to give vitamin K,' Linda said. 'I need a parent.'

'The mother's dead and no one knows who or where the father is.'

So Linda gave the vitamin anyway. She couldn't let her charge have a smaller chance because of an administrative problem.

The little girl stabilised. 'I think she's going to make it,' Linda said. 'I didn't have high hopes but now she's got a fighting chance. I know you'll do one-hour observations and with any luck all should be well. I'm going off to bed. You know when and if to ring me?'

'I know, Linda. I don't think it will be necessary.' The nurse and the paediatric consultant beamed at each other. It might be late at night but they were happy with what they had done. A good evening's work.

Three hours later Angel was hard at work. There was no end to the paperwork. But no sooner had she started than there was a tap on her door and June Wright, her assistant nurse, peered round. 'There's a man come to see that new baby—you know, the one whose mother was killed. He says he's a doctor but not for this section.'

The door to the neonatal unit was, of course, locked. No one was allowed in unless they had the code to the door or a good reason for visiting.

'It's four o'clock in the morning. That baby has seen all the doctors she needs to see. Tell this one to come back later in the day.'

June disappeared, and then reappeared two minutes later. 'That man's getting very angry, Angel. He says the dead woman was his sister, he's her only relation. He's just joined the hospital—he's the new surgeon in the cardiac unit. If we want to check on him that's fine, but do it quickly. His name's Michael Gilmour.'

'What was that name?'

June looked surprised at Angel's horrified tone. 'He says he's Michael Gilmour. Angel, are you all right? You've gone very pale.'

Angel gripped the edge of her desk, looking downwards so that the junior nurse could not see the riot of emotions that must be so clear on her face. 'I'm a bit tired,' she gasped after a while. 'Working nights is never much fun, is it?' This was an excuse. So far she had been fine. 'Let's go and see this man, shall we?'

She forced herself to stand and smile at June. Michael Gilmour wasn't such an uncommon name. How she hoped this man would be a stranger!

Rapidly she walked down the corridor, June having difficulty in keeping up with her. This was a nightmare, she needed to wake from it. If she could. At the ward entrance she peered into the little CCTV screen. The man was there, smiling unpleasantly up at the camera. He knew he was being watched. And Angel's nightmare was going to continue.

'Wait till I get to my room,' she told June, 'then let him in. Show him the baby, tell him anything he needs to know. Tell him he can't see me—that is, he can't see the sister. It's not…it's not convenient.'

'Right,' said June, obviously thinking that everything wasn't right.

Angel half ran back to her room. There was no way she could get out of the ward. Perhaps he might see the baby then leave. She was hyperventilating, her chest heaving with the unaccustomed stress. She needed to calm down. He might just go.

After ten minutes she was allowing her hopes to rise.

Perhaps he had seen the baby and left. Then there was a bang on her door, it flew open and the man stood outlined there. A tall man, casually dressed in jeans and sweater, with longish dark hair that needed brushing.

For a moment there was silence. Then he said, 'It's no good hiding. You knew I'd get to talk to you, didn't you?'

She was all right now. The fear had gone, there was only a cold anger. 'Yes, I guessed you might. And you know the reception you're going to get.'

'When I asked who was in charge your nurse said it was Angel—the sister. I couldn't believe it so I asked her to describe you.'

'That nurse could have answered all your questions. Please, sit down. Now you're here there's some paperwork we have to—'

'Paperwork! I didn't come here to...'

'I said sit down! I'm in charge of this ward now and, doctor or not, if you cause me any trouble I shall have absolutely no hesitation in sending for Security and having you thrown out. You know that, don't you?'

She could tell what an effort it cost him to contain his anger. But somehow he did it, sat in the chair she pointed to. 'Yes, I'm only too well aware of what you can do. Angel, I—'

'Angel is the name for my friends. In here I am Sister Thwaite. ''Sister'' will do if you have to call me anything.'

'Sister it shall be.' He appeared to have regained control of his temper. She knew this was when he was most dangerous.

'Mr Gilmour, first of all may I say how sorry we all are about the death of your sister. I didn't know that...' She caught herself, she should stick to being professional. 'I'm sure everything possible was done for her at A and E. If you wish, you could talk to Dr Croll. I gather he was her doctor when she was brought in.'

'I've already spoken to Dr Croll.' He pressed his hands to his face, as if he were trying to rub the tiredness away. 'My sister and I were estranged for all of our lives. Now there's no chance for us ever…I'm sorry, I mustn't burden you with my problems. Tell me about the little girl.'

Angel felt a fleeting touch of pity for him, knew she had to fight it down.

'Of course. The baby was born by Caesarean section. She's premature, about thirty-four weeks, and presented us with considerable problems, as I'm sure you gathered from seeing her. But for the moment the paediatric consultant thinks she's holding her own. Do you know what the baby was to be called?'

'I've no idea. I haven't seen my sister for fifteen years.'

'I see. Then you have no idea about her present address, where we might find her husband or partner? Are there any other relatives?'

'My sister was what they call "of no fixed abode" and there are no other relatives but me. I gather her partner disappeared the moment she told him she was pregnant. If you do find him, tell me. I'd like to come down and break his neck.'

'I'm sure you would. So you are the baby's only relation to come forward—her guardian. Do you want to come with me to see her?'

'I have seen her and I'm lost. I'm a cardiac specialist, all babies look the same to me.'

'She's tiny but she's perfect, a lovely baby,' Angel

said. 'She is a person Mr Gilmour, she needs love from the minute she's born.'

'Don't we all?' he growled.

He looked at her. She reddened under his gaze, then fought back. 'Yes, we all need love. And consideration.'

The anger seethed between them. Perhaps it was a good thing when June looked in and said, 'Shall I get coffee?'

'No,' said Angel.

'Yes, please,' said Mr Gilmour.

They spoke at exactly the same time.

'Fetch two,' Angel said reluctantly. 'Mr Gilmour is helping me with some background queries.'

After a moment's silence, he said, 'It was a shock, finding you here. You were the last person I expected to meet. The last I heard, you were running a nursing station in the mountains of South America.'

'I was there for four years. Then I came home for good. My father is dead, my mother needs me and I love this place. This is where my roots are.' She caught herself. 'Not that it is any of your business.'

June came back with the coffee, and as they drank Angel reached for the forms she knew had to be handed in. 'You're a surgeon—you know that we have to fill in all these forms. I'll take what details you can give me, and forward them to anyone else who is concerned. We don't want to cause you too much pain. You understand that the police will want to speak to you? This was originally a traffic accident.'

'I've already made a short statement to them.'

'Good. The baby is quite premature, and prems always give cause for alarm. She will need to stay here in Intensive Care for a while, and then I suspect a week or two in the postnatal ward. Are you married, Mr Gilmour?'

'No, I am not married—not now.' The words were spoken with emphasis.

'Then I expect that all the arrangements for her post-hospital care will have to be left to you, though we will have to inform Social Services. She will probably need reasonably competent nursing for a few months after she's discharged. As I said, you are her guardian.'

It appeared that this was a new idea to him. 'Of course,' he muttered. 'I'm her only relation. All she's got now is me. But I don't know how to look after a baby! I'm only here for six months then I'm taking up a post in central London. I hadn't heard from my sister for years when she phoned me last week. I didn't even know she was pregnant. I only knew that she had come to visit me when they rang through a couple of hours ago from A and E. They'd found my name and address in her purse.'

Angel hadn't realised that, and for a moment he had her sympathy. 'Oh, Mike, that must have been a shock! You never mentioned you had a sister!' She reached over, touched his arm.

'We were brought up separately. When I was younger I tried to get to know her, wrote to her and so on but it never worked.' Then he looked down at her hand. 'Sympathy?' he asked.

'For anyone who's had a loss.'

'What about sympathy for anyone who suddenly acquires an unexpected child?'

Before she could answer, June appeared. 'Sorry, Angel, but if you've a minute I'd like you to look at the monitor for baby George. BP seems just a bit low and—'

'I'll come at once, June. Will you take Mr Gilmour

to see the new admittance again? Then see him out and report back to me. Mr Gilmour, I'll forward your name to all the other concerned parties. I'm afraid there'll be rather a lot of sorting out to do. And could you give us a name for the baby?'

'A name? I'm to choose a name?'

'Who else? Apparently you're her only relative. The staff here like babies to have names. It makes their charges more real, like proper human beings.'

'A name. What should I call it? Perhaps…'

'She's not an it, Mr Gilmour. She's a she.'

'Of course. My mistake. Very well, you may call her Suzanne.'

'Suzanne?' Angel paled, as if she had been struck. Suzanne was her own middle name. He was playing mind games with her.

'Suzanne sounds a very good name to me. It's honest and reliable and it will go well with Gilmour. Suzanne Gilmour. It's got a ring.'

He stood to follow June down the corridor. At the door he turned and said, 'You don't need to worry about the…about Suzanne, Sister. It's come as a shock but she's my responsibility now and I'll do all I can for her.' Then he was gone.

Angel went to look at baby George, decided that nothing much was wrong but that she would change him. There was comfort in handling the tiny body, following the well-known procedures. This was a part of the job she loved.

But her emotions were in turmoil. Still, she could take it, she was tough. Life in South America had taught her that. And other things had made her tough, a small voice reminded her.

When she had finished she saw June outside the room and beckoned her in. 'Has Mr Gilmour gone?' she asked.

'Not yet. He's standing by the incubator, staring down as if he doesn't know quite what to do.' June giggled. 'He asked quite a lot of questions about you, Angel— you know, casually, but it was obvious what he was doing. Said there was no wedding ring on your finger. D'you think he fancies you?'

'I doubt it. And nothing on this earth would make me go out with him.'

June looked surprised at Angel's outburst. 'I think he's nice. He's got a fit body and those blue eyes, and the way he smiles…not that he smiles very often.'

'It's what's inside a person that counts,' said Angel. 'If he asks for me again, say I'm busy with one of the other babies.'

In fact, this was true. The readings on baby George's monitor had continued to fall. Angel decided to call for the SHO. She still wasn't too worried, but rules dictated that a doctor had to be called. And she wanted to be certain so she rang through. Five minutes later Barry French ambled into her room, still rubbing his eyes.

Angel looked at him with vague affection. Barry was older than the average SHO, about her age. He had been a nurse before he trained to become a doctor, he knew how nurses felt. 'Problems with baby George?' he asked.

'You asked to be kept informed, so this is me informing you. I suspect it's nothing but I want you to make that decision.'

'OK, I'll take a look.'

So they looked at baby George together, and decided that as yet there was no real call for alarm. 'Don't forget,' he said, 'I don't really need sleep. You phone me and I'll be here.'

'Keen, alert and yawning like mad,' she said. 'Want a drink before you go back to bed?'

'Might as well. I'm not going to sleep for a while.' So they sat, drinking tea and talking idly in her room. After the confrontation with Mike it was restful. There was no need to shout, no need to take care with every word in case something was said that shouldn't have been said.

'Doing anything special on Saturday night?' he asked casually after a while. 'Fancy a meal or something somewhere?'

She thought about it for a minute. Over the past few weeks she'd realised he had been trying to decide whether to ask her out. He was basically a shy young man. Her first intention had been to say no—now she wondered why. 'Why not ask June out there?' she suggested. 'She's unattached and you could have a good time with her.'

'Hmm,' he said judiciously. 'I'm not exactly looking for a good time, whatever that is. I just want to get to know you better. A lot of the time you seem a bit…reserved.'

'I probably am,' she said. 'But, yes, Barry, I'd love to come out with you. Shall we sort out the details later? You're probably too tired to make decisions about your social life now.'

'I think you're right.' Barry unfolded himself from his seat. 'Really looking forward to it, Angel. Oh! Can we help you?'

Angel looked up, behind her. Mike was in the doorway. She wondered how long he had been there, how much of the conversation he had heard. Had he heard Barry ask her out? Well, what she did was no concern of his!

'Just to say that I'm going now. Sister, thanks for your help. I'm sure we'll meet again soon.'

'Probably not,' she said stiffly. 'I'll be working nights for a while. Most arrangements will have to be made in the daytime.'

'Of course. Goodnight, then.' And he was gone.

Barry turned to her, lifted his eyebrows in enquiry. 'Brother of that woman who died after the car crash,' she explained, 'and apparently only relation of the little girl we admitted to come forward. He's a surgeon here.'

'Poor devil. There's going to be a lot of work for him.' Then Barry, too, was gone.

Half an hour later June also came in, for a well-earned break. 'Been a busy night,' she said. 'I still think that doctor fancies you. Asked even more questions.'

'He's just nervous,' Angel said, 'not sure how he'll cope with his new family.' In fact, she knew that somehow he would cope very well. He always did. She wondered if he would keep quiet about her or if it would suit him better to let everyone know. Perhaps not. Or perhaps tomorrow, when she came in for her night shift, all of the hospital would know that seven years ago, for nine brief months, Angel Thwaite had been married to Mike Gilmour, the new Cardiac surgeon.

The temperature in the neonatal unit was kept very high—certainly it was a little too warm to work in comfortably. Angel changed into her outdoor clothes, walked quickly down the corridor and out into the freezing early morning. The biting wind shocked her—but it revived her as well. From the moors above came the smell of wet heather. She loved it.

Behind her was the grey stone mass of Micklekirk Hospital. Built in the nineteenth century and built to last.

Round the back there were new, sometimes portable buildings, all the necessities for a large regional hospital. But when she thought of where she worked, Angel always thought of this frontage.

Micklekirk itself was only a small town. The hospital served much of the country area not covered by Carlisle on one coast or Newcastle-upon-Tyne on the other. There were other small towns, villages, farms without number. Angel loved the area. This was where she belonged.

Ten minutes' drive from the hospital was the village of Laxley. It was the nearest place to Angel's home. She had been christened in the parish church, taught in the village school. It was a lively village—not pretty enough to attract large numbers of visitors, but deeply loved by most of its inhabitants.

Angel turned right out of the main street and after a hundred yards pulled up outside a stone bungalow. Valley View it was called, and outside was a FOR SALE sign. Angel pulled up her coat collar, got out of the car and walked to the end of the road. Beyond was the valley—a vista of fields, little farms, grazing sheep. Valley View would suit Angel and her mother very well—if they could afford it.

She was driving back to the main street when she saw an older woman waving vigorously to her. Annie Blackett. Angel knew her quite well.

'We've just sent Jackie off in the ambulance,' Annie said breathlessly. 'I've got a few things to do and then I'll go down to see her. They say it'll be a while before the baby comes.'

Angel looked at the tired face smiling down at her. 'Jackie will be all right,' she said. 'I'm not on her ward but tonight I'll drop in and see how she's getting on. Be good for her to see a familiar face.' She paused a moment and then asked, 'How's Terry managing?'

'Not well. I think prison is worse for him than it is for most people. But I tell him, he did the crime, now he must pay for it.'

'Will they let him out to see the baby?'

'I think so. There's some sort of new release system operating. He's been out once to see Mr Martlett at Brock Farm. He's offered Terry a job as a shepherd and a cottage when he gets out.'

'That'll be good for him. And Terry can do anything with animals. Mr Martlett will get a good worker. I can remember Terry in Miss Beavis's class in primary school, he used to help me with painting.'

'He's doing a lot of it now. Says it calms him down. I hope so. Bye, Angel. You look as if you need a sleep!'

Angel sighed and drove on. Terry Blackett in prison! He wasn't a bad lad, just not used to large numbers of people. They upset him, confused him. He'd got mixed up with some people from the coast, something to do with handling stolen cars, and the police had caught him. Handling cars! Terry was the was the best animal handler for miles. His girlfriend, Jackie Taylor, was pregnant. She'd been living for a while with Terry's mother. And in time Terry would come out, marry Jackie, take on the cottage and the sheep and be happy. A local problem, a local solution. People would cope.

She drove through Laxley, up onto the high moors road. Here the wind tore across the flattened grass, shaking her car. It nearly always did in winter. This was cold, bleak country. And then up ahead she saw a blackened stone building, seemingly huddled against the winds that tore at it. High Walls Farm. The place she lived.

The warmest room was the kitchen, and there she

found her mother, waiting as usual with a hot meal. 'Ma!
I do wish you'd stay in bed, look after yourself a little!'

'I'm fine. And if you're to work all night there's no
way I'll let you cook your own breakfast.'

'I'm young and I'm strong and I haven't got a heart
condition. You've remembered your pills?'

'If I didn't you'd soon let me know. Yes, I've taken
them all. Be glad when I don't have to bother! Now,
this afternoon, I can take the bus and—'

Angel put down her knife and fork with a crash. 'No,
Ma! You're going for your appointment and I'm coming
with you. We go in my car. No argument. Don't spoil
my breakfast by trying.'

Marion Thwaite looked at her daughter fondly.
'Sometimes you remind me of me,' she said.

Fifteen minutes later Angel was in bed, giving thanks
for the invention of electric blankets but still clad in a
set of fleecy pyjamas. There was no heating on the top
floor of High Walls. She was tired, but there was still
time for a moment's worry.

Her mother had mitral stenosis, a heart condition
brought on by rheumatic fever when she was seventeen
and then a long hard life in an unforgiving climate. The
cardiologist had said that an operation was inevitable—
probably an artificial valve would be fitted. He would
refer her to a surgeon but afterwards she must have an
easier life. No way could she stay in High Walls.
Everyone knew that. The difficulty was persuading her
mother to move. Angel had hoped to move to Valley
View, the bungalow in Laxley. But worryingly, they
couldn't quite afford Valley View and Angel hadn't been
able to find anywhere else.

Just as she was going to sleep something else struck
Angel, something she should have thought of before. As

the new cardiac surgeon, Mike was the man she would meet tomorrow with her mother. Her mother had never known about Angel's all too brief marriage. At the time she'd had problems of her own. More trouble!

Angel slept then, and had odd dreams of the past.

CHAPTER TWO

'THE leaflets in this section aren't very interesting,' Marion Thwaite said cheerfully. 'The last hospital I visited had little books warning me about diseases I'd never heard of and sexual practices that I would have thought impossible. This place is very boring. Just leaflets about diet.'

'Hush, Ma,' Angel scolded. 'Not everyone has your sense of humour. This waiting room isn't so bad.'

She supposed that all visits to a hospital involved waiting—certainly her own unit was no different from any other. But Micklekirk had decided that if waiting was necessary, it could at least be made comfortable. She sat with her mother in a very pleasant area, with a television set, not playing too loudly, a pile of newish magazines and papers and a small coffee-bar down the corridor. It could have been a lot worse.

Angel had asked the receptionist—yes, there was a new surgeon, yes, he was Mr Gilmour. So be it. She had never doubted Michael's skills as a doctor. In fact, a part of her was very pleased that he was to be her mother's surgeon. She only hoped they wouldn't fight again.

She kept her eyes fixed on the door to his room. When the time came, she would walk in coolly, the professional to the end. So she was surprised and a little irritated when he walked down the corridor and came up behind her. 'Angel...that is, Sister Thwaite, what are you doing here?'

She stood, turned to look at him. Now he was every

inch the professional. Under the white coat were dark suit trousers, gleaming shirt, college of surgeons tie.

'I'm here with my mother, Mr Gilmour. She's been referred to you by the hospital cardiologist who thinks she may need surgery.'

'Of course. Please, come into my room. I've just got a quick call and then I'll be with you.'

Angel would rather have waited outside, but he ushered them into his consulting room and then left. She looked round. Apart from the usual medical appliances and computer terminal, there were academic books, surgical magazines, filing boxes. There was one unusual feature, though—a whiteboard had been installed on one wall. But other than that, nothing to show the man's personality. This was the room of a man who didn't intend to stay long.

'Mrs Thwaite!' he came back in the room, file clutched under his arm. 'My name's Michael Gilmour. I'm a surgeon here. And I've already met your daughter.' There was no double meaning, no secret message for Angel. This was a simple statement of fact. 'First of all, Mrs Thwaite, I'm very happy for your daughter to stay here with you. But this is your decision. If you'd rather she waited outside then that's fine.'

'She's my daughter and a nurse. She can stay.'

'I'm glad you feel that way. Now, I know that every time you come here the doctor does the same things, so I'm going to as well. Just a quick examination.' He took the usual pulse, blood pressure, listened to the heart. Then he sat behind his desk, riffled through the file of notes in front of him.

'You must be tired of tests, Mrs Thwaite. I see you've had a chest X-ray, an electrocardiogram, an ultrasound echocardiogram and a coronary angiography.'

'Seems a lot of tests when all that appears to be wrong with me is that I get tired easily.'

'But you also suffer from dyspnoea—sometimes it's hard for you to breathe?'

'I can always sit down.'

'But I'll bet you don't. Do you?'

'Well, I have my work to do.'

You're fifty-five, you don't smoke and never have done, you drink alcohol in moderation and you've cut down on the salt in your diet.'

'My daughter insists I cut down on salt,' Marion said drily. 'Makes food seem tasteless.'

'I sympathise. According to this sheet you filled in, you don't overeat and I see you're quite thin. You've got ruddy cheeks, but in this case that's not a sign of a healthy life outdoors. You're a widow and you...live with your daughter. Any more children?'

'I have a son who lives down near London. He works very hard, but he keeps in touch.'

'You've never fancied living near him? Say, if your daughter got married, moved away?'

Was this a gentle dig? Angel wondered. She said, 'That's not likely to happen. I'm settled here.'

'And living near London would kill me,' her mother added.

'I see.' Mike turned the sheets in front of him. 'Dr Forrester, whom you saw last, has got quite a lot to say about where you both live—High Walls Farm. Tell me about it, Mrs Thwaite. Tell me about your life there.'

Angel had to admit that Mike was good at his job. He was drawing her mother out, making her talk about her early life as a teenager in Laxley. 'So, when you were seventeen you thought all you had was a sore throat? And since the family was busy, you didn't want to

bother them. Only when you were really ill, had agonising joint pains, did they realise you'd got something
very bad—rheumatic fever. Did you develop chorea—
what's known as St Vitus' dance?'

'No. The doctor came out every day. He said it might
develop but it didn't.'

'That's good. Now, tell me about your married life—
you were married to a farmer?'

He got her to talk about life on the farm, the way she
had tried to keep some of it going when her husband
had died. And he learned about the winds that scoured
the moors, the cold in winter, the fact that the house was
almost impossible to heat and draught-proof.

'I know it isn't ideal. But it's my home, it's the
Thwaite home. My husband, my mother and my grandmother all lived and died there.'

'I know it's been your home, Mrs Thwaite, but you're
going to have to think very strongly about moving. You
know your body can only take so much. How many
times have you had bronchitis in the past ten years?'

Marion was silent, so Angel said, 'Nearly every winter, Mr Gilmour. And last year I found out that on occasion she was spitting blood.'

'Right.' He stood and went to the whiteboard, quickly
drew a picture of a heart. 'What's wrong with you, Mrs
Thwaite, is that this valve here—we call it the mitral
valve because it looks a bit like a bishop's mitre—is not
able to do its job properly. The opening here between
the left atrium and the left ventricle can't open far
enough. Now, one treatment would be to use a transatrial
balloon catheter—to put something in the opening and
try to force it open. However, I suspect that wouldn't do
much good. What I'd like to do is replace the valve with
an artificial one. Now, this is a serious operation. I have

to tell you that it could go wrong. But the consequences of not having it could be far more serious. I'd like you to go away, think about it and then let me know.'

'I'll have the operation. I'm fed up of being tired all the time, of not being able to do things.'

Mike smiled. 'I'd still like you to talk to your son and daughter, perhaps have a word with your GP.'

'She'll have the operation,' said Angel. 'I think it's a good thing, so does my brother, so does the GP. We'd like it as soon as possible.'

'Very well. But if you have second thoughts, do let me know. Mrs Thwaite, we can see to your heart. But you must take things easy now and after the operation you mustn't go back to that house. You'll be weak for quite a while and, frankly, your body won't be able to stand it. D'you fancy some kind of retirement flat?'

'I'd rather die at High Walls than live in a town,' Marion said. 'But Angel's been on at me to move and we have something in mind.'

Mike looked at Angel. 'There's a bungalow for sale called Valley View, just up the road in Laxley,' she said. 'It would be perfect for us. Small garden, central heating, no stairs. No work at all in the house. We know all the neighbours, even the GP is handy. And my mother just has to do something. She used to be a children's nurse, but there are no children near High Walls. When she has recovered perhaps we could find her a small job in Laxley.'

'That sounds ideal,' said Mike. 'So will you buy this bungalow?'

Angel shrugged. 'We're having another look round at seven this evening. But the question is whether we can afford it. It's right at the top of our price limit.'

'That's something I can't advise you on. Right, Mrs

Thwaite, I'm putting you on my list for an operation in the next three or four weeks. Carry on with your current tablets and we'll let you know the date well in advance.' He stood, leaned over to shake hands. 'Been good talking to you.'

Angel and her mother left. Just before Angel walked through the door, Mike caught her by the elbow. 'You do know that it's very important that your mother finds somewhere less stressful to live?'

'Yes, Mr Gilmour, I do know. Thank you for your concern.' She didn't want to stay and talk further to him.

They drove back up to High Walls. 'He seems a very nice man,' said Marion. 'Have you met him before?'

'I'm looking after his niece. He was in the department last night.' Angel didn't want to go into detail, she was still unsure about Mike Gilmour.

'Well, I liked him. He seemed more human than the others I've seen—although they were good, too.'

'He has what they call a good bedside manner,' Angel said heavily. She stopped in the old yard of High Walls, the wind buffeting her car. 'Now, I'm going back for another couple of hours' sleep before we go down to see Valley View. I'd sleep easier if I knew you weren't trying to clean round this place and cook for me.'

'I'll just do the kitchen,' Marion promised. 'I'll get you up about six. Shall I have something hot ready for you?'

'No, Ma. I just won't be hungry then.' Angel sighed. If there was work to be done, her mother would do it.

That evening, they wandered round the bungalow, thinking about colour schemes, wondering where their furniture would go. This place would suit them very well. The reason Marion liked it was that there was a conservatory overlooking the valley. Even in winter she could sit out and watch the changing scene below. But it was also centrally heated, double glazed and all on one floor. The rooms were large but not too large, easy to clean. And shops and friends were only a few yards away. It was perfect, Angel thought. It was also, out of a dozen places they had visited, the only place her mother would even consider moving to.

Someone rang the doorbell. The estate agent? No, he had given them the keys, told them to return them when they were ready. Frowning, Angel opened the front door and gasped at who was there. 'What d'you want here?' she asked. It was Mike Gilmour.

He smiled and took a step forward, and she was forced to let him in. 'I said this afternoon that your mother should move and you told me about this place. I thought I would call, tell you what I thought of it.'

'We don't need your approval to buy a house,' she hissed. She wondered what the real reason was for him being here. Had he come just to persecute her?

'I think it's very kind of Mr Gilmour to come and advise us,' her mother said placidly. 'Not every surgeon would do that.'

'If I'm doing anything extra, Mrs Thwaite, it's because Angel is doing something extra for me. I've got my niece in her ward. I know she'll get the very best of care and attention there.'

'She's also being looked after by many other equally dedicated nurses and doctors,' Angel snapped.

But now he was wandering round, chatting happily to her mother. 'Gas fired central heating—good. I've noticed more than a few round here are solid fuel. And what's this?' He opened a door at the far end of the central corridor.

Angel answered. 'The last owner had his father living with him. He built on this extension so the old man could live a partly independent life. There's a big living/bedroom, an *ensuite* bathroom and a separate entrance. I suspect we'd keep this closed off in winter.'

'I see.' He looked at Angel. 'You wouldn't try to live here yourself? Have some independence?'

'No, I want to live with my mother. I've been independent, been abroad, come back here and I love it. I doubt I'll ever move.'

'No well-paid job in London beckoning?'

'I wouldn't take it for double the salary. Anyway, Micklekirk is a very good hospital. It's well managed, well supported financially. I'm pleased to be here.'

She knew there was an undercurrent to his probing questions but she didn't yet know what he wanted. So she told him the truth about how she felt. Nothing would drag her away from Micklekirk hospital.

'Good. I like it when families can stay together.' He frowned. 'Though I must say that I didn't manage very well with my sister.' For a moment Angel thought she saw pain flicker in his eyes, but he went on, 'I hope you get this bungalow, I can't think of a better place for my patient to live. Are you going back home now up to—High Walls, was it?'

'For a bite of supper and then into work,' said Angel.

'Ah. I'm only staying at Micklekirk for six months so I've got myself a room in the residency. I usually dine in the hospital, which is quite good, but occasionally I need a change. Could I invite you two ladies to dinner at that pub in the main street? I've been told the food there is very good.'

It happened again.

'No,' said Angel.

'Yes, please,' said her mother.

Then, when Angel hesitated, Marion said, 'Mr Gilmour has been very kind to us, Angel. The least we can do is accept his hospitality.' To Mike she said, 'You must come to tea soon, Mr Gilmour, if you're not too busy.'

'I should really enjoy that. Shall we go for a meal, then?' Apparently, they would.

Angel and Mike had a moment alone while her mother went to fetch her coat. 'Just what are you playing at, Mike?' Angel asked in a furious whisper.

He shrugged. 'Just trying to be helpful. And I really like your mother.'

She'd been in the Cat and Fiddle quite a lot through the years, and she recognised more than a few people there. Janet Card, a girl who had been in school with her, came over to sell some raffle tickets. 'They're trying to close the village school, you know. We're getting up a petition, forming a committee to fight the closure. Miss Beavis is the leader.'

'Miss Beavis! She must be in her late eighties!' Miss Beavis had been headmistress of the village school well before Angel's time. But then she had become a regular visitor and part-time teacher after she'd retired. Miss Beavis was formidable.

'She might be getting on, but she still stands for no nonsense,' said Janet. 'Will you come to a meeting once we've got all our support? We'll pass the word round when we've fixed a date.'

'I can try,' said Angel.

Since her mother was with them there was no need to worry—if Angel had been on her own with Mike there might have been gossip. But her mother and Mike seemed to get on well. Angel was the one left out of the conversation.

The food at the Cat and Fiddle was supposed to be very good, but afterwards Angel couldn't remember what she had eaten. She still wondered what Mike was doing here—and she was still nervous in his presence. He seemed to have got over yesterday's bewilderment and Angel couldn't tell if he was intent on charming Marion or was being charmed by her.

When they parted both Marion and Mike said that they must meet again. Angel's views weren't asked.

'Seems a very nice man, Angelina,' said Marion. She was the only one occasionally to use Angel's full name. 'Why don't you go out more often? Meet more young men? You know, I loved being married.'

'Well, I'm married to my job,' said Angel. 'And, anyway, on Saturday I'm going out with a young doctor from my ward.'

'That'll be very nice,' Marion said placidly.

That night she was working with June again. At handover they had been told that things were normal—baby George had made slight progress but baby Suzanne wasn't progressing as well as had been hoped. But there was nothing much to worry about.

For the first couple of hours Angel and June carried on with the normal work of the unit. They now had six babies there—three in cots, three in incubators. All were monitored, and they had to keep a close eye on the readings.

Baby George had at first been fed on demand, now he was fed every two hours. Angel took the cap from the tube that was taped to his face, ran through his nose and down to his stomach. With a small syringe she aspirated some of the baby's stomach contents, sucking a tiny amount up into the syringe. Good, she could tell that the milk was partly digested. She returned the contents of the syringe to the stomach, got a larger syringe and filled it with the fifteen mils of milk that George was entitled to. Then she took the plunger out of the syringe and let gravity feed the baby.

There was the baby-care routine before each feed. The eyes might need cleaning, the mouth wiped out with a damp cotton bud, perhaps a little petroleum jelly smeared on the lips. Then a quick temperature check before the nappy was changed.

It was routine work, but it was a routine that Angel loved. There was something satisfying about handling such tiny human beings. And they all had different characters.

Then there was a lull. It was too early to try to catch half an hour's sleep, so she told June where she would be, made sure she was carrying her bleep and walked out of her section and into the delivery suite. On one wall of the midwives' station was a big whiteboard with the names of the mums in labour, which room each was in and the progress they were making. Jackie Taylor was in room three, a rim of cervix showing, which meant that she would give birth at any moment. Angel frowned. It seemed rather a long time since this morning, it had been a long-drawn-out birth.

Work in the delivery suite was erratic. One night there might be a couple of births, the next night seven or eight. Tonight the midwives were busy. Angel thought she'd pop into room three and see how Jackie was doing.

'May I come in?' Angel could tell that the birth was imminent. Annie Blackett, Jackie's soon-to-be mother-in-law, was standing by the bed holding her hand. Both

seemed happy to see Angel. And the midwife was most
pleased of all. 'Angel, Jackie here is about to deliver—
can you stay here ten minutes? There's no one else to
help.'

'Happy to help out. If I'm bleeped I'll have to go
back, but we should be OK for a while.'

'Ten minutes is all I need. Bless you. Now, Jackie,
push!' Angel knew that seeing a familiar face, having
an ordinary conversation, was often the best way of coping with pain and exhaustion. As the birth progressed
she chatted to Jackie and Mrs Blackett about the future.

'They think that Terry will be allowed out to see the
baby,' Jackie gasped. 'You don't know how keen he is
to see it. Funny for a man, isn't it?'

'Not for Terry. He's always loved babies. That's why
he's such a good animal man. He thinks giving birth is
wonderful.'

'I…wish…he was here with me.'

'I'm sure he does, too. But it won't be long now,
Jackie. Just concentrate on pushing and… It's a little
girl!'

As second in the room, Angel was to take the baby.
The midwife cut the cord, Angel wrapped up the little
girl, took her to the cot and gave her the regulation baby
check—just a quick inspection to see if there were no
obvious flaws, a finger in the mouth to check for the
palate, a hand run up and down the spine. When a husband or partner was present Angel liked to do the check
with him. But, of course, Terry was in prison.

Then the little girl was laid on her mother's breast.

Angel filled in the Apgar form, giving a score of nine
out of ten. A good baby, Terry and Jackie could be
proud.

Then her bleep went.

'Thanks a lot, Angel,' the midwife said. 'Made it easier for all of us.'

'My pleasure. Jackie, I'll be in again to see you, but that's a darling baby. Don't let Terry spoil her!'

She trotted down the corridor to the nearest phone. 'Angel here, June. What's the problem?'

'Well, Mr Gilmour's here again and he's not very happy that I'm the only one in charge. He wants to know when you're coming back and says your place is here.'

'Anything wrong with any of the babies?'

'Nothing at all. They're all fine. You know I'd have bleeped you.'

'Of course. On my way back, June.'

She walked smartly down the corridor, tapped in the code to let her into the unit, moved to the room where baby Suzanne was lying. Mike was there, scowling down at the tiny pink figure. 'Sister, I thought your place was here with your charges, not wandering round the building, looking up old friends.'

What a change from the way he had spoken to her not four hours ago! She ignored him, checking the monitors of each of the babies in turn. Then she said, 'At present I'm in charge of this unit. If you have any objections to the way it is run, please, make them to the senior nursing officer. I will say that I have every confidence in Nurse Wright and that had there been any emergency I was two minutes' away. Now, how may I help you?'

He was angry again—it was too bad. She could see the glint in his eyes. She remembered how his lips tightened when he didn't get his own way. They tightened now. Then somehow he forced himself to relax. 'Angel, I—'

'I told you, visitors call me Sister.'

This angered him more than ever but no way was she going to back down. Finally, he said, 'Sister, then. Might I have a report on the progress of my niece?'

'Certainly. I have her notes here. During the day she was visited by Linda Patterson, the paediatric consultant, and this is the course of treatment she has prescribed.'

'I see.' He took the notes, leafed through them. 'It looks like she's going to make a complete recovery.'

'We hope so. But even when she's discharged she'll need nursing care for a few months. She'll need... Have you any plans for her future yet?'

'None at all yet,' he said sombrely 'It's hard to call someone a problem when she's so small and helpless, but I'm afraid she is. What would you do with an un— an unexpected child?'

'I do hope you weren't going to say "unwanted child". It's not my place to advise you what to do. I can only tell you what I wouldn't do—I wouldn't even think of abandoning the child.'

'Very noble. Rest assured, nothing will make me abandon Suzanne, Sister. And I take it you only abandon those old enough to look after themselves? In spite of any promises you might have made?'

'No, Mr Gilmour, I only abandon those so selfish that they think no one but them matters. Is there anything else?' She held out her hand for the sheaf of notes.

'Nothing else, thank you. I leave the child in your very capable hands. Goodnight, Sister. And let me say again that Suzanne will have as happy a life as I can give her and I have no intention of abandoning her.'

June came into the room when she saw Mike leave. 'Why does he always look angry when he talks to you, Angel? You don't irritate any of the other parents— you're good with them.'

'Mr Gilmour is different to all the other parents, June. Very different.'

It happened, as it so often did, in the bleakest hour of the night. Baby Suzanne had her antibiotics and seemed to be happy. But then the alarm on her monitor sounded. The oxygen saturation level was down and there was a dusky look round Suzanne's mouth.

The first thing to do was check the endotracheal tube to make sure that the oxygen mix was reaching the baby. Angel tried suction, the tube was clear. When the saturation level continued to sink Angel rang Linda, at present in the Residency.

'Increase the oxygen,' Linda said with a yawn, 'and ring me straight back. I'm not going to sleep now.' Angel increased the oxygen as she'd been told, then phoned Linda back.

'Saturation level still going down and she's looking even duskier. Heart rate isn't looking good either.' It wasn't Angel's job to diagnose, but this was a job she knew well. 'I think she's blown a pneumothorax.'

'Get the cold light out. I'll be there in five minutes.'

Angel suspected that air was escaping from one of Suzanne's lungs into the pleural cavity, the space round the lungs. This had collapsed the lung—and Suzanne needed all the lung capacity she could get.

When Linda arrived Angel handed her the cold light—in effect, an intensely powerful torch that would shine its beam right through a baby's body. All other lights in the room were switched out. Then Linda directed the beam at Suzanne's chest and it revealed what Angel had suspected. A dark shadow showed that one lung had collapsed.

There was no time to confirm by X-ray. Linda at once

put in a chest drain, sliding a thick needle into the pleural cavity and then suturing it in place. The needle was connected to a flutter valve, and the two watched as the air started to drain from the pleural cavity. Suzanne's lung should now reinflate. But had the shock been too much for her? Her heart rate and the oxygen saturation level continued to go down.

Ideally the heart rate should have been about 130 to 140 beats per minute. It was now below a hundred. The oxygen saturation level had dropped from near a hundred to seventy-two. And still both sank.

June had phoned Barry as she knew Linda would want his presence. He, too, examined the tiny form and read the notes as Linda, June and Angel looked on. Even at this stage Linda remembered that she was supposed to be a teacher. 'What do you think is the right thing to do, Barry?'

He thought. 'We've just been hoping she's strong enough to survive. Now that doesn't seem very likely. But I can't see any treatment or any medication working.'

'I agree entirely. Angel, isn't the guardian a surgeon here? Perhaps you ought to get him down.'

'I'll see to it straight away.' She walked to her office. This kind of thing happens, she told herself. It's no fault of ours, it happens. We did everything possible for the little mite, now she has to fight on her own. I've got to be professional—be caring but be detached as well. But it was hard. She had taken to Suzanne, the little girl deserved some good luck.

She had Mike's internal number on her desk and she phoned before thinking about what she was to say to him. On the second ring the phone was picked up and a sleepy voice said, 'Mike Gilmour here. This is a terrible hour to call a man.'

For a moment seven years were swept away and she was back in a time when things had been so different, when she had been so happy. No matter how little sleep Mike had had, he had always been able to wake good-humoured. It was a trait she envied. Before she could stop herself she said, 'Come on, sleepyhead, you have to wake up.'

'Angel?' Only her name and yet in the way he spoke it she could read... Nothing, she decided. She had to remember who he was, why she was calling. There was no other possible emotional relationship between them.

'I'm very sorry to have to call you, Mr Gilmour. I'm afraid Suzanne has taken a turn for the worse. Perhaps you ought to come down quite quickly.'

There was a silence and she wondered what he was thinking. When he spoke again his voice seemed to be entirely neutral. But Angel had once lived with him, she could feel the emotion under the iron control. 'You don't think she's going to make it?'

'We can't possibly tell, but she is very ill.' The next question was one she hated asking but it had to be done. 'Would...would you like me to make arrangements to have her christened? Before...in case it's too late?'

Now he was fully awake, his tone metallic. She remembered that tone so well. It was the way he sounded when he was going to do whatever was necessary, no matter what it cost. It was a tone that had always upset her. Why couldn't he give way, why couldn't he show what he was feeling? But it was now no business of hers. 'It might be a good idea. I've no idea what her mother was, but I'm C. of E. I'd like her to be christened into that church. I'll be there in five minutes.'

The hospital had an arrangement with the vicar of Laxley, who was the hospital chaplain. Angel phoned him at once. He, too, was accustomed to being called out at night. She told him what was happening, a little about Mike and the baby. Then she went back to the incubator room. They had other charges that had to be fed, changed and checked. For them life was going on. Angel found that working calmed her. Nothing was worse than just standing, watching, hoping.

Mike came down. Angel left it to the consultant to introduce herself, to explain what was happening. Then, when the Reverend Whitby came in, she took him in to meet the others. She liked Eric Whitby. He was a cheerful, hard-working man, who had given up a well-paid job as a solicitor to become a clergyman.

'Mr Gilmour, this is the Reverend Eric Whitby.'

Only then did Angel realise what Mike was going through. He stared at Eric as if he had just realised why he was there. For a moment Mike couldn't speak, then she saw him take a great breath, saw his shoulders hunch and then relax.

Mike's face was completely impassive as he shook hands. 'I'm sorry you have to be dragged out at night, Reverend.'

What an empty thing to say, Angel thought, but she understood Mike's desperate state of mind, and she knew that Eric did, too.

Eric smiled. 'You're a surgeon, and I'm sure this has happened to you. Being called out is nothing when we think of the reasons for it.'

Mike rubbed his face. Angel remembered how he used to do that when he was tired or upset. He wouldn't say anything—just rubbed his face. Deliberately repressed memories flashed through her mind. Irritated, she shook her head. This was a time for work, not reflection.

'I should know that,' Mike now confessed. 'In a lot of my cases I've noticed that when people are really...concerned, they worry about the most trivial things. I don't like it when it happens to me. But I'm this little girl's only relation, and it's come as a shock.'

Eric reached out, rested his hand on Mike's shoulder a moment. Then he became businesslike. 'I don't want to interfere with any medical procedures. There's a special service for cases like this so I'd like to baptise this child, say a quick prayer, and then, if you'd like to talk to me, Mr Gilmour, I'll stay with you as long as you wish.'

From his bag he took a silk stole, draped it round his neck. This, Angel knew, was his badge of office. 'I take it there has been no time to find godparents?'

'I'm not Suzanne's father, I'm her uncle,' said Mike. 'I want to be her godfather.'

'I'll be godmother if I may,' said Angel. 'I've only known her a few hours but I've got very fond of Suzanne.' It seemed terribly sad that a two-day-old child had so few friends, so few people who cared for her.

'If you wish to, I'd like that,' said Mike.

The service was swift. Then Linda Patterson said she would go as there was nothing more she could do. Barry said he would stay a while longer. 'Would you like to talk?' Eric asked Mike. 'Sometimes it helps. At other times I know people want to be left to themselves.'

'It's very kind of you to ask, but I think I'd like to stay here, wait and see what happens. I have some thinking to do.'

No one seemed to want to leave the room. Mike, Angel, Barry and Eric all stood and gazed at the little

white-swathed figure, the tiny pink face, the almost imperceptible rise and fall of the chest. Then they would
look at the monitor, watch the tell-tale trace of the oxygen saturation level. This was the most reliable guide
to Suzanne's progress. It was still dropping. All of them
knew what it meant—Eric had asked for the equipment
to be explained to him when he'd first started this job.

Over the past hour that trace had descended from 95
to its present 60. If it continued its downward path, in
another half-hour Suzanne would be dead.

Sixty...59...58...57... A small life, trickling away,
marked by an electronic monitor. For a mad moment
Angel thought that it was the monitor that was killing
the child, forcing the take-up rate to slow. Then she bit
her lip, pressed her fingernails into her palms. The pain
brought her round. Such thoughts were not suitable for
a nurse!

Fifty-seven...57...58... No one commented. Fluctua-
tions like this were not uncommon. Fifty-nine...60...
61... Then quickly, 64...69...

The tension in the room was palpable; this kind of
recovery could happen—but it was very rare. At 69 the
rate of increase slowed, the level dropped...68...
67...but then it accelerated again and within two
minutes the indicator read 90.

Angel looked at the set faces staring downwards. She
could tell what Barry was thinking, what June was thinking, what Eric was thinking. Only Mike remained stone-
faced. Hadn't he yet learned that letting your emotions
show was not a sign of weakness? To her his suffering
was obvious; she wondered if it was to the others.

It wasn't good just to stand there. Angel took Barry
and Eric to her room for coffee. The alarm on Suzanne's
monitor was, of course, set and June was in the room,

but Mike, his face still completely impassive, said he would stay by the incubator. Angel remembered that expression well. When Mike wanted to hide his thoughts, he could do so better than anyone she knew. But then she noticed his hands, gripping the rail of the incubator. The knuckles were white. He might not be willing to demonstrate what he was feeling—but he was certainly feeling something. Angel felt a pang of pity for the solitary figure.

Coffee was welcome. After the drama they all felt the need for something calming, soothing. 'That was a very heartening experience,' Eric said. 'I've never seen anything like that before and it made me feel...' obviously he was looking for the right words '...both humbled and grateful. I couldn't ask out there—but what are baby Suzanne's chances of survival now?'

Barry shrugged. 'Who can tell? I would say pretty good, there's no reason why this improvement shouldn't continue. And don't anyone tell me that medicine is an exact science, it isn't.'

'Nothing to do with human beings is exact,' said Eric, 'I know that. D'you think Mr Gilmour will be all right on his own? Should I take him a coffee?'

'He'll be fine on his own,' said Angel, and was conscious of the other two looking at her, wondering why she spoke with such certainty. To change the subject, she asked, 'How d'you find doctors as patients, and as parents of patients Barry?'

'Terrible,' Barry said. 'They always know too much about medicine in general, and not quite enough about this particular branch of medicine. I know we're supposed to keep patients informed—but I'm a doctor, not a lecturer.'

The other two laughed. There was still tension in the room but they were slowly feeling easier.

'So Mr Gilmour is a surgeon here?' asked Eric, 'I didn't know that. He seemed very composed, but I suspect he wasn't.'

'I was chatting to him in the doctors' lounge,' Barry said. 'He's done some high-powered work in America. Unfortunately he won't be here for long, there's a post he's been promised in London. It's a pity, there aren't many first-class heart surgeons around and we've got plenty of call for one here in Micklekirk. A man could build a reputation up here.'

'Perhaps he prefers the bustle of London to the peace of Micklekirk,' said Angel. 'I know which I'd rather have.'

She looked up as someone knocked on the door then opened it. It was Mike. 'Is everything all right?' she asked anxiously.

'Everything is fine. Suzanne continues to improve and, as you once told me, June Wright is a more than competent nurse. I'm hopeful now and it's a good feeling.' He stepped into the small room and suddenly Angel felt that it was getting overcrowded. 'I'd better soon be back in bed. I've got a full list tomorrow and I can't let those patients suffer. But I wondered if I could beg a coffee.'

Angel poured him one, strong, black and sugarless, handed it over with the words, 'Just as you like it.' Then she flinched again. How was she supposed to know that? But no one seemed to notice her little mistake.

'We've been hearing that you've worked in the States, Mr Gilmour,' Eric said conversationally. 'Coming to Micklekirk must be quite a culture shock.'

'After New York, Boston and Chicago, it is a bit of a change. But there are compensations.'

Did he glance at her as he said that?

'And does American medicine differ much from our home-grown version?'

Angel knew what Eric was doing. Mike had suffered a traumatic experience—perhaps they all had—and after such a thing there was nothing better than to be forced to return to ordinary, everyday life. This was the kind of question Mike would get all the time. It would do him good to have to answer. But she suspected that he also knew what Eric was trying to do.

Mike thought for a minute. 'Technically, America is a little ahead of us,' he said. 'Over there I get more time and more funding for my work so perhaps my results are better. But I still think the British National Health Service, with all its faults, is the best system in the world.'

She couldn't help it. 'And yet you spent seven years abroad away from it?' she snapped.

'Personal reasons,' he said smoothly. 'Thanks for the coffee, Sister. I'd better get to bed.' At the door he turned. 'Barry, Sister here told me last night that when Suzanne recovers, she'll be able to go home but that she'll require quite intensive care.'

'Probably,' said Barry. 'It's early days yet, but I think at least her first year will be difficult. After that she should be fine.'

'What'll be best for her is a loving, caring family,' said Angel.

'A loving, caring family?' he said thoughtfully. 'A pity you can't get that on prescription. I'll say goodnight to Suzanne and go to bed. You won't hesitate to phone me if...'

'We'll phone you,' said Angel.

Her other two visitors left shortly afterwards and Angel and June continued with their tasks—the feeding, observations, drugs. As ever, the familiar routine calmed Angel, reasserted her confidence. She was Angel Thwaite, a competent children's nurse, doing what she knew and liked.

Just before handover the next morning, June called her to the phone. It was Mike, asking about Suzanne.

'Much much better,' said Angel. 'It's up to the doctors to say, of course, but I would think that she's definitely on the mend.'

'Good. I'll drop in to see her at lunchtime. Are you in again tonight? Start at nine-thirty?'

'Yes. It'll be the third night of my five-night rotation.'

'I see.' There was a pause, and when he spoke she could hear the doubt in his voice. 'Angel, I'd like to meet you to chat for an hour or so before you start work. Not in the hospital—somewhere on what we might call neutral ground.'

'Meet you? Why? Oh, just a minute.'

She turned and said, 'Go and check the readings on baby George, will you, June?'

June realised she was being dismissed and thought she knew why. She winked broadly at Angel as she left. Angel sighed. She could do without this.

'We haven't seen or heard from each other in seven years. Why bother trying to talk now?' she asked.

'Because it is seven years. We're both older, perhaps wiser. There are things we have to sort out.'

'But I still don't like you.'

Now she could hear the laughter in his voice. 'Fair enough. There are times when I'm not too fond of you.

Still…can you remember anything good about the nine months we were together?'

She didn't know whether she ought to answer that question. But eventually she said. 'Yes, I remember quite a lot of good things.'

'Me, too. So meet me somewhere.'

She was going to say no, but somehow the answer came out the opposite. 'All right, then. But, understand, this is just to sort out how we work together. This is not the start of something new. We're a boring old story, everything between us is past. And I have a man in my life.'

'Ah. Let me guess, the lucky Dr Barry French. He seems a very able young man. Now, this is your area, you know the district—where shall we meet? I liked the Cat and Fiddle.'

'Not there. I don't want us to be seen by anyone who knows us, either from home or hospital.' She thought a minute. 'Five miles down the main road there's a big roadside pub called the Drovers' Arms. There's a quiet room at the back, we could meet there at about eight tonight.' If she had to meet him she wanted it over quickly.

'About eight tonight, that's fine. Will you have dinner with me?'

'No, I'll have eaten, just a fruit juice will do fine. This isn't a social occasion, it's just a meeting to get things sorted out.'

'What else?' he asked.

I'm not sure what I'm doing here, Angel thought to herself as she drove into the large car park of the Drovers' Arms. Her life recently had been happy. She had settled into living with her mother, enjoyed her work, was reasonably fulfilled. Once or twice she had been out with men but she had treated her affairs with caution. She didn't really need men. She'd had one and it hadn't worked out.

Mike was there already, watching for her, and he came out to meet her. A small courtesy but a thoughtful one. He escorted her to the quiet back room, fetched her a fruit juice and himself a beer. 'I've got exactly an hour,' she said, 'and I'm still not sure what I'm doing here.'

'I'm not sure either. But apparently, unlike you, I wanted to be here.'

She couldn't trust herself to contradict him. 'Why do you want to be here? Why do you want to talk to me?'

'Because the happiest time of my life was spent with you.'

This shook her. She was sure he was telling the truth, and knew that she had felt the same way. But that had been then. 'That time has passed,' she said. 'It passed after nine months.'

'Nine months out of a lifetime isn't long to be truly happy.'

'Perhaps you should have thought that before rushing off to America!' She was angry now. 'Mike, I don't need all this, it's a complete waste of time. We were married, we couldn't agree so we got divorced. In six months you'll be gone and I can get round to forgetting you again.'

She saw the tell-tale signs—the firming of his lips, the narrowed eyes. She had angered him, but somehow he kept control. 'There was so much between us,' he said. 'I remember it often, and even if it's now gone we should…celebrate what we had.'

Celebrate. It seemed an odd word to use. Rather than

celebrate, she had tried to forget. 'Asking me to remember is hard,' she said. 'You risk making me lose my temper.'

He grinned. 'How well I know that. Do you remember telling that paediatric consultant that he might be a brilliant doctor, but that as a human being you'd seen better specimens in the zoo?'

She flushed. 'I'm older, I'm more controlled now.' She thought a moment about the incident he'd referred to. 'But I was right.'

'I suspect you were. And I also suspect you are more controlled now.' He seemed ill at ease, not sure of what he wanted to say.

She was uneasy herself, not knowing which way the conversation was going. She still didn't know what he wanted of her. More unsettling, she didn't know what she wanted of him. 'So why did you want to talk to me?' she asked flatly.

'Somehow we have to work together, not snarl each time we meet. Be friends even—in public at least. For a start, I'm going to have to make arrangements with you about your mother. Our personal feelings can't get in the way of our professional duties.'

'I can see that. All right, Mike, we'll both make an effort to get on.'

'Fine. Because I really like Marion. Right now I'm her surgeon, and that's the most important thing between us. But afterwards, when she's recuperated, I can see her becoming a friend.'

Angel looked at him anxiously. 'That might make things difficult.'

'It's that difficulty I'm trying to sort out now. The other thing, of course, is Suzanne. She's mine now, Angel, and I'm going to be as hard as any other parent, fighting for what's best for his child. You can help me—or help her—and I want to know that I can count on you.'

This was a new Mike, and one she rather liked. 'Of course you can,' she said. 'Apart from the fact that I'm getting rather fond of Suzanne myself, I suppose I owe you something.'

'Perhaps we owe each other something?'

She didn't want to go into that. She glanced at her watch. Time had passed far more quickly than she had thought. It was time to be professional now. 'Have you made any decisions about Suzanne?' she asked. 'And, incidentally, why did you choose that name?'

'I called her after you, of course,' he said. 'I could hardly have called her Angel, could I?'

'Why call her after me?'

He grinned. 'Because the two of you have caused me more trouble and more heartache than any other women I know. It's fitting that you should share a name. As to what to do about her, I just don't know yet. I want the very best for her, and I guess I want to share in her life. But she must have a happy childhood—happier than I ever had. I have to face up to my responsibilities and I'm not going to try to wriggle out of them.' He frowned. 'And I'm starting to…love her.'

'That's the word. And I'm very pleased you're going to look after her.' She still wasn't sure how she felt about him naming the child after her. 'Now, I must go, Mike, or I'll be late for work. I'm glad we've had this talk. Quite frankly, I didn't want it but I think we've got things sorted out. Incidentally, you haven't told anyone we were once married?'

'No. I thought you'd prefer not to.'

'Best for both of us, I think.' Together they stood and moved to the exit.

After the warmth of the hotel it was bitterly cold outside. She pulled her coat around her, slipped her hands into the pockets. He walked with her to her car, stood as she took out the key. They were in the shadow of a line of trees, well away from the neon-lit façade of the hotel.

She didn't know how or why it happened. Suddenly his arms were round her, pulling her to him, his mouth coming down onto hers. So unexpected was it that she responded at once. She held him as tightly as he held her, her lips parting willingly to his passionate kiss. It was a kiss that jerked back the happiest memories of her life, and yet seemed somehow new. She had been in love with a boy, but this was a man she was holding. His body was so close. She could remember... She wrenched herself away.

'Mike, that wasn't right! You shouldn't have done that!'

His reply was soft but fierce, as if each word was meant. 'Maybe I shouldn't have kissed you, but you enjoyed it as much as I did. Didn't you?'

'That's why it was wrong. There's nothing between us now, nothing at all.' Her sudden lapse had made her angry, she wanted him to know how furious she was. 'We've just had your quiet, civilised talk, trying to sort things out between us. I went along with it. But you'd better understand this, Mike, I don't feel quiet and civilised. You let me down. You betrayed me. You put your career before our relationship and that's why we got divorced and that's why I still don't like you.'

Before he could reply she was in the car, backing away so he had to move aside. As she moved out onto the road she glanced in her mirror. He was standing motionless where she had left him.

CHAPTER THREE

IT WAS good to come off night shifts. There was the usual period when Angel's body wasn't sure whether it was day or night, but that was soon over. She would be on earlies or lates—mornings or afternoons—now for quite a while. Something to look forward to.

She enjoyed her evening out with Barry. He took her to the nearest big town, where they had dinner in a newly opened steakhouse and then went to a jazz club in the back room of a large pub. She was rather touched by that. Barry had heard her humming 'St Louis Blues' and had apparently casually asked her if she liked jazz. She had said she liked traditional jazz and so he had found a club where they could listen to it.

'You listened and then you went to that trouble just for me?' she asked. 'That was lovely of you.'

'No, just for me, Angel. I think you're well worth the trouble. And it's my training. You know that medicine largely consists of making lots of small observations.'

She sighed. 'I thought he was taking me out as a woman. And all he wants to do is make large numbers of small observations. I'm just a case to you, aren't I, Barry?'

'Much, much more than that,' he said, and though they were joking, she thought that she heard a thread of truth in his voice. She would have to be careful. She was very fond of Barry and didn't want to hurt him.

'I've really enjoyed myself. Shall we go out again soon?' he asked after he had driven her home.

51

'I've enjoyed myself, too. Yes, I'd love to go out again.' But when she got into the house she reminded herself that Barry would never be more than a friend— though a dear one. She would have to tell him that.

Next morning there was a letter with the heading of the estate agent. Excited, Angel tore it open. Perhaps their bid for the house had been accepted. But the news was bad. Feverishly, she read the three paragraphs again and again. 'Another offer…an extra three thousand pounds…would like to sell to you but must look after the interests of my client…happy to sell to you if you can match this…'

So that was the end of her dreams. There was no way she could claw together another three thousand pounds, she had gone far beyond her limit already. Now she would have to start again on the long dreary round of estate agents, looking for somewhere where her mother would be happy and that they could afford. Valley View would have been perfect! Angel said nothing to her mother, stuffing the letter into her briefcase.

She was feeling rather low as she walked down the corridor towards the neonatal ward, not paying much attention to the throng of parents, nurses and porters. Then she heard a voice shout to her, 'Hey, Angel.' She looked up. There was Terry Blackett.

He looked thinner, and paler than she'd ever seen him. There was an air of unease about him, as if he wasn't sure of his welcome here. But he was obviously pleased to see her, a familiar face.

'Terry! You've come to see your new baby? Isn't she lovely? You're a lucky lad.'

'Not that lucky, Angel. I'm on my way back now— they only let me out for a quick trip. But she's a lovely baby.'

'I've dropped in to see her now and then.' She looked at him. 'Will you be able to come regularly?'

His face now was grim. 'Not regularly. This is a new scheme, letting prisoners out so they can get used to life outside. But it only upsets me, Angel. Having to leave Jackie and the baby, and deliberately walk back into that place—you don't know what it takes.'

'I can guess, Terry. Now, look, the baby and Jackie are going to be fine, we'll keep an eye on them. Your mother says you've got another six months to go. Well, I know you're tough, you can do it. And you've got such a lot to look forward to!'

'I know that, Angel. It's the one thing that I think about. But that place…you're never on your own! Sometimes I need to be by myself, and there's nowhere.'

'You can do it! You've *got* to do it, you've got a baby to think of now!'

'I know.' He glanced at his watch. 'Better go. If I'm even five minutes late I don't get the chance again.'

'Just hang on, Terry. You'll be all right.'

There are people with bigger problems that me, she thought gloomily as she keyed in the code to the neonatal ward door. I hope Terry manages. She hadn't liked his air of quiet desperation. At school Terry had been a quiet, reasonably good child. But if he was pushed too far he could run riot.

Barry and Angel stood by the side of the incubator, looking at the little form below them. Suzanne was improving day by day. Her movements were stronger, her crying louder. She just looked a healthier baby.

'I think we can stop worrying about her now,' Barry said to her later. 'She's made good progress and her breathing and heart rate are both better than we might have thought. In a week or so I suspect we would be able to discharge her but we'll keep her in till she's nearly full term. She'll need quite intensive care for a while but she should be all right.'

'Who's going to look after her?' Angel asked, 'if Mr Gilmour is her only relation.'

Barry shrugged. 'I don't know. It's a bit difficult to say anything when the guardian is a colleague. But I guess he'll have to get in touch with Social Services, see what they can do for him.'

'We do need the beds,' Angel said doubtfully. 'She can't stay here indefinitely.'

Usually, discharging a baby was a joy. She got fond of them, of course, it was hard not to have an emotional relationship with a baby who you had watched over and helped to fight its way through to health. But when she saw proud and happy parents carrying away a tiny bundle that she had nursed through to strength, she thought hers was the best job in the hospital. Discharging Suzanne would be different.

'D'you want to have a word with Mr Gilmour when he comes down?' asked Barry. 'He usually drops in at lunchtime.'

'I'd prefer it if you did it. I'll be busy then.'

Barry looked at her oddly. She wondered if he suspected something but he said nothing. 'I'll tell him. But I bet he wants to talk to you.'

She hadn't seen Mike since their meeting in the Drovers' Arms. In time she knew she'd have to speak to him—he was her mother's surgeon after all. But for the moment she'd rather keep her distance from him. He disturbed her.

At lunchtime, when apparently Mike usually called, she intended to stay in her room. There was always paperwork to catch up on. But one of the trainee nurses knocked and put her head round the door. 'Angel, there's that Mr Gilmour come in to see Suzanne. I was just going to feed her and he wants to know if it'll be all right if he does it?'

Angel thought. After her shaky start Suzanne had been gaining strength daily. There was now no need to feed her through a nasogastric tube, she could be held and fed her tiny amount of milk by hand. Often Angel did it herself. She knew was getting very attached to the infant.

'I don't see any reason why not,' she said. 'But you stay in the room and if you're worried about anything at all, tell him.'

This trainee still thought that all doctors were wonderful. 'I couldn't tell a surgeon what to do!' she gasped.

'Mr Gilmour wouldn't mind at all,' Angel said with certainty. 'But if you like, I'll tell him.' It struck her that this might be the best way to re-establish their essentially professional relationship.

He was standing, as he so often was, looking down in the incubator. As ever, there was no way of telling what he was thinking from his expression. Then Angel noticed what he was wearing, and she sighed gently. A dark suit, a white shirt, a black tie. Dress suitable for a funeral.

'You want to feed Suzanne yourself?' she asked him.

He nodded. 'I've noticed that the other...the parents are shown how to do it. I thought I should learn how myself.'

'We encourage the parents to do it as soon as it's safe. Ideally, babies should have instant physical contact with their mothers, it promotes bonding. But if they're in an incubator, it's hard.'

'I do know the theory, Sister, and I agree with it.'
There was just a touch of dry humour in his voice.

'I'll get her out, then, and we'll prepare her feed. Sit
there and let me put a towel on your lap.'

When he was sitting she waved to the nurse to fetch
the milk, opened the incubator and took Suzanne out.
There was that indefinable—to her, exciting—baby
smell. She wrapped Suzanne, offered her to his gentle
hands. Then the feed arrived.

'Nurse Fawkes here will stay with you,' Angel said
formally. 'If there's any problem or question at all,
please, ask her.'

'Of course,' he said equally formally.

'I'll be in my room if you need to speak to me.'

As she left she looked back through the glass door of
the incubator room. He had forgotten her, and was staring down at Suzanne. There was something infinitely
caring about the curve of his head and neck, the way his
arm held the little bundle. Angel felt tears prickle in the
corners of her eyes.

Twenty minutes later he did call at her room, where
she had a coffee waiting for him. 'You've been to a
funeral?' she asked directly.

'My sister's funeral. Suzanne's mother, Monica. I was
the only mourner, Angel, and I felt sad that anyone could
be buried with not a single person there who really cared
for them.'

She could feel his desolation. 'I'm so sorry, Mike.
We've had our differences, but I would have come with
you if I'd known. I've got very fond of Suzanne and, as
you say, this was her mother.'

'Well, thanks for the thought anyway. Eric Whitby
conducted the service. He was…he was helpful. He
couldn't have taken more care if the chapel had been

full, instead of just the two of us. He talked about learning from the past and looking forward to the future. The funeral was the end of something but now I've got to think of Suzanne.'

'Does Eric know about your past?' Angel was anxious.

Mike smiled briefly. 'I didn't tell him we were married. I did tell him about the way Monica and I were brought up. But now, how is Suzanne?'

Angel relaxed. His tone was friendly, their argument at the Drovers' Arms apparently forgotten. Well, this was what she wanted, a proper relationship between carer and guardian. 'We're all very pleased with her progress. She had a shaky start but now she's doing fine. Are you making arrangements about what to do when she's discharged?'

'I'm thinking about it, but it's a nightmare. Some solution will come to me—it'll have to. There are two problems really. First, I've got to find someone to look after her here in Micklethwaite, just for the next few months. I thought of asking you if you could recommend anyone, Angel. You seem to know everyone round here.'

'I'll have a think. What's the second problem?'

'The bigger problem is when I go down to London. For the first year or so I'll be working like a lunatic. The job needs—deserves—someone who can give it all their attention. But I couldn't give it that attention unless I was certain that Suzanne was happy. I'll have to find a nanny, or a set of nurses to take over. Money's not the problem, getting the right people is.'

'I wondered,' she said. 'I'm afraid I wondered…when she was first born and I knew about your plans for the future…I wondered if you'd want to keep her.'

He shrugged. 'I'll be honest, Angel—just for a while

so did I. But then I stood there and looked at her and knew I had no choice. I wanted her.'

For a moment they were both silent.

She didn't quite know why she said it. 'I told you before—I've got very fond of Suzanne, Mike. If you just can't work something out—and if you can get someone to help—I'll look after her for a while. If you need me.' Then she sat back, appalled at what she had just said.

'D'you mean that? Please, Angel, just think about what you've said. It was something you said quickly, you haven't had time to think about all of what it might entail. I'll quite understand if you realise it's quite impractical.'

She frowned. 'It was just meant as a last resort, if everything else didn't go well for you—for Suzanne, that is. It's her I'm thinking of. I've still got my mother to worry about first and, of course, we're still trying to move. Make what plans you can, Mike, and if eventually you're really desperate I'll see what can be done, depending on my situation.'

'That's very good of you, it's an offer I really appreciate. But you know, Angel, it doesn't surprise me that it comes from you.' He lifted his cup, looked at it in surprise. 'Empty? Any chance of another cupful? You always made wonderful coffee.'

She poured him one, mildly pleased by his compliment, and spoke without thinking. 'When we had a morning off together you always got up first and made us tea in bed. Then I would get up…later…and make us coffee.'

'Later?' he said without inflection, and she blushed.

For quite a while neither of them spoke. Then he said neutrally, 'You're not your usual self Angel. Your voice is a bit flat and you look…well, defeated. I won't flatter myself that I'm the cause. Not had any bad news, have you?'

She had never been able to conceal anything from him. At times his ability to recognise her moods had been almost upsetting. There were some things she needed to keep to herself but, she supposed, this wasn't one of them.

'The bungalow you looked around—the one we were trying to buy. The agents have written to me. Someone has offered an extra three thousand pounds. There's no way I can find that, I'm stretching my limit already.'

'But won't selling High Walls bring in some money?'

She shook her head. 'Not much, because we can't sell it. It's held in trust for the family—perhaps in time my brother's children or even my children might farm it. But for the moment we've agreed to lease the building to a neighbour—Mr Martlett of Brock Farm. He already leases the land.'

'So you can't buy the bungalow?'

'Not unless I can find three thousand pounds in the next three days. That's all the time the agent can allow us.'

'A pity. That bungalow would have suited your mother perfectly. Angel, let me emphasise, High Walls isn't good for your mother.'

'I know that! But I can't find somewhere suitable and she won't move. She's stubborn.'

'It seems to be a family trait. Sorry, Angel, didn't mean to be personal. I really took to your mother.'

Three days later she saw that the bungalow had a SOLD sign outside. Well, she had expected it. But it still felt hard, and she was rather depressed when she walked into the ward.

Mike came in at lunchtime as he nearly always did, and asked to have a word. 'Angel, we need to have another talk somewhere out of the hospital. Could we go to the Drovers' Arms again?'

'Why? I thought things were going well between us. And the last time we talked there we had a fight. I just don't see the point.'

'There is a point,' he said patiently, 'but standing up in the middle of a busy neonatal ward isn't the place to consider it.'

'Is it about Suzanne?'

'Partly, but there's something else a bit more important. Listen, we really do need to talk.'

Angel sighed. 'All right, then, we could go when I finish this shift—if you can get away. Ma is expecting me, but I'll phone and tell her I'll be late.'

She wasn't really sure how she felt about this. Once she had accepted, she felt almost pleased at the prospect of a drink with him. That wasn't good.

She didn't like the way her mother coughed when she phoned but knew it would be no use telling her to go to bed. Some things never changed.

Mike was waiting for her at the same place in the entrance to the Drovers' Arms. He fetched her a fruit juice as before and insisted that she have a sandwich as well.

'I want you comfortable and relaxed,' he said, 'and I want you to promise me that you won't lose your temper. You'll listen to everything I have to say before saying anything.'

She bit into her sandwich. 'That is a bad way to start the conversation. I'm curious, of course—but I'm angry already. You've got something in mind for me, and you think I won't like it. Mike, we're not married any more. You have no say in my life and I owe you nothing.'

'Are you going to listen to everything I have to say?'

'Oh, yes. I'll listen. As I said, I'm curious.'

Now he didn't seem to know where to start. 'You told me there was no chance of you buying the bungalow that you wanted?'

'That's true. And it's gone now, I saw the sold sign this morning. Someone could offer three thousand more than I had.'

'It didn't go for three thousand more. Someone else offered five thousand, in cash, on condition that they could move in immediately.'

'Good luck to them,' she muttered. 'It must be nice to have all the money you need. How did you know that, Mike?'

'Well, I was curious.' He drummed his fingers on the table a moment, looked thoughtful. 'Just for a minute I want to go back to when we got divorced. The agreement you sent out to me stated that in our settlement you made no claims on my estate, or on my present or future income.'

'I didn't want anything from you,' she said. 'I could earn my own living.'

'But you knew I was earning a vast salary in the States. When I showed the agreement to a lawyer myself he was astounded, said I was the luckiest divorced man he'd ever met. I'd even been sending you money while we were still married and you'd saved it and sent it all back.'

'I had my pride,' she said.

'How well I know that! Well, Angel, for all your pride, I felt beholden to you. Now it's only fair that you should be beholden to me.'

She was lost, she just couldn't see the point of this conversation. 'What are you talking about?'

He took a mouthful of his beer and then said, 'I bought the bungalow.'

It took a moment for what he had said to sink in. 'You did what?'

'I bought the bungalow. I have plenty of cash. I've saved most of what I was paid in America.'

'We showed you round that bungalow, Mike! You'd never heard of it till my mother told you about it. Mike, this is truly despicable! I never thought you'd stoop to anything like this. You look round the place as our guest, then creep off to the estate agent and—'

'Angel, I didn't! There was absolutely no chance of you buying the place, you said so yourself. Didn't you? Well?'

It hurt, but she had to admit he was right. 'I suppose so. Yes, I did. There was no way I could afford an extra three thousand pounds. But why do you want it? It's no good to you. You're going off to London in a few months, it's not worthwhile moving into a place for that short time. I hope you're not going to keep it as a holiday cottage!'

'Very true, it's not worth my while moving in and, no, I'm not going to use it as a holiday cottage. Now, Angel, take a deep breath, have a drink and try to listen without losing your temper! This is serious. It concerns you and your mother.'

Perfectly calmly, she said, 'Please, say what you have to, and then I can get home.'

'Right. I have a proposal for you and your mother.' He paused, took a deep breath himself. 'I have bought Valley View. Think of it as an investment if you like. I would like to offer you a long lease on the property, you can move in at once. I've got a few calculations here, this is what I think is a fair return for me.' He pushed a piece of paper across the table to her.

She looked at what he had written, then pushed the paper back. 'Mike, you know very well that that rent is far too low. My mother and I don't want charity!'

'I knew I could rely on you to get angry,' he muttered. 'Angel, can't you just take it that this is something I want to do?'

'Why should you want to be so generous to my mother and me?'

'Well, for a start, I want to help your mother. And though this might be a lot of money to you—I don't want to boast, but it isn't a lot to me.'

'There's more to it than that, Mike. This is a very generous gesture on your part. Why?'

He didn't seem to want to answer. He drank some beer, rubbed his face, gazed vaguely round the room. Then he seemed to make up his mind about something. Looking at her intently, he said, 'We were married for nine months and I was happy then. I still have some…regard for you. I am in a position to help. I'd like to because I know perfectly well that if the situation were the other way about, you would do the same for me. Wouldn't you?'

The last two words were a challenge, and she knew she had to answer honestly. She couldn't take her eyes from his face as she desperately wondered what she could tell him. But eventually she said, 'Yes, I would do the same for you. And I still have some—we'll call it regard for you. But Mike, make no mistake, it isn't love. That has gone.'

'Are you sure?'

'I'm absolutely certain.' She didn't want to talk about

this, she felt she had given away too much already. 'Now, let's get back on the subject. What else are you getting out of this?'

'Nothing. This would be a purely business arrangement between your mother and you and me. If you're interested, perhaps you would get your solicitor to write to me.'

'I'll have to talk it over with Ma, but I know she'll be delighted.' Angel thought for a minute, reviewed the conversation she'd just had. There was something she had left out. 'Mike,' she said, trying not to sound grudging, 'this is a very generous offer on your part, and you know we're going to accept. From my mother and myself—thank you very much.'

He grinned. 'There,' he said, 'that didn't hurt very much, did it?'

For a moment she looked at him in horror—but then she had to laugh. 'Mike Gilmour, you know me too well.'

'I'll fetch us another drink,' he said.

It was good to have a short break from the conversation, she was more relaxed when he returned. 'Have you got anywhere in deciding on Suzanne's future?' she asked.

'Possibly I have, there's been an offer. Sister Parkin works on one of my wards and I—'

Angel stood, leaned over the table. 'You let Grace Parkin anywhere near Suzanne and I'll phone Social Services and see that the child is adopted! Grace is selfish, mercenary, idle and a disgrace to the nursing profession. I'm shocked that you could even—'

He laughed. 'I know all that. Give me credit for some sense, Angel. Sister Parkin made me an offer, I asked a couple of questions and then refused it. I just mentioned her to show you how hard it is to get someone exactly right. But I'm still looking. Now, sit down and finish your drink.'

'Don't do anything like that to me again,' she said, 'even as a joke.' Then she took a card from her bag and slid it across to him. 'That's the name and address of someone I will recommend to you,' she said. 'Her name is Nancy Timms. She was a children's nurse for years and she'd be delighted to help you with Suzanne. She lives only a hundred yards from High Walls.'

'Is that significant?' Mike asked quietly.

She hesitated, then said, 'As you know, I've got very fond of Suzanne. If I had the chance to take her out in the pram every now and again. I'd like that. But my recommendation has nothing to do with that.'

'I know you only want to best for your god-daughter. And I'll phone this Nancy Timms tonight.'

It was three days later when he phoned.

'Hi Angel,' he said. 'I've been to have a long talk with Nancy Timms. I've asked about her around the hospital and I think she's wonderful. However, a problem has come up since she agreed to take Suzanne in. Her daughter has got to go into hospital and Nancy will be going over to her son-in-law's to help with the children on occasion. She's willing to look after Suzanne whenever needed but, of course, is not always going to be at home.'

'So now you need somewhere for her to stay in the meantime?' she asked after a pause.

'Yes. I certainly can't take her to live with me in the residency.'

She decided to take the plunge. 'Mike, you did us a

great kindness in offering us Valley View. But if you need the place for yourself and Suzanne…'

'No Angel—it's for you and your mother. I wouldn't dream of backing out of our arrangement now.'

'Thank you Mike. In that case, we may be able to help you in return. Nancy actually told me about her daughter yesterday morning and my mother and I have had a long talk. This isn't a sudden thing, we've talked it through and slept on it and talked it through again. If it all can be arranged—if we can agree—we'd like to offer Suzanne a home while you're in Micklekirk and just till you're fully settled in London and have found a nurse or something. Sort of share her with Nancy so one of us will always be available. I've got…very close to Suzanne and would love to take care of her as well.'

There was no immediate reply and the silence between them seemed to stretch on into infinity. 'Mike…are you there?' she asked eventually.

'I'm here. I'm just too— You say you've talked this over with your mother? And you're absolutely certain yourself?'

'I said that to start with,' she pointed out, 'and you know I don't say what I don't mean.'

'Yes, I know that. My first reaction is to say that I can't think of anything better. But…your mother isn't well and I'm not sure a baby in the house is the best thing for her. At least, not till well after her operation. I need time to think, Angel. Shall we have another session in the Drovers'? Say tomorrow night?'

'We're becoming regulars,' she muttered. 'All right, I'll see you there at eight.'

They now had their favourite table at the Drovers' and the barman recognised them and smiled. Mike bought their drinks and they faced each other, each obviously uneasy. 'I've thought about this quite a bit,' he said. 'Here's a proposal, but we can negotiate if there's anything you don't like. This is only a rough plan.'

'I'm listening,' she said.

'Right. Both you and Nancy would need to co-ordinate Suzanne's living arrangements and care. I can help out, too, when I'm available, but you would ultimately be sharing the bulk of the work between you. You mother's operation is due and she will need to recuperate—we must take her health into account and make sure we don't cause her any stress before or after.'

'Nancy will keep an eye on her while I'm not there and if it becomes necessary, Ma is happy to stay at my brother's for a while. We can do this Mike,' she said firmly. 'She'll be cared for as well as Suzanne will be, don't you worry, and she'll soon be back on her feet again.'

He smiled. 'That's good to hear. In return for all your help, for the time you have her, I want you to have the bungalow rent free. When I come to leave Micklekirk I'll take Suzanne off your hands. I'm going to search desperately for someone to help me look after her in London.'

'You don't want to be parted from her, do you?' Angel asked with some interest.

'No I don't. When she came into my life first I was…confused, but now things are different. I want her with me always. We nearly had a child Angel and I—'

'We're not talking about that now! This meeting is about Suzanne.'

'Yes. Of course. It would be easier for Nancy and her family if Suzanne could stay some of the time in Valley View.'

'We can work well with Nancy,' said Angel. 'We've
already talked to her about it.'

'Good. The next thing is, I want a complete set of
everything a new baby needs. You can get me a list,
can't you?'

She was overwhelmed. 'Yes, I can get you a list. But,
Mike, you don't have to—'

'Not only do I have to, I want to. And do you know
any good local workmen?'

'I know everyone round here,' she said, her shoulders
slumping. 'Anything you need doing I can get done.'

It seemed as if she was being dragged more and more
into Mike's life again. And, what was worse, she was
quite enjoying it.

CHAPTER FOUR

IT HAPPENED at nine o'clock at night, three days later. Angel had eaten the tea Marion had cooked, they had chatted for a while and then her mother had wrapped herself in a shawl and gone to watch television in the chilly sitting room.

Angel sat at the kitchen table to run through her lists of jobs to be done and things to be bought. She hadn't quite realised what a lot of stuff needed to be bought when a newborn was coming into the household. And in the past she had advised new mums what they needed! This was learning at the sharp end. But…it was fun.

Mike had been typically direct about this. 'I want to buy what is needed. I don't want you trying to economise, trying to save me money. Whatever is necessary we'll get. I have every faith in your judgement.'

'I know someone with a second-hand pram that—'

'No. A new pram. Perhaps I'm being foolish, but you can give in to my whims.'

So a new pram was on the list—with cot, bath, baby clothes, no end of things. She was taking a guilty pleasure in making the list. Shopping would be fun.

At five to nine she decided to make herself a cup of tea, called through to the living room to ask her mother if she would like one, too. No reply. Probably dozing, Angel thought with a smile, and went to ask in person.

Her mother was slumped on one end of the couch, her face white, her breathing laboured. 'Ma! What happened!'

69

She could just make out the answer. 'Worst pain yet. Don't think I can move. Help me…help me up, Angelina.'

Angel was a nurse as well as a daughter. There was no time for emotion now, she had work to do. Quickly she pulled her mother upright, after which she could breathe more easily. After a while her mother looked slightly better.

'I'm going to phone an ambulance, Ma. You should be in hospital.'

'No! I'm all right, it was just a twinge. You know I've had them before. Now I've had my tablets I'll be all right.'

'You've never had one as bad as this and I think you ought to— Not now!'

The phone was ringing. Why did the phone always ring when it was completely the wrong time? 'Answer it,' her mother commanded. 'I can't stand the sound of a ringing phone.'

So Angel answered it. 'Yes!' she snapped.

'Not the most welcoming greeting I've ever heard,' a calm voice said. 'It's Mike, Angel. If this isn't a convenient time I can ring back later.'

'Mike? I'm sorry, I didn't mean anything. I'm a bit, well, I think—that is, I know my mother's just had another heart attack and she refuses to let me ring for an ambulance…'

'Does she need an ambulance? D'you want me to send one?' His voice was harsh, efficient now.

'I don't really think so. I was scared, Mike. I thought she might have… She's had these before, but never quite as bad as this.'

'Keep her warm, keep her upright. If her condition

gets even slightly worse, send for the ambulance and ignore what she says. I'll be there in twenty minutes.'

'But, Mike, there's no need...' Too late. The buzzing noise told her that he had already rung off.

He arrived in less than twenty minutes and she shuddered to think how he must have driven. It usually took her over half an hour. He was dressed in jeans and sweater, which contrasted with the doctor's bag.

'It's so good of you to come, Mike, but I could have sent for the GP or an ambulance. But I'm glad you're here.'

He followed her as she led him into the sitting room where her mother was sitting, now bundled in a couple of blankets. 'In a sense she's my patient already,' he pointed out. 'I've got her on my list for an operation. Call this pre-op preparation. Hello, Marion. You look just a touch under the weather.'

'Round here the weather's always bad,' she said, perhaps misunderstanding him.

'It certainly is. Now, tell me exactly what happened, and how you felt.' After she told him he gave her a quick examination, then stood there, frowning. 'Marion, I don't want any argument, it won't do you any good. I'm admitting you to hospital. I'll phone and arrange a bed while Angel packs you a case. There's no real need for an ambulance, so I'll take you in my car and your daughter can follow in hers.'

'Am I really so bad that I need to go to hospital?'

'If you stay here and have another of those attacks then you'll know what being really bad means.' He turned to Angel. 'Can we leave as quickly as possible? I'd like to get her under proper observation.'

'Of course,' said Angel.

They drove in convoy down to the hospital, Mike obviously driving so as to shake Marion as little as possible. There was a bed waiting in the cardiac ward. Angel said hello to the nurse whom she knew, and then to the house officer who would book her mother in. She gave what details were necessary and then sat in the little waiting room. She knew better than to interfere with other people's work.

After ten minutes Mike rejoined her. 'How d'you feel?' he asked.

'Well, you whipping her into hospital has made me feel worse,' she said. 'I didn't think she was this bad.'

'Possibly not, but it's as well to be careful. One thing, though, Angel. I'm not discharging her back into that freezing house.'

'I know you're right,' she said dismally. 'I'll sort something out. It's a shame the bungalow isn't ready yet.' Then she smiled. 'Ma is very much looking forward to moving into Valley View and seeing more of Suzanne. She misses children. She'll be so happy to take charge when she's well enough. And I know Suzanne will be a lovely child to look after.'

'You do?' There was humour in his voice. 'You can tell how a premature baby will develop, even though you've only nursed her for a short while?'

'Yes, I can,' she told him seriously. 'Cardiac surgeons aren't expert in everything, you know. When you've nursed prems as long as I have, you get to know how they'll behave, how they'll develop. Babies are as different as people, Mike.'

'So you think you can tell her character already?'

'I certainly do. Suzanne is a fighter. Remember that night when we had her baptised?'

'I remember it,' he said shortly. 'Not a night I want to recall.'

'Quite. Well, take it from me, a lot of babies would have given up, they would have died. She didn't. And that's how she'll be all her life.'

'I like listening to you talk about babies,' he said. 'You're enthusiastic, you love them. It's a side of you that was there but I never appreciated before—'

She thought about that. 'I think I've been complimented,' she said, 'but I'm not really sure.'

'You've been visiting your mother so you know she's a lot better,' Mike said five days later. 'She could be discharged tomorrow, but the question is, discharged to where? We've agreed not High Walls. And I don't think she's ready to move into the bungalow yet. And the bungalow certainly isn't ready for her.'

'It's all been arranged,' said Angel. 'I mentioned my brother Martin to you. He lives in London, and married with two children. Ma can go to live with them for three weeks. She dotes on the kids and she gets on very well with Alice, Martin's wife. They wanted her to live with them, but she said there was no way she'd live in suburbia.'

'Marion does have definite views about some things,' he agreed. 'Martin knows how your mother is?'

'Of course! I rang him the night Ma had her attack and I've rung every day since. He's a very busy man but he wanted to fly up at once. I told him there was no need.'

'So you're a close family? You never talked about your brother before.'

She frowned. 'That time…those months we were married…somehow they seemed a different part of my life. They weren't connected to where I'd been brought up, or the friends and family I had. In time we would all have met and got on together. But it didn't happen.'

'No, it didn't happen.' They were sitting in his room at the hospital, the cubbyhole with nothing but a desk and three chairs, a computer terminal and shelves full of books and files. He rolled a pencil across the desk, they both listened to the tiny rattle. 'Do you think…because I was a different part of your life, it was easier to cut me out?'

A few weeks ago she would have snarled at Mike that her reasons for leaving him were her own business. But he had asked gently, and it was a reasonable question.

'Probably,' she said. 'When you'd gone there was a big emptiness. But I didn't have to explain to anyone, didn't have to endure people's pity or compassion or even annoyance. Since they didn't know about you they didn't miss you. And that made it easier. How did you feel in America?'

She was wary about this conversation. Somehow they had strayed from talking about her mother, which was safe, to talking about themselves. And that usually led to a fight. But so far they had managed to remain calm. And she genuinely wanted to know how he had felt.

'I had no friends out there, only colleagues. People were only interested in my work, not in me. So I guess I was able to compartmentalise you. You were a thing apart. And I worked till I dropped and when I dropped I slept.'

'I did something similar. I gave up the Buxton job, went to South America. That was hard work, too.'

'Our parting seems distant now. As if it happened to someone else.'

She thought. That was exactly right. She *could* look back on it as if it had happened to someone else. 'Perhaps it was my fault in the beginning,' she said. 'I got that really good nursing job in Buxton. I hadn't really liked living in Manchester, but because I was with you I'd managed to tolerate it. And that tolerance disappeared. Buxton was so close to the countryside I felt I could breathe again. When you didn't have to live in the hospital you stayed with me and commuted into work. Lots of people did. You could have carried on doing it.'

'But, instead, three months later I was offered a wonder job in Boston. We flew out there together to look round. I thought we could make it work.'

Now she knew her voice was getting louder, she even sounded shrill. 'I hated it. I knew it was a brilliant career move for you, but I would have been actively miserable living there. So we decided you would go on your own.'

'Did we make the right decision, Angel?'

'You would have been foolish to turn it down. It was a young doctor's dream job. But since we were going to be apart indefinitely and things weren't right between us, I decided we might as well get divorced. And now we've both been successful in our own ways and we've managed well without each other.'

'Apparently,' he said. 'Have you been happy?'

That was an unfair question. 'Well, happyish. As much as anyone is, I guess. I enjoy my work, my friends, the countryside.'

'Was there no other reason for you wanting a divorce? I mean, apart from us being so much apart? You said things weren't right between us.'

'There was the baby. Look, Mike, can we talk about something else?'

She felt uneasy. This conversation was getting too intimate, she didn't want to know how Mike had felt, or him to know how she had felt. It was important to keep their distance. Only that way could they work together.

'Anyway,' she said in a brighter voice, 'Ma will go down to stay with Martin for a few weeks. He'll fly up, stay the night with me and fly her back the next day. There's a very good air service between the coast and London.'

'Yes, I know. I use it quite often.' Now he was being practical, professional. 'When will it be convenient for your brother to fetch your mother?'

'I'll phone him at his office this lunchtime and then let you know.'

Martin was a busy businessman but he had his priorities right. He told Angel that he would fly up the next day, he was looking forward to a night at High Walls. 'Bring your fleece-lined pyjamas,' she told him. This isn't the soft, centrally heated South.'

'I know that, little sister. Remember, I grew up there, too. Now, what's the name of this surgeon again?'

She was needed for something on the ward then, so it was half an hour before she had time to phone Mike.

His voice sounded amused, as it so often did. 'I've already heard from brother Martin,' he said. 'He wants a meeting.'

'What? The three of us?'

'No. He specifically asked just to talk to me. Man talk, I suppose.'

'Mike, that's not funny! You talk to Martin about my mother, not about me. And you are, above all, not to tell him that we were married!'

'I wouldn't do that, Angel, unless you wanted me to. No, I think that Martin wants to talk about the arrangement that is to exist between you, your mother and me.

And I think that is a good thing. I'd like your interests to be well represented.'

'I can look after myself,' she mumbled.

Martin refused to be met by her at the airport. He would have a hired car waiting, as it would be much simpler. 'Not sure I trust that banger of yours, Angel. I'll come straight to the hospital, see you and this Mr Gilmour then visit Ma. Next morning I'll take her home. The kids are really looking forward to her coming.'

'It'll be good to see you, Martin, even if it is a flying visit.' She was still not sure about Martin and Mike being together without her. In spite of Mike's assurances, she wondered what they would talk about.

But everything seemed to go well. Martin arrived, looked round her ward, went to see Mike, visited his mother. In the evening he toured the bungalow then took Angel to dinner in the Cat and Fiddle. 'I like the bungalow and I like Mike Gilmour,' he said. 'We talked about the bungalow and you looking after the baby for a while, and I think it's fine. He's getting a lot, of course—I know what bringing up a child takes—but he's letting you virtually have the bungalow and has ensured Ma's future and well-being. Strange he's not married. Don't fancy him, do you, little sister?'

'No!' She knew the answer came out too curt, too definite.

'Pity.' He took a deep draught of his beer. 'I still think there's something you're not telling me, little sister, but I know you will in time. Now, since we can walk home from here, I'll have another pint of this excellent bitter.'

She liked being with her brother, they had once been very close and it was a pity he lived so far away. But she had forgotten how shrewd he could be.

Next morning she went to the cardiac ward with

Martin and together they took her mother down to his car. To her surprise, Mike had come into the ward, too.

'I'm only going for a few weeks,' Marion had said. 'It'll be lovely to see my grandchildren, but I've got work to do when I get back.'

'There's an operation you've got to have,' Mike had replied, 'then more recuperation and then you can start work. But don't worry, I've got a vested interest in seeing you up and fit.'

Mike and Angel waved goodbye as the car pulled off. 'Years of work in her,' said Mike, 'after she's had the operation.'

'Don't worry,' said Angel, 'we'll both stick to our half of the bargain.'

It was amazing how fast things could be done when people were willing to push. Mike got access to the bungalow practically at once. Her solicitor drew up an agreement between them, with a great deal of frowning and nose-pinching. He had been the family solicitor for years.

'One thing I must make clear,' he told her, 'this agreement gives you no rights of access to the child after she leaves you. I know it will be only for a few months— but whatever relationship you may have formed will then be entirely at the mercy of Mr Gilmour. Are you willing to accept that?'

'I'm a professional nurse, I know the dangers of getting too attached to my patients.'

'This is something entirely different,' he told her.

The agreement with Mr Martlett was equally speedy. He would take over High Walls at once, he had plans to turn it into a hostel for walkers. One of the outbuildings would remain in their name. They could store furniture and so on in it and there was easy access to it.

She kept away from Mike as much as possible. The last couple of times they had met she had been too relaxed in his company, she needed to keep him at a distance. When he came to the ward to see Suzanne, she stayed in her room.

But eventually they had to meet as there was much to be decided. She had already been making lists of what they needed to buy and they needed to check them together. There were also legal matters to be considered. Eventually Social Services would be involved.

Mike phoned the ward with an invitation one morning. 'So far we've had drinks and snacks at the Drovers' Arms,' he said. 'Let's see how what their dinners are like.'

She didn't really want to have dinner with him. It would be too friendly, too intimate. 'I'm afraid I'm very busy at High Walls. I've got things to do there. I don't really have the time for dinner.'

There were problems on the ward. In the middle of the night they had admitted baby Ellen, a full-term child who had been born with an exomphalos—a hernia—and some of her intestines protruded through her umbilicus. Fortunately the protrusion wasn't too large. A damp sterile dressing was draped over it and baby Ellen put in an incubator.

Because her intestines were blocked she couldn't be fed by mouth. She took nourishment from a dextrose drip and she screamed constantly.

Baby Ellen would need an operation, quite a minor one but requiring a specialist surgeon. Only the very largest hospitals had specialist paediatric surgeons, so the baby would have to be transferred. The consultant phoned and arranged the transfer.

'Angel, if it's possible, I'd like you to accompany the baby,' Linda said.

Angel checked her staffing rota, and decided it was possible. No matter how well trained the ambulance paramedics might be, the baby had to be accompanied by her own nurse.

There was a special portable incubator for the journey, with a syringe drip fitted. The baby was moved into the portable incubator and Angel checked that all was well—that the monitor was functioning, the oxygen supply ready.

She introduced herself to the two paramedics, Joe and Marge, and soon they were on their fifty-mile journey to the coast.

It was a typical moors day, overcast and cold to start with and then with heavy rain beating against the ambulance. But it was warm inside. Angel chatted casually to the paramedics and kept a wary eye on Ellen. But there was no trouble.

They were expected. The baby was transferred efficiently, they had a quick cup of coffee and set off back. She would be back in plenty of time for her date with Mike. No, it wasn't a date. It was a meeting.

It happened, as it so often did, at the worst time and the worst place. The wind and rain had increased, buffeting the ambulance as it wound across one of the least hospitable sections of land for miles. This was high country, with only a rare farmhouse to relieve the bleakness of moor and sky.

The radio crackled, she half listened to the paramedics' quiet conversation. Then Marge looked into the back where she was sitting on the stretcher.

'Got a problem, Angel. There's a 999 call been made from one of these farms. We're by far the nearest and we've got to respond.'

'No problem,' said Angel. She knew that ambulances had to answer 999 calls, no matter what else they were doing. They would have answered the call even if they had been carrying the baby and incubator. 'What's the emergency?'

Marge laughed. 'You're going to like this because you might get involved. It's a birth. A real chapter of incidents. First, the midwife was driving out but she got high on the moors and then skidded off the road into a ditch. Her mobile phone wasn't charged so it took her half an hour to walk to where she could phone in for help. And the husband has no idea what to do and he's panicking. Meanwhile, even though it's a first baby, it turns out that this is going to be one of those super-rapid births. Contractions only four minutes apart.'

'Four minutes apart! D'you think we'll get there before the baby?'

'We're certainly going to try.' At that moment the ambulance turned off the road, bumped and slid along a muddy drive towards a grey stone building sheltering under the side of a hill. There was no other building within sight. 'No neighbours to run to for help,' said Marge. 'This is a great set-up for a first baby.'

Angel didn't know what the etiquette was for these occasions. She had a vast respect for ambulance paramedics, who sometimes had to deal with the most horrendous of accidents. 'Look,' she said, 'I know you're trained for this and you've probably helped with dozens of births. But I'm also a trained midwife, and if you want me to help I will.'

'Don't want you to help,' grunted Joe. 'We want you to do it. Don't we, Marge?'

'Our own portable midwife? Too true, we want her to do it.'

After a while they skidded to a halt in the farmyard, outside the front door. Marge and Joe grabbed a bag each, ran through the rain to the shelter of the porch. Angel followed them. As they ran the door opened. A man waved to them frantically.

All three ran into the front room. 'She's in there,' the farmer cried, and pointed to another door. They could all hear a woman crying in pain.

Joe and Marge held back. Angel looked at the frightened face of the young girl on the bed and said, 'Hi, I'm Sister Angel Thwaite and I'm here to help. Don't worry, everything's going to be all right now. What's your name?'

'Jenny, Jenny Armstrong. I—Ooh!'

Angel pulled back the covers, placed her hand on Jenny's abdomen. It was obvious the waters had broken. Automatically she timed the interval between contractions. Three minutes—not a lot of time to waste. She turned and said, 'There's no way we can load Jenny into the ambulance now, this baby's going to be born right here.'

Baseline observations first. Using the kit that Marge provided, Angel took the temperature, blood pressure, pulse and respiration rate. She scribbled the results on a handy bit of paper. Then she listened to the baby with a Pinard's stethoscope and conducted an internal examination. Head was at plus two.

To one side of Jenny's bed was a cot, and nearby was the pack that the midwife had obviously left. Angel tore it open, slipped on a pair of gloves. 'Do you want to take the baby?' she asked Marge. 'I think we'll have the action in a couple of minutes.'

To Jenny she said gently, 'would you like your husband to come in?'

'Yes, yes, please. I want him here.' With a grim attempt at a smile she gasped, 'He can see what it's really like.'

After that it was straightforward.

The baby boy had been born and was on his mother's breast when the midwife arrived, wet from her earlier walk but determined. She had been driven by the proprietor of a local garage. Once she was satisfied that all was well, the farmer found her something to change into. Then Angel handed over to her officially, signed the Apgar form and left her name and hospital address. Then she climbed back into the ambulance. 'Going to be no end of paperwork to sort this out,' Joe said gleefully.

When she had a moment Angel used her own mobile phone to ring Mike to explain that she would be late. He understood at once. 'Glad for the girl that you were there. D'you want to cancel our meeting, then?'

'I'd rather not. Can I phone you when I'm nearly back? We could still meet no matter how late it is.'

'That's good. Don't worry, I appreciate what you have to do. But phone me no matter how late you are.' He rang off.

She rang Mike when they were near the hospital. It was nine-thirty and she was exhausted, but she still wanted to meet him. Things had to be sorted out.

'How long since you ate?' he asked as soon as they were sitting in the Drovers' Arms.

How long since she'd eaten? She couldn't remember.

It had been too much of a day, she'd been too busy to eat. 'Well, I had a sandwich at lunchtime. But, really Mike, I'm fine, I don't need anything—'

'You look terrible, your blood sugar level must be down in your boots. For once, don't argue, I'll get what you need.'

With his pint of beer he fetched her a brandy, and shortly afterwards there was a hot pie for her, brown-crusted and smelling wonderful, with great golden chips and salad on the side. 'You need calories and some comfort eating,' he said. 'Finish that and you'll feel better. Mind if I steal a chip?'

So she ate, and when she had finished she felt much better. 'That was good,' she said. 'I feel that I can face the world now. And whatever you propose, I'll agree to. The way to a woman's heart is through her stomach.'

'I know that. One of the good things I do remember about you is that you enjoyed eating. No lettuce-leaf diets when you'd put on half an ounce.'

'Hey, we're here to work, not trip down memory lane.'

'Very true. In fact, there's so much to remember that I've got a little notebook.' He produced it with great pride. 'I write down jobs on one side of the paper, and tick them off on the other side when they're done.'

'And then write down new things to do?'

'You've spotted the weakness in the system. And I can even envisage having to buy a new notebook. Now…surveyors' report. I told him I wanted the place fixed so that nothing would need doing once you were in. This is what he suggested.'

She peered in the book and flinched. 'Rather a lot there.'

'I want there to be no problems later. And I want it painted inside and out.'

'But I was going to decorate the inside! I'm good at it.'

'Don't I know it. Top flat, 2 Grove Street—it took you two weekends to turn that place into a little palace. I loved living there.'

The flat at 2 Grove Street. She hadn't thought about it in years. Yes, it had been a little palace and she had... 'That was then,' she said. 'Circumstances have changed now.'

'Of course. But you've got better things to do than shin up ladders. We'll get a contractor to come in. May I leave the choice of colours and so on to you?'

She felt a stirring of interest, this was going to be fun. 'If you like. Do you want to pick the colours for your room, though?'

'No, I want to leave everything to you. Now, can you recommend any good firms? I know no one around here.'

'There's a firm of contractors in the village that I know well,' she said. 'They'll do anything—gas fitting, plumbing, electrical work, painting and so on, too. They might not be the cheapest firm but they'll be the best.'

'Just what we need. Now, you were making me a list of baby things needed? I told you I didn't want a second-hand pram.'

'I remember.' She passed over a piece of paper. 'This is the list I used to hand out to soon-to-be mums. Some of the things are more important than others and—'

'We'll have everything at once.' Mike looked at the list. 'What about carpets and curtains?'

'Well, I was going to cut down the curtains we had in High Walls. And they're going to leave the carpets in the bungalow—they'll do for a year or so.' As she spoke, she knew what he was going to say.

'No. Everything new, I think, unless there's something you're particularly attached to.'

'Not really. New stuff would be fun.'

'Good. Shall we buy it next Saturday? We'll have a day shopping in the big town. I'll pick you up at about eight.'

Angel seemed to be caught in an avalanche. 'All right,' she said.

'Look, I am not short of money. Most of the money I earned in the States I saved. And I earned a lot. I want this job done right so I can be assured that my niece is having the best.'

She was enjoying herself no end. They had ordered carpets, curtains, a vast amount of baby furniture. To her surprise, he didn't just let her make all the choices, he had his own point of view, too. They had started by selecting papers and colours for the rooms from a sheet of samples, and now were getting everything else to match.

They were spending a horrifying amount of money, but he didn't seem to mind. 'When we got the flat,' she said, 'we went out one morning and spent a hundred and fifty pounds and thought we were being mad, reckless and extravagant.' Then she caught herself. 'Sorry, that slipped out. Shouldn't have mentioned it.'

They were walking down the middle of a large and upmarket department store, surrounded by women in hats looking thoughtfully at Persian and Turkish rugs.

'Angel!' He stopped, grabbed her arms, shook her slightly. 'It happened! We were married! For a short time we had everything! All right, things went sour. But if we had the happiest days of our lives there, then we are entitled to remember them, no matter what went wrong later. Otherwise we deny part of what we are!'

'Happiest days of our lives? You never told me that then.' She was curious, not argumentative. 'I wish you had sometimes.'

He let go her arms, spoke in a quieter voice, and the ladies who had looked up returned to gazing at rugs. 'We never said much at all then,' he said. 'Life was good but it was hard. It was work, sleep and sex.'

'No, it was work, sleep and making love, Mike. There's a big difference. Now I think we'd better go down to the linen department.'

He didn't say anything until they'd walked down two floors into the basement. 'They *were* the happiest days of my life, Angel. What about you?'

'Who can tell?' she asked. She didn't want to tell the truth and say yes.

The next day they went to the bungalow and met Harold Days, the local builder. Angel had known him for years, had gone to school with his son. For a while they gossiped, exchanging local news while Mike stood by patiently. Harold asked about Janet's baby, Angel told him she had seen Terry.

'Good lad at heart,' Harold said judiciously, 'a determined little devil. He worked for me one summer, and I knew that I could set him going on a job, leave him for half a day and he'd still be at it when I came back. Hope he gets himself sorted out.'

'He will,' said Angel. 'He's got a stake in life now.'

'Are you coming to the meeting next Saturday? To object to closing the village school?'

'Oh, yes, I'll be there, it's got to be stopped. Now, can you work us out a price on what we want done'

Mr Days had been following them round, measuring and listening, scribbling furiously in his notebook, a much larger one than Mike's. 'I'll phone you through a price tomorrow,' he said.

'Thanks, Mr Days. If I pay cash, can you get all this work done in the next fortnight?'

Harold consulted his notebook, made a couple of calculations. 'Yes,' he said.

'When he's finished and your mother has recuperated, you can move in with your mother and Suzanne,' said Mike to Angel. 'A whole new life starting for you. I hope it'll be a contented one.'

CHAPTER FIVE

ANGEL had never quite realised how traumatic, how time consuming moving could be. Mr Martlett sent a couple of lads to help her move the heavier stuff out of High Walls and into the storeroom—there seemed to be plenty of it. Every day she called at the bungalow to see how the workmen were getting on, and what she saw made her even more excited at the prospect of moving in. Her life was altering. She hoped it was altering for the better.

She was spending as much time as she could with Suzanne. All the staff encouraged the mothers to bond with their babies, to spend as much time with them as was possible. So now she did what she had encouraged the mothers to do, nursing, crooning to the baby, holding her as much as possible. And she found a satisfaction greater than she had realised. For the first time she truly knew the meaning of the expression she had seen on mothers' faces.

It was Barry who gave her the greatest shock of all. 'You're becoming Suzanne's mother,' he said.

'That's silly, of course I'm not! She's just one of my charges and I—'

'Do you feel the same about all the rest in here?' he asked gently.

She had to give him an honest answer. 'No,' she said after a while.

'I thought not. Angel, I know you've been very busy recently. I've asked you out three times, each time you've given me a good reason for not coming. What I

want to say is…I shan't ask again. We had one great
evening, we're going to stay friends and work together,
but that will be all. Are you all right with that?'

She sighed. 'Barry, I never wanted to hurt you. It was
a great evening, but now my life seems to have changed
and…and I do still want to be friends.'

'That's fine. Now, we've got other work to do.' He
turned to look at the reports on their latest admission.

Angel didn't know what to think. She felt sad and
guilty. Barry was a wonderful friend, that evening together had been good fun and she realised she had hurt
him. But…that spark was missing. Barry would never
be more than her friend. Perhaps it was as well to finish
like this.

Mike came down to see the baby when he had time.
Often she wasn't there, but the other nurses told her that
he held the baby, cuddled her like any of the other fathers. He, too, was besotted.

On the Friday, after he had been to see Suzanne, he
asked her how the work was progressing at the bungalow.

'It's going well, I'm really impressed. Most of the
inside is finished. I've taken some of my stuff there already and I'm going to move in tomorrow night. D'you
want to come up and look round?'

'I was hoping to, yes.'

She thought for a moment. 'There's a meeting at my
old school at ten tomorrow that I want to go to, but it
shouldn't last very long. D'you want to meet me at the
bungalow at twelve?'

'Sounds ideal,' he said. 'I'm looking forward to seeing
the place.'

She found it odd to go back to her old primary school.
She had so many fond memories! And there were so

many faces that she remembered. This had been a community school and the community was here. It didn't want its school to close.

They crowded into the main hall, some sitting at the little desks, others standing round the walls. After being welcomed by the headteacher—a Mrs Simms—they were addressed by the chairman of the Save Our School committee, Miss Beavis.

Miss Beavis had been headmistress of the school for many years. After having to leave and taking a world cruise, she had come back as an unpaid assistant teacher. She still came in for three afternoons a week. She was now eighty-seven and as alert as she had been thirty years before.

'Children I have been proud to teach came from this school. We have produced doctors, architects, nurses, farmers, lawyers, no end of good mothers and fathers. Among many others I have two messages of support, from an old boy and an old girl. One is a government minister one is a vice admiral in the navy. And they tell us this school isn't financially viable. Rubbish!'

'That's a good argument,' a voice whispered from behind her.

She turned her head. To her surprise, there behind her was Mike. 'What are you doing here?' she whispered back, rather annoyed, 'I thought we arranged to meet later!'

'I found an extra couple of hours. Now, hush while I listen to this speech.'

What *was* he doing here? Mike never did anything without a definite motive. She wondered uneasily exactly what it might be.

After the speeches he wanted to look round the school

where she had spent six formative years. They looked at the solid old stone building with BOARD SCHOOL written proudly above its front door. And there were three smaller portable classrooms, neatly arranged on the old playground. People were wandering round, meeting old schoolmates and reminiscing.

'I came here and I learned a lot,' said Angel. 'It's still a good school, supported by everybody around. They should judge a school by how well it does, not by how much money could be saved by closing it.'

'I agree. But education is like the health service. You count the cost before you do anything.' His voice was cynical.

'You don't really believe that?'

'No. But sometimes I think that every other medical manager does. Tell me more about growing up here. You never mentioned it before.'

'As we both agreed, we didn't do too much talking at all.' She pointed to the bell-tower on top of the main school. 'You see that slab of darker stone just below where the bell used to hang?'

He peered upwards. 'Yes? The one with some kind of mark on it?'

'That's something scratched on the stone. It says "Herbert Thwaite, 1923". My great-grandfather. He climbed up there when he was nine, and got very soundly smacked for it. He won a posthumous DCM in Africa in 1943, his name's on the memorial outside the church.'

He looked at her thoughtfully. 'You're telling me this for a reason, aren't you?'

'I'm trying to get you to understand something about belonging to a place. Shall we go and look at the bungalow now?'

He was impressed by what had been done. He peered at the new boiler, inspected the pile of baby stuff that had not yet been unpacked. The curtains and carpets were due to be fitted during the following week, but the place was beginning to look homely. Angel's bedroom already had her double bed in it, and she blushed when Mike glanced at the chaos of her dressing-table. There were things that still had to be put away.

Finally he stood in the conservatory, looking at the great vista of the valley below. 'This is why my mother will feel at home here,' she told him. 'She needs to feel she can breathe, have space.'

'I can almost understand.' For some reason his voice was harsh. 'She thinks this is better than nothing but chimneys, better than anything London can provide.'

'That's right,' she said, surprised at his apparent anger.

'So show me what's so wonderful, Angel. All I've done since I got here is work and take a trip shopping with you. I'm on call at seven tonight but till then I've got the afternoon off. So see if you can prove to me that this is better than a big city!'

It was a challenge. 'All right,' she said, 'I'll show you what this place means to me. We'll probably end up arguing, but I don't mind trying.'

He seemed to want to argue at once. 'You were happy enough in Buxton. And then you went even further—to South America.'

'I always knew I'd come back here,' she said quietly. 'I enjoyed wandering but this place was always home and I wanted to come back. When I was away I wrote every week, phoned whenever I could. I'm a local girl. I don't know how my brother managed to leave. I know he regrets it. And Ma...she just couldn't cope.'

He thought about this for a while. Then he changed the subject. 'I see. How is your mother? I gather that, since I've heard nothing, that she's doing all right.'

'She loves being with her grandchildren, and they love having her there. But she says the constant roar of traffic is getting her down.'

He looked across the valley. 'What about the constant bleating of sheep?' he asked, and she had to laugh.

They started by looking round the village. 'Do you know everyone?' he asked after a while. 'That's the tenth time you've said hello to someone.'

'I know a lot here. People tend not to move, or if they do move they come back. Like I did, in fact.'

She took him to see the memorial outside the church, showed him Herbert Thwaite's name. Then they went inside the church. 'Not locked?' he asked. 'A lot of churches have to be these days.'

'Someone will have seen us come in. If anyone looking a bit dubious went into the church, there'd be a phone call to the verger, or someone would come in after them. This is our church, we look after it. Mostly it was rebuilt in the nineteenth century, but there are bits of it that are much older.'

'I like it,' he said. She was pleased when she saw him put something in the box for the church restoration fund. She knew from their earlier life together that he wouldn't have done it unless he liked the building.

Outside again, she pointed to a tree at the bottom of the churchyard. 'My brother Martin broke his arm when he fell out of that tree. My mother said he shouldn't have been birds'-nesting anyway.'

'Obviously the Thwaites are a climbing family.'

'We are. But you'll have to do some climbing now. Do you still carry a pair of walking boots in your car?'

'You remember,' he said softly, and she looked away.

'I thought we'd go up on the moors,' she said to change the subject. She looked at the sky with an expert's eye. 'The weather's quite good and I think it should hold. Do you fancy a walk?'

'Part of the guided tour,' he said. 'I'd really like that. I've been stuck in the hospital for too long, I need to smell fresh air instead of antiseptic.'

'We'll get all the fresh air you want,' she said.

They went in her car, driving up past High Walls and then into the corner of a field where they could park. 'The main car park is at the top of the hill,' she said, 'a place called Pike's Ridge. This is a short cut.' Then she led him up the shoulder of a hill and onto the ridge. 'You asked for fresh air,' she said. 'Now you've got it.'

They could see for miles, a bleak but dramatic landscape of rolling moors with only the occasional sign of man. In the valley the wind had been gentle, intermittent. Here it blew steadily, chilling them after the exertion of climbing. Both buttoned up their anoraks. 'Believe it or not, this is an old Roman road,' she said, 'and it might be even older than that. These valleys were once full of forests.'

'And wild people like the Thwaites, who didn't like interlopers?'

'Probably. But we do accept the odd visitor. If he behaves himself.' She considered a minute. 'In fact, the Thwaites were probably interlopers themselves. It's a Viking name. The Vikings sailed up the river and then marched up here. Now, that's enough history.' She set off along the ridge path and he had to follow behind.

After half an hour they reached a high point, an outcrop of rocks standing high in the heather. She led him round the side, squeezed through a narrow passage between two tall rocks and there was the opening to a cave. 'Not a lot of people know this is here,' she said. 'They call it the smugglers' cave, though what smugglers were smuggling up here I don't know. I remember coming up here with my class and Miss Beavis once.'

'Quite a lady, Miss Beavis. I admired her performance this morning. Can we get in the cave? When I was a little boy I wanted to be a pirate and spend a lot of my time in caves.'

'If you want. It seems to get bigger inside.'

He stepped carefully down through the opening and then held out a hand to steady her. They were able to stand upright once inside. They didn't move, waiting for their eyes to acclimatise to the dark. He still held her hand and they were face to face, but all she could see of him was a vague blur.

'You didn't tell me anything about your childhood— about all this—when we were married,' he said. 'I would have liked to have known.'

It was easier to have a half-intimate conversation when they were in the dark. She didn't have to look at him, register the expression of his face. 'When you're younger different things are important,' she said. 'Remember what we agreed before—our life was work, sleep and—'

'Making love,' he supplied.

'You've got it right now. And after we'd made love I often wanted to talk, but all you wanted was more sleep!'

He laughed, sadly. 'I know. I'm sorry. I used to lie on my back. And after a while you'd lean over me, you'd giggle a bit and then you'd brush your breasts across my face. It was…'

'It was what?'

'Well, it certainly stopped me sleeping.'

The memory flashed into her mind, so strong it might have been yesterday. Suddenly she could feel the warmth of his body, the gentle rasping of his beard on her face, that infinitely exciting smell that meant they had been together.

She could still see nothing of his face. But his voice, the very way his body was next to hers, told her that he was remembering as she was. 'Well, we'd better get out and walk a bit more,' she gabbled. 'There's another main road about four miles away and—'

He took her in his arms and kissed her. The shock was so great that she gave in at once. And then she responded, holding him to her as he clutched her. She didn't know what she was feeling—it was an odd mixture of sensations, both familiar and strange. But she loved it.

For a while they kissed. Then she felt his hand at her back, sliding under her anorak and sweater, tugging at her shirt, feeling the warmth of her skin. In a moment he might... She had to stop this...but she would wait just a few seconds more.

It was so hard to do. Gently she pushed him away, stepped back a little.

'We must stop now, Mike,' she whispered. 'There are so many memories coming back and I couldn't stand the pain again.'

'I like kissing you so much.'

There was no way she could hide the truth, she had just fully realised it herself. 'And I like kissing you. It's not just the kissing, it's because it's you. Mike, I've tried so hard not to let things start again between us. But it's no use, I can feel...feel what we had creeping back. And I got hurt so much!'

Slowly he released her and there was only silence in the cave. The vagueness of his figure loomed above her; to one side a thin streak of sunlight illuminated the cave floor.

'Perhaps,' he said, after what seemed liked an eternity, 'perhaps you can never recapture the past exactly. Life moves on. But I would like you to be part of my future. What now?'

'Now I need time to think. Shall we carry on with the walk?'

'It's the reason we came here,' he said. 'You get out first.'

Walking was different after that. The path was broader here and they walked side by side. There was no excuse for not talking to him. But Angel couldn't get over the excitement of his kiss and the truth that had been torn from her. What was she to do now?

Mike appeared equally puzzled. She thought he might be feeling exactly the same way. Surely he knew exactly what he wanted? Desperately she cast about for something to say.

'Tell me about your family,' she said. 'We never talked about our families at all.' Then she paused. Perhaps this subject would pain him. But, in fact, he seemed ready, even eager to talk.

'I think I had told you my family was of no consequence when we met,' he said. 'I believe I told you that they wouldn't interfere with us.' His face was set like stone. 'In fact, all I had was my sister—about four years younger than me. Our parents were both killed in a gas explosion when we were very young—I have no memory of them whatsoever. My father had an older—a much older—sister who said she could take Monica but not me. I don't think she really wanted Monica. Anyway,

I went to an orphanage. When I got older I tried to get in touch but the aunt had died and Monica was starting on the third of a set of foolish relationships. I learned very quickly not to interfere. We exchanged Christmas cards, that was all. Then I got this new job and out of the blue Monica phoned. She wanted to come to see me.'

'Did she want to get to know you again?' Angel asked curiously. 'D'you think she was hoping for some kind of reconciliation?'

'I suppose that was possible, I'd certainly like to think so. But I suspect she just wanted to borrow more money. She'd done it before. I would have sent her some, I have in the past, but...but now she's dead.'

'That's a sad story,' Angel said. 'Apart from Suzanne, you're now completely alone.'

'Being alone isn't too bad. Having relations has only ever meant trouble. Look at me and you.'

'We had our moments,' she said, thinking that that was a mammoth understatement.

'I know we did, Angel. And now I have Suzanne to love.'

Angel didn't ask him if the love of a child was enough. Perhaps she didn't want to know the answer.

After that they talked of less troublesome things, of the running of Micklekirk hospital and how it was better than most. They enjoyed the rest of the walk and then she drove him back to the bungalow. Then she remembered why they had been walking the first place.

'I've showed you round a bit of my background and history,' she said. 'Do you understand now what it all means to me?'

'I think so,' he said carefully. 'I can see you love this place. The trouble is, love so often goes sour. What will you be left with if it does?'

'It won't go sour,' she said confidently.

She felt relaxed with him now, so much so that she asked him if he'd like to stay to tea. There were some rooms habitable in the bungalow, and she had brought plenty of food. They had a cup of tea together and then she left him in the living room while she cooked. When Angel went back after ten minutes to ask if he wanted more tea, he was asleep in the rocking chair. She smiled and left him.

At twenty past seven she heard Mike's mobile ring and then there was the mutter of his voice. He came into the kitchen at once, rubbing his face.

'Well, I suppose I am on call,' he said. 'It's my senior reg—we're going to have to open a chest. A farmer's just been sent up from A and E. Apparently he was working under a vehicle when it slipped and crushed him. The SR thinks he can cope but he wouldn't mind if I was standing by. I'm afraid I'm going to have to miss tea, Angel.'

She indicated the array of pans on the stove. 'Tea's far from ready yet and I'm not very hungry. If you want to…why don't you come back when you've finished? This will all keep warm.'

He smiled. 'I'd like that, Angel. See you later.'

For a moment she wondered if he would kiss her, just a gentle kiss on the cheek perhaps. There was something about the way he was looking at her, as if he wanted to. But he didn't. He turned and left.

Mike drove out of Laxley village, down the hill towards Micklekirk Hospital. He wasn't happy with himself. This situation was ridiculous!

He had come to Micklekirk almost expecting a rest. For years he had worked and trained in America; he had learned certain techniques there that no one else in Britain could perform. Others were in America training now, but he was the first, the one who was expected to take the chair in a prestigious London hospital. It was what he had worked towards for so long!

Working at Micklekirk was supposed to be easy. In fact, he had found an excellent team of co-workers and a very demanding workload. No matter, he liked work. But his personal life…

The first shock had been the death of his sister. He could have coped with this; he knew she had no regard for him and that she was only interested in what money she could get from him. In the past he had tried so hard to become close to her and it had always ended badly. Even though she had been his only living relative, he couldn't honestly shed much of a tear for Monica.

And, as ever, she had left him in more trouble. He was the only living relative of a baby. This he didn't want; he'd had enough of family responsibilities! Well, that had been his first reaction. His second reaction had startled even him. He'd looked at this tiny scrap of humanity who was his only living blood relative and—he loved her! When he looked down at her he felt emotions that had been dormant since…since he had thought he was to be a father. He loved her. And he wouldn't be parted from her.

And now the biggest problem. Angel. The woman he was once married to. Looking back, he seemed to have been a different man then. They had both been different, thinking of only two things—their work for most of the twenty-four hours, each other for the rest. Then work had come between them.

He realised that he had cut himself off from his feelings, had worked with an intensity that now bothered him. Uneasily he wondered if he had lost something. He was happy, proud of his accomplishments, he had an international reputation. But was he happy?

He had never asked himself that question before.

He drove into the car park, hastened up to the cardiac centre. His senior reg was waiting there. 'Things are a bit more complex than I thought,' he said.

CHAPTER SIX

THERE was a full team waiting—anaesthetist, scrub nurse, assistants, SHO and the SR himself. As Mike showered, dressed in greens and scrubbed up, he listened to the SR's report. Of course, he would examine the records himself, But an initial overview was always a useful thing to have.

'Name's Jake Lauren,' the SR said, 'a farmer from further down the valley, aged thirty-seven. He had this heavy trailer jacked up, he was lying on his back underneath it, greasing one of the axles. It wasn't the right jack for the job and it slipped.'

'Now, there's a surprise for us all,' said Mike. The number of injuries that came into A and E because someone hadn't been using the right lifting tool was enormous.

'I've had a word with the family. Apparently he's in good health, very fit, no history of heart trouble, doesn't smoke. His chest wasn't crushed for long—there was someone nearby who jacked up the trailer and got him straight out. They called an ambulance at once. He was still conscious but in severe pain and complained of not being able to breathe. Consciousness was altered also.'

'Classic,' said Mike. 'Do you think the heart is lacerated or just contused?'

The SR said he wasn't certain. Mike was glad. Although you might suspect what was wrong, he knew there could be no way of knowing fully until the chest was opened. He didn't want an over-confident assistant.

'Investigations?' he asked.

'I found hypotension, distended neck veins, paradoxical pulses. Radiography, ECG, echocardiogram all suggest cardiac tamponade and possible disruption of the vena cavae.'

'Good,' said Mike. I'll have a look at them all and have a quick word with the man and his family. Then we'll get started.'

'There's a message for you, sir,' said one of the porters, 'which was only to be given to you when you'd quite finished. It's not urgent, not bad news, but will you, please, ring the neonatal unit?'

Not bad news. So Suzanne wasn't ill or anything like that. He rang the unit. He recognised the voice of the nurse who replied—he'd spoken to her once or twice. 'Mr Gilmour? Can you hold on a minute? We've got someone who wants to speak to you. At the moment she's asleep in our parents' room.' Then there was a giggle and a moment later a sleepy voice said, 'Mike? It's Angel.'

Of course, he had said he would be back for tea after a couple of hours. 'Angel! It's two o'clock in the morning, I thought you would have guessed—things were a lot worse than we anticipated.'

'I'm a nurse, remember. I know how operations can change. In fact, I phoned up the theatre and they explained what was happening. How was it, by the way?'

'I think a success,' he said carefully. 'You never know what might happen—but I'm pleased with what we managed.'

'That's good. Mike, I'm so glad.' He could tell by the warmth in her voice that she meant it and it pleased him. 'Now, I baked a quiche for you in my new oven and I really wanted you to try it. So I thought I'd come down here and wait for you and try to persuade you to come back and see if you liked it. Then things went on and I decided to sleep. By the way, how d'you feel?'

How did he feel? 'My nerves are jangling,' he said honestly. 'I'm tired but there's no way I could sleep for a while. It was just an ordinary operation—not a simple one, quite complex really, but I'd done it before and I thought it went well.'

'I remember when you used to work a late night, sometimes you'd wake me up and tell me all about it.'

'Yes, and you never complained,' he said thoughtfully. 'You'd always look interested and listen.'

'It seems like it's happening again. I didn't think you'd be this long, but if you still want to come back to the bungalow and eat, it's all ready and waiting. Of course, you might be better off in your bed.'

'I'm coming,' he said. 'I've just realised I'm ravenous. I'll have a quick word with the family, then a shower and I'll see you outside in fifteen minutes.'

'We'll take my car,' she said. 'You're not safe to drive.'

He had been up for twenty hours.

Angel quite liked eating with Mike at this odd hour of the morning. He didn't want the beer or wine she offered him, just water. Working for hours under those lights tended to dehydrate him. For a while she listened while he talked about what he had just done. She understood that it was a relief from tension, a way of calming down.

They finished the meal then she cleared away while he sat in the rocking chair again. 'Tea or coffee?' she asked.

'No. They're not what I want,' he said.

He was dressed in shirt and jeans, the outfit he had worn when they'd gone for their walk. His hair was slicked down after the shower he'd had, and his cheeks were darkened—it was a while since he'd shaved. His blue eyes were tired, but in them she recognised a spark that flared in her, too. And how well she remembered those lips. As he stood he swayed slightly.

'What do you want, then?' she asked. She knew the answer to the question but she had to hear him say it.

'I want you.' A simple, stark answer.

Just for a moment she hesitated. Then she walked towards him, put her arms round that firm waist. 'Then you can have me,' she said.

For a while they just stood there in the living room, their bodies pressed together. Even though they were both dressed it seemed that she could feel all of him, her calves, thighs, hips, breasts all touching him, filling her with desire. When he kissed her it was so gentle at first that she sighed, it was like a spell turning her body to liquid. She had to lie down.

With her arm around his waist she urged him to her bedroom. He kissed her more passionately now, but she stopped him. She loosened his belt, pulled his shirt over his head as if her were a child. Then she pushed down his jeans so that he stood naked before her. 'Lie on my bed,' she said. 'Lie on my bed and wait.'

He did as she told him, unashamed of his nakedness, unashamed of his obvious need for her. She pulled off her own clothes quickly—they must be equal as soon as possible. Then she stepped to the bed and knelt astride him.

'Do you remember this?' she asked. Leaning forward, she trailed her breasts across his face, letting their fullness touch his cheeks, his lips. She could feel the roughness of his growing beard. The tiny pain hardened her nipples, made them full, as excited as she was.

He sighed underneath her, wrapped an arm round her shoulders and crushed her breasts to his face. Then he pulled her head to his and his kiss now was hard, demanding, a response to equal his own desire.

They remained locked there together and her body rested on his, feeling the fire of his skin.

Then slowly he rolled her onto her back. To her this now seemed entirely proper, the thing they should do. All other thoughts had left her. She knew only that she wanted to give herself to this man. She spread her body out beneath him, felt him pause, knew he was looking down at her. She heard him catch his breath, a sound almost like a sob. Then she took him to her.

It was half remembered, half new and all wonderful. It didn't last long. There was no time for gentleness, just a craving that both needed to satisfy. And then a joint cry, and it was over. He lay on his back now, pulled her half on top of him with her head on his shoulder, his arms round her. And in no time he was asleep. She had no time to think, she didn't want to think. She pulled the duvet over them both and soon she too slept.

Angel woke early. For some time she lay still, forcing herself not to think about the warmth of the body next to hers, the deep breathing and the relaxed hand that lay so casually on her waist. Then cautiously she slid out of bed, took her clothes from where she had dropped them and walked into the next room. She dressed quickly, then sat at the kitchen table to write the letter she had already planned.

Dear Mike,

I have gone for a walk round the village. When you wake take my car to drive back to hospital. Leave the car by the babies' unit and put the key on the front wheel.

Last night was so lovely but it was also a dreadful mistake. I am sorry, I know it was my fault, but if you think anything of me, please never mention it again. I don't want to talk about us or our past. Can we carry on as friends and colleagues, as we were before?

Yours, Angel.

She tiptoed into the bedroom and, carefully avoiding looking at his face, left the note on the pillow. Then she took her coat and walked out into the village.

What had happened between them? Was it sex, or love, or sex and love combined? She just didn't know. She walked round the village, trying to decide how she felt. Making love with Mike had been so wonderful that it threatened to displace everything else. But she couldn't let that take place. Look what had happened the last time. They had parted because they hadn't been able to get their two lives to work together. It would be even harder now.

When Angel got back to the bungalow her car was still outside. She turned and went for another half-hour's walk. After that the car was still there. She was angry now. If he wanted a confrontation he could have one. But he wasn't there. Instead there was a note on the kitchen table.

Dear Angel,

Thanks for the offer of the car, but I think I also need a walk.

Last night was wonderful. I was happier than ever I have been in my life before. Now I will never mention it again unless you do first.

I would have thought that we did have things we had to discuss, but this I will leave to you. In the past you have accused me of making decisions on my own. Now you must do it.

Please forgive me if I sign this,

All my love, Mike.

Well, he had always been able to write a good letter. She tried to get on with her work in the bungalow. But as she worked the tears ran down her face.

Next day Angel was told by the paediatric consultant that Suzanne would soon be ready to leave the hospital. 'I know about the...sad circumstances of this case,' Linda said, 'but we'll still have to know what arrangements Mr Gilmour is making for Suzanne's future.'

Angel took a deep breath. 'Mr Gilmore is going to keep Suzanne,' she said. 'In time she'll move down to London with him. But until that happens she'll stay with me or with Nancy Timms. I'll be taking some of my holiday time soon to get things settled.'

'I see,' said the consultant, who obviously didn't see. 'It's a lot to take on, no one knows that better than you, Angel. Does this mean that you and Mr Gilmour are...?'

'No, we're not. This is a purely temporary arrangement. We're just helping each other out.'

'Well, you know how demanding a baby can be. Having said that, Angel, there is no one I would rather discharge a baby to.' She frowned. 'There will be quite a few formalities to see to and I suppose Social Services will have to be consulted. More forms to fill in!'

'I know Judy Harris, the children's social worker, quite well,' Angel said thoughtfully. 'We've had plenty of dealings with her in the past. We should be able to get something satisfactory sorted out.'

'I'm sure we shall. I'll phone both her and Mr Gilmour and then see if we can set up a case conference. Can you arrange for Nancy Timms to come in, too?'

The building and decorating work on the inside of the bungalow were finished, much earlier than expected, then on one day the curtains arrived and on the second the carpets were fitted. She laid out all the baby requirements in the little room she had decided would be the nursery. It was different from doing it in a ward, she felt far more personally involved. This was going to be *her* baby.

Angel had only seen Mike at a distance in the past few days. But they met the paediatric consultant just before the social worker arrived for the conference. To her relief he treated her in the same friendly way they had treated each other before *that* night.

'I hadn't realised that doing a simple thing like looking after a family was so complex,' he said, 'but I guess we have to put up with it. Good of you to go through all this, Angel.'

There was a questioning look in his eyes, but she ignored it. 'I'm sure we're all happy with the situation as it is,' she said. 'It seems to suit all parties well.'

Judy Harris arrived with Nancy Timms—the two were old friends—and seemed equally happy. 'For once I'm happy to cut corners,' Judy said. 'This seems an arrangement that benefits everybody. Suzanne here is a very lucky baby. Now, all I need are vast numbers of forms filled in. Angel, I'll have to make a visit to both the new homes, and I'll be visiting again, as will as the district nurse. Are you happy with that?'

'Come whenever you want. You know you'll always be welcome.'

So it was quickly done. 'Perfect,' Linda said. 'I'll be looking at Suzanne in a couple of weeks and regularly after that, but for now she can be discharged. Friday be all right, Angel?'

It was suddenly all very, very near. She gulped. 'Friday will be fine,' she said.

In the past she had seen parents come in to take their babies home for the first time from the neonatal unit. Often they had been nervous, unhappy, not sure that they could cope. Angel and the rest of the team had done their best to encourage and support. Now she was taking a baby home. There could be few people better qualified than she was. And yet she found herself as nervous as anyone.

There were specific rules about handing over a baby. Before letting any parent take a child from the neonatal unit, the staff had to be certain that the parents or guardians knew how to look after the child. Even though Angel was a children's nurse, and Linda Patterson had known her for years, Linda still came down to have a couple of words before baby Suzanne was discharged on Friday. Another nurse carried the baby out of the hospital, Angel wasn't allowed to. Now she was guardian, not nurse.

It should have been easy. Suzanne wasn't her child. There was no blood bond linking them. But over the past weeks Angel had fallen in love with the little girl.

Suzanne had a character, Angel could respond to it. She knew the two of them would get on together.

While they were going through the necessary procedures, Mike came into the ward. 'Just dropped in to see that everything was all right,' he said. 'Tell me if I'm in the way and I'll go.'

'You're not at all in the way,' Angel said. 'It's good to see you here. I was going to phone you. If you have the time, would you like to come home with us? See how things are going, watch her being fed. In fact, you can feed her. Suzanne will stay with me for the next couple of weeks.'

'I'd very much like that,' he said quietly, 'but I need to be sure that I wouldn't be a nuisance. Wouldn't upset you in any way.'

Another coded message. 'You won't upset me,' she told him. 'I've looked after babies all my professional life. I can cope with you easily.'

So he drove up after her, watched as she put the baby to bed in the new nursery. Suzanne cried, but that was to be expected. Afterwards Angel took him on a quick tour to see the curtains, the carpets, the way she had tried to make the bungalow a home.

'It's just what we need,' she said, 'and my mother will be coming back on Sunday. She's feeling much better and really looking forward to looking after Suzanne.'

He frowned. 'Well, I'm very pleased about that,' he said, 'but as her surgeon I know that the time between now and after she's had her operation will be just the time when she can't really cope.'

'No problem. Nancy's only down the road.'

After a while he had to leave, and she was left alone with the baby.

*　*　*

It seemed odd to be on her own and working. For the first time her personal and her working life were mixed. Later in the evening Angel bathed the baby, fed her again and then put her back in her cot. She made herself a quick meal and sat down to watch television. She felt restless. It's just the novelty, she told herself, just the mixture of home life and work. But something seemed to be missing. Perhaps it was her mother.

She went to bed with the cot by her bedside, but she couldn't sleep. Like so many of the mothers she had observed, she was fascinated by the sound of the baby's breathing. There was something calming about it. But she still couldn't sleep.

She had used the new washing machine that Mike had bought for her. Two nights after the night with him she had stripped off the sheets and thrown them in the dirty linen basket. When she had climbed into bed the next night, there had been the faintest of scents there, not of her but him. In the middle of the night she had risen, torn off the sheets and replaced them. She couldn't sleep, tantalised by that living memory.

This bed, this room, this house were all so much more comfortable than High Walls. But it was hours before she slept.

At four in the morning she had to wake to feed and change Suzanne. No problem to this, she had done it so many times before. Afterwards Suzanne wouldn't go back to sleep. Angel rocked her, cuddled her, walked with her. Still the crying. So Angel did what she had sometimes recommended to her new mums.

She lay on her back on the bed, put the baby between her breasts and let her rest there. Quite quickly Suzanne went to sleep. Angel felt her hunting for a while, felt the tiny hands on her naked breasts.

This was something she had never done before—she had nursed many babies when she was clothed, but never this most intimate of contacts. Suzanne couldn't suckle, of course, but she tried. It was the oddest of feelings. Angel remembered the peaceful, happy faces of her nursing mums. She knew why, of course, it was just one effect of prolactin—a hormone produced by the pituitary gland to make milk flow. But she found she loved the feeling herself. When she put the sleeping baby back in her cot she found tears running down her face. Just tired, she told herself.

Her mother came back on Sunday afternoon and settled into Valley View at once. Mike came out to see her, he said both as her doctor and as the guardian of his child. He took her into the bedroom for a quick examination and said that the stay down South had done her no end of good.

Angel thought she hadn't seen her mother so happy in months. She sat in the rocking chair and fed Suzanne as Mike and Angel had a quiet word in the kitchen.

'She's still not a hundred per cent fit, Angel,' said Mike quietly. 'Make sure she keep up with her medication, and don't let her do too much. Use Nancy as much as you like. And I'd like to see her in hospital later in the week. I'll consider bringing her operation forward a little.'

'You're frightening me,' she said. 'Are you saying that there's something seriously wrong with her?'

'No, I'm not saying that. But remember, there's always the tenth of one per cent chance that something might go wrong. And that tenth of one per cent means one in every thousand people.'

'I'll look after her.'

So when Angel went back to work on Monday morn-

ing she felt a little apprehensive at leaving her mother
behind. But Ma was more than happy and Nancy was
going to call round and stay for most of the day.

'Are you missing High Walls?' asked Angel.

'No. I've started a new life here.'

What sort of a new life have I started? Angel wondered to herself.

CHAPTER SEVEN

SOMETIMES he was delayed because of work, but otherwise Mike came every evening. After Angel had showed him how—Suzanne was still tiny—he would feed the little girl, bathe her, dress her and hold her before putting her into her cot.

He had a surgeon's delicacy and dexterity and Angel knew at once that Suzanne would be safe in his hands. But she liked to sit and watch as, absorbed, he tended his little girl.

Late on Friday afternoon it was raining, blowing half a gale, another typical late winter night on the moors. As she moved from warm kitchen to equally warm and draught-proof living room, Angel thought of High Walls ands shivered. This was the way to live!

The phone rang. She thought it would be Mike, he usually phoned to say if he would be delayed. But to her surprise it was Mr Martlett. He sounded worried. 'Angel, have you got a minute to talk to me? There's a problem—a big one—and you might be able to help.'

'You couldn't have been more thoughtful over High Walls. Anything I can do to help you, I will.'

He sighed. 'I'm not the one in trouble, I'm afraid. You know Terry Blackett? I gather you've seen him and his baby from time to time.'

'I've known Terry since primary school. Why? Is the baby all right?'

'The baby is fine. Terry isn't. I'm at the police station,

116

Angel. They've called me in as they think I might be able to help. And I will if I can but—'

'Just tell me what happened,' she said. 'Then we'll see if I can help.'

'Terry was allowed out again, on his own, to see his baby. Part of this new scheme they're trying. He had left the hospital and was walking through the rain to catch the bus. An old Land Rover apparently deliberately swerved across the road to splash him—there was a witness in a car behind, that's how we know all this. Anyway, the Land Rover stopped, someone in it leaned out and jeered at Terry.'

'Not a good idea,' said Angel. 'Terry can't control his temper.'

'He didn't. He got to the car, pulled someone out of the passenger side and thumped him. There was a bit of a mix-up, another man from the car joined in the fight, it was hard to see. Then a shotgun was fired. We think Terry was hurt.'

'You *think* he was hurt? Don't you know?'

'No, we don't. You know Terry's a big, strong lad. Apparently he flattened both these two louts in the car. Well, someone had phoned the police. They arrived in a car, lights flashing, siren blaring. Terry panicked. He fired the shotgun at the police car, then got in the Land Rover and drove off.'

'It wasn't his fault!' Angel cried. 'Anyone can see he was provoked he didn't know what he was doing!'

'We know that. The police see it as a convicted criminal firing at a police vehicle and then going on the run. Apparently there were more shells in the Land Rover. Anyway, the police followed the vehicle onto the moors and Terry abandoned it at Pike's Ridge, got out and ran. Now there's a big police operation in progress. Men with guns are going to try to surround him, they think he might shoot someone.'

'If Terry sees men with guns hunting him, he'll panic more,' Angel said decisively. 'He's likely to fire back. All they need do is leave him alone. He'll turn himself in in time.'

'They daren't risk that with a man with a gun. I just phoned you on the off chance that you might have some idea where he'd go. If I could talk to him perhaps...'

'Pick me up here in ten minutes,' she said. 'We'll go up onto the moors ourselves.'

She briefly explained the situation to her mother, who said she'd look after Suzanne. Then she changed into her hard weather clothes, packed a torch, some chocolate and a small first-aid outfit. She was ready when Sam Martlett arrived in his four-wheel drive.

When they got near Pike's Ridge they found a police car drawn across the road. At Sam's insistence a constable took them to a large van fitted as an office. From inside it a Superintendent Wragg was directing the operation. Through the rain Angel could see other cars further on, with some policemen in hard hats and bulletproof vests, carrying guns. She shivered.

'We might need your help,' said the superintendent. 'It could be useful when we've got him pinned down. We have sent for our own negotiator and until we have something more to go on I'll have to ask you keep well away.'

'You know he panicked,' Angel shouted. 'All this is making things worse. If you just go away he'll come to you.'

'Possibly. But we daren't take that risk with a man with a loaded gun. I'm sorry, miss, I'll have to ask you to wait here. I'll send for you if I think we need you.'

She thought the man sounded sympathetic, but she knew he was right. It was a risk no policeman dared take. 'You stay with the superintendent,' she said to Sam. 'I'll drive your car down the road a way.'

He handed her the keys. 'We have to do what the police say,' he said. She nodded and went to his vehicle.

She only knew afterwards what happened next. So far the police had only gathered, they hadn't started their hunt yet. Sam was talking to the superintendent when a constable came up and said, 'Excuse me, sir, we've just seen a woman in a red anorak running across the moor towards the ridge. What would you like us to do?'

The superintendent turned to Sam. 'This is that nurse woman of yours, isn't it? Doesn't she know how to obey orders?'

'Not really,' Martlett said calmly. 'She'll do as she thinks best. And before you ask, no, I didn't know this was what she was going to do.'

The superintendent could hardly contain his anger. 'Doesn't she know she's jeopardising an entire operation? I'll have her arrested for this!'

'You'd better catch her first. Now, you may not want it, but this is my advice. Don't try to stop her. If Terry Blackett is on those moors, watching you, and he sees his friend being dragged away by your men, he's not going to be very happy. He might even try to rescue her. And you wouldn't want that.'

For a moment the two men stared at each other. Then the superintendent said to the patiently waiting constable, 'Don't do anything, Kenton. Tell the others.'

'Sir!' The man disappeared.

'I hope you know what you're doing,' the superintendent said.

'So do I,' said Sam.

* * *

Angel ran through the heather, her heart thudding, her chest heaving, the wet plants catching at her ankles. She knew she'd be seen pretty soon, that she only had a short start. But it might be enough. She had to get to Terry first. He just couldn't cope with large numbers of people. She remembered even at school how he'd hated crowds, how they'd made him uneasy. If he could just get his cottage, with his wife and child and sheep to look after. If she could get to him first.

She looked over her shoulder. The police were there, in the distance, now coming towards her along the ridge. But they didn't seem to be moving too quickly. If she could just maintain her lead. If she was right about where Terry might be. If Terry would listen to her.

Eventually she reached the little rock outcrop where she had stopped with Mike, the outcrop where there was the smugglers' cave. This was her only hope. She pulled herself onto a rock, tried to signal to the advancing men in rain-stained blue uniforms that they were to stay back. Perhaps they slowed a little. All she needed was a little time.

It was surprisingly difficult to find the entrance to the cave. When she slid between the two tall rocks she realised that there was little daylight left and darkness would come soon. That would make things even more tricky. And someone had cleverly pulled stones and bracken round the little cleft in the rocks. You needed to know the cave was there. But there would be policemen who knew.

She pulled at the stones in the entrance of the cave and shouted, 'Terry! It's me, Angel Thwaite! Don't shoot, Terry, it's me—Angel.'

There was no reply. Two thoughts struck her. Perhaps

Terry wasn't there. And if he was, perhaps he was angry enough, desperate enough, to shoot her. It was the first time this had crossed her mind.

She wasn't backing out now. She stepped into the darkness, her hands outstretched in front of her. 'Terry, are you there? I've got to talk to you before the police come.'

The voice was so close that she screamed. 'Angel? What are you doing here? You've brought them here after me. I thought you was my friend.'

She listened to his voice. It was high, fluttering, as if hysteria was not far away. The last thing Terry needed now was excitement.

'Terry, they were coming here anyway. Now, I've got a torch here. I want to look at your arm. I've brought some—'

'No! You leave and they might follow you. Then I can slip away and—'

'Terry, we're surrounded. No one's going to slip away and I'll be in trouble for coming to try to help you. Now, I'm going to switch the torch on and look at your arm.'

She switched on the torch she had decided to bring. Terry was a sorry sight. He was wearing a light raincoat, now sodden with the rain and stained after his flight through the heather. His hair was matted and his face unnaturally white. A scarf was wrapped round his left arm, above the elbow.

In his right hand he held the shotgun. He was a countryman so he held it broken, safe. But it would be too easy to snap it together again.

'Take your coat and jacket off, Terry. I need to see that arm. You've lost blood already, you'll probably need a transfusion.'

'Where will I get one of those?'

'In hospital, Terry. That's where you'll be going ultimately. I can't deal with a gunshot wound here. Now, coat and jacket off!'

He placed the gun behind him—within easy reach, she noticed. Then, his face twitching with the pain, he pulled off the coat and jacket. He was shivering.

'We'll have to get you into something warm and dry,' she said matter-of-factly, 'otherwise you might get pneumonia as well. Here…' From her pocket she took a bar of chocolate and handed it to him. 'Eat this. You'll feel better.'

As best she could, she cleaned up the wounds on his upper arm. Two pellets had cut through the flesh which would at some time have to be sutured. She was pretty sure that two more were still embedded deep in the flesh.

'Terry, you've been shot. You're in a bad way, you've got to see a doctor!'

'In a bad way! Not as bad as those following me.' He reached for the gun, snapped it closed.

'Terry! Those policemen have done nothing to you, a couple of them know you. Now, break that gun again and sit here by me.'

He did as she asked. After a moment he said, 'Would you like a piece of this chocolate? I'm sorry I didn't share it.'

She thought she would burst into tears. This was Terry twenty-odd years ago, the boy who would share everything.

'I've got more chocolate here if I need it,' she said. 'Terry, what are you going to do now?'

His smile was ghastly. 'Well I've missed my train back to prison so I guess I'm in trouble. Might as well make a fight of it.'

'Don't be silly. You're in trouble but things could get

worse. Mr Martlett is out there, he wants you to come out. He's not asking through charity, he thinks you're the best shepherd for miles. And what about Jackie and your baby? What is she going to think of this? Your mother says you're going to get married.'

'When? Angel, I'm going to spend the rest of my life in prison! And I can't stand it. I'd rather be dead than go back to be locked up there.'

His mood seemed to alternate between reasonable and hysterical. She knew this was probably a result of shock, blood loss and the run along the ridge. He needed urgent medical help—but he wanted to fight.

'I think we can sort something out,' she said, 'if you—'

Suddenly, the entrance to the cave was floodlit. He grabbed the gun again, snapped it shut. 'I'll shoot that light out, I'll—'

'No you won't. I'll go and see what I can do.' Feeling both foolish and frightened, she put her hands high over her head, then stepped into the beam. ' Don't shoot! Can you see me? I'm Angel Thwaite.'

'We can see you, miss. Are you alone in there?' The sound of another voice upset her, the man sounded so normal.

'No, I'm in here with Terry Blackett. We're having a talk. Now, this is the only opening to the cave. He can't escape. That light is disturbing us. Can you turn it out?'

'I don't think so.'

'Look, we're both all right. We can sort this out if you just take your mates with guns away.'

She had seen it all on TV. The thought that there were men nearby with their guns trained on her, or near her, was horrible. And it wasn't necessary.

'Just wait a minute,' the voice called. 'We can turn it

down. Would Terry like to talk to someone? We've got someone here.'

'He's got someone to talk to,' she said tartly. 'Me. Now, leave us alone.' A minute later the bright light dimmed. She went back into the cave.

She knew that Terry must be weakening fast. But there was a glassy look in his eyes and she wondered if he might try to do something heroic, or stupid, before he fell unconscious.

'They've got someone to talk to you,' she said. 'I wonder who it could be. The only person I can see doing any good is Miss Beavis.'

Then it happened. He laughed. 'Miss Beavis! I liked her. She didn't half smack me, but she never made me cry. I took what was coming to me.'

'Yes, you did. So are you going to cry now?'

This was it, she felt, her last chance of getting through to him. The silence between them went on and on. She shivered herself, became conscious of her own wet hair, of the unpleasant trickle down her spine, of the damp in her boots.

'So what do I do?' he asked.

'Give me the gun and the shells and I'll take them out. Then you come out with your arms over your head. They'll grab you, hold you on the ground and handcuff you. Don't fight back.' Once again, she had seen all this on television.

'Sounds just like shearing a sheep,' he said. 'Angel, my little girl—'

'I told you I'd keep an eye on her and I will. Now, pass me the gun and the shells.'

He had made up his mind now. He broke the gun, slipped out two shells. It had been loaded! She had wondered. Then he handed her the shotgun and took a box of shells from behind him. 'That's the lot,' he said.

She went to the entrance and shouted, 'I'm coming out with the gun in my hand. Don't shoot.'

Suddenly the light was bright again. The voice said, 'Keep coming forward then put the gun on the ground and step back.' She did as she was told. Someone rushed up and took the gun, then she walked forward.

There was a group of men in shiny coats there. She gave one the box of shells and said. 'He's coming out with his hands up. He hasn't got a gun. He realises he made a mistake and he certainly doesn't want anyone hurt so keep those guns down. He also needs hospital treatment quite quickly.'

She turned, and there was Terry behind her. 'Sheep-shearing time,' he said, and fell to his knees.

Angel was taken, politely but firmly, a little distance from Terry. The police did handcuff him but she was pleased to see that they weren't as rough with him as they might have been. Sam Martlett was standing nearby, and he had a quick word with Terry.

It was now quite dark. The scene was lit by torches carried by the police, which shone eerily on their shiny wet coats. And the rain still slanted down.

'We appear to have more or less a happy ending,' Superintendent Wragg said to her. 'But, Miss Thwaite, you interfered with a police—'

'That can wait till later,' a voice snarled. 'There's no need for it now. Anyway, she saved you from a very nasty job. Angel, are you sure you're absolutely all right?'

What was Mike doing here? He sounded very angry. 'I'm wet and a bit cold,' she told him, 'but I'm all right. Mike, can you look at Terry's arm? It looked as if…'

It obviously took him an effort to be calm and polite, but Mike turned to the Superintendent and said, 'My name's Mike Gilmour. I'm a surgeon. Would you like me to have a quick look at that man? He appears to have been hurt.'

'We have a paramedic handy, but I'd be obliged,' said the superintendent. 'After all, this appears to be amateur night.'

Mike walked over to Terry who was now sitting on a rock. He looked at his eyes, checked his pulse, asked a couple of low questions. 'Don't undo that dressing on his arm,' Angel called. 'I've just put it on. But I think there are pellets still inside him.' Mike turned and nodded.

'He'd better go to A and E,' he said to the superintendent, 'but otherwise he's reasonably fit.'

'In that case, let's all get back to the road and out of this rain. Then, sir, perhaps you could take this woman away.'

Angel felt that she was perhaps not the police's favourite person.

Walking back along the ridge path to the cluster of vehicles at the car park seemed to take for ever. Mike was by her side. He said nothing but supported her when she stumbled. Now she was tired, and all she wanted was for this thing to be over. And what was Mike doing here?

Some of the police vehicles had already gone. She saw Terry being loaded into a van and managed to wave to him. Mike went to talk to Sam, then came back to join her with the superintendent.

'Well, am I under arrest, too?' she asked the superintendent.

He didn't smile. 'No, Miss Thwaite, you are not. But

I'm still going to warn you. This affair has had a reasonably successful ending. It could have been an awful lot worse. The police presence was very carefully organised, with the primary aim to ensure that no one got hurt. Unlike the popular idea, we do not shoot people at random—it's the last thing we want. Eventually we would have arrested this man and I very much doubt if anyone would have been injured.'

He stopped to take a deep breath. 'You got him out and I'm very glad. But just for a minute, think of the consequences if you hadn't succeeded. Guns go off, Miss Thwaite, even when people don't really intend to shoot. How d'you think I'd feel, my men would feel— even that poor devil down there would feel—if you'd been shot? How would your relations feel? You're a nurse, Miss Thwaite. I hope you don't take these risks with your patients. Now, you'd better get home.'

'I told Martlett that I'd run you back,' Mike said. 'After all, I'm going that way.' He took her arm and led her away. She couldn't resist. Somehow she was bundled into his car, the seat belt fastened across her. Then he was driving down the hill, and the car heater slowly warmed her chilled body. She didn't have to cope any more, she could relax. Reaction set in and she burst into tears.

'Here,' he said, and handed her a handkerchief. He didn't seem very comforting and she would have liked comfort from him.

'What were you doing there?' she asked after a while.

'When I arrived, your mother said Martlett had called for you as there was trouble up on the moors. So I came up to see if I could help.' His voice suddenly grew angry. 'Then I found you were out chasing a man with a gun! Who d'you think you are? You're a nurse, not a soldier!'

'He's a friend of mine and I help who I like!'

There was a squeal of brakes as he jerked the car to the side of the road, bouncing up onto the verge. 'How d'you think I felt when I heard what you'd done?' he yelled. Then he kissed her passionately.

She rather liked it.

'I can't cope with this,' she said when finally he released her. 'I want a hot bath and something to eat.'

'Sounds like a good idea. Your mother invited me to tea.' Then he drove on in silence again.

Something was nagging away at her, something the superintendent had said. She asked, 'You heard what that policeman said about me. I'm feeling guilty now. Well, was he right?'

'He had some good points,' Mike said judiciously. 'I thought he was a very competent and a feeling man. The trouble with you, Angel, is that when you think you're right you tend to be absolutely certain.'

'Oh,' she said, feeling rather subdued.

It was late. Her mother had sent for Nancy and they had fed Suzanne who was now sleeping. Marion said hello to Mike, kissed her daughter and said that there was a casserole in the oven but that she was going to bed.

'And I'm going to have a bath,' said Angel, and took a cup of tea in there with her. After a long soak she felt tired but much better. She could cope with whatever else the evening might bring. She put on a long robe and went back into the living room.

Mike was still there. He had laid the table and when she came in he fetched the casserole from the oven. After she had eaten she felt even better still.

'It's been an eventful evening,' he offered after a while. 'I was very concerned about you. I didn't want anything to happen to you.'

'Nothing did happen to me and now I'm fine. Thanks for your concern and in future I will try to think before I do anything hazardous.' She paused a minute and then said, 'We don't need to talk about it any more. We revert to how we were. There's no need for more talk.'

'Then it's time I was leaving.' At the door he turned and said, 'But I feel the need for talk. You might have your feelings firmly under control, Angel. I haven't. When I heard you were out on the moors, looking for a man with a gun, I…I wondered what I would do if anything happened to you.'

'Suzanne would still have been well looked after,' she said feebly.

'You know damn well that I'm not talking about Suzanne!'

Then he was gone.

CHAPTER EIGHT

OCCASIONALLY it happened. Angel was a paediatric nurse, with the 405 qualification—there were only three of them at Micklekirk Hospital. None was on duty and one was needed urgently. The phone rang at seven next morning. She listened to the message then said, 'Right, I'll be there in half an hour.' Then she phoned Nancy, to ask her to collect Suzanne earlier than expected.

The mother had been brought in the day before with a urinary tract infection. She was twenty-five weeks pregnant and a scan had shown she was having twins. And then, in spite of efforts made to stop it, it became horribly obvious that she was going to give birth—at twenty-five weeks. The twins had been born, one weighing 700 grams, one weighing 750 grams. Between them they weighed about the same as a bag of sugar. They needed ultra-specialist care, and would have to be sent to the coast when they had been stabilised.

Would Angel come and special one, and then ride with her in the ambulance? Of course she would. But it made for a hard day.

Looking after Suzanne was fun. Marion, of course, doted on her—this was the kind of work she had been trained for. Mike called every night and now they had things sorted out between them Angel quite looked forward to his visits. He would come to play with his little charge, feed her and bathe her, rock her to sleep and then perhaps have tea with them.

It happened late one night when her mother had gone to bed. Suzanne had been crying. Mike had lifted her from her cot and was walking up and down with her in his arms. Angel was sitting on the couch, watching him—and suddenly the tears were running silently down her face.

It was a while before he noticed. 'Angel, sweetheart— what is it?' He was concerned.

It took her a while before she could say what she was feeling. 'I had a baby of my own once.'

He stood motionless. '*We* had a baby,' he said.

He looked down at the now silent Suzanne, then with extra care took her out of the room to lay her in her cot. When he returned he sat on the other side of the couch, reached out and took her hand.

'We were two students living together,' he said, 'both studying, both working like fury, both dedicated. The little spare time we had we spent together. And…did we love each other?'

'Sort of,' she said eventually. 'We were two young animals, we loved each other's bodies. It used to excite me just to see you walking towards me down the corridor, looking all sleepy and dozy-eyed.'

'Everything you did excited me. We were great together, and then we discovered you were pregnant.'

Pregnant. More than seven years ago but she could still remember how it had felt. A kind of guilty joy. It hadn't been a good time for her or Mike's career to have a baby, it would have been troublesome—but she still remembered the joy. She had felt fulfilled. At first Mike had been shocked, but then he, too, had looked forward to being a parent.

'Both of us were a bit wild,' she said, 'a bit careless. It wasn't your fault or mine, it was both of us. We wanted each other so much that we took a risk. The number of girls I've warned against that!'

'I'll never forget that day we decided to get married. Just we two at the registry office, two friends, Mark and Penny, with us. Do you remember, Angel? A meal together in a Chinese restaurant and no time for a honeymoon. Almost as if nothing had happened.'

'I didn't even tell my parents. Dad was very ill, Ma was worried sick about him—it wouldn't have been right to worry them. And I thought that when things were easier we could have had a blessing in Laxley Parish Church and a proper party.'

'And we both worked that night.'

They stopped for a moment, memories churning through their minds.

'I lost the baby,' she said. 'At about three months. I'd barely got used to the idea of being pregnant.'

'That's what you told me,' Mike said. 'I remember coming home. You were in bed, white-faced, and you'd been crying. But you said you were OK, and I told myself I believed you. But it wasn't true, was it?'

'No! It wasn't true! I felt my life had been torn apart. And after the first time I couldn't even weep for my lost baby. I didn't want to upset you. You were working so hard!'

He looked stricken. 'You never said. I loved you, Angel, you could have leaned on me more.'

'I told myself that it was just hormonal, that in a couple of weeks the pain would go away. All I had to do was work, work like you were doing, and the pain would pass. But it didn't go away—not ever, really.'

'Is that when you started to dislike Manchester—why you wanted to go to Buxton?'

The question startled her, it was something she had

never thought of. But then she said, 'Yes, I suppose it was.'

'Now I realise I never knew fully how you felt about losing the baby. Angel, I'm so sorry. But did you ever wonder how I felt?'

Another startling question. No, she had never wondered how he'd felt. She had been so wrapped up in her own misery, but trying to keep up a happy front, that she had never really thought that Mike might have been affected.

'No,' she said after a while, 'I wanted to protect myself and just kept pushing you away. You mean that…'

'I mean that I thought the best thing for you was not to show any emotion. But I certainly felt it.'

'We *did* make a mess of things, didn't we?' she said.

Other than his visits to them, Mike didn't appear to have any social life at all. He was a handsome man and many of the female staff in Micklekirk would have been delighted to go out with him. But he appeared dedicated solely to his work and his new child. Angel knew there was gossip about the pair of them, but she didn't care. The people who mattered to her knew exactly what the situation was.

'You could stay overnight if you wanted,' she said to him. 'We keep that room warm and it would be a change from your bare little place in the residency.'

'Thanks, Angel. But for the moment it's better if I sleep in hospital.'

There was tolerably good news about Terry. The two men who had jeered at him were well-known local trouble-makers—in fact, Terry had been mixed up with them before. Their Land Rover turned out to have stolen goods in the back. The witness to the affray said that

Terry had been assaulted first, and the police decided that he had not fired the shotgun at their car on purpose, it had been an accident. Terry would have to serve a little more time but he felt he could take it.

Angel wrote to him and got a letter back, which she showed to Mike. 'Terry knows who his friends are,' he said.

'He'd do the same for me,' Angel replied.

About a fortnight after her evening on the moors Mike phoned her on the ward and asked if she could come up to his consulting room. 'I want this to be official,' he said, 'doctor to patient stuff.'

'Properly, I should be talking to your mother,' he said when she was sitting opposite him, 'and I will later. But I want to discuss this with you first. I've scheduled your mother's operation for next week. But I've been seeing a lot of her recently and she's become a friend. I'm still wondering if I ought to carry out the operation. We could transfer her to a larger hospital on the coast.'

'No way,' Angel said. 'I can sympathise with your point of view, but I think you're the best surgeon around and I want you to do the job. Anyway, Ma wouldn't be happy in some distant place, she wants to be here among friends.'

He thought for a minute. 'All right, then,' he said. 'Next Wednesday?'

'That's perfect. I've already arranged things with Nancy and there'll be no difficulty looking after Suzanne. She'll move into Nancy's house for a while. What time next Wednesday?'

'In the afternoon, I think. It should take quite some time. We'll have her in overnight on Tuesday, though, for the usual preps. We'll send her an official letter.'

'I'll tell her myself,' said Angel. 'She's been getting a bit restive recently. She wants to get it over with.'

That night she told her mother and then phoned her brother. Martin offered to come up on the Tuesday but she told him it wasn't necessary. 'She'll be comatose for quite a while so there'll be little point in you coming. I'll phone you with any news. But if you could get up for the weekend, that would be super.'

'I'll fly up next Friday,' he said.

Angel accompanied Marion to the hospital on Tuesday and saw her settled in. As a nurse herself, she knew how to draw the fine line between supporting her mother and getting in the way of the staff. Her mother was supremely confident, already planning her new life when she was fully fit.

'I love looking after Suzanne,' she said. 'I wouldn't mind looking after a couple more children at the same time.' She looked at Angel speculatively. 'What do you think?' she asked.

'I think you should concentrate on one thing at a time,' said Angel.

Her mother was prepped the next morning. Angel stood by the trolley, holding her hand just before Marion was to be wheeled to Theatre. Her mother smiled up at her. 'I know who he is, you know,' she said.

'Know who who is?' Angel asked, puzzled.

'Mike, of course, the man who's going to operate on me. He's your ex-husband.'

Angel looked down at her mother in horror. 'How d'you know that? Has he told you? He said that—'

'He's never said a word to me. But eight years ago, while you were training, I came over to Manchester to see you just for the day. You father was very ill and I...I needed a change. I was going to surprise you. Then I saw you in the distance with Mike, and I asked someone who it was with you. They said it was your new husband. You were so obviously happy that I decided not to talk to you, not to spoil your happiness.'

Angel's eyes filled with tears. 'Oh, Ma! You should have come over! You came all that way and then you went back? That's terrible!'

'It doesn't matter now. Then your father died and I kept on expecting you to confide in me, but you didn't. Instead, you got withdrawn and remote, and then you went to South America.'

'I thought I'd forgotten him,' said Angel. 'Mike turned up here by accident and it was a shock to us both.'

'So how d'you feel about him now?'

'Right now I don't feel anything about him. I'm only interested in getting this operation over and you back on your feet again. I'll worry about Mike when that's done.'

A nurse and a porter arrived. 'Time to go to Theatre, Mrs Thwaite.'

'Listen,' her mother said, 'I don't want you hanging around, worrying. Go and do some nursing or some shopping or something. It'll only annoy me to think of you sitting brooding here.'

'Ok, Ma, I'll do that.' She stooped to kiss the smiling face. The trolley was wheeled away.

She wasn't on duty but she went down to her ward, changed and generally made herself useful. She had arranged that when the operation was over she would be contacted, but three hours and then four passed so she phoned the ward. Mrs Thwaite wasn't back from Theatre yet.

Still in her uniform, Angel crossed over to the cardiac centre. The theatre doors were still closed so the operation was presumably still be in progress. She went round the back to where there was a viewing gallery. A handful of medical students were watching intently. Angel kept her eyes from the brightly illuminated figure in the centre. She sat next to a student. 'How're things going?' she asked.

'Fantastic! It started off as a routine valve replacement for a mitral stenosis, then the patient arrested and there were all sorts of complications. That lady there should have died, but this fellow Gilmour wouldn't let her go. He tried everything and I guess he succeeded. She might still make it, but I'm not sure.'

'Now I have to repair this vein insertion. Notice how little room there is for manoeuvre. You never move fast here.' Suddenly Mike's voice echoed round the gallery. Angel remembered that surgeons could give a commentary to help anyone who might be watching. It made things even more unreal.

She became aware that the student was talking to her, his voice concerned. 'Are you all right, love? Put your head between your legs and I'll fetch you a glass of water. We don't expect nurses to faint, do we?'

'That's my mother being operated on,' she said.

The student was young but in time he'd be a good doctor. He put his arm round her, lifted her bodily. 'Come on, out, this is no place for you.'

'No. I mean, I want to—'

'You can tell me outside.' She was half helped, half dragged out of the viewing gallery.

He found her somewhere to sit and fetched her a drink. 'Look,' he said, 'I'm sorry for what I said but, with you being in uniform, I thought you were just a nurse with an interest.'

'That's all right. I'll stay here now. Will you come and tell me how she's…how things are going?'

She could even admire the casual good nature of the man. 'Of course I will. I'll be back to see you at intervals. Now, can I get you another coffee?'

In fact, he came to see her three times. 'I would say she's well out of danger now,' he said after the second visit, 'bearing in mind that things can always go wrong. But that was a brilliant bit of surgery.' Later he came to say that things were over. The operation had been a success.

Her mother was in the recovery room and because Angel was a nurse she was allowed in. She had seen people after operations before and was expecting how her mother would look, so pale as to be almost grey, with a sense of the entire body being diminished. But she was going to survive.

Then she went looking for Mike. His greens were covered in blood. 'I want to change before I talk to you,' he muttered. 'Things were harder than I had expected but she should be all right now.'

'I know it was harder. I was up in the gallery.'

'You were what?'

'It was OK. A student took me out.' She looked at him. He was swaying slightly, and grey with fatigue. 'You look terrible,' she said.

'It's nothing to what I'm feeling,' he said honestly, 'but the job is done and I'm glad.'

'Have your shower, get changed, then come back to the bungalow and sleep there. You can bring your mobile with you. If you're needed you can get back.'

'I'm very tempted. But why are you inviting me?'

'Because I want you there. I need you there. I don't want to be on my own tonight. Because you're dead on your feet and I don't want you to go to your impersonal little hospital room. Let someone else look after you for a while.'

'Angel, I'm all right!'

'No, you're not. You look terrible. Any minute now you're going to fall down.'

'Well, the last time I came back to your place feeling like this I—'

'Whatever,' she said. 'You seemed to be happy enough.'

Mike was still very tired but she could see him coming round, see the spark of intelligence alight in his eyes again. 'One thing,' he said. 'No, two things. First, I don't want simple gratitude, I'm a well-paid surgeon. Second, whatever this night brings, afterwards we talk. I don't feel like being silent any more.'

It only took her a moment to decide. 'Fine,' she said. 'If you want to talk then we'll talk. I've been frightened of it but I know we'll have to. See you back at the bungalow.'

She went to see her mother again, though she knew there was little point. The nurse in charge knew her, and after five minutes chased her away. 'You know there's nothing you can do! If we need to, we'll be in touch.'

So she phoned her brother, who had said he wanted her to get in touch at any time. 'It took a little longer than we expected, Martin. But Mike thinks she should be all right.'

'That makes me feel easier. I like that guy and I've got a lot of confidence in him. See you on Friday!'

She went home, undressed and showered. The clothes she was wearing seemed sticky, though they had all been fresh on that morning. It was as if emotion had seeped out of her very skin. She changed into a tracksuit.

Mike arrived ten minutes later. He, too, was freshly showered, and was dressed in jeans and sweater. But there were still dark marks under his eyes and he seemed to move more slowly than usual.

She made him tea, and then served him the soup her mother made in large quantities. Good stock, a variety of vegetables, a thickening of green lentils and a selection of herbs and spices that was a family secret. When he had eaten he looked less fatigued. She took him to the sitting room and sat beside him on the couch.

'Just before the anaesthetist did his bit I had a word with Marion,' he said. 'She winked at me and said, "I've got every confidence in you, son." Have you told her about us?'

Angel said, 'She knows we were married but I didn't tell her. Apparently she came to Manchester one day and saw us together.'

He looked at her, amazed. 'And she never said anything to you?'

'No. She knew that if there was any reason to tell her anything I would do so. But there wasn't.'

'No, there wasn't,' he said bleakly. Then he frowned. 'Why has your mother chosen this time to confide in both of us? It seems odd.'

'I've no idea,' Angel said, 'but you can bet there is a reason.'

For a while both of them thought about this. Then he said, 'Your mother is a truly remarkable woman. You know I never knew my own mother. If I had, I hope she'd have been like yours.'

'That's a true compliment,' she said quietly.

There was another short silence and then Mike said, 'Look, I've got work tomorrow. I just have to go to bed.'

This was it. She knew after the last time she couldn't

hope for or expect help from him. Steeling herself, she said, 'D'you want me to come with you?'

'You know I do, Angel! But why do you ask me? What d'you want? Last time was…well, better than anything that has ever happened to me in my life. And then your letter was so stark. I could sympathise, of course. With what we'd both been through before, I didn't want that again.'

'Nor me,' Angel said. She laughed nervously. 'Mike, are you asking me to persuade you to get into my bed?'

'You never used to have to do that, did you?' he asked, and she blushed. He went on, 'I'll answer your question. I want you now. I wonder if I ever really stopped loving you. Now I want you desperately, but not just for tonight and with no future. I want your promise that we talk some time, and your promise that we go out together all of this coming Sunday.'

'Go out where?' she asked curiously.

'I want to keep that a secret. But I think you'll be interested.'

'All right, then, so long as Ma is OK.'

'She will be,' he promised.

'Right. Decision time. Mike, will you go and get in my bed and I'll be with you in five minutes? I just can't go and leave the washing-up.'

'Just like that? Get up and walk to your bed?'

'If it's hard then I'll take you.' She stood in front of him, pulled him to his feet. Then she kissed him, softly, gently, a kiss with the promise of good things to come. Slipping an arm round his waist, she urged him towards the door. In her bedroom she lit the bedside lamp, slid her nightie from under the pillow. 'Five minutes,' she whispered.

'After six minutes I'll be asleep.'

Angel needed that short time to herself. The washing-up was done practically at once, and then she went to the bathroom to clean her teeth. She undressed and looked at herself naked in the full-length mirror. She was twenty-eight. Her waist was as trim, her breasts as firm and high as they had been when she was eighteen. She picked up her nightie, then put it down again. It wouldn't be needed.

She wasn't sure where this would lead, why she was doing it or what it would mean to her. She only knew that she wanted it—needed it—more desperately than anything she had needed in years.

Naked, she went to her bedroom. With only the bed-side lamp on, it was in half-darkness. Mike was lying there, obviously naked himself but with a sheet drawn up to his waist. As she looked at him his expression was unreadable. He was tired but there was a glimmer in his eyes that said that he was as interested in her as she was in him.

She slid under the sheet and for a while they were content just to lie there, hands gently stroking each other's bodies. Both were weary, and she felt something infinitely comforting in the way he touched her. His hands strayed across her shoulders, lovingly caressed the slopes and peaks of her breasts, squeezed her waist and then trailed downwards. She sighed, then gasped. Suddenly she wasn't tired any more.

His body felt electric beneath her touch, she wondered at the effect even the least little contact could have on him. She smiled to herself, did it again.

'If you carry on doing that,' he panted, 'if you don't stop doing that...' So she did it even more.

'Do it like this, you mean?' she asked. 'What will you do, Mike, if I do it like this?'

For someone so fatigued he could move remarkably quickly. One moment they were side by side, smiling, kissing, touching gently. And then he pushed her down, stretched across her naked body and was poised above her. For a moment she felt almost afraid, but… 'I want you Mike,' she muttered.

She wrapped her arms round him, pulled him to her, into her, for this was something they should do together. For her then there was only the desperate urge to a swift and longed-for climax.

She kissed him softly on the lips. 'You can sleep now,' she said.

'You'll be by me in the morning?' Even though he was so tired she could hear the anxiety in his voice.

'Oh, yes, my love,' she promised. Within seconds he was asleep.

Once again Angel woke early. Mike was fast asleep, there was no way he would wake on his own. Just to be wicked she leaned over and kissed him lightly on the lips. He didn't even move. She looked down at him. His face was now relaxed, more youthful-looking in sleep. In the past she had often done this. Of the two of them, he was the heaviest sleeper. She felt a great surge of— it was love.

Trying not to disturb him, she crept out of bed, put on the kettle and then phoned her mother's ward. Marion had had a good night. She was still very tired but her condition was fine. Angel should visit her later in the day when she would be better able to talk.

A sleepy voice came from her bedroom. 'Do I hear the sound of a kettle boiling?'

'Stay in that bed,' she shouted back. 'There's at least an hour before you need to leave for the hospital.'

'Talked me into it.'

She took two mugs of tea to the bedroom, slid again in beside him. 'Before anything,' she ordered, 'especially before talking, you drink your tea. You make more sense when you've woken up.'

'Whatever you say, miss.' He pulled himself up in bed and she reached over to drop a pillow behind his head. As she did so he leaned forward and kissed her breast.

'Mike! Tea first, I told you.' Firmly, she placed the mug in his hand.

They drank in contented silence, again aware of naked legs, hips, shoulders, just touching. It was gently arousing.

'Last night I was tired,' he said sleepily. 'I felt my manhood was under attack. I need to reassert myself in a very positive manner.'

'Your manhood seemed to be as certain as my womanhood,' she told him, 'but what did you have in mind? Oh. I see.' Her body arched in ecstasy.

This time their love-making took longer, was more inventive, finished in a joint climax that seemed to throb inside her and go on and on and on. For ten minutes they lay there, content just to hold each other. Then she decided to be practical.

'We have five minutes for a bacon sandwich each,' she said. 'That'll be a pleasure of an entirely different kind.'

'Being with you is always so exciting and so different,' he said. 'What else can we do?'

'We can go to work. Mike, last time I think we took things in too much of a hurry. Don't worry, I'm not going to leave you another note. But I want us to go carefully, to decide what we can give each other, as well as what we want. If we're to have any kind of relationship I want it to be one that will last. Don't you agree?' Her voice was pleading.

'Yes, I do,' he said. 'That is, I suppose I do. This time work isn't going to get in the way of what we have for each other. Tonight I'm on call and tomorrow I'm off to run a clinic at that place further south for the day. When did you say Martin was coming up?'

'Tomorrow. He'll stay overnight, visit Ma and go back late Saturday. And I'm not having noisy sex with you if he's in the spare bedroom.'

'Pity. I'd like to see him, though. And remember you're spending Sunday with me. It'll be a sort of test.'

She was curious. 'A test? What sort of test?'

'One that I think you'll enjoy. Wear something nice and feminine—we're not going for a walk. Oh, and bring a hat.'

'A hat! What will I do with a hat? Mike, where are you taking me? I want to know!'

He grinned. 'I love teasing you when you're stark naked,' he said. 'Somehow it makes everything different.'

CHAPTER NINE

MIKE said Angel should visit Marion after he had seen her. He would be making a routine visit to check up on her progress at about eleven. So she waited till he had been in the ward and talked to him afterwards.

'Nothing to report,' he said, 'which is good. As you know, it was a serious operation and there were complications. But everything is as it should be now. I see no reason why she shouldn't make a complete recovery and have a much enhanced lifestyle afterwards.'

'You just want her to look after Suzanne,' Angel grumbled.

'And look after me a bit,' he said urbanely. 'I could live on that family soup that she made.'

Angel was a nurse and she knew better than to be intimidated by the battery of instruments that monitored her mother's progress. Most of them she used herself with her neonates. But it was different when your mother was the patient.

Marion was awake, but still drugged. Angel sat with her for a while, held her hand and thought she saw a spark of recognition when her mother's eyes slowly opened. Then she had a quick word with the nurse and went to her own ward. Everything was going well. It would take time, of course, but everything was going well.

She felt the prick of tears in her eyes and had to stop and run into a cloakroom. It was relief, of course, but only now did she understand what kind of a strain she had been under. Now was a time for celebration! Well, it would be in a week or two.

Martin had sent her strict instructions for his arrival on Friday. He was not to be met and again he would hire a car at the airport. He would go straight to the hospital to see their mother and then come to the bungalow. Angel considered for a minute, and then invited Mike to join them for a meal that evening. She knew the two men got on well.

Mike arrived early, carrying a bottle of wine. She let him in, snatched a kiss, then sent him into the living room. 'Go and chat to Martin,' she said. 'I'm going to be another hour doing exciting things in the kitchen and I don't want to be disturbed.'

A couple of minutes after he'd gone into the room there was a burst of laughter, and then her brother put his head round the kitchen door. 'If you're doing wonderful things in here for a while, us two men are going to the pub for half an hour.'

'If you do then you wash up!'

'We were expecting to do that anyway. Be back in time for tea!' And they were gone.

She was pleased that the two got on so well. But then she wondered if they would talk about her. Her brother was a shrewd businessman, she knew it wasn't easy to fool him. If he asked Mike what his relationship was with her, what would Mike say? She shrugged. Nothing she could do about it now.

It was a good meal and the three of them had a pleasant evening together. Mike left quite early, saying he had some work to do before the next day. Martin, too, was ready for an early night as the travelling had tired him. Angel sat up in bed, thinking about what had passed. Yes, it had been a good evening—casual but interesting. She couldn't remember the last time she had sat down to a meal with two men.

When Angel and Martin went to see her next day, their mother was much better, sitting up in bed and talking about the future. They arranged that when she was discharged she would go to stay with Martin for a further fortnight.

My life's taken a new track, Angel thought as they walked down the corridor. I knew Ma would have to have her operation, and I knew we'd have to leave High Walls, but I hadn't expected half the excitement that I've had. And all due to Mike. My ex-husband, the man I'd almost forgotten.

No, you hadn't, an honest little voice told her.

She was sorry that Martin had to go back so soon. But he had enjoyed his trip, he said, and he was much happier now he'd seen his mother. 'I'm glad to see I'm leaving the family in such good hands,' he said. She wondered what exactly he meant by that.

When Martin had gone Angel phoned Mike and boldly asked him if he'd like to come to stay the night.

'You know how much I want to stay,' he said, 'but I'm not going to. First reason—I'm on call and I've got a very good idea I'm going to be hauled out of my bed at least twice. Second reason—we still have to talk. I don't want to spoil what we've got again, Angel.'

'1 suppose you're right,' she said gloomily. Then she brightened up. They were to spend all the next day together. 'Tell me about this hat I've got to wear tomorrow. And won't you give me just a hint as to where we're going?'

'We-e-ell—no. But make the hat a frivolous one, and I will tell you we'll spend some time in church. Another thing, we're going to be in the car for quite a while, so if you want to travel in something comfortable and then change in a pub or something, that'll be fine.'

Stranger and stranger. But he wouldn't tell her where they were going, only that she'd find it interesting.

She picked a light blue dress that went well with her blonde hair, and matched it with a darker blue hat with a golden ribbon round it. Both were draped in a polythene cover and she dressed in her normal sweater and jeans.

She spent a couple of hours round at Nancy's, helping her with a very contented Suzanne, and then came home to go to bed early, but not to sleep. She was intrigued. What *would* tomorrow bring?

As promised, Mike picked her up early next day. He was wearing a sweater over the top of a white shirt and dark trousers. The jacket and tie hung behind him. They set off at once, and for the first hour or so she was content to enjoy the drive and be with him. But then her curiosity got the better of her. 'Come on,' she said, 'you've tantalised me long enough. Where are we going and why?'

She thought he seemed a little uncertain. He paused before he answered. 'We're going to a christening,' he said. 'I'm going to be a godfather again. There will be a little party afterwards.'

Now she felt uneasy. 'A party for your friends, obviously,' she said. 'Which friends are they?'

He spoke slowly, as if each word were carefully considered. 'We're going to Manchester. Where we first met, where we first trained and worked. We're going to the christening of Jennifer Joanne Haliwell. Mark and Penny Haliwell's third child.'

Angel sat there, unable to speak. Mark and Penny were doctors, once friends of theirs. They had been the couple who had witnessed their wedding and had shared the Chinese meal afterwards. Shortly after the wedding they had left for posts in the South and she had seen or heard nothing of them since. They had trained with Mike and had been his friends, rather than hers.

She didn't know what to say. She wasn't sure what she felt. Now she realised why Mike hadn't told her where they were going, he'd known she wouldn't have consented. This shifted the way she was beginning to think about him, to feel about him. She had been thrown back into a time she had tried to forget, tried to put behind her.

It was hard to recognise her own voice when she finally did speak. 'Will there be anyone else there that I used to know? Any more old friends?'

He shrugged. 'There might well be. Mike and Penny came straight back to Manchester after they'd finished a tour down south. They kept up with a lot of people we used to know.'

A vast anger was building up inside her. 'Mike! Stop this car! Stop it now! I want to get out. How could you do this to me?' I said *stop*!'

Fortunately there was a lay-by handy. He pulled into it and she scrabbled at the doorhandle. 'Unlock this door! Unlock it now!'

Flatly, he said, 'There's a bench over there. Go and sit on it and get your breath back. When you're ready, come back and we can talk. If you want we'll turn round and I'll take you straight back home, and not say another word, I promise.'

'Just shut up! I need to be away from you.' She scrambled out of the car, walked up and down the lay-by, taking deep breaths. Her heart was pounding. Taking out her handkerchief, she wiped away tears, tears of anger not of suffering. How could he do this to her?

After a while she tired of walking and sat on the bench, looked up at the blue sky. She could hear the cry of birds, the hum of traffic on the road behind her. And slowly she calmed down. She couldn't remain angry for too long. But a deep determination grew inside her.

She walked back to the car, sat in the front without looking at him. 'You said we could talk?'

'We can talk, Angel, we have to! I knew this would be a bit of a shock for you—but I think it's for the best.'

'*You* think it's for the best. But there's two of us here. I'd almost forgotten your habit of making decisions and just expecting me to go along with them. Have you learned nothing?'

The stone face he had presented so far now looked worried. 'I thought things between us were moving. I wanted us to see together how things might have been if…perhaps I'd acted differently.'

'You, be different? Mike, couples take decisions together. It's not just you deciding what is best. I might think differently.'

He sighed. 'I'm sorry, Angel, I know you're right. But would you have come if I'd told you?'

'Probably not. Not yet. In a month or two, perhaps.'

'I suppose that's fair enough. Right, if you want I'll turn round and take you back. It's entirely your decision, and I shan't say a word.'

She couldn't bring herself to say it. For a while she was silent and then she said, 'Tell me about Mark and Penny.'

'I've kept in touch with them for years. They've both done rather well. He's a senior registrar in Manchester and she's done a variety of locum jobs while bringing up the kids.'

'Did you tell them I was coming with you?'

'Yes. They're both looking forward to seeing you. We'll call at the house first for a quick bite, then there's the church service and then back in the afternoon for a little party.'

She guessed that didn't sound too bad. Besides, she was curious. 'All right,' she said, 'let's go. I'd like to see them—I think. Do they know what our situation is?'

He said nothing but his relief was obvious. 'They know we've just met again by accident. Don't worry, they won't say anything that might be unfortunate.'

'Doesn't leave much to talk about, does it?'

Most of the rest of the journey took place in silence. When they got nearer Manchester they stopped at a motorway café and had coffee, then she went to change into her navy dress. Once in the car she put her hat on.

'Am I allowed to say I think you look absolutely gorgeous in that?' he asked.

'Don't push your luck, Gilmour. I have neither forgotten not forgiven.'

Once they came off the motorway and started to drive through the suburbs, she felt a little restless. 'Where do they live?' she asked.

'Rather a pleasant district on the east side. You can see the Pennines from their back garden.'

'Anywhere near where we used to live?'

It was a while before he replied. Then he said, 'Their house would be about twenty minutes' drive from Grove Street. Do you want to pass there? We're in plenty of time.'

Did she want to see where she had lived? And if so, why? She just didn't know. Now she was edgy. 'No,' she said… 'That is, I don't know, it was only a flat. But there again…yes, I want to see it again.'

Angel's mood became even more uncertain as she started to pass landmarks she recognised, places she had visited. 'I've not been to Manchester since we split up,' she said abruptly. 'I guess I've avoided it.'

'I've done the same,' Mike said laconically, 'and, anyway, they say you can never go back.'

Finally they drove down the High Street. This district of Seaton had once been a small town of its own. It had been swallowed up by Manchester but still seemed to be a community of its own. And she found that the memories that returned were all happy.

'There's the chippy we used to go to,' she shouted. 'Remember the James's Special? We used to get extra pork because the owner's daughter had been very well treated in hospital. And we went in that pub…and that one… Remember how we used to play darts?'

'I remember very well,' he said.

On an area of waste ground a gigantic new supermarket had been built, open twenty-four hours a day. 'We could have done with that,' he said. 'Remember the number of times we needed something to eat and there was nowhere open?'

'We used to keep emergency supplies of beans and crisp breads. Beans and crisp breads! What a diet!'

'I can think of far worse meals,' he said.

He looked at the passing pedestrians. 'I think this is still the same kind of district,' he said. 'It has the same feel to it. Look, I'll swear that bunch are medical students!'

'They have that look. They all have that superior look that they teach in medical school.'

'Angel! I said I was sorry.'

He turned right into a short cul-de-sac. There on their right it was. Number 2 Grove Street, part of a short terrace of three-storey houses. Angel looked up at the first-floor flat where she had lived with Mike. That was their living room with windows on two walls, that was their bedroom that only got the sun last thing at night on summer days. But the curtains had always been shut anyway...

'I've had enough of this,' she said sharply. 'Those times are gone. We're not students now, neither of us are.'

'I agree. But don't you want to get out and walk round for a while?'

'No. I have a new life now. I don't want to waste time looking back at an old one.'

He drove on then, and neither of them spoke. She thought he was as affected by memories as she was. There was a bitter-sweet sense of what had been, of what had happened and of what might have happened. She realised that there was so much she had forgotten, probably deliberately. Going back was dangerous.

She was glad when they entered a hilly, leafy suburb. If you had to live in a town, this would be the place. They turned into the drive of a detached house and now she felt nervous in a different way. What would her welcome be? Mike had said that Mark and Penny were looking forward to seeing her. Why should they?

'Uncle Mike, Uncle Mike!' Two little girls came running out, aged about five, one in a long pink dress, the other in a long blue dress. Obviously they were twins.

Mike jumped out of the car, picked one up in each arm and swung them round. 'How's my two little girlfriends? I want a kiss from each of you.' Solemnly they each leaned forward and kissed him. It was easy to see that he was a favourite.

Angel got slowly out of the car, holding her hat in her hand. She was aware of two sets of eyes looking at her steadily. Mike said, 'Samantha and Sarah, I want you to meet Angel. She's a very special friend of mine and she's helping me look after a little girl.'

After a moment, either Samantha or Sarah said, 'She can't be an angel. Angels have long white dresses on, and wings.'

The other Sarah or Samantha said, with the air of one trying to be fair, 'But she's got the right colour hair, hasn't she?'

Angel bent down and said, 'I'm sorry I'm not a real angel. But first can you tell me which of you is Sarah and which is Samantha? And then can I have a kiss anyhow?'

She was duly kissed by Sarah—in pink—and Samantha—in blue. Then a voice behind her said, 'And can I have a kiss, too? I'd recognise that lovely hair anywhere.'

She turned, and there was Mark. He was a bit older, a bit fatter, had lost a little hair. But there was that cheerful expression she remembered so well, and that genuine pleasure to see her. She put her arms round him, and as he hugged her she discovered that that was just what she wanted. She hugged him back hard. This was how it always had been. 'Angel, it's been far, far too long,' he said, and she had to agree.

She had missed Mark, had missed the rest of the friends she had shared with Mike. She had given them up, if not willingly then with determination. They had been a part of her life that had ended. She had cut it out ruthlessly, and now she found herself wishing she hadn't.

She turned to see Penny in an apron, smiling at her. I want to be kissed, too,' she said. 'Then both of you come in for a while before lunch.'

There were just a couple of relations for lunch, and Angel was introduced as an old friend. Then she put on her hat, went to church and enjoyed the service and christening. She couldn't help comparing the happiness and the ease with the last christening she had been to—when she and Mike had become godparents to a child that both had thought would die.

Afterwards there was a party at the house. Angel played with the twins, talked with Penny, thoroughly enjoyed herself. In fact, she didn't see too much of Mike—he seemed to be monopolised by some important people from Mark's hospital. But from time to time she was aware of him looking at her.

Eventually they had a moment together. 'Why are you looking at me as if you're worried?' she asked. 'Every time I look up you seem gloomy, and I'm having a wonderful time.'

Soberly he said, 'I really am pleased you're enjoying yourself. I'm very pleased. But bringing you here was a gamble, and I'm still worried about it not coming off.' He glanced at the two dark-suited older men who had been talking to him so seriously. 'And things aren't being helped by people who are determined to talk shop.'

'Ah, well, that's your fault for becoming so important. But if you're worried about your gamble, then I should stop. I think you've won. I'm having a super time.'

'Things aren't over yet. You promised me we could have a talk soon. How will coming here affect us, d'you think?'

'I can guess what you want to talk about. I want to talk, too, but I'm afraid that when we do things will be clearer that I want kept in the dark. But I do agree that coming here has made things a bit more complex. If nothing else, it has made me rethink things I once was certain about. And I'm not sure I like that.'

'All I want is to—' But then they were disturbed again and she never found out what was troubling him.

Eventually most of the guests disappeared. The twins sat and watched a video and there were only Mark and Mike, Penny and herself sitting holding cups of tea. Mark and Mike were now talking shop. 'I've been working towards this for years,' Mike was saying. 'I've had the training in America. I can start in London and introduce a whole new programme.'

'When d'you expect to start?'

'As soon as I can. I'm very happy in Micklekirk—there's a great team there and it's one of the best run hospitals I've ever seen. But I need to get back into the heart of things. I'm going to buy a flat in the centre of London—you'll have to come down and visit, stay with me and Suzanne.'

'Look forward to it,' said Mark. 'We like the occasional visit to the capital.'

Angel drank her tea and considered. She knew this already, but she'd had a tiny hope that perhaps, just perhaps, Mike might have thought again. After all, he was back in her life again. Mike and Suzanne—her temporary family…

So he was still going to buy a central flat in London. Where did that leave her? Was he going to invite her to live with him—so far away? Could she to go with him? Might she be falling in love again, or was it just a case of realising her feelings for him had never truly died?

One thing was certain. Before she did anything she had to be sure she wasn't on the same destructive course as she had embarked on before.

'It's been so lovely seeing you again,' Penny said, just before she and Mike left. 'We always thought of you as our friend, you know, not just…not just…'

'Not just Mike's wife,' Angel finished cheerfully. 'Don't worry, now I know where you are I'll be here again, either with him or not. You've no idea how much I've enjoyed being here. Bye, Penny.'

After a shaky start it had been a good day. And now there was so much to think about. 'If you don't mind,' she said as they drove back, 'I want to postpone this serious talk we're going to have. I don't want to have it now, I don't even want to have it tonight. I need at least one night's sleep to get my mind round what's happened today. It's altered no end of things.'

'Altered things—or brought them back?'

'That's what I want to consider,' she said firmly. 'Now, leave it till tomorrow night. I want to decide if I've been deceiving myself for the past seven years. Mike, it's very easy to believe that you're right and all the rest of the world is wrong.'

'Don't I know it. All right, Angel, I'm quite happy to wait. You've got to feel comfortable.'

'Just one thing, though. I want you to stay at the bungalow tonight. If you want to, that is.'

'Oh, I do. I most definitely do. Especially if you cook me some more of that wonder soup that your family makes.'

'Is that the only reason you want to stay?'

'What other reason could there possibly be?' he asked.

They called at the hospital. Mike needed to check on

one or two appointments. She went to see her mother and found her almost her old self. 'Nancy brought Suzanne in to see me. I think that little darling has grown since I saw her last. She looks a really healthy baby now, Angel. How have you spent the day?'

'I've been to Manchester with Mike. We saw some old friends of ours.'

'Ah,' said her mother. 'Well, don't tell me all the details now, I'm still a bit tired. But when you're ready—and if you want—I'd like to hear everything.'

Angel leaned forward to kiss her mother. 'You're one in a million,' she said.

She made Mike the soup he wanted when they got to the bungalow, but the evening was still early. 'There's a play I really want to see on TV,' she told him. 'D'you want to sit and watch with me? It's an adaptation of a nineteenth-century novel.'

'A play! I haven't watched a play on TV in years!'

'Then this is a good time to start. You can sit by me and read the paper if you like. We'll be together and I think we need a bit of time when all we do is just sit with each other.'

He put his arm round her, kissed her gently on the forehead. 'That's a nice idea. You watch, I'll read.'

So they sat side by side on the couch, mugs of tea in front of them. She thought it was a good adaptation— the clothes, settings, even language gave the feeling of the times. But the emotions were so easy to recognise. Love was universal.

At first he merely glanced at the screen occasionally, reading the paper most of the time. But then she saw him become more and more interested, more and more intent. The paper was dropped and ignored. When she reached for and held his hand, he squeezed it almost abstractedly.

When the play was finished she sighed with delight and said, 'It's lovely, watching with you. I feel so relaxed, so…well…togetherish.'

'Togetherish it is,' he agreed. 'Now, it's not very late, but shall we go to bed?'

This time she bathed and got into bed first. It was quietly arousing, lying there, waiting for him. He came into the bedroom with only a towel wrapped round him and knelt on the bed by her side.

'I know what we're going to do now,' he said, 'and it will be wonderful. But I want to say something first. And I don't want you to say anything back because you might feel obliged. I love you, Angel.'

She looked at him, wide-eyed. When she opened her mouth he gently put his hand over it. 'No more talk now,' he said. 'We can talk tomorrow. Just remember, I do love you, Angel.'

Then he slid into the bed by her side and this time their love-making was more explosive than ever before.

They were early to bed again the following night. But this was to be a serious meeting. To emphasise this fact, Angel had put on a nightie, one she called her Wee-Willie-Winkie nightie, long-sleeved, high-necked, in thick pink material.

'It doesn't work. I'm afraid you look sexier than ever,' he told her glumly.

At hospital she had told him that if he was going to stay the night, he had to bring pyjamas. 'For the first hour anyway,' she said.

He'd looked panic-stricken. 'I haven't got any pyjamas,' he said. 'Shall I wear a long shirt?'

'If that's the best you can do.'

But this was to be a serious meeting, and she knew as he sat upright in bed beside her that he would treat it seriously. This was the talk he had asked for. 'You asked for this—you start,' she told him. In truth, she wasn't sure what she would say herself.

It seemed hard for him to start. 'I feel we should be at the Drovers' Arms,' he told her, 'where we've had our other heart-to-heart talks.'

She giggled. 'You couldn't dress like that in the Drovers'. This is a good place to negotiate. Neither of us will get angry, we can each see what there is to lose.' Then she grew serious. 'When we were married we didn't talk enough,' she said. 'We just kept on being happy, working and hoping that things would sort themselves out. And they didn't. So this time we get a clear idea of each other's point of view. OK? Then it's you first.'

Mike stared at the bedroom wall opposite the bed, and his voice changed to being reflective. 'I told you last night, I love you. I think I always have. Over the past few years I've had a couple of affairs, neither of which was really serious because I just couldn't get involved. I hope no one got hurt—certainly I tried to part as gently as possible. And I always had my work. Then seeing you again was a terrific shock. I never expected to run into you again. I deliberately tried not to think of you. Now I want you more than ever but I'm not going to rush into...'

'Marriage?' she asked softly when he hesitated.

'Yes, marriage. There's a lot we have to sort out first, a lot of problems. Suzanne for a start.'

'Suzanne isn't a problem,' said Angel. 'She's a baby and she's lovely. We'll make a good life for her.'

'Good. Now it's your turn. You tell me what you feel, what you want in the future.'

There was no problem as to what came first. 'Well, I love you, too. I thought I didn't. I've spent seven years deliberately trying to forget you, but it just hasn't worked. I even tried to fight against it when you came back, but it did no good.' She pondered a moment. 'I've not had any actual affairs. I've been out with the odd man, but that's all. I was wary, I suppose. I didn't want to get into anything I couldn't handle.'

'So do we have a problem now?'

This was the heart of the matter. 'Yes, we do, a big problem. I heard you talking to Mark and you've made no secret of your ambitions—you're going to work in central London. It's a job you've always wanted and you'll be good at it. But I'm settled here. This is my life, I'm part of a community. There's no way I could live in the centre of a big town. I've done it and I hated it. So what do we do?'

He had changed in the past seven years. Once he would have instantly insisted that she give way. Now he could see her point of view, was willing to think about it. He reached over, ran his hand down her arm. Not a sexual gesture, a reassuring one.

'The first thing we do is remember that there's no need for a quick decision. I've got months of work left here in Micklekirk. We can think about things, take our time. This time we'll get things right, we'll talk them through.'

He leaned over again and this time he kissed her. 'Here's a suggestion. I'm going down to London next weekend. Come with me. Fly down Friday, come back Sunday. You can look at the hospital I'm going to work at, I'll show you the area I want to live in. Incidentally, once I tell people what you are, you'll be offered a job at once! Meet a couple of my friends, get an idea of the kind of life I'll be leading. All you have to do is look— there'll be no pressure. Think of it as a little holiday.'

It didn't take Angel long to consider. 'I'd love to come,' she said.

Marion was doing very well. She was making the most of her stay in hospital. Even Angel was surprised at the number of people she knew, the casual visitors who just turned up.

'You're an item of juicy gossip,' she cheerfully told Angel the next day. 'Everyone's got you paired off with Mike. They know about the arrangements for Suzanne and that's a good thing, but they think that now he'd better marry you.'

Angel sighed. Could anything stop hospital talk? 'What do you say?' she asked.

'I just smile sweetly and say I'm sure that everything will turn out all right in the end. I'm afraid I've irritated no end of people by not having any little titbits to tell them.'

Angel remembered that not once in seven years had her mother mentioned that she'd known her daughter had been married. This was a woman who would only say what she wanted to.

'Why did you never ask me about being married?' she asked. 'You must have wanted to know.'

'Well, I did. But it was your story, dear, and if you'd wanted to tell me you would have done. And lately I thought you'd got it beaten. Did Mike come looking for you?'

'No. This is the frightening thing. It was a complete

coincidence, him coming to Micklekirk. We might never have met again in our lives.'

Marion took one of the oranges Angel had brought her and started to peel it. 'Coincidences happen, of course. Perhaps Mike believes that coming here was a coincidence. But I'm sure you must have mentioned to him where you were born. Then he was looking for a job, just for a few months, and…perhaps he put the two ideas together without realising it.'

'You mean he subconsciously wanted to come here? He wanted to find me?'

'Yes,' Marion said with a smile. 'But don't tell him I said so. He thinks he's master of his own destiny.'

'Isn't that what we all think?' asked Angel. Could her mother be right?

'Just let me know what you think I ought to know,' her mother went on. 'I know you, you'll go your own way. You've got the strength to stand up for yourself. When you were younger I never had to worry about you the way I had to worry about Martin.'

'Thanks, Ma,' said Angel.

She was looking forward to her trip to London, she hadn't been there for quite a while. It was fun packing her bag, deciding which clothes to take, wondering what they would do when they got there. Then Friday came. Mike drove them to the airport where they had dinner, a quick flight down and then coach and taxi. It seemed to take no time at all.

He'd booked them into a hotel—a double, she had insisted. They went to their room to freshen up and then he said they'd go for a walk round, just for an hour. 'Get the feel of the place,' he said. 'You do that best by walking.'

The first thing she noticed was how hilly it was. Streets seem to climb in every direction—she liked it. She didn't like flat country.

'This is called Crouch End,' he told her. 'It's about ten minutes from the M1 and the A1M, and in the other direction a short bus journey and six stops on the underground to central London. But there's still a village atmosphere here.'

'Show me,' she said.

They went to a pub on a main road first. It was large, seemed pleasant enough and wasn't too crowded. There was a large selection of beers on offer and a chalked menu—it didn't seem too different from her own local.

Mike had a beer and bought her a red wine. She sipped, looked round and choked on her drink. She nudged him. 'Mike! Look there in the corner!' she whispered excitedly. 'That man's on TV! He's an actor in that police serial.'

Mike glanced over. 'So he is,' he said. 'Quite a lot of TV people live round here. It's pleasant but it's central, too. Don't look now, but there are three girls sitting together behind you. The one at the end is a children's programme presenter.'

When she had a chance she looked round. Yes, there she was. Smaller than Angel had thought, and not looking much out of the ordinary.

'You notice no one's staring at her,' Mike said, 'not like they would in the Cat and Fiddle in Laxley.'

'They wouldn't stare in Laxley,' she said. 'They'd look but they wouldn't stare.'

After a thoughtful pause, he said, 'You're right. They wouldn't stare.'

'Mike! I thought I'd find you here! And with a lady, too!'

Angel looked up to see a rotund looking man in a black cableknit sweater smiling cheerfully down at them. It was odd, but she liked him at once. He seemed to radiate good humour, as if he found the world, on the whole, a pretty good place to be.

'Tim, come and join us. Meet my friend Angel Thwaite—she's a trained neonatal children's nurse with midwife training and has her 405 certificate. She's vaguely, thinking—just vaguely mind you—of moving down here in a month or two. Angel, this is Tim Beckett, paediatrician at the hospital I'm interested in.'

She shook hands with Tim, noticing that although he was smiling more expansively than ever his brown eyes were alert. Tim put his pint of beer on their table and sat down.

'Always remember that I saw you first,' he said. 'I see you've got a drink. Could I ingratiate myself by fetching you a packet of crisps? Or even two packets? Angel, I would like to think that this is the start of a long and fruitful professional collaboration.'

She laughed. She'd never quite met anyone like this man.

'Among other things, Tim runs the hospital neonatal unit,' Mike explained. 'Like yours in Micklekirk but a bit larger.'

'It doesn't run, it staggers,' Tim said. 'If you say you're looking for a job now, Angel, I'll interview you in the next five minutes and you can start work tomorrow.'

'It can't be that bad!' With a slight shock she realised that Tim was only half joking.

'It is that bad. And it's a good department. We have a good medical staff, state-of-the-art equipment, a large training budget. We'll send you on any course that will benefit us. Say you'll join us tomorrow!'

All three were laughing now. 'If I come down I promise I'll work for you,' she said. 'But yours is a prestigious hospital. Why can't you get staff?'

'The young ones just can't afford to live round here,' he said bluntly. 'And we don't have any nurses' subsidised accommodation. Last week I had to pay five hundred pounds for a suitably qualified agency nurse to cover the weekend. She came down from Stafford.'

Angel winced. 'I can see you have problems.'

They spent the rest of the evening with Tim. He was an entertaining companion and they had lots to talk about. When he heard that they were going to visit his hospital the next day he pressed her to drop in at the neonatal unit.

'I'm off to the south coast early in the morning,' he said, 'but I could phone the sister in charge so she'll be expecting you.'

'I'd like to go then,' Angel said.

'I didn't set you up with Tim,' Mike said as the two of them walked back to the hotel. 'Our meeting there was pure chance.'

'I know that, Mike. And I'd like to look round his unit tomorrow.'

Mike left her in the unit next morning while he conferred with someone in senior management. 'I promise not to be longer than an hour,' he said. 'In fact what I have to say to this man should take ten minutes. The question is, will he listen?'

Sister Bell was about fifty-five, and had no thoughts of retiring. 'I started when I was sixteen and I have no intention of giving up when I'm sixty. I need this job almost as much as it needs me.'

'Tim Beckett said you couldn't get staff because they couldn't afford to live around here.'

'He's right! I've been in my little house for thirty-one years now. It's not special but no incoming nurse could afford anything like it.'

Mike picked her up shortly after that and they wandered round the area. There were outdoor cafés—not much use at this time of year—bookshops, boutiques. She bought herself a dress for a surprisingly small amount. 'There are a lot of boutiques, they compete or go under,' Mike told her.

'Not exactly like Laxley. We've got a wool and haberdasher's there.'

Then, holding her new dress in its startlingly shiny purple carrier, she saw more of the area. There were a couple of parks, one of them with a fantastic view of the city of London. She could see many famous buildings, appearing like shadows in the grey mist.

In the evening they went into central London and saw a show, then had supper in a bistro afterwards.

On Sunday morning they met an estate agent who showed them round three different luxury flats. Angel quite liked them all—until she saw the price of one. 'You could buy a farm for that in Laxley,' she squeaked. 'Quite a good farm, too.'

'I'm into hearts, not animals,' he told her.

Then they had lunch and made their way back to the airport.

'How did you like your trip?' he asked her, once they were airborne.

'You know very well that I had a fabulous time. I thought you were really good, Mike—you just showed me round and never once tried to sell me on the place.

And I loved it. London's so exhilarating—it's like swallowing neat vodka.'

'I never knew you'd tried that,' he muttered. 'Don't forget, Angel, millions of people live quiet, ordinary lives in London. They do the shopping, they go to school, they see their friends. Just like in Laxley.'

'I know that, Mike. And I'm thinking.'

The weather in London had more or less been good—it had been warmer for a start and they'd had sunshine for most of the time. But when they got out of the plane it was raining. They set off in the car, and after half an hour Angel asked Mike to stop for a minute. He did and she stepped out. They were in the middle of the moors, only the odd distant light shining in the blackness. She stood, letting the rain touch her face, smelling the wetness. It was good to be back, she thought.

When she was back in the car she looked at Mike. He knew what she was feeling. But she remembered how he'd looked when he'd been talking about his work in the new wing of the hospital in London. This was his life's ambition come true. She couldn't ask him to change.

'You've got another three months here,' she said. 'At the end of that time, if we're still together and you ask me, I'll come down to London with you and Suzanne.'

He knew what it had cost her to say this. Gently he said, 'Just think about it, Angel. I'm not going to pressure you about it this time. We've got time to think, to consider. There's no reason why we should do what I want. You are a partner in this. And I still want above all to do what is best for Suzanne.'

That night, as she lay in his arms, she couldn't sleep. What should she do? She had loved her weekend in London. But she had loved coming home even more.

CHAPTER TEN

FOR the next two weekends Mike went back to London. There were things at the hospital he had to advise on, suggest, ask about. This suited Angel fine as she could take her turn in the Saturday and Sunday shifts and thus free herself for weekends later.

After the first trip he came back to tell her that one of the flats that they had viewed—in fact, the one she had liked the best—had gone. The agent had said that these days flats were at a premium, you had to jump while they were available. 'So I told him not to bother looking any more, I'd wait until I was in the job.'

'But I thought you were in a hurry?'

'I am in a hurry. But I thought if you were going to come with me, if there were to be three of us instead of just two—then I'd prefer a house to a flat. But I'm not pushing you, Angel. I said I would give you time.' He leaned over to kiss her. 'Never again will I pressure you.'

Her mother was discharged and came home. To Angel's amusement she seemed to have missed looking after Suzanne more than she had the company of her own daughter. She was still weak, of course, and Angel had to insist that Nancy still did most of the work. But their little family group was working well. She told Mike, 'Ma is really going to miss Suzanne when she goes.'

'I know,' he said sadly. He still came to see the baby every night, but he told Angel that he wouldn't stay the

170

night while Marion was there. So every now and then she crept into his room in the residency. It was furtive and it was childish and she loved it. And she was getting to love Mike more and more.

'You're not the man I married,' she told him. 'You're more caring, you don't think you always know what is best.'

'Thank you for that compliment,' he said. 'Now it's my turn to be back-handed. You're more willing to listen to both sides of an argument. You can conceive that you might be wrong.'

'Only with great difficulty,' she told him.

They were so happy together. But she was aware that his time at Micklekirk was coming to an end. The hospital management committee had written to him asking him if he would like a full-time post as they would be pleased to offer him one. Typically, he showed the letter to Angel. 'This is a great hospital, Angel,' he said. 'The work here is hard but you've got a marvellous back-up and the management here is first rate.'

'But it's not introducing the work you want to do in London.'

'No. In a couple of years the techniques will be up here—but London will have to pioneer them. And I still want to do that.'

She would go to London with him if he asked her, she had promised him that. And she now knew that she wouldn't have been able to give up Suzanne. But as they gradually moved from winter into spring, she knew that it would be hard to tear herself away from this place.

They were invited to take Suzanne down to see Mark and Penny. Angel thought it was a lovely idea. Mike bought an expensive new baby seat for the car—he thought cheap ones were a false economy. 'I've heard of cheap ones breaking,' he told Angel. 'If it's safety you're worried about, you should get the best.'

Suzanne was a source of great interest to the twins, Sarah and Samantha. Judiciously, they compared her with their own little sister, Jennifer. 'You're not getting married, then?' Sarah asked. 'I thought you were supposed to be married if you had a baby.'

'She's not quite our baby,' Angel said, 'but we love her and we look after her.'

There was time to chat to Penny about the difficulties of bringing up a young child. 'I used to give out advice to young mums when I was a doctor,' Penny said. 'I feel quite guilty about it now. The facts were all correct, of course—but I got the feelings wrong. I never knew just how hard work babies were.'

'You can tell me,' Angel said feelingly, 'but at least we've got lots of help, and my Ma and Nancy are wonderful.'

Penny was sitting in a rocking chair, Jennifer on her lap. 'I don't care what the experts say,' she said, rocking a little faster, 'I think every baby needs a father. Certainly every mother needs a husband—or partner, if you like. Work is so much easier if it can be shared.'

'If the partner knows what he's doing,' Angel pointed out. 'In fact, many of my mums don't have much idea. They bring their own mothers sometimes, and that way we get some sense out of them.'

'Which brings us,' Penny said slowly, 'to young Suzanne there having both a mother and a father. Poor little mite didn't do very well the first time round, did she?' Mark and Penny had been told the circumstances of Suzanne's birth.

'We—well, Mike and me together—are doing the best we can,' Angel said, 'though there are problems.'

'Hmm. Mark tells me that Mike has this offer of a wonder job in London. Tell me if you don't want to talk about it, but it's obvious from seeing you and Mike together that you're…you're…'

'Yes we are,' Angel said. 'I love him and I'd marry him again tomorrow but… D'you mind if I tell you all about it?'

It was surprisingly helpful, talking to a third person. Penny wasn't involved and she could see both points of view with equal clarity.

'You've got a problem,' she said. 'I'm not going to offer any advice, because I can't think of anything to say. Just one thing. I don't think any marriage is off to a good start if one partner sacrifices everything to please the other. There's always some room for negotiation if you can find it.'

'I hope so,' said Angel.

They had intended to stay till late evening, but the weather forecast was bad and Mark and Penny encouraged them to make an early start. 'You have to cross the Pennines,' Mark pointed out, 'and that can be tricky. Don't worry, we'll be over to see you soon enough.'

In fact, the journey over the M62 was easy. Mike had a four-wheel-drive car. Angel felt very safe in the warmth, and the lashing wind and bitter rain hardly affected them at all. They made good time, dropped down towards flatter country and turned left onto the A1M. Then they had to turn left again. This was still a main road, but more lonely, crossing through wilder country. And then a warning cut in on the radio. There had been a crash ahead. Long delays were anticipated. Mike pulled in. 'Let's have a look at the map,' he said.

This was her home country, they were only about thirty miles from Micklekirk. 'We can turn off here,' she said pointing. 'It's only a small road but it'll get us there. And in winter there'll hardly be a vehicle on it. It's mostly a summer road for walkers.'

'That sounds fine. We'll be home in time for an early supper.'

Five minutes later they did turn off. The road was narrow, with frequent bends, and he had to slow down. There was nothing to see but blackness ahead, cut only by their headlights. And the rain drummed down on them. Nothing passed. The only sign of life was an occasional roadside farm building and all were without lights.

Angel wound down her window a little and sniffed the night air. 'I love it up here when it blows,' she said. 'There's nowhere else like it. In London when there's a wind all you get is cars crashing and slates falling off roofs. But here you feel as if you're one with nature.'

His voice was amused. 'Are you trying to tell me something?'

'No! Not at all. What I said, it just slipped out. I said we would decide later and I meant it.'

She could tell he wasn't angry. 'It sounded as if you were saying that you couldn't be happy in London.'

'No. Well, perhaps… Mike, what is most important is that I want to be with you. Wherever you are, that's where I'll be happiest. I want to spend my life with you…if you want me.'

He reached over to stroke her hair. 'Oh, I want you all right. Life without you would be insupportable. I can't imagine…'

He wasn't driving fast. They were skirting the top of a small valley. In it was a stream, now swollen by the rain. Gently, they turned a corner. The car slowed and lurched to the left. Angel thought they had skidded. Then she screamed as they rolled over sideways. For a moment she knew they were upside down, her body flopped forward against the restraining seat belt. She heard a curse from Mike, a wail from the terrified baby. Then there was a crash, the sound of rending metal and an agonising pain in her shoulder. Then she lost consciousness.

She was lying on her side. She was cold, she was wet, and when she tried to sit up the pain in her shoulder was so great that she screamed again.

'Angel, Angel, don't lose it now! Angel, you've got to stay awake. Just lie there, feel your body a bit at a time, tell me where you're injured.' Mike's voice was desperate, coming from somewhere above her. Then there was another noise—the cry of a baby. How was Suzanne?

Injured and frightened though she was, her professional training came through. That wasn't the sound of an injured baby. For the moment, Suzanne was all right.

'Just give me a minute, Mike,' she muttered. 'I don't think I'm too badly hurt. Yes, I am! My clavicle is broken!' When she ran her hand over the shoulder bone she could easily feel the fracture. 'What happened?'

'I don't know. We came off the road, but I just don't know why. Now, if I can wriggle round... There should be a torch in this side pocket—got it!'

A moment later the torch flicked on, and by its dim light she could see the plight they were in. The car was on its side in the stream. Water was pouring through the broken windscreen and across her body. Dangling precariously above her was Mike, held fast by his seat belt, his body twisted in what must have been an agonising position. And behind her was Suzanne, still in her safety seat. But the seat was wet through. The tiny girl must be soaking.

'I had my mobile on the dashboard,' Mike said. 'It must have fallen—can you feel around see if you can find it?'

The pain and the cold were as strong as ever, but she was slowly growing more conscious of things. Mike's voice was clear enough, but there was a roughness to it that made her realise he was in pain.

'Are you injured, Mike? Are you all right?'

This time she heard his gasp of pain. 'I have been better. My leg is smashed—in at least two places, I think. One thing is certain—I can't walk. Now, can you find the mobile?'

She felt round about, underneath herself, being careful not to cut herself on jagged bits of metal or glass. A small, oblong piece of something—the mobile! She lifted it into the thin light of the torch. 'Broken,' she said, 'completely, utterly broken. With a mobile we could have sent for help. We could have—'

'Angel!' Mike's voice echoed through the car. 'We are trained medical staff and we have the life of a child in our hands. Now, we don't panic and we don't give way to shock. You can fight it! Wriggle into the back of the car, next to Suzanne. Then I'll drop down next to you.'

His words about Suzanne had made her determined. She pulled herself half-upright, managed to use her legs to push herself into the back of the car. If she held her shoulders back the agony was... Well, it was endurable—just. She was still half in the water, just below Suzanne. Almost automatically she reached for the wailing infant, stroked her cheek and muttered, 'There, darling, there. Soon have you dry and warm and comfy again.'

Mike managed to undo his seat belt and somehow broke his fall as he dropped to where she had been. 'On the back shelf behind you, Angel. There's a first-aid box—can you pass it to me?'

She screamed again when she had to twist. There was crepitus—the two ends of her broken clavicle grinding against each other. But she found the box and she passed it to him. 'Now, turn your back to me,' he said.

She felt him knotting bandages round both shoulders and then pulling them tight across her back. It hurt a bit, but she knew that for a while it would stop the bone ends rubbing together. 'And here's a plaster for your forehead.' She hadn't known she'd been cut. What was one more drip among all the others?

'Why has Suzanne stopped crying?' His voice was anxious again. Angel felt for her little charge, put her head close to the baby's head.

'She's getting chilled,' she said. 'All her bedding is wet through and there isn't anything dry on her. Mike, she'll get hypothermia!'

'I know that! Can you get her out, strip her and pass her to me?'

'That'll make things even worse!'

Now there was a tremble to his voice, the tremble of pain. 'She is cold and wet, I am warm and dry. I'll warm her for a minute. Now get her!'

Angel's fingers were now beginning to numb, the cold affecting her more and more. But she managed to fumble the straps undone, pull away the damp clothing and pass the wet little body to Mike. He undid his anorak, pulled up his sweater and crammed Suzanne next to his skin.

'I can spare the warmth,' he said. 'She's chilly but there isn't much of her.' Only his laboured breathing told her what he was suffering.

'Now, Angel, this is up to you. I can't walk and no one else is going to come down this road tonight. We have to look after ourselves—and Suzanne. You'll have to get out of the car, then you'll have to walk back down the road. You can carry Suzanne. We passed an old climbing hut about three miles back. Break a window and climb in. There should be blankets there, perhaps something to eat. You and Suzanne get dry, get warm and then wait.'

'What about you?'

'I'll be all right. Don't, whatever you do, leave her. You've both got to get warm and dry. I'm big and strong, I'll survive.'

'But I can't leave you here. You might…you might…'

'Angel, listen to me, my love. You're going to need all your strength. Now, pass me that baby seat—just the bare plastic—throw all the wet stuff out. Then get out of the car.'

She was past arguing now. She did as he'd told her, somehow pushing open the door that was above her, managing to climb out into the rain, sitting on the side of the car and then sliding off. It was agonising.

'Now, reach through the front windscreen and take Suzanne.' She paddled through the stream and leaned down to do as he'd said, peering at the little bundle he pushed out to her. 'Mike! You've wrapped all your clothes round her! You'll freeze to death!'

The baby was wrapped in his shirt and sweater and round the seat he had placed his anorak.

'I won't freeze to death as quickly as she could. I'm

fit and strong, I can do sufficient exercise to keep the blood circulating. Now, stop talking and move! Here, take the torch.'

'I can't leave you to—'

'You can and you will. And Angel...I love you!'

Was his voice weaker now? He had said he loved her. She wondered if...if he was giving her something to remember him by. With a sob she stooped to pick up the baby seat. 'I love you, too, Mike. And I'm leaving you.' Then she started to scramble upwards.

As she did so Angel saw what had happened to them. The road was undercut, the earth underneath it had just dropped away. Then the tarmac had broken when the weight of the car had driven over it.

She couldn't climb straight upwards, she had to follow a diagonal course, aiming for where the slope was easiest. A couple of times she fell, but she kept going and she held onto the baby seat.

She could only bear to hold the seat in her right hand. Her left hand, the side of the fractured clavicle, she tucked into the top pocket of her anorak. This eased the pain just a little.

In time she made the top of the slope and climbed onto the road. The wind was blowing stronger up here, chilling her even more. Perhaps the exercise would warm her up. She remembered having passed the climbing hut. She could make it. She had to make it.

Walking was agonising, and the wind was against her. She clutched the seat to her and walked on. The bandage across her shoulders made holding the seat harder—but Suzanne didn't weigh very much. She could do it. She had to.

For how long she walked she didn't know. Then suddenly she found herself slipping, tripping over into the heather. Perhaps she should sit and rest for a while. She was exhausted. She tried to dry a hand and slipped it inside the seat. Suzanne was still warm. That was good.

So she crouched by the side of the road for a minute. Only when she started to feel warm and sleepy did she know she had to move. If she could feel pain then she was still alive. She managed to stand, managed to walk on. She was cold, she was wet but she had to keep moving. Mike and Suzanne needed her.

After a while she knew she had to stop to rest again. But this time she wouldn't sit down. She'd just turn her back to the storm and wait a couple of minutes. If she sat down she knew she might not stand again.

She walked, one foot in front of the other, just one foot at a time, then another. Don't think about how far there was to go. Just one foot in front of the other, that was all. And she had to keep her eyes open! The rain and the wind lashed them, but if she tried to shut her eyes she staggered off the road.

And she was so cold.

Finally she could go no further. She had to sit down for a minute, she had to rest her eyes, her weary legs, do something to ease the chill that invaded her whole body...

'What are you doing out on a night like this?'

What? That was a stupid question. Everyone knew she was... What was she doing out on a night like this? No, it was an interesting question. And suddenly she was bathed in light.

She managed to open her eyes again. There were men, tough-looking men in bad-weather gear, men who knew what they were doing. She saw a four-wheel-drive vehicle, its lights shining on her.

'Get out of the way and let me take a look at her.'

Interesting. That was a female voice. So they weren't all men. The female seemed to put an arm round her and said, 'What're you carrying that's so—? My God, there's a baby here!'

She had very little strength left, but she knew she had to say something before she went to sleep. 'Two miles up the road there's a car in the river. There's a man inside it and he's…he's… Please, keep the baby warm, her name's Suzanne and—'

'We'll see to everything now,' a voice said comfortingly. 'Let's get your baby inside where it's warm and you climb in here.' An arm came round her shoulders, the broken bone rubbed and she screamed again. Then there was only comforting darkness.

It was like a weird dream. Angel wasn't sure what was happening, she only knew that she didn't have to worry any more. Other people would worry and she could rest. There were people around her, the sound of car engines and wonderful, wonderful warmth. Later on there was a tiny chill as her clothes were pulled off and people were doing things to her. But soon she was warm again. Then more comforting darkness.

She felt as if she had been beaten with a mallet. She was weaker than she had ever been in her life before, all she wanted to do was rest. But there was something she had to do. With an effort she opened her eyes, gazed at the white ceiling. What was she doing here?

'So you're awake at last.'

A cheerful voice. She turned her head to see a nurse. Angel thought she vaguely recognised her, she'd seen her somewhere… Recollection came flooding back!

'Suzanne! Where's Suzanne?'

The nurse heard the terror in her voice. 'Suzanne is fine,' she said. 'She's down in the baby unit, as happy as anything and no worse for her experience. Your mother is fussing round her. They're keeping her in just to make sure—but she should be discharged this afternoon.'

'And Mike? Is he all right?'

This nurse seemed to know everything. 'Mr Gilmour is two floors down in the orthopaedic ward. He's got plaster up to his thigh and a bandage on his head, but he seems to have survived well enough. When you've had some breakfast and the doctor has had a look at you, perhaps he'll let us put you in a wheelchair and you can go down to see him.'

'So I'm in…'

'You're in your own hospital, Micklekirk. Brought into A and E earlyish last night. You were lucky. A party of walkers found you as they were driving to a climbing hut. They got to you just in time.' For the first time the nurse's face was serious. 'They say you couldn't have walked much further. And if you'd stopped…'

If she'd stopped? Angel thought about it, and burst into tears.

The doctor came to look at her and then her mother called in to see her. She said that Suzanne was fine and that she would take her home later. Nancy would help, as always. Marion was serene, confident that now all would be well. Angel was glad of that, she didn't want any more emotion.

Slowly, the feeling of weakness and the weepiness disappeared. 'You've given your body a bit of a battering,' the doctor said. 'Now it's getting its own back. But you'll feel a bit better later on today.'

As a nurse, she was curious. 'Just what is wrong with me?'

'When you were brought in you were in shock,' the doctor said. 'How you kept going along that road I just don't know. But you did. Sometimes, when you've just got to do something, the body finds that it can do it. Anyway, you're paying it back now. You had a nasty bang on your head, but you weren't seriously concussed. You were suffering from hypothermia, but one of those climbers was a paramedic. He knew just how to keep your condition from getting worse until we got our hands on you.'

'And my shoulder?'

'Fractured clavicle. Did you know that of all the bones in the body, the clavicle is fastest to heal? Interesting, isn't it? No one quite knows why. And of all the bones on the body it is probably the easiest to knit, even though it's almost impossible to control movement.'

'Fascinating,' Angel muttered. In fact, it was fascinating, but she found the doctor's enthusiasm just a bit hard to bear. She was the one suffering the pain. 'So how will you set it?'

'We won't. We took X-rays last night—there was some overlapping and shortening but there was no need for any great effort at reduction. What we've done is just an elaboration of those bandages you had on when you came in. You can feel there's a stockinette pad over each shoulder? Well they're tied together across your back and pulled tight to keep your shoulders back. That's all we need. Oh, and you'd better keep the injured arm in a sling for a day or two.'

When she learned that she wasn't seriously injured she felt better. 'Have you seen the man who was brought in with me?' she asked, 'Mr Gilmour?'

'I've seen him but he's not my patient. His leg is in a worse state than your shoulder, but ultimately there's absolutely no reason why he shouldn't make a complete recovery.' The doctor grinned. 'He refused to be anaesthetised until he'd heard that you and the little girl were all right.'

She felt much better after a light lunch. Her lethargy wasn't so pronounced and the nurse decided she could be taken to visit Mike. 'I'll just phone to see if he's fit to receive visitors,' she said.

So Angel was wheeled along the corridor and down in the lift. She didn't like it very much. This was her hospital, usually she walked along fast and proud like the other nurses. She'd rather be a nurse than a patient.

Mike was in a side ward, a little room to himself. The nurse wheeled Angel beside the bed, so that Angel could hold his hand, perhaps even lean over and kiss him.

'I'll leave you, I'm going to pinch a cup of tea,' the nurse said. 'Back in a quarter of an hour and don't over-excite yourselves!'

'I'd like the chance,' muttered Mike.

'You look like I feel,' Angel said candidly. She hadn't realised before, but he had injured his head, too. There was a patch where the hair had been shaved, and a dressing covered it. His leg had been plastered, she could see the outline under the sheet. And his face looked—well, battered. Not physically but emotionally. 'How do you feel, anyway?'

He considered. 'My leg itches and my head aches but I'm warm, reasonably comfortable and I know I'll survive. Compared to how I was last night, I'd say I was in pretty good shape. How're you, Angel? I know Suzanne's OK.'

'Fractured clavicle and a head injury like you. Also

like you, I know I'll survive.' Then she burst into tears yet again. 'Mike, why are we talking to each other like this? I love you and you nearly died!'

He reached for her hand, squeezed it. 'It's only emotion, sweetheart. Too much to face up to. You can't help thinking about what might have happened. But it didn't happen. We're all right.'

She found a tissue, wiped her eyes. 'Yes we're all right. And it makes all our other troubles seem trivial! Whatever happens, we've got each other.'

'And Suzanne,' he said.

'Yes, and Suzanne. My mother said she was gurgling with pleasure when they put her into her cot last night.'

'Something to tell her children in years to come.' He had twisted his head to look at her, now he let it drop back to the pillow and stared at the ceiling. 'I've been doing some thinking this morning, Angel. The orthopaedics man has been in to see me. He said I wasn't fit to make any kind of decisions yet but that after a couple of days I can have my secretary in to take letters.'

'You and decisions,' she said.

'Last night I forced you out into the rain with a baby. I did it because I thought that was the best chance for you and Suzanne to survive. And when you'd gone I lay there, listening to the rain and wondering if I'd sent you out to die. We could have clung together, there was some body warmth between us.'

'Not enough. Suzanne would probably have died. You forced me out but I needed it. You made the right decision, Mike. Be pleased about that.'

'I heard that at the most you could only have kept going for another ten minutes.'

'Ten minutes was long enough,' she muttered.

'Just. Now, I'll tell you what I've been thinking.

When I get my secretary here, when I'm allowed to make decisions, I'll write to the London hospital and say that there is no way that I'll be able to take up the post in the foreseeable future. They must find someone else. If necessary, I can recommend someone.'

'But, Mike! You've been working towards this job for years!'

'And I'm turning it down. It's a question of priorities, Angel. I want to be with you and I want to be with Suzanne and I want to stay here.'

'You're just saying that to please me!'

'Can you think of a better reason to do something? Don't worry about my professional future. Micklekirk is an excellent regional hospital. I want to stay and work here. In a couple of years I'll be able to introduce the techniques I studied in America.'

It was too much to take in. This was the best news she ever could have imagined—she couldn't have written a better scenario herself. But did she believe Mike? Was he still affected by the accident, still weak? She couldn't take advantage of him if he wasn't sure of what he was saying.

'We'll forget you said that,' she said. 'In another week or two, when you're a lot better, you can tell me again. You know it's what I want to hear, but I want you to have time to think, to decide. I love you Mike. I can wait for you.'

'If I had lost you, out there is the wilderness, I would have wanted to die, too. I won't allow myself to risk losing you again, so I've made my decision,' he said. 'I love you Angel. Suzanne and I belong here, with you. I'm asking you now…will you marry me?'

Looking into the clear depths of his eyes, Angel knew

for sure. Mike had meant every word he had said, and he heart lifted.

'You're asking me to become your wife and Suzanne's mother,' she murmured softly, with a smile. 'How could I ever refuse, my love?'

THE MIDWIFE'S SECRET

by

Fiona McArthur

A mother to five sons, **Fiona McArthur** is an Australian midwife who loves to write. Medical romance gives Fiona the scope to write about all the wonderful aspects of adventure, romance, medicine and midwifery that she feels so passionate about – as well as an excuse to travel! So now that the boys are older, her husband Ian and youngest son Rory are off with Fiona to meet new people, see new places, and have wonderful adventures. Fiona's website is at fionamcarthur.com

The Surgeon's Special Gift **is a fabulous new novel from Fiona McArthur available in September 2006 in Mills & Boon Medical Romance™.**

TO MY MOTHER THE ADVENTURER
– WITH ALL MY LOVE

PROLOGUE

DR SINCLAIR MCPHERSON glanced down into the smoky depths of the bar with a grimace.

Wine bar nightlife was something he didn't often make the effort to investigate, but he had to stay over for the next day's medical presentation anyway.

He should have driven back to Southside. One of the local obstetricians had made the music here sound promising, but Sinclair wasn't so sure he needed the lung cancer.

The bar was crowded and noisy when he descended and he almost returned to his motel television but then the music started up again.

The haunting wail of a lone saxophone infiltrated his irritation with gossamer fingers the way sirens pulled ships to the rocks. But the real siren was oblivious to his presence as she stood in the far corner under an overhead spotlight.

Her body swayed in a slinky red dress, while her glorious copper hair floated in a thick cloud around her head. He could feel the music vibrating in his veins and shook his head to break the spell. It didn't work. She seduced the saxophone and Sinclair with her eyes closed.

She seemed vaguely familiar, and his brow creased as he tried to place where he'd seen her, then he shrugged. She embodied every fantasy that he'd held of the perfect woman—and that made her an old friend.

Sinclair eased to the bottom of the stairs and leant on the rail to drink in the sound and sight of her. He couldn't look away, and even tried closing his eyes, but her image was still there, burning in his brain.

People pushed past him and he restrained the urge to tell the chatterers to shut up and listen.

When she finished the notes drifted away on the chatter and he sighed. The spell was broken.

His hand reconnected to his body and released his grip on the rail. Wryly, Sinclair shook the tingling out of his fingers as she stepped down from the stage.

Her smile was like sunlight in the dimness of the bar and she continued to sway to some inner beat as she moved towards a boisterous table at the side of the room. Unable to stop himself, he cut through the crush towards her.

Unexpectedly, a drunken reveller's hand landed on her shoulder to detain her and Sinclair's response to the sight surged up irresistibly like a kick in the gut. Close enough, he stepped forward and between them so that the wine-saturated breath of the drunk blew in his face instead of hers. One hundred per cent alcoholic garlic. Sinclair coughed and turned his head to look down at her, his smile quizzical. 'Would you like this gentleman to leave you alone?'

Eyes wide and voice husky with confusion, she turned to him with relief. 'Yes, please.'

Sinclair glared into the unfocussed eyes below him. 'Sorry, friend. You're not welcome.' Even in his alcoholic haze the drunk backed off.

Sinclair watched the man stagger away for a moment before looking back at her. Then the vision laughed up at him and he felt the bands around his heart expand along with the silly smile on his face.

'A he-man? I haven't seen that side of you, Dr McPherson.' Her voice was deliciously playful and it was a moment before he realised she knew his name. Then, like a light switch flicking on inside his head, he knew where he'd seen her. She was one of the quieter midwives at Southside—Sister Robin—but he'd never seen a glimpse of this side of her.

Sinclair clamped his lips together to stop his mouth falling open. He probably saw the woman briefly several times a week but he couldn't remember a non-patient-related conversation with her.

'I'm sorry. Letty Robin, isn't it? I didn't recognise you.' Great comeback, McPherson, he chided himself. But she still had him stunned. He'd never have believed it. The mouse? He couldn't relate the painfully shy woman—well, he'd always assumed she was shy—with the vibrant vision in front of him.

'Scarlet, are you OK?' The rest of her party, more musicians or hippies by the look of them, surged around her. Sinclair allowed himself to be swept with them back to their table, still bemused by the strength of his reaction to someone he worked with. He strained his memory for the last time they'd spoken, and the only visual memories he could come up with seemed to be of him talking to the bun on the top of her head. He must have been asleep for the last few years. Maybe it was all a strange dream but he didn't want to bypass a second of it. He frowned. Why did they call her Scarlet?

He asked her once they'd sat down, her by his side.

'Letty is short for Scarlet and these friends have always called me that,' she shouted over the din. 'We've jammed together a long time, but not in public.' Her eyes sparkled with excitement. 'We've just made our own CD. The local music shop has sold a whole six copies.'

He grinned back at her delight. 'That's an occasion.'

'It's also my birthday, and tonight they arranged for me to play in public to get the feel of it.'

'Happy birthday. So how did it feel to be up there?' He couldn't look away as she swallowed what looked like apple cider in a soothing draught and relaxed back in the chair.

Her lips were soft and shiny and eminently kissable. He felt like picking up her glass and pressing his own lips to the spot where her mouth had been. Or, better still, those lips. Then she spoke again and he dragged his gaze back to her eyes.

'Performing live is scary. And not something I want to do on a regular basis. But I'm breaking out tonight.' She smiled that broad-daylight sunbeam right at him and for the first time he wished he could play a musical instrument or at least sing a note so he'd have something in common with her.

Until he realised he did have something in common with her. He worked with the woman. He couldn't believe he'd never felt the pull of attraction to her before. Pull? He felt like a bullock team was dragging him along.

He wanted to see that smile again. 'My voice makes a dog howl.'

She grinned at him and then one of the others at the table drew her attention and Sinclair sat back and just watched her. In this company she was vivacious and witty and vibrantly alive. He'd never seen her like that at work. It was still difficult to fathom but, then, he'd always been at the centre of the crowd and at work the more outgoing staff, and more lately, Tessa, tended to take over the conversations.

The motel's television was long forgotten as he bought her another cider and chatted with her friends, his eyes always searching for her smile.

When he finally managed to secure a dance with her, he realised what had been missing all the years he'd danced before. The soft material of her dress shifted seductively beneath his fingers and their bodies swayed together perfectly. Scarlet against him was a whole new way of dancing.

Reality receded even further as she leant into his shoulder and he smoothed the fabric. 'I love your dress,' he murmured.

She twirled in his arms and laughed up at him. 'A present to myself on my twenty-fifth birthday. Wicked, eh?'

'As sin,' he said huskily and pulled her closer into his arms. Scarlet filled his senses like a potent wine yet there was an air of innocence about her that baffled him.

The time raced away and when her friends left to go home he looked at the clock with indecision. He felt like a randy sixteen-year-old and just as unsure of himself. He couldn't let her go yet.

'I don't want this evening to end, Scarlet. Stay with me.' He gazed down at her and her eyes were like blazing jewels in her face, almost glittering as she stared up at him. Then she laughed and swept up her bag and her saxophone case.

'Let's make a night of it we'll never forget then, Sinclair.'

*　　*　　*

When he woke in the morning, she was gone, as if she'd never been. Yet his body could still feel the pressure and pleasure of hers. He knew for a fact that she didn't make a habit of sleeping with strange men—so why would she leave? He ran his hand over the slight indent her head had made in the pillow beside his and caught a faint wisp of her flowery perfume on his fingers. His feeling of loss caused a lump of disquiet in his usually cast-iron stomach.

Later that afternoon, when he took the steps to Southside's Maternity Ward two at a time, Sinclair looked at the place with new eyes. Someone here would be able to give him Scarlet's address. Unfortunately, the first person he saw was Tessa, sitting alone at the desk.

'Sinclair? You're back early. I thought the conference went for another day?' The tall midwife's pleased smile reminded him and a twinge of guilt pulled a frown between his eyes. They'd been out for dinner a few times but he'd never promised Tessa anything. He knew now what he'd been waiting for.

'Something came up.' He watched her lift one sculptured eyebrow. Clinically, he could see her beauty, but she couldn't compare with the joy he found in Scarlet. It was only fair that Tessa knew that. Be honest with her, McPherson, he chided himself. 'Actually…someone…came up.' He couldn't help the smile that followed or the implication that his change of plans had been because of a woman.

Her face stilled and she looked away for a moment before turning back to him.

'I'm pleased for you. Anyone I know?'

Sinclair hesitated, an uneasy reluctance warring

with his desire for the information he wanted. He'd have to ask someone.

'You wouldn't have Letty Robin's home phone number and address, would you?'

'Letty Robin?' The eyebrows went up again in disbelief. 'My, my.'

Sinclair heard footsteps approaching down the corridor and frowned at her. 'That's enough.'

'Captured her heart, have you? I went to school with Letty—she's always been a funny, shy little thing. What a good catch for someone like her. I understand her father never acknowledged her. You do know her mother was unmarried?'

'No, I didn't.' If Tessa didn't shut up he'd strangle her. Sinclair's voice became very soft so only she could hear him. 'I hope you're not going to play the woman scorned, Tessa.'

Tessa stood up and draped her arm around his shoulders before whispering in his ear.

'Me? Scorned? Never.' Then her voice returned to normal. 'I know you'll come back to me.' She moved away from him around the desk and her lips curved in a smile of greeting as someone he didn't see left through the front door.

He ignored Tessa's conceit, too immersed in his own world to take notice of her. 'Address, please.'

'The staff book is on the shelf—she lives in the nurses' home.' Tessa laughed and he squashed the feeling of disquiet that grew with her smile. Lord, save him from all women—bar one.

As she walked down the steps of Maternity, Scarlet's face felt frozen. There were a lot of reasons she regretted the night she'd spent with Sinclair McPherson.

And conversations like the fraction she'd just over-heard between Sinclair and Tessa only emphasised her regret.

She'd hoped she'd grown out of her inferiority complex about her birth but hearing Tessa's snide comments to Sinclair took Scarlet back to her school-days. The last five years had been peaceful until Tessa had resettled in Southside a few months ago.

She needed to get away and think this thing through, Scarlet realised. She'd been a fool last night and it was the lack of any future in it that was the worst. But when Sinclair had looked at her finally, with all the admiration she'd ever dreamed of, she'd felt beautiful and worthy of him.

A one-night stand with a man she'd fancied for years. How stupid could she get? His eyes had been on Tessa since she came back and from the way she'd been draped all over him, whispering sweet nothings in his ear, it seemed like they were right back where they belonged at this moment.

Scarlet had watched him drifting into a relationship with her nemesis and she'd really thought she'd ac-cepted the cruel fate that had spelt the end of any fanciful dreams she'd held. She just didn't have it in her to fight Tessa for him.

Then last night, drunk not on wine but on Sinclair's undivided attention, she had gone back to that motel with him. Knowing what she did and risking what she had, she'd weakly thrown away the self-esteem she'd painstakingly earned over the last five years.

Self-esteem and respectability might not seem dif-ficult to most people, she thought bitterly, but when you'd had the loss of it rammed down your throat by a bunch of school bullies for years it assumed enormous importance.

Her love of midwifery had done a lot to repair the damage but obviously her own illegitimacy was something she still hadn't come to terms with. She had to get away.

Sinclair was frustrated, more so than he had ever been before in his life. Letty, or Scarlet as he now thought of her, was gone. She wasn't home, didn't answer her messages and didn't come to work. As suddenly as she'd entered his life she'd left it. Later in the week, when he questioned the charge nurse about the midwives' roster, he was told that Letty was on leave for two weeks. Then it had been extended to twelve months. Her nurses' home room was deserted. Eventually one of the other midwives mentioned a phone call from her about a whirlwind courtship with some geologist up in the hills and that she was married!

CHAPTER ONE

LATE in August, Sinclair McPherson, Director of Obstetrics at Southside, rubbed the bristles on his chin, unaware his life was about to change again.

Four o'clock in the morning was too early to shave, he defended himself, not breaking stride down the hallway.

He glanced up at the 'birth imminent' red light that glowed gently outside Labour Ward One, knocked briefly and stepped around the door into the room.

He frowned, momentarily confused. The labour ward bed was empty and there seemed to be an inordinate number of women present at first glance. Then he realised the birthing woman was kneeling on a mat at the side of the room. He sighed.

Times were changing. Still, the good news was that it seemed he'd made it with a few minutes to spare to be present for the birth. Surely she'd hop onto the bed at the last minute. A natural, uncomplicated birth was always a pleasure, even at this time of the morning.

The woman he'd been called to see—Mrs Connors—was earthily naked and he could hear the tiny puffs as she pushed gently with the contraction. He couldn't remember seeing her name antenatally, so she must have visited one of the other practitioners. He shrugged. It wasn't uncommon to meet a woman for the first time in labour if you covered as many calls as he did.

A cascade of deep copper hair screened her face and there was something beautifully primal about her that touched him. He shook his head at the unusual thought.

In fact, the whole room had a peacefulness that wasn't common at this time. Sinclair opened his mouth to speak and then decided against it. She was too busy for him to introduce himself at this moment. He heard the longer exhalation of her breath as he made his way to the sink where he began to wash his hands and gown up as usual.

'Get him out of here!' The woman's words were strong and clear and vehement with intent.

Sinclair froze and turned back towards the group huddled around the woman on the floor. He reached for the towel and bit back a sigh. Hormones. Women in labour were known to be irrational at times and he'd taken his fair share of abuse over the years. He smiled slightly. They usually apologised profusely once their babies were born.

A tall woman, probably her mother, Sinclair guessed, brushed the sweep of thick hair off her daughter's face. She soothed her. 'It's OK, Scarlet.'

Sinclair looked into his patient's face for the first time, recognition hitting him like a freight train. He squeezed the towel between his fingers.

Here, in the final throes of labour, were the delicate cheekbones and luminous eyes that had haunted his thoughts.

Now, only the second time he'd seen her beautiful hair loose from its usual bun, she was in labour!

'Scarlet—I mean Letty?' Sinclair was unaware of the speculative glances the others in the room cast his way at his use of her birth name.

When she'd been a midwife here, her actions had always been controlled, and she'd never raised her voice above a low murmur. But that night, and now in the throes of childbirth, it was as if someone had turned a light on. Her strength and vitality shimmered from her.

Don't go there, he warned himself, and dragged his mind away from the memories.

Another breath whooshed between her lips but there was no problem understanding her next words. 'I *said* get him out. He's the last person I want here.'

This was ridiculous. Sinclair quelled the flicker of pain her request caused. 'I'm here to help you, Letty.' He tried to establish his role as doctor and benign father figure. 'It will all be over soon.'

Her look seared him with scorn. 'I know that,' she said and her gasp, as a new wave of pain engulfed her, made him wince. She looked away from him, to some hidden place, to concentrate on the progression of the baby's head. Then she sighed again as the contraction ebbed. 'This is all your fault.'

Sinclair's heart skipped a beat and then galloped off in a bolt. Surely not? She would have told him. November, December, January... It was late August now... Sinclair's usually analytical brain scrambled as he tried to work it out. No. He'd used protection.

He shook his head. He was inferring too much here. 'All right, Letty. I know it hurts.' He forced the next words. 'But I'm sure your *husband*—' he couldn't help the hardness he injected into the word 'husband' '—is more at fault than I. Now, perhaps you could let me see where you are up to.'

She gave a slightly hysterical laugh and then gritted

her teeth. 'The midwife will deliver my baby. Please, leave—before I say something I'll really regret.'

Now he could feel the hostility from the other women in the room. He glanced at Michelle, the midwife in charge, and she shrugged wryly as if to apologise for calling him.

'Fine.' He erased all expression from his face. 'I'll be outside in the corridor if you need me.'

The sound of the door as he pulled it shut coincided with the unmistakable sounds of the last moments before birth. Then he heard a baby's cry and the murmur of congratulatory voices.

Sinclair pushed himself off the door. He felt as if someone had burst a large paper bag in his face. What the hell had that been about? But most disturbing of all—Scarlet was back. With a baby!

Scarlet Robin sank back in the bed and clasped her new son skin to skin against her breast. He snuffled to match her own ragged breath and she realised at last the wait was over. 'I'll call him Cameron.'

A great wave of love for the infant lying against her took her by surprise, and she brushed her lips across his damp hair. She'd done it. Scarlet caught the tears in her mother's eye.

'Thanks for your help, Mum.'

'Congratulations, darling. Welcome to motherhood,' Vivienne said.

Scarlet smiled and glanced at two other women, both dressed in brightly tie-dyed sarongs. 'And thanks, both of you, for bringing me in from the valley and down the mountain. You made me strong with your presence.'

The younger of the two was heavily pregnant and

ran her hand nervously over her bulging stomach. 'You were wonderful, Scarlet. And you were right. It wasn't so bad at the hospital.'

Scarlet relaxed back against the beanbag. 'Good girl, Leah. At least you'll have some idea what it's like here, just in case.'

Leah glanced guiltily at her friend. 'I'm sure I'll be fine with Crystal at the community.'

The other woman, long-faced and expressionless, nudged her. 'We'd better go and leave Scarlet with her new son. It was interesting, seeing the hospital side.'

Leah nodded and her long plaits swung around her face. 'Bye, Cameron. Bye, Vivienne.' She smiled shyly at the hospital midwife. 'And you, too, Michelle.' As they left, Crystal said nothing.

Michelle waved and followed them to the door to shut it after them. 'Is Leah having her baby in the valley?'

'Baby is breech at the moment and she's hoping it will turn before labour. But she's promised she'll come here if it doesn't.' Scarlet ran her finger down the incredible softness of her baby's leg.

'Who's the other woman?' Michelle's voice made Scarlet look up.

'Crystal is the new valley midwife, she's determined Leah will have her baby at the community.'

Michelle raised her eyebrows. 'I noticed a bit of attitude.' The other midwife slid the blood-pressure cuff over Scarlet's arm and pumped it up. Stethoscope in ears, she asked the question that Scarlet knew had been burning to get out. 'So what was all that business with Dr McPherson?'

Scarlet glanced pointedly at her constricted arm.

'Um, Michelle? Could you let the air out? Otherwise my arm will drop off.' The slow hiss of deflation made them both smile.

The few seconds gave Scarlet time to formulate an answer. 'It was nothing personal. A tirade against men. You know what women in labour are like. Forget it.' She glimpsed her mother's raised eyebrows and frowned her to silence.

Cameron chose that moment to make his presence heard and the women all hustled to pacify him. Within moments he nursed quietly at his mother's breast with a warm blanket tucked securely around them both.

Michelle stepped back. 'He's got the hang of it. I'm off to empty my trolleys before we get you showered. Press your call button if you need me. It's great to see you back. Congratulations, Letty. Or should I call you Scarlet?' she teased.

'Whatever strikes your fancy.' Scarlet gave a wry smile and shook her head. 'I'm not sure who I am at the moment. Thanks anyway and I'll call you if I do need help.'

That left three generations of the Robin family alone in the room, and the silence lengthened between mother and daughter.

Finally Vivienne could stand it no longer. 'So what are you going to do about his surname on the birth certificate? Are you going to call him Connors after your absent husband, Robin after you or...' Vivienne paused and squeezed her daughter's hand '...perhaps McPherson after his father?'

Scarlet refused to meet her mother's eyes. 'What's Sinclair McPherson got to do with this?' But her voice lacked conviction.

Her mother raised her eyebrows. 'I've had my suspicions and the reactions of both of you today confirmed it. I really couldn't swallow the travelling-geologist-husband story. I'm sorry, darling.'

Scarlet raised her own eyebrows, not realising how much she resembled her forthright mother when she did so.

Then she sighed. 'It was my fault for weakening when Sinclair turned up at the nightclub. Just one let-my-hair-down vulnerable moment and the last five years here, spent trying to be perfect, were wasted.'

Vivienne shook her head. 'Well, stop trying to be perfect. I never liked you shortening your name to Letty. Scarlet is a strong name. Blaze a trail and be yourself.'

Scarlet narrowed her eyes. 'I always knew he was dangerous.'

'Did you, now?' Vivienne bit back a smile. 'I wonder why that is?'

Scarlet was too immersed in her own problems to notice. 'I'd hoped by creating Mr Connors I could protect my child from the rumours.' And me from Sinclair. But she didn't say it. She looked up at her mother. 'It seemed like a good idea at the time.'

Vivienne sighed. 'I can't help feeling you'd be better to face the gossips and be done with it.'

Scarlet sank back in the bed. 'Of course you do. You called me Scarlet. I've worn my illegitimacy branded on my forehead all my life. I won't have that for my son. I like being unobtrusive Letty, and it feels like I've spent the last twenty-five years avoiding scandal like the plague. It's so pathetic that one mad loss of control ruined it all.'

'I'm sorry you feel that way, Scarlet.' Vivienne bit

her lip. 'But I think you'd find that you're the only person who can read the writing you're so sure is there. Sinclair may even surprise you and I believe he should have the chance.'

Scarlet watched her mother stand up from the bed and stroke her new grandson's cheek. 'At least you came back to have him here. I'm grateful for that,' she said. Vivienne picked up her bag from the side bench. 'I should have minded my own business. I'll see you later this morning. Try and get some rest.' Scarlet watched her mother blow a kiss and leave.

Scarlet sighed and closed her eyes. She hadn't meant to hurt her mother. She'd felt more attuned to her in the last twelve hours than she ever had. Maybe Vivienne did understand what she was going through? This was probably the first time she'd let Vivienne get really close to her. Now that was an unattractive thought. Had she really been that obsessed with her own problems?

Cameron had settled to infrequent sucks and Scarlet knew she should detach and burp him to protect her nipples from damage. She slid the tip of her little finger into the side of his mouth and broke the suction—just as she had shown the technique to countless new mothers.

It was strange, being the mother and not the midwife.

A lot of the assurance she'd shown as adviser to inexperienced mums seemed to have slipped away somewhere. Now she held this child who was totally her responsibility, she could feel the fear of doing the wrong thing threaten to overwhelm her. Was this how all mothers felt—or just those who were parenting on their own? She cupped his tiny foot in her hands and watched his toes spread at the sensation.

She wished there were someone there she could share her delight with as she smiled over his perfect tiny feet. Which brought her back to Sinclair.

What about Sinclair? Should she have told him? Given him a chance? Was her mother right to advise her to brazen it out? The problem was, she wasn't the brazen-it-out type. Not like her mother.

And when Sinclair married someone else, as he would one day, would that woman's children bully Cameron like she'd been bullied?

Scarlet shook her head. She couldn't face it. She imagined the furore if Scarlet Robin named the town's most eligible bachelor as the father of her child. She shuddered.

Then there was Tessa. How ironic that the taunting child of her schooldays was practically engaged to the only man she'd ever slept with. Now there would be another illegitimate child for Tessa's children to taunt. But even more ironic was the fact that the person who had undermined Scarlet's confidence for so long was her half-sister. Only Tessa would never know that.

A wave of fierce protectiveness for Cameron rose in her heart. Nobody would victimise her son. This way Scarlet Connors would be a respectable married woman and Cameron would be like every other child. She'd never shared with her mother how virulent the jibes had been right through her school years until a wall of suppressed emotion had blocked true communication between mother and daughter.

And this morning, when Sinclair had walked in, she'd nearly blown it at the last moment.

With his presence in the labour room she'd felt her

control slipping through her fingers like silk through a loop. What she'd lost, what might have been—it had all been there for distraction at a time that hadn't permitted distractions.

In a perfect world, he would have been beside her to grip her hand for the last twelve hours, to wipe her brow and moisten her mouth as she'd struggled and strained and finally exulted in the birth of their child.

But it had been a mockery to see him enter a few moments before the end. To see the glory and not the journey it had taken to get there. Instead, he'd stood tall and straight, in his work suit and tie, every inch the distinguished country specialist, here to 'attend' another birth.

It was hard to imagine the two of them so lost to sense and reason that Cameron could have been conceived.

She shook her head at the memory. Sinclair's fleeting touch leading to a whisper of a kiss, leading to the first sign of the impending storm.

But lightning was like that.

A cataclysmic mating of passing storms—wild winds of passion interspersed with miraculous rainbows of joy—but even the most perfect storm had to end.

She could remember lingering the next morning, despite the shock of what they'd done, to catch a last sight of him with his dark hair tousled on the motel room pillow. His ridiculously long lashes had rested on his cheeks as she'd slipped away. It had been then that she'd known that she couldn't face him without the world finding out how she felt. Or face the fact he'd never be hers. She'd needed to get away—from

Sinclair and what she'd done—just for a week or two to come to grips with her own weakness.

The nurse manager had been baffled but understanding over her sudden need for a short leave of absence. Then Scarlet had found out about her pregnancy and she'd extended it to twelve months.

The strange thing was, even though the last nine months spent at the valley community had been special, Scarlet had never felt tempted to have her baby anywhere else but here at Southside. She must be a masochist.

Hopefully, Gerry the geologist—she grimaced wryly at the alliteration she jogged her memory with—her fictitious husband, would protect her son. She really must get her story straight.

With more luck, now Cameron was born, she wouldn't be as scatterbrained as she'd felt during pregnancy. She had to remember to tell people he was in New Guinea—or was that New Hebrides? Or should she just kill him off? Ditch him? Her eyes closed. It was all too hard at the moment and she dozed with her son as the sky turned pink in a beautiful dawn.

'How are you now, Mrs Connors?' Sinclair stressed the 'Mrs' but Scarlet wasn't sure if it was for her sake or for Tessa standing beside him as he did his ward rounds.

She could feel herself turn back into inconspicuous Letty as he towered over her, and she frowned. Why would that annoy her? Wasn't that what she wanted?

She looked down at the sheet crumpled between her fingers and smoothed it. 'I'm fine, thank you. I must apologise for my rudeness in the labour ward this morning, Dr McPherson.' She looked up and caught a brief flash of emotion cross his face before he schooled his expression.

'Not a problem.' He stepped forward to the little cot and peered in at her baby. 'What are you calling him?'

Scarlet couldn't help comparing Cameron's naming process to the usual father-mother discussion. 'I've called him Cameron.'

'A good strong name,' he said, and untucked the baby sheet. 'I'll do a newborn check on this fellow now, too, as I missed doing it at his birth.' He turned to the midwife. 'Perhaps you could find me one of those infant stethoscopes from the nursery, please, Tessa?'

Scarlet suppressed a wince at the glowing smile Tessa bestowed on Sinclair as she hurried to do his bidding. Some things never changed. He'd always been everyone's grey-eyed boy and then favorite man—even Scarlet's. He'd never noticed her and she hadn't pushed it, as if she'd sensed how easily he could have broken her heart if he had. It had been safer hiding in full view—as dull and dutiful Letty.

She looked from baby to father. Earlier, Scarlet had been sure that he had his father's determined chin and beautiful mouth. Now she found herself searching Sinclair's face for other signs of paternity. Or was she filling a need to drink in the sight of the man who affected her so deeply?

Affected her so profoundly that she'd run.

A headlong flight that had meant leaving Southside where she'd finally carved a comfortable niche for herself—until, of course, Tessa had moved home—in a profession she adored. A need to leave rather than face a loss of control that had rocked the foundations of the safe life she'd built for herself.

Now she had come to terms with what she wanted out of life. She still believed she had done the right thing. It had been time to come home.

Sinclair's black hair was slightly shorter than she remembered and his face seemed thinner. Those straight brows were drawn together as he competently undressed and examined Cameron for any signs of abnormality. His intense concentration made his cheekbones more prominent, and her fingers itched to run down the side of his face as she remembered doing that night. She must have been mad.

His sudden stillness warned her and she glanced away from his face to his hands. He'd turned Cameron over to run his finger down his spine and he'd seen the small dark brown mole glistening on the baby's buttock like a tiny brown paint spill.

Sinclair lifted his head and stared at her. She could tell his mind was racing and a cold fear clutched at her stomach. She moistened her lips and strove for a calm voice. Those birthmarks were quite common.

'I saw that this morning. Apparently my father had one.'

He answered almost absently as if his mind was still elsewhere. 'It's a congenital melanocytic naevus. They occur when melanocytes, the cells which produce skin pigmentation, accumulate in large numbers, producing a dark patch of skin. Usually greater than one centimetre in size, it's basically a mole that tends to run in families.'

'That was impressive.' Scarlet couldn't keep the tinge of sarcasm out of her voice. 'Obviously you've seen them before.' This wasn't an interesting case they were talking about. This was her baby!

Sinclair's beautiful grey eyes narrowed and a grim smile played across his lips. 'Yes, I've seen them before. Both my father and I have one, and we're fine.'

Tessa swept in with the stethoscope and Sinclair looked back at Cameron as he held out his hand.

Scarlet sagged unobtrusively against the pillows and resisted the urge to clutch her chest. That wasn't proof. She was being foolish. He'd said 'tends to run in families'—not *always* run in families. He didn't suspect anything. She hoped.

The examination was soon over and Sinclair stepped back for Tessa to re-dress the baby. Cameron's indignant cries filled the room.

Scarlet curled her fingers and resisted the urge to snatch him from the other woman and dress him herself. It was only a moment later before she had him safe in her arms but it was illuminating. So this was how new mothers felt!

That was another basketful of empathy she would have when she came back to work.

Sinclair wrote in Cameron's newborn health book and slipped it back under the cot. 'Everything seems OK. Cameron is a fine healthy baby. So when does his father get to see him?'

Scarlet jumped and her mind went blank. 'I'm sorry?'

Sinclair's gaze drilled into hers and she sat, transfixed like a rabbit caught in headlights on the road. 'Your husband? I believe he's overseas at present and couldn't be here for Cameron's birth.'

Right. 'Of course. In New Hebrides.' Scarlet

stretched a smile across her frozen face. 'I'm not sure, but he was thrilled when I spoke to him this morning.'

Sinclair smiled but his eyes were hard. 'I'm sure any man would be proud to have a son like Cameron. Have a restful day, Letty.' He nodded and gestured for Tessa to precede him from the room.

Scarlet felt sick. She had to get out of here before rounds the next day. Please, God, she would handle seeing Sinclair more easily when she wasn't so emotionally drained from labour.

On his way out of the hospital Sinclair's mind wasn't on where he walked and he almost bumped into Scarlet's mother as she entered through Reception. She was taller than her daughter or perhaps it was just the way she carried herself.

But, then, he was beginning to wonder if that depended on whether the young woman in question was playing Letty or Scarlet.

'Good morning, Mrs Robin.'

'Good morning, Dr McPherson. And it's Miss Robin not Mrs.'

Sinclair blinked but recovered quickly. He could feel a small smile tug at the corner of his mouth. 'Miss Robin.' He inclined his head. 'I've just checked your new grandson over. He's a fine young lad.'

Vivienne smiled. 'Ten fingers and toes, I assume. He'd better have. Scarlet couldn't have tried any harder to be healthy.'

'Just the congenital melanocytic naevus on his buttock. Any family history you know of for that?'

'Come again?' Vivienne's brow wrinkled.

Sinclair grinned self-mockingly. 'Sorry, brown mole.'

The older woman raised one arched eyebrow and gave her own small smile. 'Not that I'm aware of, but perhaps Scarlet will know. I haven't met her husband's family. Have a good day, Doctor.'

'Please, call me Sinclair.' He shrugged and shook his head. 'I feel like I've known you for a long time.' He could have sworn she looked startled.

'Funny, that. I'm Vivienne. I'll see you later, then, Sinclair.' She moved on, head high and no backward glance.

He continued on his way but the tension in his shoulders ached for release. Why had Scarlet/Letty lied about the mole unless she had a reason? Was he just being paranoid? Or was Scarlet hiding something? Like he had a son!

Hell. He'd finally started to get his life back together since she'd crashed into his world like a destructive comet and had left just as quickly. He'd been out again with Tessa a few times since then—and been congratulating himself on his good sense at returning to normality. He'd even started to think of those grandchildren his father kept asking for. Until this morning.

Once he'd seen Scarlet again, he'd had a hard time resisting the urge to return to the hospital to interrogate her. He'd probably worn a path in his carpet as he'd waited for normal round time because he hadn't trusted himself to see her that first time alone.

But he was no nearer the truth of why she'd disappeared than he'd ever been. And now it was too late.

At the thought of that magical night, his hand slid up to rub his neck and he dug his fingers into the knot of tension there. He couldn't believe how she'd affected him or how he'd behaved. That he, who'd never lost control before—or immersed himself in someone until the outside world had disappeared—had been so powerless to resist a woman.

His only hold on sanity had been the fact he'd used protection when they'd made love. Almost infallible.

But it must have been very shortly after their night together that she'd met her husband. An idea that didn't bear thinking about froze his steps. If Cameron was his own son, had he, Sinclair, forced her into a marriage she hadn't wanted and was now stuck in—because of the consequences of that night?

Surely not. She would have told him. Sinclair started walking again. And if that had been the case he would have married her himself! That stopped him cold.

Sinclair realised now he hadn't come to grips with the fact that Scarlet had disappeared before he'd even been able to attempt to repeat the experience of making love with her. Could he really consider spending the rest of his life with a woman he barely knew—not counting the little he'd seen of her at work?

When he'd received the news she'd married some geologist, the depth of his dismay had been a sobering realisation.

As the months had passed, the whole incident had become even more illusional until he'd almost convinced himself it had been a dream—a warning to be careful.

Well, that little indulgence had certainly come home to roost. It was a nightmare.

CHAPTER TWO

'I SAW Sinclair on my way in.' Vivienne placed the small blue-wrapped present on the bedside locker before she reached over to kiss her daughter on the forehead.

'Yes, he checked Cameron over.' Scarlet tried a smile but her face felt stiff. 'Mum, I want to go home. Today. You said we could move in with you.' She realised she was twisting the sheet again and stopped.

'Of course I'd love to have both of you.' Vivienne pulled the chair up beside the bed. 'I never understood why you lived in the nurses' home all those years. But why today?'

Scarlet met her mother's eyes. 'I'd feel more relaxed away from here.'

'Away from Sinclair, you mean.' It was a statement not a question. Vivienne frowned.

Scarlet sank back against the pillows. 'It doesn't matter what the reason is. Take us home, please.'

'If that's what you want.' Vivienne patted her hand. 'Give me time to make a few preparations and if it's OK with your doctor, I'll pick you up this afternoon. I must take home those bags the girls brought in with you. You said one had the baby things in there?'

'Everything's there.' She pointed to three cases beside the bed. 'Thanks, Mum.' She kissed her son's head. 'We'll go home to Nana's, OK, darling?'

Vivienne mock shuddered. 'Don't you dare teach your child to call me Nana! Vivienne, please.'

* * *

31

The McPherson Family Practice was run from the front of what used to be four units overlooking the river. Sinclair had purchased and restored the outside of the block to its 1950's grandeur on his return from Sydney five years ago. Inside, renovations had converted the top floor and rear of the ground floor to spacious living accommodation with wonderful breezes and views.

This year he'd finally convinced his father to move in so they could see more of each other. Privately, Sinclair was concerned about his father's health.

The phone rang as Sinclair was about to go through to his consulting rooms. He listened, frowned at the news and then replaced the phone gently in the cradle afterwards. So Scarlet wanted to go home. Already? Funny how he now thought of her as Scarlet and not Letty. Was she trying to avoid seeing him or was her sudden wish for discharge for another reason altogether? He laughed self-mockingly. As if he understood her.

Of course, she could do what she liked and he couldn't stop her. But he had to see her once, alone, to settle what had been between them or he would go crazy.

He wished her bloody husband would come back, covered in naevi—the thought made him smile at the mental picture—so he could stamp on those suspicions that wouldn't leave his mind. The timing of Cameron's birth was too close for comfort but the real problem was that he couldn't get Scarlet out of his mind. He had to remember she was a married woman and out of his reach. Technically he shouldn't see her.

He heard the front door open and he followed the

sound of slow footsteps through to the kitchen. When he walked through, his father's shoulders had an unaccustomed droop to them. Sinclair frowned as the older man lowered himself heavily into a chair at the table.

'You OK, Dad?'

Dr Frank McPherson looked nearer to seventy than the sixty he was. 'Just in need of a holiday, my boy.' He looked up from under a tufted set of straight brows. 'I heard you go out in the early hours. Get there in time?'

'Technically.' There was that word again. Sinclair sat down at the table beside his father. He didn't want to elaborate on his eviction from the labour ward by his ex-lover.

'You deserve more than a holiday, Dad. You should be out having the time of your life now.'

His father ignored his son's not too subtle suggestion of retirement. 'What do you mean—technically?'

Sinclair sighed. 'Do you remember Letty Robin? She used to be a midwife from the hospital.'

'Daughter of Vivienne Robin?' A strange smile flitted across his lined face. 'Now, there's a woman. I haven't seen her for a while.'

Sinclair tilted his head. 'Is that a glint I see in your eye, Dad?'

'She's a dangerous woman. I almost lost my head over her—sometimes wish I had. I wonder if she's still got that fire that draws a man like a moth to a flame. I've never seen it in young Letty.' He glanced up at his son. 'But still waters run deep.'

'And I always thought you were pining for Mum.'

'Your mother was a good woman and didn't deserve to die young. We had a good marriage.' He changed the subject. 'Which reminds me! When are you going to provide me with some grandchildren?'

'Diversional tactics, Dad?' Sinclair couldn't help his thoughts going straight to Scarlet. He grimaced. 'I had hoped to give you a daughter-in-law before the children, if that's OK.'

'Well, mind I'm not dead before you do. So what's last night got to do with young Letty?'

'She had a son and I was called in.'

'Uncomplicated, I hope.' He didn't wait for an answer and had lost interest in the original question. 'So Vivienne's a grandparent before I am, eh?' His eyes twinkled and he stared off into the distance.

Sinclair tested the idea of saying there was some complication but not the type his father was talking about. He decided against it. That was between Scarlet and himself.

Scarlet heard her mother's doorbell ring just after six that evening. The murmur of voices didn't enlighten her and when Sinclair walked into the room she could only stare. Her breath caught and with her hand at her throat, she panicked for a moment. He seemed to fill the room from where she sat.

'Good evening, Scarlet.' His voice was calm and deep like she'd remembered, and it still activated the nerves all over her body. Would she ever be able to forget that night?

He was frowning at her. 'May I sit down?' He indicated the chair beside where she was sitting with Cameron.

She tried to crane her neck unobtrusively to see around him in case her mother was still available to rescue her, but his strong shoulders blocked any view of the hallway.

Sinclair's voice, at least, was amused. 'If you're looking for Vivienne, I asked her to give me a few moments alone with you.'

She straightened her head and nodded at the chair. When he sat down, he looked very relaxed as he crossed one well-shod foot over the other. Damn him. Scarlet licked dry lips and carefully met the cool grey of his eyes. 'Why are you here?'

'A little unfinished business.' The subtle undertones raised the hairs on her arms and she suppressed an urge to clasp Cameron closer to her chest.

She raised her chin. 'I'm sorry, I don't know what you mean, Dr McPherson.'

If anything, his eyes became cooler. 'I've handed your case to the women's health nurse to follow up. I thought you might be more comfortable. So I'm not here as your obstetrician. Please, call me Sinclair. You at least owe me that.'

At his words, her eyes flashed and she looked more like the Scarlet he remembered. 'I owe you nothing.' Then she looked away for a moment and when she looked back she still looked beautiful, with her copper hair loose around her shoulders. She also looked tired. He stifled the sudden urge to gather her in his arms and offer her a safe haven. Maybe he should leave her to rest?

He hardened his heart. She was married and this could be his last chance to talk to her alone. This was too important.

Her voice was flat when she went on, 'The Scarlet you met has gone. You caught me at a mad, vulnerable moment and totally out of character for me. I'm just plain old Letty whom you've walked past for years.'

He stared at her for a moment, and weighed her words. She'd never be plain anything to him again. But that wasn't her problem with a new husband and son. When he spoke, his voice was very quiet. 'I hope we can still be friends?'

Her startled gaze met his. 'I'm a married woman, Sinclair.'

Her voice lacked conviction and his pulse leapt with the subtle underlying implications. Did she already regret her marriage to this other man? Then she pressed on as if to cover her lack of fervour.

'And I'm a respectable mother who has come home for some peace and quiet until my husband comes back from New Guinea. And now, if you'll excuse me, I need my rest.'

He stood up and replayed her words in his mind. 'As you wish. I'll leave you to rest.' His final look was enigmatic. There was something not quite right here but he couldn't pinpoint it. 'My regards to your travelling husband—he certainly gets around.'

Scarlet stared after him and then heard the door close. Blast. She'd been rude and that wasn't like her.

Why did Sinclair always do that to her?

Her brain felt scattered to the four corners of the earth. A bit like her absent husband who should have been in New Hebrides, not in New Guinea. She sighed but was too preoccupied with what Sinclair had said to care.

Sinclair McPherson wanted to be friends? What did that mean? He wanted an affair while her 'husband' was away? That thought was too big to contemplate even if there was some truth in it, which she couldn't believe, because if she did, she had a whole new set of problems.

The man could have any woman in Southside—why would he want her? She winced. Because she played good sax? She gave a strangled laugh. Good sex was more like it. Well, she'd learnt from the master. It was probably always that good for him.

She sighed and the tears scratched at the back of her throat. Cameron stirred in her arms and gave a little whimper. Grateful for the diversion, she lifted him over her shoulder to gently rub his back. He burped and the loud noise drew a smile from her.

'What a well-brought-up boy.' The oft-repeated phrase slipped out and the true meaning of it crashed in on her.

Her spine stiffened. Cameron would be well brought up. There would be no scandal attached to his name and the best way to achieve that was to remain in control. And that wasn't something she could guarantee if she let Sinclair McPherson into her orbit. Perhaps he was attracted to her, but lust wasn't love.

She was an unmarried mother and the daughter of an unmarried mother. Not exactly the perfect partner for the director of obstetrics at Southside Hospital. Especially if the truth came out that she'd fabricated a husband.

The only option was to remain in control of her life. Alone. Control was something she didn't seem to have much of when Sinclair was around.

'Are you OK, sweetheart?' Her mother broke into her thoughts and Scarlet looked up.

'I am now.' There was a new firmness in her voice.

She tightened her arms around Cameron. 'I'll be a mother my son will be proud of.'

'I never had any doubt of that, darling,' Vivienne said, her brow furrowed.

Scarlet sank her head back against the pillows of the lounge. That's it, then, she thought. 'I think I'll go to bed early.'

Vivienne hid her disappointment. 'It's only just dark.'

Her daughter gave an uneven laugh. 'At the community we slept and rose with the sun. No electricity there. I guess I'm used to it now. Sorry, Mum. I'll be better company tomorrow.'

Vivienne shrugged philosophically. 'You must think me a selfish old woman if you expect me to keep you up after the day you've had.'

'No. I know you have my best interests at heart.'

Two pairs of hazel eyes collided. 'Do you?'

'Goodnight, Mum.'

The first days blurred together and then a week had passed since Cameron's birth. Cameron demanded Scarlet's full attention for those early unsettled days, and all she seemed to do was feed him and sleep. Or lie in bed and think about Sinclair.

Another week passed and Cameron settled down to more regular feeds. But Scarlet couldn't seem to get her bounce back. She felt like she was living in a thick grey cloud.

Vivienne provided meals and support unobtrusively, and a new rapport began to build between mother and daughter.

Sinclair stayed away and Scarlet told herself she

was glad. The emptiness inside had to be because she was used to being busy.

'So, tell me what you did at the valley community. I imagined it's changed since I was there for your birth. We haven't had a chance to talk about it.' Vivienne was buttering her daughter's toast as Scarlet tried to eat breakfast and breastfeed at the same time.

'It's still very isolated from the world—utopia for the establishment haters—although they do have one mobile phone for emergencies. But the theme is still self-sufficiency and clean living.

'The majority of the food is grown there, as it was in the early days. Everyone made me very welcome when I turned up.' Scarlet remembered the moment when she'd decided that escape from Sinclair was harder than she thought. Until she'd remembered the commune where she'd been born.

Vivienne smiled. 'I remember when I arrived, too. Though there was only half a dozen families living there then. I'd just discovered I was pregnant with you and wanted to do everything right for the pregnancy.' Another piece of toast popped up in the toaster and Scarlet realised she'd eaten the last one already.

She accepted the new slice and smiled at her mother. 'We've never talked about it.'

'No. You haven't wanted to know.' Vivienne's voice was soft. 'But women change when they have their own baby. And we'll talk about it soon. Tell me about your time there.'

Scarlet stared at the food in her hand as she remembered. 'The previous midwife had just left and they were glad to see me. I took over the running of the clinic and ensured we had what was needed in first-aid supplies. But mostly I was the midwife. It's the same as when you lived there. Everyone has a task and certain responsibilities and it runs surprisingly smoothly.'

She smiled at the memory of her first couple of weeks. 'The maternity side was so different to the medicalised version of childbirth I was used to.' She shook her head. 'It was as if all the rules I had been taught had been ripped away. The true concept of midwifery in all its glory. But sometimes it was scary.

'These women didn't want me to deliver their babies—they wanted me ''with'' them while they did it themselves.' She laughed at the shock she had first battled with.

'It became the most incredible thrill to see them empowered by birth and not treated as *patients*.' She curled her lip over the word 'patients'.

Scarlet looked up to catch her mother staring at her.

Then Vivienne smiled. 'The time away has done you good. I've never seen you so passionate about anything before, except perhaps your music.'

Scarlet laughed, slightly embarrassed, and played with her toast. 'It certainly changed the way I feel about my role in childbirth. In fact, I think it actually changed me.' She looked up. 'I grew into being myself in the time I was there. There was no need for the rigid control I'd always thought essential when I worked at Southside.' But there was no Sinclair McPherson either, her thoughts mocked her. She pushed the disturbing concept away. 'I could be who I wanted and nobody thought any less of me.'

Vivienne shook her head. 'I've said that all along but you had other ideas. I admired your self-control but I could never understand it.'

'That's the joke. My self-control was important to my self-image. When I lost it with Sinclair I had to get away and see what was left of me to feel good about.' Scarlet laughed bitterly. 'And that was before I found out I was pregnant and the whole world was going to know how pathetic I was.'

Vivienne's eyes were suspiciously bright. 'Darling, I hate to hear you talk like that. If you feel that way because I didn't marry your father then I have a lot to answer for.' She met her daughter's eyes. 'Tessa's father would have married me, though I'd never tell his widow that.' A grim little smile hovered over her lips. 'But the man I should have married long before I met your father came back into my life and I wouldn't settle for second best. And except for your lack of a male role model as you grew up, and the fact that this is a small town, I don't regret that. Was your childhood so bad?'

Scarlet looked away and then her brows furrowed. She'd always believed her father hadn't wanted to marry the pregnant Vivienne. Scarlet thought of the few times she'd met the man she knew was her father accidentally in the street—unspoken conversations thick in the air between them. And her mother had refused him? She tamped down the hurt that he'd never wanted to know her. Well, it was his loss. Had her childhood been so bad? One day soon she would tell her mother about Tessa and her friends.

But here was something it didn't hurt to think about. Who was the other man? And how had she not known? 'Why didn't you marry the man you loved?'

Vivienne shrugged and stared down at the teacup in her hand. 'When his wife died, he didn't ask me and I was too proud to pursue him. Pride has a lot to answer for. But enough about me.' She offered to pour more tea and the subject was closed. 'Do you plan to resume at the hospital as a midwife or return to the valley?' The wistfulness in her voice was plain to both of them.

'Back to Southside—part time—as soon as I can.' Scarlet looked down at Cameron. 'My time at the valley is over. Crystal is the midwife now and in charge of the births. They don't need me.' Scarlet shrugged. 'Do you know that people come from all over New South Wales to spend the last few months of their pregnancies in the community because of the kind of births we have there?'

Vivienne patted her daughter's hand. 'It still sounds a wonderful place to be a part of—although I enjoy the creature comforts and the outside world myself.'

Scarlet nodded. 'For a time I thought I could stay for ever, but I must be a townie like you, Mum.' They both laughed. 'One of the good side issues about my time there was the opportunity to show that people who work in hospitals can be on the same wavelength as those in the valley community. I just hope I left the women with enough confidence that if they need to come to Southside for specialist care they'll rise above their reluctance. Or Crystal's reluctance.' She shook her head.

'It's something they haven't felt comfortable with, even in emergencies. I've promised to try and ensure their needs and choices will be respected. Hopefully, they'll realise that sometimes sick newborns will benefit from care that can't be provided in the valley.' She sipped the last of the tea and stared thoughtfully into the empty cup.

'That was the worrying part—no back-up if something did go wrong. Luckily it didn't in my time there. But I don't want to waste what I've learnt at the community.' She looked up at her mother and her eyes and voice showed the enthusiasm missing since she came home from hospital.

'I want to encourage change at Southside so that the women who choose to give birth there have the same chances as the community women to feel empowered by their births. It won't be easy but I'll fight for what I believe is their right.'

She grinned cheekily. 'I'm not sure how that's going to fit in with Southside doctors.'

Her mother sighed with relief. 'I love it when you're like this, Scarlet. I'm glad you're going back to Southside.'

Scarlet squeezed Vivienne's hand. 'The valley was a wonderful place to take time out from the world and have a healthy pregnancy, but I want Cameron to grow up able to hold his own in any setting.' She stroked his cheek and he stopped drinking for a moment to gaze into his mother's eyes.

'That's how I felt when it was time for you to start school,' Vivienne said.

Scarlet nudged her son under the chin and Cameron resumed his breakfast. 'He can visit when he's older, like when you took me back in my teens, but I've still got the money I saved before I left. I might buy my own house in town.'

'If that's what you want,' Vivienne said. 'But this house is too big for one person. It would be crazy to run two households.'

Scarlet searched her mother's face. 'I don't want to intrude. Cameron and I would make a huge change to your lifestyle.'

Vivienne laughed. 'No bigger than when you were born. I enjoy having you both. But it's up to you.' She stood up. 'They say mothers and daughters get on even better when the first grandchild hits the household.' She smiled down at her grandson.

'We missed out on a lot of that closeness when you were younger. I was so busy showing the world I didn't care what they thought, and you were tucked behind a wall I couldn't penetrate—maybe it's our time now. But that's enough soul-searching. Here…' She held out her hands. 'Give me my grandson and you go and shower. How do you feel about the three of us going to the shops today?' She smiled. 'Get us all out of the house.'

The shopping expedition was a disaster. Scarlet ran into three nursing friends who hadn't seen her since she'd left. She kept muddling her marriage story and Cameron grizzled as he picked up on his mother's tension.

Vivienne just smiled to herself as she ushered her daughter back to the car. 'The problem is, Scarlet, you're a terrible liar. Stick to "it didn't work out" and be done with it.'

'Making up a husband seemed like a good idea at the time.' Scarlet wiped a tense hand across her forehead.

'That's how most trouble starts. And here comes Dr McPherson.'

Scarlet's pulse rate jumped and she twisted her neck to search. 'Sinclair? Where?'

'Not Sinclair. Frank!' Vivienne smiled at the older man approaching and Scarlet felt like a fool as she recognised Sinclair's father. He was shorter than his son but one could see he'd been handsome when younger. And that he only had eyes for her mother.

'Hello, Vivienne. It's good to see you.' His greeting seemed unusually warm and Scarlet's forehead creased at the undercurrents between the older couple.

Even her mother's voice was softer than usual as she inclined her head. 'Frank, long time no see.' She turned towards Scarlet. 'You know my daughter, Scarlet?'

He smiled paternally at Scarlet and Cameron. 'I hear this chap dragged my son out of bed a couple of weeks ago.'

He smiled benignly down at Cameron and Scarlet hoped his son hadn't told him the full story.

He went on, 'Congratulations on your baby, young woman. He's a fine-looking lad.'

'I've recently acquired a son-in-law and a grandson,' Vivienne said. 'Scarlet's home with me while her husband's overseas.' She moved onto a new topic before he could comment. 'I hear you moved in with your son, Frank? No more wild parties for you.'

'I haven't a wild bone in my body, Vivienne. As well you know. It's at times like this that I regret it but I'm too old now.'

Scarlet looked from one to the other, feeling the conversation was on another level. The couple were oblivious to her presence and Cameron started to fuss. She stepped away to unlock the car and let the cool air in.

As she slid Cameron into his car capsule, she heard her mother say, 'We're not spring chickens any more but I don't like to hear you talk like that, Frank. Why don't you drop around for sherry this evening? We could catch up on old times or maybe play Scrabble.'

Scarlet heard innuendo in the suggestion, then the couple laughed.

'I'd like that.' His voice had picked up a deeper undertone and Scarlet smiled to herself.

She'd never actually seen her mother in action before and it was illuminating and even amusing. Until she heard her next suggestion.

'Bring your son. Scarlet is housebound at the moment and would welcome some company from the hospital.'

Scarlet lifted her head in shock and whacked the back of it against the doorframe. 'Damn!' She rubbed her head and tried to catch her mother's eye. Cameron started to cry and Scarlet sighed. She'd kill her mother. She wished she'd never left the house.

'I can't believe you did this.' Scarlet was viciously chopping celery, still fuming thirty minutes before the visitors were due.

Vivienne was her usual serene self. 'It will be fine. If you hate it that much, take yourself off to bed. But I was hoping you'd change out of your jeans into a dress. Make an effort to brighten yourself up.'

The doorbell rang. 'Oops, they're early.' Vivienne glanced at her reflection in the microwave door and tidied her hair.

Scarlet glared. 'I'll get it and I'm not changing.'

Her mother just laughed. 'It's good to see a bit of fight in you, dear. All this moping around was starting to worry me.'

When the door opened Sinclair thought Scarlet looked sombre but fabulous in tight black jeans and a ribbed sweater.

Her 'Please come in' belied the fire in her eyes and

he wondered if he should turn around and come back another time. Then his father pushed past, smiled blithely at Scarlet and sailed into the house. That was it, then.

He cleared his throat. 'Pleased to see me, I gather.' Sinclair watched her grit her teeth and the funny side of the situation caught up with him. She was no more impressed when he smiled.

'My mother's idea and it *is* her house.' She gestured him in with her hand. 'Please come in.'

He looked around with interest. It was a welcoming house with lots of plants and interesting knick-knacks. The last time he'd been here he hadn't noticed anything but Scarlet. 'Well, that deflates any pretensions I may have had.'

'I'm sure you have enough to go around.' The sound of a baby's cry floated down the stairs.

She shot a look at his face and then away. 'Excuse me. I have to attend to *my* baby.' She spun on her heel and left him.

Sinclair stared after her. Had she stressed the 'my' in 'my baby'? Her jeans clung lovingly as she took the stairs two at a time and he was sure they said, Come hither.

It had been hell staying away from her the last two weeks and he didn't fight the impulse to follow her now.

Sinclair tracked the soft croon of her voice and when he found the room he leant on the doorpost of the baby's nursery. The walls were pale blue but he was more interested in the big white wooden rocking chair facing the window.

The black sweater she'd been wearing lay in a heap on the floor and the light shone off the paleness of her slender shoulders as she sat in the chair. The white lace of her bra strap bisected the soft curve of her breast as she bent over the baby in her arms, reminding Sinclair of a Renaissance painting.

He swallowed the lump in his throat. How could he have walked past her all that time? It was still difficult to fathom how he'd never thought to look beneath the mask of the meek midwife to the true Scarlet inside.

Maybe she hadn't heard him come up the stairs, and for a fleeting second he wondered if he should creep away.

But he couldn't. The empty hollow in his heart formed by that one night with Scarlet began to ache as if the raw edges had just been exposed again. She was married, damn it. He should never have come.

Sinclair watched her rest back into the chair and sigh as her hair fell across her face and breast. The sight of her clenched his gut with desire and he knew he had it bad. For a man who spent most of his days around breastfeeding or labouring women, the sight of Scarlet and her baby blew him away like no one ever had.

Scarlet must have sensed his presence because when she turned her head she didn't look surprised.

He felt like a peeping Tom. 'I'm sorry,' he said, 'but you both looked so beautiful I couldn't leave.' The simplicity of the statement embarrassed him but it obviously upset her. A tear rolled down her cheek and he cursed himself for an insensitive monster. 'I'll go.' He turned to leave.

'It's all right, Sinclair.' She sniffed. 'Perhaps you could pass me one of those tissues. I seem to have

the labile emotions of the post-partum period off pat.'
She pointed to the dresser top.

He moved into the room and passed them to her.
She looked so alone with her baby. He wanted to
gather them both up in his arms—which should have
surprised him, but didn't. Even the realisation that he
wished Cameron were his own son didn't surprise
him. 'Why isn't your husband here for you?'

She remembered her mother's advice. 'We're going
through a rough patch. Let's leave it at that.'

His eyes narrowed with concentration at the first
positive news he'd had. 'How far can I leave it?'

'A lot further than you are at the moment.' He
sensed her mood change and almost sighed as she
glared at him. Back off, he warned himself.

He held up his hands. 'Sorry.' He crouched down
beside her chair and some herbal scent drifted from
her hair. It reminded him of the night he'd buried his
face in the fragrance of it and had felt silken strands
slither across his chest. The band around his heart
tightened.

He couldn't prevent himself from moving closer to
breathe in her scent and she turned her face towards
him. Her soft lips were so close and his hunger
gnawed at his control like a trapped rat. But that's
what he would be if he took advantage of her vul-
nerability.

Instead he sat back on his heels. He still had to ask
and his voice was husky when he spoke. 'Can you
tell me why I never saw you again after that night?'

Scarlet closed her eyes and he thought she wasn't
going to answer him.

She didn't look at him when she spoke. 'What can
I say? It was a turning point in my life and out of

character for me. Afterwards, I needed some time to find myself again.'

The answer was disappointing but he couldn't leave it alone. 'You can't deny it was special. Can you?'

She turned towards him and her eyes narrowed. 'If you want me to say that, I will. But it's in the past, so let it drop, Sinclair.'

Her attitude confused and, he had to admit, infuriated him. His eyes hardened. 'What if I don't want to drop it?'

Scarlet glared. 'Then leave and don't come back.' They glared at each other and neither of them softened. Finally she tossed her head in disgust.

'Perhaps you could inform my mother I'll be twenty minutes or so on your way out.'

That had been dumb. He had no right to harass her because of one incredible night. He needed to think this through and he couldn't sit across the room from her tonight and stay sane. He stood up. 'If that's what you want,' he said, and after one last glance at the baby in her arms he left. He heard her blow her nose as he walked down the stairs. All he'd achieved had been to upset her and most likely stop himself from sleeping for the next few nights. He should stay away from her.

Scarlet dried her eyes. Damn the man. How was she going to cope with him when she went back to work? She could ask him to leave her mother's house but she wouldn't be able to evict him from the ward. Maybe working at Southside wasn't such a good idea.

CHAPTER THREE

FOUR weeks later on her first day back at work, Scarlet couldn't calm the butterflies in her stomach. She dreaded her first contact with Sinclair.

To settle back into being inconspicuous was harder than she'd imagined.

Irritated by the length of her hair, Scarlet had decided to cut it to a short bob. She didn't realise that her shoulders were straight and her chin pointed up instead of down as she walked in with her bag.

'Welcome back, Letty.' Michelle stepped up and hugged her, and Scarlet hugged her back. 'Love the hair.'

Scarlet put her hand up to her neck and smiled. She had missed the camaraderie that flourished in the unit.

'Thanks.' She grinned at her friend. 'Do you think you could call me Scarlet? I'm used to that now. And I kept Robin as my work name.'

'No problem. And when do we get to meet Gerry the geologist? Still in some out-of-this-world place?'

'I'm afraid so. It's not working out. Marriage may not have been the brightest thing I've ever done.' Scarlet could hear herself rambling again and she looked away. 'I don't want to talk about it.'

Michelle hugged her again. 'No worries. How is your gorgeous son?'

'Gorgeous.' Scarlet's eyes softened. 'He's six weeks old now and takes the expressed breast milk from the bottle really well as long as I'm not the one trying to give it to him.'

'Well, it's going to be busy today, so yell when you need your lactation break. We don't want you to explode.'

Scarlet laughed. 'At least you guys understand. So what's on the agenda for the day?'

'Two kids in the crib in oxygen, one first-time mum in the birthing unit whose waters broke yesterday evening but she's taking a while to establish labour and a oxytocin induction of labour is booked for this afternoon.'

Scarlet was itching to get into it. 'Can I take the birthing unit?'

Michelle grinned as she agreed to work in the nursery for the shift. 'But you won't get it all the time.'

'I suppose it's a bit different from when I used to say, "whatever you want",' Scarlet acknowledged wryly. 'I've changed in the last few months working away.'

'What was it like, not having medical back-up, when you lived in the valley community?' It was obvious Michelle was fascinated by the idea.

Scarlet smiled at the memories. 'Sometimes it was scary, but it was an incredible experience, being present for the births there. Before I went, I knew I was midwifery-trained but now I have so much more confidence. Confidence that when women are left to their own devices, they'll progress in their own time. When they listen to their own bodies they are capable of directing their own labours, as opposed to being patients who have their labours managed for them. I'm afraid I've become an advocate to let the mother do it herself.'

Michelle's eyes danced. 'Well, good luck. This should be a hoot. Sinclair McPherson is coming in to start a drip to speed labour for the woman in unit two—in half an hour.'

'Sinclair McPherson, eh?' Scarlet supposed it was too late to ask to work in the nursery now without making an issue out of avoiding Sinclair. She squared her shoulders. 'In that case, I'd better go help her find some contractions—then he won't need to interfere. Catch you later, Michelle.'

Scarlet scanned the written notes as she walked down the corridor. She could handle this. She had to. When she opened the door to the birthing unit Scarlet smiled warmly at the young couple. They looked very nervous as they waited for the doctor to arrive—with mother-to-be on the bed and her husband holding her hand as he sat beside her on a chair. Scarlet shelved her own nerves. This was a prime example of people lacking confidence by not being in their own environment.

'Hi, Jill. Hi, Peter. I'm Scarlet and I'm your midwife today.' She walked over and shook both their hands before perching on the edge of the bed.

'Before the doctor comes, I'd like to have a chat about the type of birth experience you were hoping for. It really helps if you can fill me in on what you expect today will bring.'

They both looked at her as if she'd just spoken Russian until finally Peter took one chewed fingernail out of his mouth and grinned. 'We expect a baby. The ultrasound people told us it's probably a boy—and they said he was about eight pounds.'

Scarlet's eyebrows lifted. 'Crikey. They didn't leave much to the imagination, did they? Don't be surprised if some of that's different. It's pretty hard to judge until a baby is naked and on the scales.'

She smiled encouragingly at Jill. 'He left the labour part to your imagination. What are you imagining today, Jill?'

The two women looked at each other and Scarlet saw the apprehension behind the younger woman's smile.

'We went to antenatal classes so we have an idea now how it works,' Jill said. 'But I guess—more pain than I have now.' Jill pleated the sheet. 'Heaps more. And my mum said it would probably be hard—and I'd get stitches because the baby's eight pounds and I'm so small.'

Scarlet glanced at Peter's face as he paled. She noticed him squeeze Jill's hand. Good. He'd be a worthy support for his wife. She'd love to get her hands on Jill's mother with a few suggestions about induction of fear before labour.

'OK. How about I give you some good news?' She smiled at them both. 'Your body is designed to give birth naturally, and your baby is designed to fit through whatever size pelvis his or her mother has. So we need a little faith here. Yes, there are exceptions to the rule and that's why you're in a hospital and not out in the desert, doing it by yourself. But that's for your doctor to worry about—not you. We have to give them some job while you carry on and do it yourself. So believe you can do it— I do!'

They both nodded, Jill almost relaxing.

'OK. The next thing is to actually allow your body to set or establish itself into labour. There are a few things you can do to encourage that. Most importantly, you have to trust it. If you're lying down, all tense, waiting for pain, do you think your body is going to think this is a safe place to let out all your hormones? It's a hard place to begin labour.'

Jill nodded. 'So what do you think I should do?'

'I'm not being smart here—' Scarlet's voice was gentle '—but what is your body telling you to do?'

Jill looked at her husband. 'Well, it is difficult to lie still when the pains do come. Maybe I should get up and walk around?'

Scarlet smiled. 'Let's do it, then.' She hooked a small footstool over to the bed with her toe.

Jill bit her lip. 'But aren't I supposed to wait here for the doctor? The night nurse said that he was coming to put in a drip and make my contractions come more quickly.'

Scarlet glanced at her watch. They still had twenty minutes. She was pushing it. 'If you have faith in your body and relax, maybe your body will move into labour by itself. Then you wouldn't need any synthetic hormones to start what your body can do for itself.' Time was against them and she had to temper it. 'Or less of them if you do still need a drip.'

Jill scrambled to the edge of the bed. 'I like the sound of that—I hate needles.'

'Me, too.' Peter stood to help his wife off the bed. 'I faint at the sight of blood.'

They all laughed and Jill started to waddle around the room. The look of surprise on her face when the next pain came more quickly made them all laugh again.

'I think I should have been doing this all morning,' Jill said as she slowly rocked her hips during the contraction. 'It's much less painful when I stand up than when I lie down.'

'Remember that for later in labour.' Scarlet turned to Peter. 'If you notice her complain about the pain then it's time for her to think about doing a different activity.'

She looked at Jill. 'The shower is terrific as a change from walking. But stay off the bed for long periods. Think lots of positive thoughts and trust your body. OK?'

They both nodded.

'I'll slip out and get you some ice and water. Fluids are important, too.' She waved as she left the room.

Scarlet crouched down to get ice from the ice machine and she could feel her nerves tighten. Sinclair would be here soon.

She hadn't seen him since the night he left early from her mother's. Old Dr McPherson had continued to call on her mother at least once a week—at least that relationship seemed to be sailing along smoothly—but he hadn't mentioned his son to Scarlet.

She scooped another paddle of ice into the jug and nearly tipped it all out as she tilted her watch to check the time again. She grimaced. Today would be the worst—it would get easier over time. She hoped.

'Sister Connors?' The deep voice came from behind her left shoulder and she dropped the jug at her feet. Ice skidded across the polished floor in all directions and she didn't even notice the cold on her own legs. She stared at the splashes of water across Sinclair's shoes and up his trousers—then she looked at his face.

He wasn't a happy camper. 'Damn,' he said as he brushed the water off the material with the back of his hand.

His annoyance stiffened her spine and she stood up. 'Damn yourself—you scared the living daylights out of me. And it's Sister Robin at work.'

To her surprise, his eyes creased with a brief flash of amusement. 'My apologies, Sister.' He was at least eight inches taller than she was and his good posture used it all.

'What did you do to your hair?' He raised his hand halfway to her face before he seemed to realise what he was doing and it fell away.

Typical man. Why did men rave about long hair? She frowned. 'Had it cut.'

With the brevity of her answer he blinked and his face became his usual professional mask. 'When you've finished with the ice, perhaps you could escort me to see my patient.'

Scarlet winced at the word. At that moment a domestic assistant bustled up to Scarlet with a mop. 'Don't you worry, dear. I'll sort this out if you want to go with the doctor.'

Scarlet sent her a grateful smile. 'Thanks.' She quickly scooped up some fresh ice from the machine and dashed after Sinclair. She caught up with him down the corridor and had to skip a couple of times to match his stride. That didn't improve her mood.

Scarlet glared at Sinclair. 'You know, I've never mentioned it before but when you call a healthy pregnant woman a "patient", I find it offensive.'

His eyes widened and she looked away and then back again. What the heck was she doing? The actual concept was true but to blurt it out at this inauspicious moment was bizarre.

Sinclair blinked, gave her a strange look, looked around as if for inspiration of what had caused that little outburst and then ignored her. He continued down the corridor towards the birthing unit.

Scarlet gritted her teeth. He was going to overlook her comment. How big of him. And she'd just decided to pull her head in, too. If he was going to ignore her then she might as well go the whole way.

'I'd like you to consider withholding Jill's intravenous Syntocinon until lunchtime to give her body a chance to do the job itself.'

That made him stop. 'Do we have a problem here?' He looked her up and down. There was no amusement now and a long moment of silence fell as they glared at each other. There was a brief softening in his eyes and for a moment she thought he might be willing to discuss it.

Then his face hardened again and he finally spoke. 'What happened? Did you wake up this morning and decide to be an obstetrician?'

Not likely. She stared levelly back. 'What a ghastly thought.' Scarlet winced in exaggerated horror. 'No. I'm much more useful as a midwife! I thought I might advocate more strongly for my client's wishes. If that's all right with you, Doctor?' The words tumbled out unbidden and afterwards she decided she must have had a devil in her.

In the past, she'd tried to steer the doctors unobtrusively towards a less dogmatic approach to birth, often with little success. While the desire to help each woman find the most rewarding birth had always been there, now it consumed her and she guessed she'd have to pay the price with a less peaceful existence. More pushing, less steering. Oh, brother, life was going to be interesting if she couldn't control herself.

Sinclair just looked at her. 'Ah. But is this your

client's wishes or yours, Sister? I gather your time among the valley dwellers has altered your hospital values.' She had his full attention now and he actually snorted.

'Nevertheless, I've found that the suggestion of hastening the first stage of labour does seem attractive to *most* women. But let's find out, shall we?'

Sinclair knocked on the door and then stood back for Scarlet to precede him into the room. He didn't leave her much room. She wasn't sure if he'd done it on purpose, but she was determined she wouldn't brush against him as she slid between him and the door. It was a tight fit.

Jill was smiling at something Peter had said and Sinclair raised his eyebrows at Scarlet as if to say he couldn't see labour starting on its own.

'Good morning, Peter, Jill.' Sinclair shook Peter's hand.

'Good morning, Doctor,' the couple chorused, and Scarlet had to resist the urge to roll her eyes.

Scarlet really hadn't taken any notice of the ritual of doctors' visits but this one was getting right up her nose. Jill was the most important person in this room, not the fellow in the suit. Or was that just *her* attitude this morning?

Sinclair must have remembered that because he turned towards Jill. 'How are you, Jill? Night Sister said you've been bothered by contractions for the last few nights and your waters broke last evening?'

Jill nodded as she unobtrusively settled herself on the bed and clasped her hands over her stomach.

'And now Day Sister Robin thinks you might progress on your own if we give you more time before we start a drip. How do you feel about that?' To give

Sinclair his due, he didn't try and influence Jill either way when he spoke to her.

'I'd like to try, if you don't mind the wasted visit this morning.'

Sinclair's smile was noncommittal. 'I'll just have a feel of your tummy if you don't mind. I like to see which way your baby is pointed on the way out.' He smiled and Jill eased down in the bed, eager to please.

Scarlet lifted two pillows out from behind Jill's head to help her lie flat and she heard Sinclair rub his hands together to warm them. The sound drew her eyes to those long-fingered hands she remembered so well. They were almost elegant as they gently palpated the mounds and hollows of Jill's stomach to draw a mental picture of the baby's lie.

A warm knot formed low in her belly and Scarlet grudgingly conceded his technique was excellent—and not only in palpation of pregnant abdomens. She frowned at the wayward thought and shifted her feet to distract other areas of her body from responding.

'I'll come back at lunchtime and we'll see how you're going.' His voice brought Scarlet back to the present and she rubbed the sudden rush of goose-bumps on her arms to make them disappear before he noticed them. Thank goodness goose-bumps didn't come out on your face for everyone to notice, she thought grimly.

Snap out of it, woman, Scarlet admonished herself. She followed Sinclair but paused to smile reassuringly at Jill. 'I'll be back in a minute.'

'Thanks, Doctor.' Peter was out of his chair to accompany them to the door and to close it after them.

Sinclair stopped a few paces up the corridor and held Jill's chart out to Scarlet.

'Happy?'

Just that one word and the inflection he used sent her blood pressure soaring. She bit back a very un-Letty-type expression and contented herself with a less inflammatory comment.

'Yes, thank you, Doctor.' She took the chart without touching him. 'We'll see you at lunchtime, then.'

It was as if he could read her mind. The side of his mouth quirked but that was the only sign she could see to make her think he found the conversation amusing. He turned and left her staring after him until he walked out the front door.

Sinclair whistled as he went down the steps two at a time. Well, that had taken her by surprise. It looked like Scarlet was having problems getting the mouse back in the cage. He grinned.

He was pretty sure things weren't going smoothly with the husband, who still hadn't showed. He was beginning to wonder if there really was a Mr Connors. And she hadn't changed her maiden name at work.

His brow furrowed. He wondered how much chance there was that it was true. If there was no husband then who was Cameron's father? Maybe he and the baby should get better acquainted.

When Vivienne opened her front door, she had the little man he'd come to see in her arms. Perfect.

'Hello, Sinclair. To what do we owe the pleasure of this visit?' Scarlet's mother stepped back and gestured him in.

'I had a few minutes before I'm expected back at my rooms and wanted to thank you. Your company has really cheered my father's state of mind.' He watched Cameron's bright eyes follow the voices from face to face and he couldn't help the grin that softened his face.

'That's very sweet of you. Come through to the lounge. I'm just giving Cameron his bottle.'

He walked after her and sank back into the lounge, trying to relax. He searched his mind for something to say. 'So he's on formula now that Scarlet is back at work?'

Vivienne shook her head. 'No. Scarlet wouldn't have that. He's on expressed breast milk and takes it well.' She looked up at him with a smile. 'If you'd like to finish giving him this feed I'll make us a cup of coffee, if you have time.'

'No problem. I don't get to do this part much.' He reached up and took the baby from her arms, along with a bib and the warmed bottle.

Vivienne was strangely quiet for a moment but then seemed to rouse herself. 'Black and no sugar, like your father?'

Sinclair was staring down at the infant in his arms. He looked up and replayed the question in his mind. 'That's right, thanks.'

As he watched her leave the room he could feel the weight and heat of the baby in his arms. It felt good. He looked back at Cameron making little slurping noises as he greedily sucked on the teat. As if aware of Sinclair's interest, the baby stopped for a moment and gazed solemnly back at the big person above him before his face broke into a huge gummy smile that dribbled milk around the edges.

'You're a cheeky boy, aren't you?' Sinclair heard the soppiness in his voice and shook his head. What was he doing? But the kid was a real cutie. He jiggled the teat in the baby's mouth and Cameron looked away and started sucking again.

'Here you are.' Vivienne carried a teatray into the room. She placed it carefully out of Cameron's accidental reach on a small table beside Sinclair's leg, and he could smell the fresh scones from three feet away. His mouth watered.

'You'll end up with me as a permanent visitor if you spoil me like this,' he said.

'You're welcome any time. As is your father.'

Which reminded him. 'I've been concerned about Dad for a while. He doesn't seem to have the get-up-and-go he used to have. Though he's much brighter since he started coming over here.'

'We're all getting older and our needs change,' she said as she poured his coffee and even jam-and-creamed his scone for him. 'I think he needs a new interest.'

Sinclair frowned. 'I think he should retire. I know he'd like to see me settled and he's mentioned grand-kids a few times.'

'That's natural.' Vivienne smiled at her own grand-son.

'I've even started thinking the same thing myself. Lately.' He looked down at the tiny bit of milk left in the bottle and took the teat from Cameron's mouth. 'He finished that quick!'

'Give him to me, and I'll wind him. Have your coffee.'

Sinclair found himself strangely reluctant to give up his charge but handed him to his grandmother. He had to get back to work soon anyway. 'Thanks. I enjoyed the experience.' Cameron's gaze stayed on Sinclair's face as he was handed over. His little head

swivelled for one last look before his grandmother
tucked him up over her shoulder to bring up his wind.
Sinclair picked up a scone and gazed thoughtfully into
his coffee. Five minutes later he left.

Back on the ward, Scarlet frowned as she dropped
into the ward nursery to update Michelle.

'How'd you go with Dr McPherson?' Michelle
flashed her a look as she juggled the syringe she held
connected to the tube into the baby's stomach and the
bottle of warmed milk that kept the syringe from
emptying.

'We've got until lunchtime to see if Jill establishes
labour on her own.'

Michelle wiped off a droplet of milk that had fallen
on the roof of the incubator. 'Well, that's a win. You
know that anyone draining amniotic fluid is usually
sped on their way if they haven't started labour by
daylight.'

Scarlet grimaced. 'Yes, but when you think about
it, why?'

Michelle frowned at the syringe barrel. 'Because
the safety bag's broken. Risk of ascending infection.
You know that. What's your point?'

'My point is—what's the rush? As long as basic
hygiene is maintained, the risk of infection is much
smaller than the risk of interference from a synthetic
induction of labour. She could even go home to wait
for labour to begin if she knew how to watch for signs
of infection.'

Michelle disconnected the syringe and capped the
end of the tubing. The tiny baby that lay in the incubator was still asleep. She straightened the kink in
her back and turned to look at her friend. 'So you'd

like to teach her to use a thermometer and take her own temperature at home until she goes into labour?'

Scarlet nodded emphatically. 'A mother should know how to take a temperature anyway, and she could at least have a little longer to let nature take its course.'

'That's fairly radical, mate. They'll be screaming about germs in the outside world.'

'Right. So there's no germs in a hospital?'

Michelle laughed. 'I'm not against you. And I'll admit you do see a run of interventions like epidurals once they start with inductions. It's just a new idea, that's all.'

Scarlet was emphatic. 'And after epidural can come the inability to push as efficiently, leading to maternal exhaustion and forceps which moves us on to episiotomy.'

Michelle bit her lip to stop a laugh escaping. 'The poor woman. You're full of doom and gloom. I hate to think how radical you'll be by the end of your first week.'

Even Scarlet had to laugh at that. 'Sorry. Softly, softly, used to be my motto. I think I've been possessed by a demon.'

Michelle put her hand on her shoulder. 'Nah. You've always thought like that, you just didn't say much before. It's amazing how having your own baby stiffens your spine for the women you care for.'

'Thanks, Michelle. I'd better go and see how Jill's contractions are coming on.'

Michelle waved her away with a grin. 'Go get 'em. Can't wait for the lunchtime episode when Dr McPherson comes back.'

*   *   *

By one o'clock, Jill's contractions were more regular but not as close together as Scarlet would have liked. Jill was pacing the room and resting during the contractions by leaning over pillows stacked on a bedside table.

Peter was coaching Jill to sigh before and after each pain. Scarlet listened to the baby's heartbeat with a handheld Doppler every half-hour and she'd been careful not to unintentionally apply pressure on Jill to perform a miracle.

Jill sighed after a particularly strong contraction. 'Do you think he'll still want to start the drip?'

Scarlet hoped not. They could progress from where they were now, although it could take a few more hours. 'I really couldn't say, Jill. If he does, it will shorten your labour but sometimes the pains can be stronger than you would normally expect so quickly.'

'My mum had all her babies induced. But, then, she had epidurals as well.'

'People weren't as ambulant years ago. They had to endure most of their labours on the bed. Let's cross the epidural bridge if we come to it.'

There was a knock at the door and Sinclair walked into the room.

He didn't look at Scarlet and she couldn't tell by his voice what he was planning. 'So how's it going, Jill?'

'I think it's coming along.' Unlike the doctor, she didn't have a problem looking at the midwife for confirmation.

Scarlet supported her. 'Five-minutely regular contractions, lasting forty-five seconds and moderately strong. Foetal hearts are fine at 140 beats per minute.'

Sinclair turned to face her. 'Have you a foetal heart monitor printout for me?'

'No, but I could do a quick trace for you now if you need one. When Jill lies down the contractions go off a bit and we wanted to establish labour.'

The paper readout he'd requested showed the baby's heart rate and heart rate reaction to the contraction of the uterus. It was also proof of the regularity and length of contractions. Scarlet wanted to say monitors caused intervention but thought she might have used up Sinclair's tolerance for the day. It had been a calculated risk that he wouldn't ask for a foetal heart trace as she'd wanted to keep Jill off the bed as much as possible.

Sinclair narrowed his eyes for a moment then turned to Jill. 'What would you like, Jill? I can start the drip and you'll probably have your baby by teatime or you can continue on your own which could possibly take up to the early hours of the morning.' He smiled. 'Of course, there's always the chance you'll be quicker than any of us expect. Perhaps you'd like to discuss it with your husband.'

Scarlet's mouth almost fell open. She had to admit, Sinclair had done a turn-around and she admired his ability to be flexible.

He gestured for Scarlet to move to the side of the room to give the couple some privacy. He looked at Scarlet sardonically and his voice only carried to her. 'I'm on call tonight so I can still be here for the baby's birth. Of course you, Sister Robin, will be off duty.'

The smart comment slipped out. 'You could always pick me up on the way through if it made you feel any better.'

He surprised her again when he grinned.

'I'm sure we'll manage.' He looked back towards the bed and saw that the couple was ready to tell him their decision.

'Well?' Sinclair smiled to imply it didn't worry him either way.

Peter squeezed his wife's hand. 'Jill would like to let nature take its course, if that's OK with you, Doctor?'

There wasn't a flicker of surprise on Sinclair's face. 'Not a problem. I'll drop in to see you both after work and, of course, the midwife on duty at the time...' he shot an ironic glance at Scarlet '...will call me if you need me.'

Somehow Sinclair drew Scarlet out the door with him. When she shut the door behind them, he stopped and turned and she almost ran into him. There was nowhere to go. As she tried to step around him, she realised again how broad his chest was. But he didn't touch her.

'So the gloves are off, are they?'

She could detect the faint trace of his aftershave and it brought back memories that seemed to surface when she least wanted them. She moistened her lips with her tongue until she noticed him staring at her mouth with an arrested expression on his face. Her heart thumped and her tongue hid.

'I'm not sure what you mean, Dr McPherson.' Scarlet's voice almost squeaked and she cleared her throat. Drat the man. He was invading her space *and* her brain.

'With your new-found zeal for natural birth it looks like the chance of you fading back into obscurity is really not an option. Is it, Scarlet?'

'If you mean I'll defend the mother's right to have as natural a birth as possible then I suppose I'll be noticed. Yes.'

She heard him mutter, 'It should be interesting.' And with one more sardonic smile, he left. The guy was winning the exit-line stakes and it was starting to annoy her.

After lunch, Jill's labour suddenly took off and Scarlet, Jill and Peter spent the last of Scarlet's shift in the shower.

'I've never spent two hours in a bathroom with two women before,' Peter commented as he rubbed soap on Jill's lower back during a pain.

Jill was holding the hand-shower directed on her bikini line. 'And you never will again,' she said, and sprayed his shirt. Then she closed her eyes and moaned gently with the force of the next contraction.

Scarlet murmured encouragement when Jill needed it during the height of the contractions. She also tried to keep her soaked nursing shoes from under the erratically aimed water stream.

Jill's eyes widened and her breathing changed. Scarlet looked up and smiled at Peter.

'It's getting close now. I'll go and give Dr McPherson a ring.'

She nudged the delivery trolley closer to the bathroom door and dialled Sinclair's number.

'Dr McPherson.'

'Hello, it's Scarlet in Maternity. Jill's in second stage.'

'That was quick. Isn't she clever?' She could hear the smile in his voice. 'I'll see you soon,' he said, and hung up.

CHAPTER FOUR

ONCE committed to birth, Jill's baby boy decided to be born in a hurry. Sinclair arrived in time to see the delivery of the placenta on the shower chair in the bathroom. The horrified expression on his face was a picture Scarlet would treasure.

'We do have perfectly good labour ward beds. Patients are upright just like a chair—only they're designed for this.' He gestured towards Jill and her baby then he shrugged. 'I'm obviously not needed here at this late stage. Congratulations, Jill and Peter.' He inclined his head towards Scarlet. 'Sister Robin.' Then he returned to his rooms without saying anything else to her.

Scarlet had to admit she was disappointed she hadn't had the chance to rub it in a little, but the new parents were over the moon with the course Jill's labour had followed.

'Thanks, Scarlet.' Peter kissed her in his exuberance.

'He's gorgeous. You were both wonderful.' For Scarlet, Jill's obvious pride in her accomplishment was all the thanks she needed. And Sinclair's interference had been avoided. She felt like pumping the air with her fist.

At changeover report late that afternoon, Michelle introduced Scarlet as the new 'bathroom' midwife of the unit. The only fly in the ointment was Tessa, who

70

sat with a disapproving look on her face through the recital of the excitement.

'People come into hospital because they know we'll deliver their babies in a safe place. Would you call the bathroom safe?' Tessa raised elegant eyebrows.

Michelle frowned and Scarlet looked at Tessa with a calm smile. 'Women don't need to be flat on their backs to give birth in a protected environment. They assume more control for the birth if they're in an upright position.'

Tessa shrugged. 'That's right, you're the one who advocates home births.' She glanced around at the other midwives. 'That's even more unsafe.' She tossed her hair. 'I don't understand how any midwife could agree with such a risky undertaking.'

This was one duel she wouldn't lose. Still serene, Scarlet replied. 'I don't suppose you would.'

Michelle raised her eyebrows and stifled a grin. She stood up. 'Well, that's report finished. I have to go. Come on, Scarlet.'

Scarlet spoke to the frowning Tessa. 'I know you've been back around a year now, but you haven't had the chance to see the side of midwifery that exists on the home-birth front. It's wonderful and exciting. Treat those people with respect and they'll treat you with respect.'

'I don't need respect from them.' Tessa looked Scarlet up and down. 'Or you.'

For the first time the barb slid off harmlessly. Scarlet shrugged. 'That's attractive.' And she walked away to follow Michelle.

When they were outside, Michelle touched Scarlet's arm. 'Sinclair was taking her out before you came back. But I don't think things are running as smoothly as they were. She blames you, I'd say.'

'We've always been at odds.' Scarlet stopped as Michelle's incredible words sank in. 'Why would she think I have any influence over Sinclair?'

Michelle shrugged innocently. 'Maybe it has nothing to do with it.'

Scarlet brushed that reasoning away. 'I think Tessa looks down on home-birth clients, home-birth midwives and, at a guess, me in general. For a change, it doesn't worry me. I just hope that if any of the women from the valley come in with complications, Tessa isn't on duty.'

By the time Scarlet arrived home that afternoon she was glad to sit down to feed her baby.

Later, when she rested on the settee with a sated Cameron over her shoulder, her mouth twitched. There had been some moments of unusual interest today, not the least being those involving Sinclair.

Cameron stirred and Scarlet patted his back.

'Did you miss me? Your mummy had a good day. I missed you.' She kissed his tiny fingers. 'Were you a good boy for your nana?'

Cameron burped and Vivienne caught the conversation as she carried in a tray with fresh tea and scones. 'He was fine. So all went well, then?'

'It's great to be back, and we had a lovely birth today.' She propped Cameron up on two pillows beside her on the settee.

'I'm glad. So how many shifts have you been rostered for?' Vivienne poured the tea and set it down in easy reach of Scarlet.

'Thanks, Mum.' She took a sip and sighed as the

cinnamon and apple flavour hit her mouth. 'They want me to do six shifts a fortnight. Is that too much childminding for you?'

Vivienne reached across and tickled Cameron's foot.

'No. As long as it's not too much for you. I enjoyed looking after him. He can come with me if I want to go somewhere when you're working.' She lifted her own cup. 'Did you see Sinclair today?'

'Yes.' She compressed her lips and left it at that. Then she caught her mother's look and smiled. 'OK, it was a bit awkward in the beginning, but I got so busy I didn't have time to worry about him.'

'Did he mention he dropped in to see me this morning?'

Scarlet's cup clattered on the saucer and some of the tea splashed over the edge. Suddenly she felt sick. 'He what? Why? Did he ask to see Cameron?'

Her mother continued to serenely sip her tea. 'Calm down, you're overreacting. He was on his way back to his rooms and dropped in to have a few words about his father.'

'I don't believe it. He suspects something.' She shot a look at her mother. 'You didn't say anything to make him suspicious, did you?'

Vivienne lifted her head and raised an eyebrow. 'I'll pretend you didn't say that, Scarlet. If you think I have a problem with my loyalties then I'm surprised you're happy to leave your son with me.'

Scarlet rubbed her brow with her free hand. What was she thinking? 'I'm sorry, Mum. You're right. I had no right to say that. My only defence is that man makes me crazy. I don't want him to have rights over my baby.'

'I think you'll come to realise that he *does* have rights over the baby who belongs to *both* of you, but it's up to you to come to that decision, not me. Now, drink your tea and I'll tell you about his visit.'

Scarlet's hand shook slightly but she obediently picked up the cup and took a sip. That was one decision she'd never come to. Cameron didn't need a trapped father in the background and Scarlet needed to remain in control.

Vivienne went on. 'Sinclair's father has been depressed and unwell lately and Sinclair wanted me to know that he felt Frank's visits here seem to be helping his state of mind.' She glanced across at her grandson. 'Sinclair didn't ask to see Cameron, perhaps because he didn't have to. I was giving him his bottle when Sinclair arrived.'

'Did he look at him?'

Vivienne frowned. 'Will you listen to yourself? The man is an obstetrician. He loves babies! Of course he looked at him. He took over the feed while I made some coffee.'

Scarlet shook her head. She wasn't sure what upset her the most—the fact that she was frightened Sinclair might decide Cameron could be his baby or that he had nursed her baby and she hadn't been here to oversee it. 'Well, Sinclair should get married and have children of his own.'

Vivienne sighed and gave her one of those I-do-not-understand-you looks. 'Perhaps you should picture him with another woman and think about how it would make you feel. It may just happen. Sinclair seems to think if he settles down his father may retire and start to take it easy.'

'Good. If Sinclair married that would be the best thing. Then I could get on with my life the way I want to.'

Vivienne snorted. 'That sounds fascinating. Why should Sinclair's marital status affect the way you get on with your life?' Scarlet didn't answer. Vivienne put down her cup. 'I think I'll go out. I have a letter I want to post. If you think of an answer to that question I'd be interested to hear it.'

Scarlet watched her mother leave the room. Cameron was asleep and she should put him to bed before he woke again. She sighed and picked her son up carefully to walk with him balanced over her shoulder. She didn't want to think about her mother's words but they followed her up the stairs.

Would Sinclair suddenly decide to marry? He'd been perfectly happy as a bachelor all these years. And whom would he marry? She remembered Michelle's words. Tessa?

How ironic if she was frantically worried about trying to keep him from finding out about his son when his present plans didn't include a baby by another woman anyway.

But the voice inside whispered that it would be easier for her to plan for her future with the temptation gone if he was married to someone else. She flinched. Yeah—like cutting off your leg so you didn't get an ingrown toenail.

No. Sinclair was his own problem. Gerry the geologist was here to stay as her baby's father and she wasn't going to be Sinclair's last fling before he settled down and married some perfect doctor's wife.

*   *   *

Just before tea, the doorbell rang, and Scarlet had a premonition. When she answered it, she found she was right. Her eyes narrowed.

'My mother's not here, Dr McPherson.' After a quick glance at Sinclair's face she concentrated on the top button of his shirt but had to fight against the urge to linger at the gap in his unbuttoned collar. There was something incredibly attractive about a strong man's neck.

'I've asked you before to call me Sinclair.' He stepped closer. 'I haven't come to see your mother. May I come in?'

Scarlet drew a breath and stepped back out of his way. 'Mum said you'd already dropped in this morning.' Scarlet caught a curious look from the neighbour across the road as the woman stared at the doctor visiting twice in one day. 'For goodness' sake, come in before the whole town wants to know why you're here.'

He brushed past her and she was sure it was deliberate as the heat from his body went right through her.

His voice was casual. 'You'll really have to practise your door greetings, Scarlet. Your welcome lacks a certain warmth.'

She was warm all right. Damn him. She willed herself to relax as she walked in front of him into the lounge room. Scarlet gestured for him to take the armchair and when he had she perched on the settee furthest away from him. 'And your visit is inappropriate—I'm a married woman.'

'Are you?' The words were almost inaudible. He settled himself into a lounge chair and crossed his long legs.

At least one of them was relaxed, she thought bitterly, and then his words sank in. Her heart thumped and she shot a look at him. 'What did you say?'

He looked back at her innocently. 'Your husband. Yes, I want to ask you about him, but before I do...' He brushed that subject away and smiled his killer smile at her. 'Congratulations on the birth today. In fact, my clients were very clever and think you're wonderful. Note I didn't call them patients.'

Scarlet's guard slipped a little as she remembered her own pleasure at Jill's baby's birth. Her voice was earnest. 'I'd wanted to talk to you about suggesting that women go home again when they're in early labour. Even those with broken waters like Jill. We would explain about risk factors and safety issues. Give them a chance before speeding up their labours artificially.'

Sinclair's gaze was sceptical. 'Maybe early labours we could think about, but ruptured membranes need more discussion. Write me a protocol—I promise I'll read it and we'll see.'

It was better than nothing. She didn't know whether to go on or not. 'Drugs aren't always necessary. Women are very powerful when they set their minds to it.'

He gave a half-strangled laugh and sat forward in the chair. 'They're powerful all right. It was an interesting morning.' She could tell he wanted to change the subject.

Scarlet was trying to keep track of all nuances but his humour kept her off balance.

'So your mother told you I visited. Did she mention I spent some time with Cameron?'

Scarlet's heart started to thump again and the nausea was back. 'In passing, she did.' She swallowed a lump in her throat. 'So?'

Sinclair stared back at her blandly. 'He's a fine boy. Don't you think he's handsome? Like me?' His question dropped onto her without warning and she jumped off the settee as if scalded.

She dared a glance at him. 'Cameron?' Her mind went blank and she couldn't think what to say. 'Cameron has nothing to do with you.' She looked away, straightened her shoulders then forced herself to meet his eyes. 'He looks just like his father.' She had her voice under control but the rest of her was like jelly. She needed a minute to think. 'I'm sorry. Would you like a cup of tea or coffee?'

He looked at her consideringly and to her relieved surprise he accepted the diversion and nodded his head. 'Yes, please. Coffee, black, no sugar.'

A trivial thought crossed her mind. She'd slept with the man and didn't know how he took his coffee. Snap out of it, she told herself. At this moment she felt as if she'd played into his hands but she couldn't think how. 'I won't be a moment, then.' She turned towards the kitchen but before she'd gone three paces he was walking beside her. She could feel the heat from his body again against the skin on her outer arms and shoulders. And everywhere else in her body.

His voice came from beside her ear. 'Let's have it in the kitchen, shall we? It's much friendlier in there.'

Alarm bells were ringing and she couldn't think how to get rid of him. Where was her mother? Scarlet fell back on the only defence she had. 'I don't think my husband would want me to become too friendly with you, Sinclair.' She stressed the 'husband'.

'Ah, yes. The geologist you've been going through

a rough patch with. I've been meaning to ask about him. When is this elusive traveller coming home?' He moved to the small kitchen table and sat down.

Thankful for a little more space from him, Scarlet tried to settle her nerves. She kept her back to him as she filled the jug and plugged it in because she could still feel him watching her every movement. 'Probably some time in the next month.' She stared blindly out the kitchen window.

Sinclair's voice made her blink. 'Tell me about him. He must have swept you off your feet.'

Scarlet forced herself to leave the safety of the sink and approach the table. 'Yes, he did.' She laid out the cups. 'Coffee, you said?'

He nodded, undiverted. 'Let's see. Your birthday was in November and Cameron was born in August...'

He was playing with her as well as the dates, and suddenly Scarlet refused to let him have it all his own way. She cut him off. 'Look, Sinclair. If you want to get sordid here, let's do it! I met, fell in love with and slept with Gerry a fortnight after I slept with you. You used contraception, he didn't. End of story. Now, if you don't desperately need this coffee, I'm not enjoying this conversation and would appreciate it if you left.'

'So you're saying there's no way that Cameron could be my son.'

She wasn't ready for this. 'Good Lord, did you think that?' She crossed her fingers behind her back and prayed she wouldn't get hit by lightning. Then she looked him straight in the eye and said in what she hoped was a firm, convincing tone of voice, 'Cameron is not your son.' She switched the jug off and took his cup away. 'You have no right to come here and make these accusations. Please, leave.'

Sinclair rose and looked down at her as she stood rigidly in front of him. Her beautiful hair was shining like a cap and she had a hunted look in her eyes. Had he put that look there? Sinclair sighed. Wishing Cameron were his son wouldn't make it true. And now she'd categorically stated he wasn't the father he'd better accept that. But he was still having trouble doing so.

'Yes, I'll go. I'm sorry if I've upset you.' He hid the depth of his disappointment behind his bland smile. 'I won't bother you at home again. But I'll watch for the next instalment of alternative birthing at Southside.' He stood up but had time for one more parting shot. 'Perhaps you could try and have a birth on the bed for a change.'

The next day at work began calmly. Scarlet was on shift with Tessa and the air between them was chilly. The good news as far as Scarlet was concerned was that Tessa preferred the orderliness of the nursery and the doctors' rounds with the postnatal women. Scarlet preferred the emotions of the labour ward.

There were only two women in labour. Apparently Sinclair had been in and had offered one the option of going home for a few hours until the contractions were stronger. Scarlet couldn't keep the grin off her face when she heard that.

So there was no problem with the delegation of the work. As long as Tessa stayed out of her way, Scarlet was happy. She was about to move down the hallway to meet her clients when the phone rang.

'Maternity, Scarlet speaking. Can I help you?'

'This is Nina Wade. I'm an independent midwife.' The name rang a bell. Scarlet had heard good reports of Nina during her time in the valley. The woman's voice was brittle with tension and Scarlet felt her own nerves tighten. 'I'm bringing a client of mine—Karen Wilson—in for a probable emergency Caesarean section for ante-partum haemorrhage and foetal distress.'

'How long before you get here, Nina?' Scarlet began to weigh up what she could achieve to streamline the admission before they arrived.

'Fifteen minutes, if not quicker. We're about to leave.'

Scarlet frowned. 'What about the ambulance?'

'There isn't time. She started bleeding heavily ten minutes ago and I haven't been able to locate the baby's heartbeat since the bleeding started. I think it could be a marginal placenta praevia. Karen didn't want any scans during pregnancy, so I can't be sure.'

Placenta praevia was when all or part of the placenta was across the cervix in front of the baby's head. If the cervix dilated, as it had to in labour, the edges of the placenta would start to separate from the womb and open blood vessels would be exposed.

Scarlet winced. Without the empty uterus needed to clamp down on itself and control bleeding after placental separation, both mother and baby were in serious trouble. Caesarean section was the only way out for baby or mother. 'OK. I'll see you as soon as you get here. Is there a doctor that your client has seen at all?'

'No. She refuses to see a male doctor because of a past history I'll fill you in on when we come in.'

'Right.' Scarlet glanced at the big hospital clock on the wall. Seven-ten a.m. Theatre staff wouldn't be in for another fifteen minutes. 'I'll start the wheels turning. Good luck.'

'Thanks. You never know what reception your client's going to get when you bring her in for a complicated home birth.'

Scarlet nodded to herself and tried to send positive thoughts down the phone line. 'We're here for you both. See you soon.'

'Thanks, Scarlet.' But the foreboding in Nina's voice was easy to hear.

Scarlet pressed for a new line and punched in Sinclair's direct office line. She'd been worried how she would face him after his visit yesterday but now she would be glad to see him as soon as possible.

'Dr McPherson.' Sinclair's voice was calm as usual and Scarlet drew a breath to match his own even speech.

'It's Scarlet here. I've an unbooked, complicated home-birth admission with query placenta praevia. She's bleeding quite heavily and no foetal hearts have been heard since the bleeding started ten minutes ago. She should be here in ten to fifteen minutes.'

'Contact Theatre. I'm on my way. Has she had any previous ultrasounds?'

'No. The midwife said the client hadn't wanted a scan.'

Scarlet heard him sigh. 'Right,' he said, and hung up.

Scarlet punched in the nursing supervisor's number and repeated the information. The supervisor would contact the theatre staff and arrange for another midwife to cover the birthing unit while Scarlet was in Theatre with the new admission.

The phone settled into its cradle and Scarlet looked

up to see Tessa. She'd caught the gist of the conversation and was glaring at her.

Tessa curled her lip. 'The parents should be ashamed of themselves for risking their baby by having a home birth in the first place.'

Scarlet winced and shook her head. 'You know, Tessa, your attitude sucks.' Scarlet would have laughed at the expression on Tessa's face if there hadn't been an emergency coming in. She'd relive it later. 'It's people like you whom home-birth parents are afraid of meeting if their instincts tell them to come here for help.'

Tessa shrugged. 'That's just tough. If they want us to fix their mistakes, they'll have to wear it. If I was the doctor expected to save the day, I wouldn't be happy either.'

Scarlet struggled to contain her anger. 'You're wrong. Choosing home birth isn't a mistake—it's merely a choice. Those parents deserve our unbiased support because they haven't taken that decision lightly. I don't have the time to discuss it with you now, but after this is over I'll make the time.' Scarlet met the other woman's eyes. 'And if you allow these people to feel your displeasure I'll make sure the nurse manager and every other person who works here knows that your professional attitude is severely lacking.'

Tessa drew herself up to her full height. 'Are you threatening me?'

'If you like,' Scarlet threw over her shoulder as she hurried down to the spare birthing unit to set up for the admission. 'Are you going to help or not?'

'I still don't know how you could consider risking

a child's life by encouraging home births,' Tessa said
as she grudgingly followed her down.

'When any woman in labour rings here in trouble,
it's just the same as if they'd had an emergency in
the birthing unit. I can't see how any self-respecting
midwife or doctor could withhold the support and
comfort a woman and her family need.' Scarlet
flipped down the hinged cover that disguised the
oxygen outlets and hung a mask over the nozzle before moving over to the bed.

'I'm not encouraging home birth, I'm respecting
parental choices and providing support in a medical
emergency to people who need it. Now, truce till
later.'

Scarlet was only giving Tessa a small portion of
her thoughts as she stripped off the bed and organised
intravenous fluids to be ready for insertion as soon as
the mother arrived. Depending on the size of the hae-
morrhage, the mother could be in hypovolaemic
shock by the time she got there, which would further
decrease any placental function that was left for the
baby.

Tessa assembled the notes, gown and trolley for
immediate transport to Theatre, and both midwives
looked up when the doorbell rang to signal the arrival
of the newcomers. They sprinted up the hallway.

'I'll get the resuscitation trolley ready for baby.
That I believe in. You can look after *them*,' Tessa
said, and peeled off to the nursery.

Good, thought Scarlet as she grabbed a wheelchair
and hurried to the door to help the pale woman, supported by her husband and the midwife.

'Hello, Karen. I'm Scarlet. Sit in the chair here and
we'll get you to bed.' As soon as the woman had half

collapsed into the chair, Scarlet wheeled it around and pushed her swiftly down the corridor back to the birthing unit. 'Doctor is on his way and will confirm what we can do for you as soon as he gets here.' She sent a brief reassuring smile towards the woman's frantic husband. 'We do have a theatre on standby.'

The next five minutes were hectic as Nina changed Karen out of her clothes into a gown and took Karen's blood pressure while Scarlet inserted an intravenous line into the free arm. The oxygen mask blew cool oxygen into Karen's face as she lay back with her eyes closed.

'Her blood pressure is stable at 90 on 50 but her pulse rate is still 130. The bleeding seems to have slowed a little on the way in,' Nina said, 'but I still can't hear baby's heartbeat.'

Scarlet looked up from where she was taping the cannula in place. She turned the fluid rate up to maximum and gestured with her head towards the large foetal heart-rate monitor. 'Try ours. It's pretty powerful—you might have more luck with the larger transducer.'

'Thanks.' Nina handed over an antenatal card. 'Here's the information I have for your records.'

Scarlet took it and reached behind the bed for the notes Tessa had assembled to be filled out. Nina gently slid the ultrasound cap over Karen's stomach to try and pinpoint baby's heartbeat.

Tessa came in with Sinclair at the same time as a very faint clop-clop of a slow foetal heartbeat finally emitted from the cardiotocograph machine.

Everybody sighed with relief because at least now they had a hope to cling to that the baby would be all right, though the heart rate was half of what it should have been.

'I'm Dr McPherson.' Sinclair stepped up to the bed and met Scarlet's eyes for a moment as he lifted Karen's wrist. He grimaced at the maternal pulse, which was galloping along at twice the baby's speed.

'This is Karen and George Wilson,' Scarlet said, 'and their midwife, Nina Wade. Karen's baby is due in two weeks by dates and has had no previous problems during the pregnancy except for this sudden painless bleeding which started after her first contraction today.'

Sinclair nodded and shook George's hand. Karen looked up briefly, and the fear in her eyes when she saw the male doctor must have alerted him. He was very gentle and explained everything he was going to do. His examination of Karen was brief but thorough and afterwards his voice was decisive.

'Right, Karen and George. Your baby needs to be born by Caesarean section as soon as possible. I imagine your midwife mentioned the possibility?' He looked at Nina, who nodded. 'We'll need to use a general anaesthetic as there isn't time for an epidural to work for baby to be born with you awake. That also means George can't come in either.' He looked at them to make sure they understood. George nodded and Sinclair continued, 'Have you eaten anything in the last four hours?'

Karen didn't answer or meet his eyes, but George spoke up.

'She didn't feel like breakfast and all she's had is half a cup of water about an hour ago.'

Sinclair nodded. He briefly ran through the risks of a Caesarean and anaesthetic and the immediate postoperative period while Scarlet completed the paper-work.

Karen signed the consent and the theatre wardsman arrived with the trolley to transport them across to the theatres.

'Let's go, then. I'll brief the anaesthetist and see you over there.'

'Is it all right with you if Nina comes in with me, just to observe?' Scarlet wasn't hopeful of his response but again he surprised her when he looked at the other midwife and smiled.

'Karen might feel less anxious among strangers and I'm sure Nina would like to see this birth through. I don't have a problem if that's what Karen wants.'

This time Karen did meet his eyes, although it was only a frightened glance from under her lashes. Sinclair acknowledged her mumbled thanks with a nod and left to prepare the theatre for their imminent arrival. Scarlet spared a second to stare after him thoughtfully. The man had potential.

The convoy of patient trolley, midwives and George, whom they would leave outside the plastic theatre doors, was rolling along the corridors.

Nina touched Scarlet's arm and mouthed a 'thank you' for including her in the theatre group. They both knew how much of a relief it would be for Karen to know that her own midwife would be there, too.

George leant over and kissed his wife's cheek as they entered the theatre complex. 'I'll be right here,' he said, and his voice shook. He gazed longingly after them as the trolley pushed through the swinging doors.

CHAPTER FIVE

SCARLET squeezed Karen's hand. 'Nina and I are going to get changed into special clothes and this sister here will ask you the same questions that I asked you over at Maternity. By the time she's finished with you we'll almost be ready. We'll see you inside. OK?'

Karen's eyes were filled with tears as she nodded her head. Scarlet smiled down at her. 'We won't be gone long.' She met Nina's eyes. 'We'd better move fast.'

Within minutes they were pushing open the operating-theatre door, garbed in hats, masks and gowns like everyone else.

The midwives were just in time to help the staff move Karen across to the operating table. Karen's limbs quivered with fright and her eyes stared, wide with fear, but she settled a little when she recognised Nina's familiar face behind her mask.

'Not long now, Karen. Hang in there,' Scarlet said quietly. 'Think welcoming thoughts for your baby for when you wake up.'

The anaesthetic took effect and Scarlet and Nina stepped back out of the way. Scarlet checked the resuscitation trolley equipment after its trip over from Maternity. The overhead lights and heater were on and the oxygen and sucker were ready to use as soon as baby was born.

'I'll get scrubbed to take the baby when Doctor gets him or her out,' Scarlet told Nina, and hurried into the scrub room. When she returned in sterile gloves, Sinclair hadn't wasted any time. It was only a few minutes until the baby's arrival.

Scarlet winced at the pea-soup green meconium-stained amniotic fluid that gushed out of the now exposed uterine cavity, and tightened her grip on the sucker. Meconium, or the first blackish-green stool passed by the newborn, was sometimes released inside the uterus. This was usually because of post-maturity—a pregnancy that extended past the time the baby should have been born—or sometimes because of the infant's stress in the womb. A baby became stressed when the usual placental function of oxygen supply was impaired by a medical condition or hae-morrhage. Karen's baby had probably been stressed and passed the meconium stool when the placenta had started to separate from the uterus and the oxygen supply had decreased.

As a birth attendant, Scarlet's job was to prevent the meconium that floated in the amniotic sac from sticking to the baby's lungs when it took its first breath.

'Here it comes.' Sinclair's voice drifted quietly across to Scarlet and she angled her sucker into the baby's mouth as the head appeared at the surgical opening of the uterus. Thick meconium covered the baby's face and the scrub sister quickly wiped it away with a sponge. The sound of the sucker was the only noise in the theatre.

As the rest of the baby—a boy—was born, Sinclair quickly clamped and cut the cord so that Scarlet could carry the newborn over to the resuscitaire. The child was limp and pale as Scarlet laid him on his back and the anaesthetist left his unconscious patient with his anaesthetic nurse to intubate Karen's son. A thick glob of meconium slithered up the sucker tubing as he viewed the baby's throat and vocal cords with the laryngoscope to check for further meconium.

'Good thing he didn't take a breath before now, with that sitting there,' the anaesthetist commented, and Scarlet silently agreed.

But *now* would be nice, she silently urged the baby.

The anaesthetist slid a breathing tube into the baby's throat and after only a few puffs on the air bag on the other end the baby started to twitch and grimace. Suddenly the baby coughed and a weak cry could be heard over the sound of the sucker and oxygen flow.

Scarlet looked up and caught Nina's expression as the other midwife sagged against the wall. Nina had squeezed her eyes closed but tears trickled down her cheeks as she realised the baby was alive.

Unfortunately, baby wasn't out of the woods yet, Scarlet thought grimly as they removed the tube and placed the oxygen mask over his nose and mouth. His breathing was rapid and shallow and his little ribs receded with every breath.

'Let's get him over to the nursery crib and into some decent oxygen as quickly as we can,' the anaesthetist murmured, and Scarlet nodded.

Scarlet looked back towards Sinclair. 'His respiration rate is over eighty. I'd like to transfer him into the crib.'

Sinclair's forehead was creased. 'Do that. I've rung the paediatrician at the base hospital and he should arrive by the time you get baby settled. I'll come over as soon as we finish up here.'

*   *   *

The next hour passed in a blur. Scarlet had to admit that Tessa was an experienced neonatal nurse and used to handling very sick babies. She took over the care of Karen's baby but was less than welcoming to Nina and George. Scarlet drew the father and midwife away for a much-needed cup of tea as soon as the baby was settled.

'He looks a little better already, don't you think?' Scarlet said as she removed the teabag from Nina's cup.

'His colour's better but I wish I knew how his lungs are.'

'The X-rays will be back soon,' Scarlet said.

Nina took the cup gratefully and sipped at the hot fluid. 'Thanks, I needed this.'

'If he's fine, it will be because you and George brought Karen in so quickly. You did a great job. Have a break and I'll let you know as soon as Karen is back from Recovery.' Scarlet squeezed George's shoulder. 'I have a new admission in labour so I'll catch you later.'

As she walked down towards the birthing unit, Sinclair stepped out of the nursery.

'Sister Robin? The X-rays are back.'

Scarlet tried to pick up the prognosis from his voice but he was going to tell her anyway. 'The paediatrician doesn't think we need to transfer baby to the base hospital if he stays stable. Where's the father?'

'That's wonderful.' Scarlet gestured with her head. 'They're both in the tearoom.' Sinclair nodded but before he could turn away Scarlet reached out and put her hand on his arm. 'Sinclair?' The warmth of his body seeped into hers. Unconsciously she tightened her grip on him without realising what she was doing.

He tilted his head. 'Scarlet?' The amusement was back on his face.

She grimaced. 'Be nice. Don't be hard on them because they wanted a home birth.'

He looked at her thoughtfully. 'You must be thinking of someone else. I'm always nice.' He squeezed the hand on his arm. 'Don't worry,' he said, and walked away.

Her hand dropped and she stared after him. She was beginning to realise how many preconceived ideas she'd had about him. And not all of them had been right.

By the time Scarlet made it home that afternoon, she was mentally exhausted. They'd had another quick birth by a first-time mum and Scarlet had been the birth attendant. Again Sinclair hadn't made it on time but at least they'd been standing beside the bed when the baby had been born. She smiled tiredly. Sinclair hadn't said much except that she was getting closer to the bed.

When Scarlet came in for her next shift, she sighed when she saw Tessa.

The ward was busy and neither midwife said anything as they sat down to hear the night sister's report. Without discussing it, Scarlet went off to the birthing unit and Tessa took the nursery. When she had a moment, Scarlet promised herself a long talk with Karen.

Carrie and Jim were having their third baby in three years and Scarlet had met them with their previous children. They'd arrived just after midnight and both looked exhausted this morning, even before the baby was born. It had been a long, hard night.

Scarlet smiled sympathetically at the grey smudges under their eyes. 'Hi, guys. It's lovely to see you again.'

'Hi, Letty.' Jim peered at her badge. 'How come it says Scarlet?'

She laughed. 'I used to shorten my name but I'm going the full Monty now. So that's my name.'

She sat on the edge of the bed and smiled at Carrie. 'I've had my own baby since I last saw you, so now I'm sure you must be Superman and Superwoman to cope with your two daughters, let alone another one almost here.' She took Carrie's wrist and felt her pulse. 'So, how are you doing, Carrie?'

The huge grey smudges under her eyes were even larger than her husband's. She could barely raise enough energy to speak. 'I'm tired and I'm sick of it. Everything aches and I don't think I can handle many more of these contractions.' Two tears slid down her cheeks along the faint line where others had been. 'How long do you reckon it's going to be?'

'Night Sister said Dr McPherson's been in. She said he suggested an epidural and that you were five centimetres.' Scarlet picked up the hand-sized book with circles to illustrate the dilatation of the cervix. She pointed to the one that was five centimetres wide.

'Five centimetres is excellent. The slow half of labour is finished with and we get to the exciting half now. Can you hang in for a little longer?'

Carrie sighed. 'I'm terrified to have an epidural but I've felt so uptight this pregnancy, and now this labour has been so slow. The idea of it all happening without me knowing about it is becoming attractive. I don't think I can do it any more.'

Scarlet frowned and stroked the woman's leg in

sympathy. 'Can I just do some observations and then we'll have a think about your options and how you can get more comfortable?'

'OK. But I'm cold and I'm not getting up and walking around later. I know what you're like, Letty-Scarlet.' The weak grin that accompanied the comment drew one from Scarlet in response.

'I'll get my thinking cap on.' She busied herself and took Carrie's blood pressure, which was slightly elevated, and her temperature, which was down.

Baby's heart rate was steady on 140 and unaffected except by a nice increase in rate at the start of the next contraction. Scarlet kept her hand on Carrie's tightening abdomen, timing the contraction from start to finish. Carrie gave a shuddering sigh at the end of it.

Scarlet lifted her hand and wrote down the timing. 'That was a big one. OK. How does this sound? If I run you a big warm lavender bath, you could just lie in the water and rock with the contractions and you wouldn't have to walk around. The heat all around you will ease the pain and it should make you feel a bit sleepy, which isn't a bad way to spend the next hour or so. It won't take all the pain away but will help.' She spread her hands. 'I throw myself on the mercy of the court.'

Carrie smiled. 'That sounds pretty good, actually. But I thought if I lay in the bath too soon it could slow my contractions.'

'Your contractions are strong and regular, so it should be fine. Actually, half-dilated or more is the best time to hit the water.'

'OK. I'll try it.'

The next hour Scarlet spent sitting on the side of

the bath with Jim as they reassured Carrie that she was doing brilliantly. The pains were coming long and fast and Scarlet could tell when the stormy time of transition hit Carrie. Transition was that time at the end of first stage and before the start of the pushing contractions.

Carrie sat up in the bath and her eyes widened. 'I want to go home.' She looked at her husband. 'Now!'

Scarlet caught Jim's glance and smiled. 'What does that sound like to you, Jim? You've seen Carrie go through this twice before.'

'Transition?' His eyes were hopeful and he looked at his wife with love and sympathy in his eyes. 'Hang in there, honey. You're nearly home.'

She met his eyes and nodded. 'You'd better be right—or you're dead,' Carrie muttered as she sank back in the water.

By the end of the next contraction Carrie's breathing had changed and Scarlet could tell she'd moved on to second stage. It would only be a couple of pushes before the baby was born.

'OK, Carrie,' Scarlet reached for the towel. 'Time to get out and have this baby.'

Carrie didn't open her eyes and Scarlet could tell she was pushing. She couldn't help her own excitement. She'd always wanted the option of water birth at Southside but there was no policy for them in the hospital and that meant it wasn't on. 'Hello, Carrie? We have to get out of the bath, friend. We're not allowed to have water babies here.'

'Sorry. Can't do it,' she gasped. 'I'm not moving.'

Scarlet rubbed her neck. 'OK…' She stood up and reached for the cordless phone and dialled Sinclair's number. He wasn't going to be happy about this.

'Dr McPherson.'

'Sinclair?' Scarlet didn't even realise she'd called him by his first name. 'It's Scarlet.' She didn't pause for him to answer because this baby wasn't going to wait. 'Carrie Wright has just started second stage and she's in the bath.'

'Well, you got her in there—get her out!' Scarlet winced at the bark.

She tried to make her voice soothing. 'I have tried.'

'Try harder. You know it's not on. Don't do this. I'm on my way.' Scarlet lifted the phone away from her ear as he slammed his receiver down.

She looked across at Jim who was trying to coax his wife out of the bath. Carrie wasn't having any of it.

Scarlet couldn't help a tiny grin at the thought of Sinclair driving grimly up the road towards them. But she might find herself out of her job if she didn't think of something fast.

Carrie was pushing steadily now and Scarlet knew that most of the time third babies knew their way out quicker than their siblings had. 'Right, then, Carrie. That's fine. As long as you're comfortable. If you won't leave the water then the water is going to have to leave you. Sorry about that. There's no policy to say we can't have the baby in the bath without water, though.' She grinned and reached in to pull the plug out of the bath to let the water drain away.

'Grab me a couple of warmed towels so she won't get cold, please, Jim, and press the buzzer for the other midwife to come in.'

Scarlet had a fair idea what Tessa was going to think of this development but the other midwife was the least of her worries. The water was taking for ever to disappear and she could see a small crescent of baby's head between his mother's legs.

She couldn't figure out why the water wasn't lower then she noticed that a facecloth was stuck in the plughole. Scarlet reached in and plucked it out but couldn't help thinking that the situation was turning into a farce.

Tessa arrived on the scene, took one horrified look at the baby's scalp showing under the water and had a fit. 'Get this woman out of the bath.'

Jim jumped. Scarlet glared and said, 'Thank you, Sister.' She used the first thing that came into her mind to prevent a scene at what should be a wonderful event. 'Dr McPherson is aware of the situation.' She gestured to the bath. 'The water is draining now, as you can see. Perhaps you could manoeuvre the delivery trolley in here so we'll have something to cut the cord with.'

Tessa opened and shut her mouth before turning away to get the trolley.

The water was below the level of the baby's head now, and Scarlet settled back down on the side of the bath. 'Pop the towels over Carrie, Jim. We don't want her to get cold. OK, Carrie, nice and gentle now.' Scarlet cradled the baby's head in her hand as the last of it eased out of the birth canal. She slipped her finger in beside the baby's neck to feel for the cord then drew back again.

'No cord. Gentle push when you get the next pain, Carrie.'

The outer door opened and closed and Sinclair appeared at the bathroom door. There was no room for him to come in with the trolley barring the door. His eyes met Scarlet's over the top of everyone else and promised retribution later. But his voice was calm. 'Well done, Carrie.'

Scarlet looked back at the baby and watched the tiny head swivel forty-five degrees to restitute the shoulders under the pubic bone.

First the anterior and then the posterior shoulder slipped out and she lifted the rest of the slippery baby up onto his mother's abdomen, where he slid around a bit until his mother held him. The thick umbilical cord trailed after him.

Jim's voice carried over the baby's cry. 'It's a boy. We've got our boy.' He leant over, kissed his wife and son and wiped the tears from his face.

'Congratulations,' Sinclair said dryly. 'Perhaps you should call him Neptune.'

Scarlet kept her head down to hide her smile as she waited for third stage to be complete. Once the shiny placenta was accounted for, she checked Carrie for any grazes and pronounced herself done. She straightened her shoulders and glanced up at the door.

Sinclair indicated with his head that he wanted to see her outside, and she nodded resignedly. He spoke to Jim. 'I'll just borrow Scarlet for a minute. Enjoy your family in private for a few moments.'

Tessa shot her an I-hope-he-gives-you-hell look and sashayed back to the nursery.

Scarlet sighed and looked back at the family in and around the bath then slowly removed her gloves and gown. Carrie was proud of herself because she hadn't needed an epidural and that made it worth everything.

She closed the birthing-unit door behind her and leant against it. Sinclair was standing, tapping his foot in the corridor.

She lifted her head and met Sinclair's eyes. 'Yes, Doctor?'

He stared at her for a moment and the silence lengthened uncomfortably. Scarlet refused to blink and for a moment she thought it was going to turn into a children's staring contest. Her eyes were starting to water and a bubble of laughter was tickling at the bottom of her rib cage. Nervous laughter. He might make her crazy but she knew she was alive when he was around.

Then he spoke. 'Congratulations, Sister Robin. Two bathroom deliveries in your first week. Perhaps you'd like to have a baby over the sink next?' He tilted his head in query.

Scarlet narrowed her eyes. 'The object of the game is for the mother to be confident and comfortable wherever she wants to be, Doctor.'

'No. The object of the game, Sister Robin, is to maintain sense and safety for all concerned. And that rules out water birth. If you'd left that water in I would have seen you out of your job. You do realise that?' He glared at her.

Her shrug was infinitesimal but he saw it. His lips thinned. Scarlet felt a small thrill of satisfaction at penetrating his control, but hastened into speech before he blasted her. 'That was a consideration in the removal of the plug. But mostly I did it because I'm inexperienced at water birth and it wasn't safe practice to learn at that moment.'

He seemed to have regained control. 'Well, then, we can be thankful for small mercies.' But the sarcasm was thick in his voice.

Scarlet wasn't finished. 'But I am planning on becoming accredited in water birth.'

He narrowed his eyes. 'Not in my hospital.'

'Perhaps it's time Southside and you moved into the twenty-first century, Doctor.'

'We don't need you to push us. Like you're pushing your luck at the moment.' He stared at her for a moment then shook his head and his voice changed. 'What are you doing?'

She could feel the depth of his look, as if he were trying to see inside her. For a minute it threw her and he took advantage of her shock.

'Are you trying to make me notice you?'

That made her head fly up. 'You amaze me. Dream on, Dr McPherson. If I was trying to make you notice me, you wouldn't have to ask. You'd notice. I'm here for my clients and no other reason. I'm sorry if you don't agree with my philosophies and I will try not to contravene any hospital protocols.' She took a deep breath, astounded her response had come out coherently. It might be time to beat a strategic retreat, though. 'If you've finished, perhaps I could return to my client.'

He gave a short harsh laugh and Scarlet winced. 'By all means, Sister, carry on. But, please, remember that they are my "clients", too.' He spun on his heel and presented her with his back.

Scarlet could feel the adrenaline pumping around her body as he walked away. A sudden film of tears pricked her eyes and she dashed them away. Like hell she'd cry over words from that man. She turned back to the birthing room and leant her forehead on the door for a moment before going in. She took three calming breaths and plastered a smile on her face before turning the handle.

Sinclair passed the sister's desk without even noticing it.

'Excuse me? Sinclair.'

Tessa's voice intruded on his thoughts. He dragged his mind away from the image of Scarlet standing up to him in the corridor. 'Yes, Tessa?'

'I'd just like you to know that I didn't realise Mrs Wright was in second stage while still in the bath. I was just as horrified as you were.'

Sinclair's brow furrowed in distaste. That was strange. A minute ago he'd been furious, but he wasn't sure he liked to hear someone else condemn Scarlet's midwifery. 'Thank you, Sister. And I thought all you midwives here stuck together. Good evening.'

He watched her sink back into the chair and realise that it hadn't gone as planned. He even felt sorry for her. But he wasn't in the mood to do anything about it. He had enough trouble trying to stay one step ahead of another certain midwife.

As he walked down the steps towards his car he suddenly smiled. At least Scarlet had pulled the plug out. The last few days had been anything but boring.

She amazed him with her newfound zeal for natural labour and delivery. He didn't have any real objections as long as the patients were happy and he didn't consider it dangerous. And preferably if it didn't involve him crawling around on the wet bathroom floor to deliver a baby. As long as all these alternative birth positions didn't get out of hand. He certainly couldn't call Scarlet a mouse now!

She had looked so beautiful when she'd been spitting fire at him that he'd wanted to kiss away her anger and turn her passions to a more desirable avenue—but she was married to some absent idiot and adultery was a sin.

But there was Cameron. Regardless of whether Scarlet's husband was in the picture or not, Sinclair felt a special affinity with the child.

After spending that short time alone with Cameron the other day, he'd needed Scarlet to categorically confirm that Cameron wasn't his son. She'd done that. He just wished he could accept it!

The next week passed quietly by Scarlet's standards. Dr Roe was on call for the two evening shifts Scarlet worked, and except for his morning rounds, Sinclair wasn't seen by the maternity staff at all.

One client was booked for a Caesarean section and, except for suggesting the family bring their own music choices into the operating theatre, Scarlet kept a low profile with the medical officers.

The cold war between Scarlet and Tessa reached new heights when Tessa continued to recount Sinclair's fury at Scarlet's attempted water birth.

After the morning staff, including Tessa, had gone home, Michelle took Scarlet aside to hear the full story.

'So did he rip through you like Tessa says?'

'No. The woman's a witch. He just mentioned that if I hadn't pulled the plug he would have taken it further.' Scarlet's eyes brightened. 'But it was so close. We nearly had our first waterbaby.'

Michelle grinned. 'Maybe we'd better get someone up from Sydney to give us an in-service on it in case accidents happen.'

'I said I'd go away and get accredited—but imagine if we held our own seminar here. I'm sure Sinclair would love that.'

'Sinclair, eh?' Her friend looked her up and down. 'So what's the story between you and Sinclair McPherson?'

Scarlet shrugged. 'Nothing.'

'Yeah, right.' Michelle tilted her head. 'On his side, when you disappeared, he sure was interested in where you went.'

Scarlet shot a look at her friend. 'What makes you say that?'

Michelle rolled her eyes. 'He asked if we'd heard from you every couple of days until we started to ask why he was so interested. Then he shut up. When I mentioned your phone call about you and Gerry getting married, he started the third degree again until people began to notice.'

Michelle watched her expression. 'Tessa's telling people they're secretly engaged but haven't announced it yet. I'm not sure if I believe her but I'd hate to see you get hurt again.'

Scarlet met her friend's eyes. 'I'm immune to Tessa at the moment. I'd say I was doubly immune to men. Though I've had a nasty reaction to the immunisation process.' She tried out her new decision on her friend. 'My marriage is over. Gerry isn't coming back.' She desperately wanted to say there never had been a marriage—she hated the way one lie turned into many. Was her mother right? Should she have brazened it out? But then she'd have to tell Michelle who the father of her child was. Not a good idea when the father himself didn't know.

Michelle compressed her lips sympathetically. 'I'm sorry, Scarlet. I'm rabbiting on and men are probably the last thing you want to talk about.'

'I'm fine, really, Michelle. Actually I'm sort of relieved. Just not into men at the moment.' They both looked up as the front door opened.

A handsome young man in cut-off jeans waved at Scarlet. He placed a large brown-paper-covered parcel on the floor.

'Speak of the men-devils.' She glanced over her shoulder at Michelle with a smile as she walked towards the door. 'Come and meet Keir. He's from the community and is the daddy of one of our little success stories up there.

'Hi, Keir. This is my friend Michelle. What are you doing here?'

He leant across and kissed Scarlet on the cheek. 'I've brought you a thank-you present.'

Scarlet looked down at the large parcel and felt the tears prick her eyes. Presents in the community were made and not bought so receiving them was doubly special. 'You didn't have to do that, Keir.'

'Of course I didn't but this is something I think you'll really love.' He crouched down and stroked the parcel and a big grin stretched across his face. 'I made it myself. It's waterproof. Open it.'

Scarlet bent down and untied the woven ribbon. Suddenly, the paper fell off to reveal a curved wooden stool. It was thickly lacquered and looked almost like an open fronted toilet seat.

Scarlet laughed in delight. 'It's a birthing stool. How fabulous.' She looked up at Michelle and her eyes sparkled. She looked back at Keir. 'I can't wait

to use it. Thank you, Keir. That's the best present I've
ever had.'

They both stood up and she threw her arms around
Keir just as Sinclair walked in the door.

CHAPTER SIX

SINCLAIR had been watching Scarlet's animated face through the glass in the door as he approached Maternity. He couldn't see whoever it was she'd crouched down to talk to but just watching her made him smile. Until he opened the door and had a perfect view of her launch herself at some man beside her.

When he saw her kiss the man he felt the sickness in his stomach like a sudden bout of food poisoning. He grunted, glared at them both and stepped past them to the desk. To complete the picture he nearly tripped over what looked like a wooden garden seat in the middle of the corridor.

'What is happening to this place?' he almost snarled at Michelle as she appeared at his shoulder. She looked startled.

He sighed and held up his hand. 'Sorry, Sister. Bad day. I've dropped in to see my antenatal patient, Mrs Jones, so let's do it.' He picked up her chart and shot Scarlet a disapproving look as he stalked past with Michelle on his heels.

He didn't know what he was going to say to Mrs Jones, but he'd think of something. He'd really come to see Scarlet. Another bad idea in a long line of bad ideas. Sinclair ground his teeth. He had to find out who the guy was.

He looked down at Michelle. 'I suppose it is about time the husband came back.'

Michelle shook her head. 'Scarlet said he's not coming back.'

Sinclair shot a look at her from under his brows but she didn't elaborate. 'Then who's he?'

'Keir's from the valley community. He brought Scarlet a present.'

Another man in her life. He frowned when he heard the laugh in Michelle's voice. Now, what did she think was so amusing? 'I gather the present is that thing I nearly fell over?'

He had the feeling there was something going on here and he'd get to the bottom of it soon. But all she said was, 'Yep.'

They walked into the two-bed ward, and he focussed himself enough to make general enquiries, but the whole time, peripherally, he was aware of Michelle's statement that Scarlet's husband wouldn't be coming back. He concentrated again on Mrs Jones and made sure he didn't rush the visit. They agreed on a suitable discharge date and said goodbye.

Michelle shrugged as she walked ahead and he could tell she thought he was acting strangely. He knew that he was. He'd been unstable since November the previous year.

When they came around the corner of the ward, the corridor in front of the entrance door was empty.

Now where were they? he thought grimly. Probably in some room, kissing.

Scarlet appeared from the unit manager's office. She looked so vibrant and happy he couldn't tear his eyes off her.

No one else was with her and she grinned cheekily at him. The sickness cleared from his gut like magic.

'Dr McPherson. I've something I want to show you.'

He thought he heard Michelle mumble something as she walked away but he didn't ask her what she'd said. Sinclair moved towards Scarlet, drawn by invisible strings. When he entered the office and the door shut behind him with a click, he realised he'd pulled it closed as he'd come through.

The mood in the room swung from Scarlet's exuberance to mutual awareness of their cramped isolation from the rest of the ward.

Her tongue passed nervously over her lips and his eyes were drawn to the sheen of moisture left behind on the erotic pink roundness. Unable to help himself, he reached out and stroked the dampness on her bottom lip gently. It was incredibly soft.

She flinched and her eyes widened.

His hand snapped back to his side and he shook his head. What the hell was he doing? 'I'm sorry.'

At least she looked as pole-axed as he felt. He jammed his libido back in its box and tried to remember why he'd shut himself in a room with Scarlet if he wasn't allowed to touch her. The garden seat was on the unit manager's desk. He glanced at it and then back at Scarlet. 'Is this what you wanted to show me?'

'Yes,' she said, and her voice shook. She cleared her throat. 'Um. It's a waterproof birthing stool.'

He looked at it again and realised that what she'd said was true. 'I see that now.' He was back under control and he could concentrate on what she was saying. 'What is it you want to do with it or maybe I don't want to know?'

She smiled and the force of it slipped in under his

rib cage. 'Don't be like that, Sinclair.' She had herself in hand as well, he could tell.

He just wished he didn't feel so shattered from that one touch. He tried to maintain concentration on the stool—a stool he wasn't interested in at that moment.

'So?' he said.

'So I want to use it here, and I'd like your support.'

He opened his mouth to comment but she held up her hand.

'Stop. Don't say no until I've finished. Just listen for a minute.' Her lips tilted and she smiled that devastating smile he remembered from their first night.

He could almost agree to anything if she looked at him like that again. He refocussed. He needed to get a grip here. He must be still off balance from Michelle's bombshell about Scarlet's husband.

She was talking and he tried to concentrate. 'Since I spent time at the valley community, I've really learnt to appreciate the difference made when a labouring woman is coping in the position of her choice. When she feels in control.'

She gestured to the stool. 'Whether it's in the bath, or a shower chair or a birthing stool. It takes a little getting used to when the woman's pelvis isn't in the position we're familiar with, but the results are worth the effort. I'd like you to agree to a trial of the stool until you see what I mean.'

'So the trial goes on until I agree—is that what you're saying?' Sinclair queried.

She laughed and the contagious sound made his lips twitch.

The humour was still in her voice when she spoke. 'It did sound a bit like that but that's not what I meant.'

'Really? Could have fooled me.' He was smiling, too. Of course he'd agree. He had no choice, in fact. He couldn't think of a good reason to deny the request, and if the women liked it, and the infection control people were happy, then he'd agree.

Who knew? Even Scarlet might be appreciative.

He patted the stool. 'One month. Then we'll have a ward meeting and see what the general consensus is.'

Her eyes lit up and he pressed his advantage. 'On one condition.'

Scarlet couldn't believe he was putting a condition on this. She put her hands on her hips. 'What condition?'

'You have to come and have dinner with me and tell me about your time in the valley.'

Scarlet's mouth went dry. That wasn't what she'd expected. She'd thought he might have insisted on being present when the women were on the stool or something equally cautious. But to ask her out. He'd said he wanted to hear about the community but just the two of them? She couldn't do it.

She could see it now. 'That would give the gossips something to talk about.'

He shrugged his shoulders. 'Is that your biggest fear? The gossips talking about us? My father would be in the house. Even your husband couldn't complain about that.'

Thank you for the reminder about 'Gerry'. That's another good reason why not, she thought. But it wasn't a good time to tell him she'd decided the marriage was finished. 'I'm sure he wouldn't like it.'

Sinclair started to turn away. 'I thought you wanted to promote your ideas on natural birth?'

Salvation came. 'I can't. I'm away from Cameron when I'm at work, I don't like to leave him when I'm home. I certainly wouldn't expect my mother to mind him when I'm not working.'

Sinclair wasn't fazed. 'No problem. Bring him with you. I'll get my housekeeper to prepare the meal before she goes home—she loves organising dinner parties. We'll go to my house and Cameron will be fine. I'll pick you both up at seven tomorrow evening.'

'Tomorrow?' Scarlet realised she'd squeaked as soon as the words left her mouth.

His face remained serious. 'That's the condition. Let me know if you can't make it or I'll see you then.' She watched him turn the handle and open the door.

She could smell a rat. Scarlet searched for signs that he was pleased with himself now that he'd outmanoeuvred her, but his face was expressionless.

'You'll need a bolt in your car for Cameron's baby capsule. As long as Cameron can come, we'll be there.' This might not be all bad. At least she'd have a chance to promote her views on the changes she had in mind for Southside. 'You could be sorry you invited us,' she warned.

He stood back to allow her to precede him from the room. 'I'll take that risk.'

Michelle was sitting at the desk and glanced up at them.

Sinclair rattled the keys in his pocket. 'Bye, ladies.'

Michelle said, 'Bye.'

Scarlet said nothing and Sinclair whistled as he went down the steps.

Neither woman said anything until Michelle looked across at her friend. 'He looks pretty happy for a man who's agreed to a newfangled idea.'

'What makes you think he agreed?' Scarlet said sourly.

Michelle blinked. 'Didn't he? I can't imagine that he wouldn't. He's always been fair and he hasn't got a closed mind like some. Now, his father I could understand. You must be slipping.'

Scarlet half laughed. 'You're right. He agreed to a month's trial.'

'So why the glum look? I'm confused. I thought you'd be jumping for joy with a new toy to play with.'

Scarlet slumped back in the chair. 'You're right again. I am pleased. I've just got something else on my mind. Do you want the nursery or the birthing suites?'

'Nice of you to offer, seeing as there's no one in labour,' Michelle teased. 'I'll take the mother-crafting on the floor. There's Karen's baby with meconium aspiration in the nursery. He'll keep you busy.'

Scarlet stood up and turned towards the nursery door. 'I need busy at the moment. See you later.'

Baby Wilson's X-rays were clipped up in front of the X-ray light.

Scarlet could see the two dark areas that indicated poor lung function. She moved over to the crib and stared down at the tiny infant. He had barely any hair and it made him look even smaller. 'Hello, Toby. Poor little fellow. I bet your mum misses having you with her in the room, though you are getting better.'

She checked the site of insertion of the intravenous cannula. His heart leads appeared secure and his heart rate and respirations were stable, although a little faster than normal. She changed the pulse oximeter clamp from one foot to the other to ensure the reading of his oxygen saturation was true.

Oxygen, measured and mixed with air, hissed into his Perspex head box and she checked the water levels and temperatures on the humidifier. He was getting it moist and warm.

It was a bit like painting the harbour bridge. By the time you finished all the hourly observations and tasks it was time to start again. Karen hobbled in and when she saw Scarlet her eyes filled with tears.

Scarlet held out her arms and the young woman buried her head in Scarlet's shoulder.

'I hate it here. I don't understand why Toby is sick. They all told me but I just can't seem to understand.'

Scarlet squeezed Karen's shoulder and sat her carefully in the chair before crouching down beside her.

'Hey, it's normal to feel like that. Do you want me to try and explain it again?'

Karen nodded.

'OK.' Scarlet grabbed a footstool and sat beside Karen, facing the crib so she could watch Toby.

'At birth, babies who have passed a bowel motion, called meconium, inside Mum's uterus have their mouths sucked out as soon as possible after birth. We use a thin tube to try and prevent the baby breathing in the meconium otherwise they could breath in meconium and gum up sections of the lungs, which leads to breathing problems, pneumonia and even worse.

'Unfortunately, sometimes there's already meconium inside the lungs.' Scarlet paused to see if Karen understood that much.

'That's what the doctor said, but how could it get in there if the baby hadn't breathed yet?' She wiped her nose with a tissue as she looked at her baby behind the Perspex wall of the crib.

Scarlet gestured with her hands. 'In normal circumstances, unborn babies have a shallow and rapid respiratory movement as they float inside their mother and lung fluid flows through their lungs.

'If, like your baby, something happens to cut down on the oxygen received, the foetus conserves energy by stopping these movements. Unfortunately, if the lack of oxygen continues, these gentle movements are replaced by deep gasping underwater breaths.'

Karen nodded her head as Scarlet mimed the breath movements.

'The foetal lung fluid is replaced by gasped contaminated amniotic fluid.'

Karen nodded.

'OK. So stressed babies, like Toby was after your bleed, often have meconium floating in the amniotic fluid. At birth, breathing difficulties are caused by the globs of meconium, which stop air entering the tiny tubes in the lungs, and inflammation is caused by the chemicals in the meconium that damage lung tissue.' She looked at Karen. 'Is that clearer?'

Karen nodded. 'So how long does Toby have to stay in there?'

'Until his breathing doesn't speed up when there's no extra oxygen added to the air. Luckily he only has a few small, inflamed areas and he's getting better all the time. Probably a few more days and he'll be able to come out. If he'd been much sicker we would have had to send him away to a larger neonatal intensive care unit.'

'I feel so lost without a baby like the other mothers, and I miss George.'

Scarlet squeezed Karen's hand. 'That's normal too. You've been very brave. Just spend as much time down here as you can without making yourself too tired. Don't forget you had a big operation, too.'

The next seven hours flew and Scarlet explained all the leads and lines connected to Toby. She even encouraged Karen to hold the syringe barrel while the expressed breast milk was run into Toby's stomach. By the end of the shift Scarlet was tired but satisfied with Toby's progress and Karen looked much more at ease around her son's equipment.

But the downside of a busy shift was the leftover tension that accompanied her home. Scarlet lay in bed and contemplated the night lamp of diving dolphins that rotated in the corner of the room.

She couldn't help thinking of the evening with Sinclair looming on her horizon, and it wasn't surprising that she couldn't sleep. If she was honest, her insomnia was more Sinclair-related than work-related.

If she was going to be honest, she'd felt good talking to Sinclair today. Once she'd got over him touching her. The feeling created by that one finger he'd laid on her bottom lip had resonated around her body and stunned her into silence. It had coloured the rest of her day. It had brought back a million tiny memories of a night she'd tried to forget and hadn't been able to. Damn him.

Which brought her back to the sweet consequences of that night. Did any reason justify the fact that she'd lied to Sinclair about Cameron's paternity? Had she presumed too much that Sinclair would feel trapped by her and her son? What it all boiled down to— wasn't it time she got over her gossip phobia? Was she too obsessed about what people thought and said?

Scarlet twisted her pillow in confusion. Why was everything so complicated?

By the time she finally drifted off to sleep Cameron was ready for another feed and Scarlet couldn't face getting up to sit in the chair. She snuggled him into bed with her and she fed him with her eyes closed.

He was still there when she woke in the morning. The breast that he'd snacked on for the rest of the night felt as flat as a pancake and the other looked like a balloon.

She started to giggle. Whatever she wore tonight would look funny with breasts like this. Another giggle escaped and Cameron woke up.

She shifted him up onto her shoulder. 'Did you have a party last night, son? Look at your poor mummy's breasts.'

He burped so loudly it set Scarlet off again.

When she went down for breakfast she was still smiling. 'Morning, Mum.'

'You look like you're in a good mood today,' Vivienne remarked.

Scarlet's brow creased. Had she been that hard to live with? 'Why? Am I normally bad-tempered?'

Vivienne patted her shoulder and placed a cup of tea in front of her. 'Just weighed down with the worries of the world on your shoulders, that's all.' She sat down beside Scarlet at the table and pushed the cereal and milk towards her.

'So what brought on this lightening of your mood?'

'I've decided to lose my husband.'

Her mother shook her head. 'Poor Gerry-the-geologist. I never liked him anyway.' She met her daughter's eyes. 'What about Sinclair?'

'Sinclair is an unknown factor. I'm not ready to tell

him about Cameron but my wish for the day is that we can find some common ground and friendship to-night.' She told her mother about the birth stool and Sinclair's condition.

Vivienne looked sceptical. 'Friends don't lie to each other. So be careful what you wish for.'

By the end of the day, Scarlet's nerves were getting the better of her and she wasn't smiling any more. What on earth had possessed her to agree to go to Sinclair's house? She should have suggested they eat here at her mother's—at least she'd be safe. Wimp, she told herself.

'What are you wearing?' Vivienne came in and sat on Scarlet's bed while her daughter was riffling through her wardrobe.

'I thought maybe my black jeans and sweater.' At her mother's look she laughed. 'Just kidding. Seriously, whatever I wear needs buttons in case Cameron wants a feed.'

'Everything in that wardrobe seems either grey or brown. Don't you have any brighter clothes?' Vivienne's nose wrinkled.

Scarlet sighed. 'Sinclair wants to hear about the maternity care in the community. It's not a fashion parade.' She watched her mother poke around her wardrobe.

'What's that red material I can see in there?'

Scarlet tried unsuccessfully to bury the swathe of material back behind an overcoat. 'That dress has a lot to answer for.' She pulled out a blue-green shift in linen. The straight lines would be flattering and it buttoned from hem to neckline. 'What about this?'

'It's not frivolous but I like it.' Vivienne scrutinised it. 'It will crush, though.'

Scarlet shrugged. 'He can see me ironed and then deal with the wrinkles later.'

Vivienne stood up and held out her hand. 'Sounds like a marriage to me. Give it here and I'll press it while you dress Cameron. You've got thirty minutes before he arrives.'

Scarlet felt the sudden thump of her heart. She was acting like a nervous teenager on her first date, not a twenty-five-year-old mother. She didn't need this.

At the McPherson Family Practice, Sinclair paced the kitchen as the clock ticked slowly on the mantelpiece. The table was set upstairs. All he had to do was take the cold platters out of the fridge and the hot ones out of the oven when he needed them.

His father frowned. 'For goodness' sake, sit down. I had no idea you felt this way about Letty Robin.' Frank McPherson's voice at least stopped the pacing.

Sinclair paused to lean on the back of a chair. 'Her full name is Scarlet. We're just discussing changes in obstetric care.'

Frank's voice was stern. 'Of course.' The scepticism was clear in his voice. 'I thought she was married? I expected better of you, Sinclair. I have all the time in the world for her mother but young Letty has proved herself flighty this last year.'

His father shook his head. 'I understand she moved into that hippie commune and goodness knows what she got up to there.'

The corner of Sinclair's mouth twitched. 'The marriage didn't work out, and as for the community...' He grinned. 'People who live there aren't called hippies and they don't call them communes any more either, Dad.'

'Humph. Well, I wouldn't know about that. You do have a certain standard to uphold, Sinclair. The McPhersons have been doctors here for three generations and we've never had a bad word said against us.'

Sinclair grimaced. 'That makes us a boring lot, then, doesn't it?'

His father snorted and it turned into a laugh. 'Wish I'd thought of that answer when my father warned me off Scarlet's mother.'

The older man stood up, slapped his son on the back. 'Goodnight. I'm off to read the papers on my bed and you needn't think I'll disturb you. Be careful. Those Robins are dangerous birds.'

He grinned at his father's pun. 'It's not even seven o'clock. And what do you mean, Grandfather warned you off Vivienne Robin?'

'It was after your mother died. Vivienne was a good friend to me. More than that. But your grandfather didn't like it and I could never stand up to him. But that's all water under the bridge.'

Sinclair had a horrendous thought. 'Do you know who Scarlet's father was?' Sinclair held his breath.

'One of the town's best-kept secrets. But, yes, I do.' He ran his finger across his mouth, pretending to zip his lip and winked. 'It wasn't me. Wish it had been. But there you go. Goodnight, son.' Frank sailed off to bed, unaware that his son was frustrated by his answer but relieved all the same.

Sinclair sank down on the chair and his breath eased out as he listened to his father walk along the hallway to his downstairs flat. Thank God for that. He certainly didn't feel brotherly towards Scarlet.

His grandfather had been dead ten years and his

own mother at least twenty-five. He couldn't remember much about his mother except that she'd sung to him when he'd been little. His childhood had been rock solid with amenable housekeepers but now he came to think about it he couldn't picture even one instance when he'd seen his father out with a woman. It was a long time for a man to be without female companionship.

But, then, he himself hadn't stayed home that much to see. He'd had a fairly active social life, although none of the women he'd known had struck that special note with him—until Scarlet.

It hadn't been a musical note he'd heard that night—it had been the complete jazz band.

He glanced at his watch. Time to go.

CHAPTER SEVEN

SCARLET was waiting for Sinclair when he arrived. He'd been hoping she'd wear the red dress. Unfortunately, it looked like his estimate of his chances was spot on. She looked beautiful in the blue.

Scarlet was very businesslike. 'Did you get the bolt for the baby seat?'

Luckily he had. 'It's all ready. My housekeeper minds her grandson and she lent me hers.'

She bent down to pick up the contraption from the floor beside the door. 'Here's the seat. I'll bring Cameron out while you fit it to your car.' It was as if she wanted to get the evening over and done with. He couldn't decide whether she didn't want to come with him or was frightened. Neither was a good sign for the evening.

'Can I come in first and say hello to Vivienne?' He watched the changing expressions on her face as she battled with her obvious desire to say no. Finally she stepped aside and gestured him in.

'As you wish. She's in the kitchen.'

'Thank you.' He smiled at her and she sighed. Her shoulders loosened and she sent him a tentative smile of her own. 'I won't be a minute,' he reassured her.

Scarlet heard him greet her mother and the sound of laughter. She sighed again. She'd been more wound up than she'd realised. She tried a couple of soothing breaths and felt a little better. This was stupid. What did she have to be afraid of?

The voice inside her head was quick to answer. How about the only guy who has managed to break down your defences and who also has the power to claim half your son?

This was a bad idea.

Sinclair's voice came from beside her shoulder. 'Ready?'

She jumped and the pounding of her heart in her ears disorientated her. She stared at him for a moment and drew some reassurance from the kindness in his eyes.

His voice was soft. 'Did I startle you? I'm sorry.' He looked around. 'Where's Cameron?'

She glanced up the stairs. 'I'll just get him if you take the baby seat and that nappy bag beside it.'

'Done.' He touched her arm. 'I don't like to see you this nervous, Scarlet. I'll bring you home whenever you want. All right?'

When he was sweet he was deadly and she could feel herself soften towards him. 'You must think I'm an idiot. I'm just out of practice.'

'Didn't your husband take you out?' She could tell he wanted the words back as soon as he'd said them. At least she wasn't the only one who put their foot in it. She felt guilty in her lie and almost felt sorry for him but chose not to answer—that way she couldn't say the wrong thing. She wished she'd never started that charade—but it was for Cameron's protection. Not hers.

The trip was short, and in no time Sinclair had parked his car in the driveway.

He came around and opened her door and Scarlet realised she'd been sitting there, staring up at his home, dreading their time alone. But then she remembered his father was there. She clutched the nappy bag as she got out of the car.

'I'll carry Cameron up the stairs if you like,' he said, and opened the rear door.

'No!' She realised she'd spoken sharply but it was too late now. 'I'll take him, in case he wakes.'

Sinclair stood back for her to lift the capsule out of the car. 'Give me the little bag, then, and I'll lead the way.' That was all he said.

She followed him in through the entrance and even in her nervous state she had to pause and admire the beautiful lead-light panels each side of the heavy door.

By the time they'd climbed the stairs, her arm was aching from the weight of the capsule. She unobtrusively swapped arms to flex her cramped fingers, hoping he wouldn't notice after his offer. Of course he did.

'Independence can be a pain sometimes, don't you think?' There was a glimmer of amusement in his eyes but she refused to bite.

'Where will I put him?'

'As I don't suppose you want to go into my room, perhaps the guest room would be appropriate.' He indicated a hallway at the end of the large open-plan room and she followed him through.

By the time she'd settled a sleeping Cameron on the bed, surrounded by pillows, Scarlet was starting to feel more in control. After all, this was her big chance to bend Sinclair's ear about natural birth in a calm and sensible manner.

The table was set in one end of the huge dining-lounge room with full-length windows taking advantage of their height over the river. The furnishings were a little spartan and lacked a woman's touch. Scarlet could see the streetlights from across the river reflected in the water and somewhere a motorboat chugged upstream.

They stepped out onto the covered verandah, and the breeze felt good on her heated face. It was quite cool for a spring evening, with a hint of storm in the air, and after a few minutes, while he pointed out local landmarks, she was glad when Sinclair suggested they go back inside. He slid the glass door across behind them to stop the light breeze.

'It must be beautiful here in the summer.'

'It is. But the view inside is better at the moment.'

She'd never been one to consider herself good-looking but she couldn't help believing he found her so. It was in the way he looked at her. 'Thank you, kind sir,' she said lightly, but the comment made her nervous.

As if he realised it, he changed the subject. 'Would you like a drink? Or I have non-alcoholic wine.'

She concentrated on the question. 'Non-alcoholic, please.' She went over to the lounge to perch on the edge of the black leather.

Scarlet noted the lined bookshelves and the latest stereo equipment in the room. 'So, what do you do in the evenings when you're not attending births?'

He smiled and the tingle it gave her travelled all the way down to her toes. There should be a law against a smile like that. She almost missed his answer. 'I socialise and play squash, or listen to music. I'm very boring.' He passed her glass and their fingers brushed.

Startled, her eyes met his and looked away. She was starting to feel like she was sitting on a low-voltage electric fence, with Sinclair zapping her every couple of minutes. Yeah, right. 'Boring isn't a word I associate with you.'

There was a smile in his voice when he spoke. 'So tell me about your time at the community.'

She felt her shoulders relax slightly. This was safer ground and she gathered her thoughts. 'It was different to what I imagined it would be,' she said. 'My mother had friends who built the first house in the valley, and Mum spoke of it as a good place to find yourself. A place without prejudice.'

He sipped his own wine and wondered out loud, 'Can any place really be without prejudice?'

He offered her some pretzels and she considered her reply while she crunched. The salt was tangy on her tongue—or was it just that all her senses seemed hypersensitive in his company? 'Most community dwellers are reluctant to come down the mountain to a hospital to give birth—I suppose that could be a prejudice against conventional medicine—but I believe that's because they have faith in the birthing process.'

He frowned. 'What happens when it goes wrong? Like Karen's pregnancy?'

She tilted her head. 'How often do you see a case like placenta praevia? Once a year in our three hundred births, which would be once every ten years for the amount of home births we have around here. That's why it's so important to be non-judgmental when these clients come in. They have to be encouraged to come if they need help.'

'I can see that. But what if they still decide not to come?'

'Then they accept the outcome as the natural course

of birth.' She could see he didn't like that answer. She wasn't thrilled with it herself.

He shook his head. 'This is where I have a problem. In Karen's case, ultrasounds for all women effectively remove the risk of undiagnosed placenta praevia. Don't you think personal preference against ultrasound is a bit harsh on the child or mother that might have been saved?' He shook his head and muttered, 'Personally, I'd say it was criminal.'

Scarlet saw his point. 'Well, to be honest, that's my dilemma as well, although I would say ''ill-informed'', not ''criminal''. And that wasn't the case with Nina's client. Nina did everything right and actively encourages her ladies to have at least one ultrasound. But George is the only man Karen trusts and our radiographers are all men. She refused on those grounds. But besides Karen's case, I know women who did everything their obstetrician suggested, including ultrasound, then spent the whole pregnancy worried about a deformed baby. All because the ultrasound thought it picked up something that wasn't there to start with. There has to be a happy medium.'

'I'll buy that,' he acknowledged. 'But I could never accept a child's death as natural attrition.'

Scarlet spread her hands. 'Hospitals have their own tragedies and sometimes all the technology in the world won't save a baby. But apart from obvious high-risk pregnancies that require a doctor, most healthy women are capable of giving birth to healthy infants at home.'

Her stomach rumbled, probably more from nerves than hunger. Embarrassed, she looked up at him. He grinned and offered her another pretzel.

'You were saying?'

She searched for her train of thought. It had been important. Got it. 'Where the community women are enormously strong is in their beliefs. I've come to believe the power of the mind is undervalued in medicalised birth.'

She would have loved him to pick up on this concept but it was a hard one for the medical profession to take on board. Especially if, from a doctor's viewpoint, someone was going to sue you if you didn't interfere and something went wrong.

Scarlet could see Sinclair had major problems with mind over matter. He paced across the room before turning to face her. 'I don't get that. If the mother's pelvis is too small, no amount of thinking about it will make that baby fit through.'

Scarlet watched his face. 'Maybe not. But if the mother listens to her body and assumes the positions to encourage optimal presentation and position as the baby moves into the pelvis, she could possibly avoid the disproportion by presenting the baby's smallest diameter.'

He swirled the liquid in his glass and then looked down at her. 'Did you have any shoulder dystocia while you were up there?'

A shoulder dystocia was when a baby's shoulders became wedged in the mother's pelvis at birth, usually after the head was born and was a life-threatening emergency for the baby if it couldn't be dislodged. Scarlet met his eyes unflinchingly. 'About the same amount as we have in Southside, but with less traumatic outcomes.' The conversation was hotting up.

'So what did you do there that was different to

what we do here?' He was every inch the consultant as he disdainfully glared down at her.

Scarlet refused to be cowed and glared right back at him. 'Get her upright.' At Sinclair's look of disbelief she nodded her head. 'That's right. Standing! It is amazing to see what positions a woman's body will tell her to assume when a baby's shoulder is caught. I've seen women squat or kick their legs out sideways until the baby dislodged and was born. The mother is just as aware as we are that something isn't right. If we gave her the opportunity to assume the position her body tells her to adopt in this kind of crisis, maybe the morbidity would be reduced.'

He shook his head. 'Give me scientific data to back that up. That's a bizarre picture.'

She shrugged. 'The baby was fine.' She placed her empty glass on the table and leant back. It was important that he grasp this concept.

'The picture is no more bizarre than a woman on her back with her knees jammed into her chest, someone pushing on her stomach and someone else pulling her baby's head.'

His eyes were cold and steel grey now. 'That scenario is a very rare occurrence and only used in dire emergencies. Many a baby is alive because of it.'

'And to think it might not have been necessary even then is a scary thought for those it happened to. Isn't it?'

'Where do you get off? I studied for six years of medical school, worked as an obstetric registrar for four years and have been here as an obstetrician for the last five years.' He glared at her. 'So don't tell me that some hill woman knows how the mechanics of birth work better than I do.'

Scarlet tried to hold back the smile but wasn't very successful. 'Poor Sinclair. Of course she does. She's been there and experienced it. And if she has a choice between listening to a textbook or listening to her body, I hope she takes the body every time.'

Sinclair smiled back at her but it wasn't amused. 'Pul-lease. Next you'll say women have a collective race memory stretching back to Eve.'

'I'd forgotten about that.' She grinned and they both laughed. The tension eased and their eyes met for a moment in recognition of how heated the topic had become.

Scarlet patted her stomach. 'Perhaps you should feed me before we come to blows.' Her smile was sweet this time. 'One more thing, though. As a mid-wife, for the rare occasions when something does go wrong, it is nice to know where to find you.'

'Gee, thanks.' He rubbed his jaw and his own rue-ful grin appeared. 'That was a pretty spirited pre-dinner conversation. I think I may suffer from indi-gestion.'

Cameron let out a cry in the bedroom and Scarlet stood up. 'I warned you might regret inviting us. I'll leave you to sort out my dinner while I do the same for my son.'

'You really do want your food,' he teased. 'I'll be back with it soon.'

Scarlet watched him disappear down the stairs and she couldn't help a small smile. That had been exhil-arating and obviously a conversation that would never have occurred on a ward round. She moved quickly through to the guest bedroom but Cameron had stopped crying and was staring at the ceiling.

'Hello, baby.'

His little face creased into a giant toothless smile as he saw his mother. She picked him up and cuddled him before putting back down to check his nappy. He had that warm and powdery baby smell that could weaken a mother's heart from ten paces.

She kissed the top of his head and carried him back to the lounge room, resettling herself on the lounge. Sinclair had already made one trip from the kitchen downstairs because there was a beautifully decorated garden salad in the middle of the table with rock-melon and kiwifruit around the edges. But no sign of Sinclair.

She positioned Cameron at her breast and closed her eyes for a minute. There was some very quiet jazz playing in the background and with a start she realised it was her CD. Hers and the band's! He'd bought it. She grinned. That meant they'd sold at least seven copies now.

She savoured the familiar notes of the saxophone but it felt strange, knowing it was her playing. For the first time since Cameron's birth she itched to play again. She grinned once more. He'd bought their CD!

Scarlet ran her finger down the side of Cameron's soft cheek and her lips curved yet again. She was enjoying herself.

Spirited conversation was something she'd discovered she had a knack for at the community. Without television or nightclubs, nightly musical jams and conversation took over for amusement in the evenings.

As a child and as Letty Robin of Southside Maternity, she'd shied from the limelight of being outspoken. But at the community it had been a free-for-all and the hilarious and sometimes heated discussions stood as some of her most treasured memories of her time there.

It was strange to feel that same animation with Sinclair here tonight. That explosive night they'd spent together, they hadn't talked much. After the first light kiss and spontaneous combustion, she'd been so blown away that conversation had been limited to the half-sentences and murmur of lovers. All night.

Scarlet's eyes flew open. It was as if she'd peered behind a closed door and been blinded by what she'd seen. Now was not a good time to go there. Never would be soon enough—or perhaps one last glimpse on her deathbed just to know that she'd lived, she mocked herself.

Sinclair's footsteps sounded on the stairs and his head and shoulders came into view. His smile twisted her stomach into a heavy lump that ached. He placed the crockery platter on the table with a flourish and then poured two glasses of water from the carafe. 'Dinner is served and, please, note the easy portions that can be managed one-handed.'

'It looks wonderful, Sinclair. I'll be there in a minute. Cameron's nearly finished.'

He hovered between her and the table. 'Would you like a glass of water while you feed him?' He handed her one.

Her tongue felt dry as she slid it over her lips. She nodded. 'How did you know?'

He stood up. He gave her an evil grin. 'I didn't. But I love it when you do that with your tongue.' He moistened his own lips.

She almost choked on the sip she took and Cameron lifted his head and looked around. Scarlet met her son's bright eyes.

'Your daddy is one sick puppy, Cameron.' Although softly spoken, the words reverberated around the room and nausea hit Scarlet as soon as she'd said them. It was too late to call them back.

There was a deathly silence in the room then the sound of Sinclair putting down his drink. Her hand began to shake and the water in the glass rocked and splashed against the sides and threatened to spill on the baby.

Sinclair's voice was like a blast from the arctic. 'What did you say?'

Scarlet swallowed the prickle of fear in her throat and tried to make her brain function. The water was splashing out of the glass. 'Take the glass, please.'

He reached across and took it and she could tell he'd been careful not to touch her. She put Cameron over her shoulder, fastened her dress one-handed then closed her eyes. When she opened them he was standing in front of her.

His grey eyes were icy and a muscle twitched at the corner of his mouth. In all the years she'd worked with him she'd never seen him in such a rage. The air seemed to vibrate around him.

It was all the more frightening because his voice was so quiet, like an icy breeze from outside the glass doors. 'What did you say?'

She wasn't ready for this but obviously her subconscious thought she was. Her voice shook and she tried to put off the moment of truth. She had a mental picture of him staring down at her as she sat below him. 'We must look like the snake and the mongoose.'

His lips thinned even more. 'Don't even think

about joking.' His voice was clipped and slightly louder. She flinched.

That shocked him even more. He stepped back a pace and then walked around the room once as if searching for control.

He grabbed a chair, plonked it in front of her and straddled it backwards, but his hands gripped the sides and his knuckles showed white. He lowered his voice. 'I'm sorry.' The muscle twitched again at the side of his mouth and his eyes pierced her. 'Tell me.'

Scarlet drew herself to sit upright with a deep breath, met his eyes and watched for the words to sink in. 'Cameron is your son. There is no husband— I made him up. You were the only one. I went to the valley after our night together and that was where I found out I was pregnant. The end.' Her shoulders dropped as she let the breath out. It was done.

For a moment he didn't say anything. But his re-action to her news was all there in his face. In-credulity, suspicion, wonder and finally anger.

Anger. She'd known it would come but she didn't care now. He had the truth and he could do what he wanted with it. She knew what she was going to do.

'How nice of you to mention I have a son.' His voice was cutting and he glared at her, shook his head, looked at Cameron and then back at her. He laughed harshly. 'I actually suspected it but stupidly convinced myself you wouldn't exclude me if that was so.' He shook his head again. 'Did it occur to you, at any stage, that I might be interested in the fact that Cameron was my child?'

She could see the pulse beating against the vein on his forehead. Cameron had one just like it.

Scarlet tried to stay calm. 'Being interested that

Cameron is your child and being interested in Cameron are two different things.'

His eyes flared at that. 'Oh, I see. Tried and convicted of being a bad father without a chance to state my own case. How democratic of you. Where do you get off, lady?' He snorted.

She gave her own harsh laugh and Cameron stiffened in her arms. She drew a deep breath and soothed him. Her voice lowered and she almost snarled. 'Democracy was the last thing on my mind. With your help, I managed to achieve the one thing I swore I would never inflict on a child of mine. Illegitimacy. I'm dealing with that in the best way I can.'

His eyes narrowed. 'So it's my fault for seducing you?'

'No.' She met his gaze unflinchingly. 'It's my fault for allowing myself to be seduced. And the thought of the whole town knowing you are his father and the fact that we aren't together are unpalatable for me. I will not have him ridiculed like that.'

He was incredulous. 'So how is that different with the bogus husband?'

Her voice was matter-of-fact. 'I'm going to kill him off.'

He laughed. Once. 'Priceless. I suppose I'm lucky you didn't try to kill *me* off.' His voice was full of sarcasm.

Scarlet could feel the tattered edges of her control slipping and her eyes were prickling. The roughness in her throat was getting worse and she had to get out of there. 'You said you would take us home when I wanted to go. I want to go home. Now.'

He straightened and drew a deep breath before looking down at his son in her arms. His expression was harder than she'd ever seen it. 'Perhaps it is the most sensible thing,' he bit out. 'I feel like strangling you at the moment.'

She'd truly alienated him now. But she would probably do the same thing again if she had to. She looked at the beautifully prepared meal. 'I'm sorry about the food,' she murmured as she stood up.

His eyes flared. 'Damn the food. I'm sorry for me—and what I've missed out with my son.'

Tears shone in her eyes. 'He's my son and I'll deny it was you.'

He flinched but was in control again. His hands sliced the air. 'Time out. We're both upset. I'll drop you home now and call around tomorrow.' He swept up her things and picked up his keys. He didn't offer to carry Cameron and it was a silent trip home.

He left her at her mother's door, his face impassive. 'Cameron is mine as well as yours—get used to it.'

She watched him drive away and her heart felt like a cold fist in her chest. She trailed up the stairs with the baby capsule and Cameron asleep in it. A roll of thunder followed by a flash of lightning that lit the windows seemed appropriate to her mood.

After Cameron was settled, she changed into her nightgown like an automaton. Her brain seemed stuck in a vacuum of inactivity. When she slid open the wardrobe door to hang her dress up, a sliver of red mocked her from the back of the wardrobe.

She hated that dress. She wrenched it off the hanger and screwed it up. Her arm rose to throw it in the waste-paper basket but she realised her mother would comment so she jammed it in the bottom of her tote bag to dispose of in a charity bin the next day.

How had she been so stupid to let Sinclair find out that way?

Sinclair stood on his balcony, watching the storm, until the small hours of the morning. The rail was cold under his fingers and the lightning flashed images out of the darkness at him. Like the images he held of Scarlet and now Cameron. A flash and then gone. All he'd dreamed of was there in front of him but somehow poisoned with Scarlet's insecurities.

If only he'd tried harder to find her. If only she'd told him she was pregnant. If only...

Pathetic words and an exercise in futility. How could he salvage his family from this mess? And he realised the more he thought of Scarlet and Cameron as his family, the more the idea seemed to jell.

He could sort it out. It was a mathematical equation that needed breaking down and he needed to leave the emotion out of it.

But it hurt that she hadn't trusted him enough to tell him. She'd excluded him from her pregnancy, and he winced when he remembered she'd ensured he hadn't been present at Cameron's birth. He felt the anger rise up again in his throat and he stamped it down. That memory would forever be missing and no amount of wishing could restore his presence at that special time.

The simple answer to all their problems was for him to marry Scarlet. Except that the walls she'd erected against him seemed insurmountable.

But he had one advantage—he could provide what was best for Cameron! The spin-off was that he could then care for Scarlet as well.

His first impulse was to demand she marry him. It

would end her concerns for Cameron's illegitimacy. She wouldn't have to work. Naturally he could support his own family and Scarlet could care for their son full time. Maybe he should present it to her like that. As a trade-off.

He thought of his father. He'd be pleased once he'd recovered from his shock at the unconventionality of it. The grandchild he wanted was closer than the old man realised.

But Sinclair didn't want to buy Scarlet's hand in marriage—he wanted her to come to him with an open heart and loving arms. And if he couldn't have that? Then he'd take whatever he could get and worry about the rest later.

He massaged his neck. Scarlet loving him might be a dream but it was worth fighting for. He slid his hand along the wet rail and the water splashed off in spurts.

The best news out of this whole disaster was the removal of the fictitious husband as a rival.

She'd said he had been the only one and that was one nightmare he could stop imagining. The thought of her with another man had torn him apart.

He flicked the droplets off the rail again as the wind changed and drove the rain in towards him under the awning and he had to step back. It was time to go to bed.

Today was the day he started to woo Scarlet.

When Scarlet woke next morning, she'd decided to return to the valley. A couple of hours in Sinclair's company and all she had tried to salvage lay in ruins at her feet. She was pathetic around him and couldn't even keep her damn mouth shut. She'd be a basket case if she let him into her life.

The next thing he'd be saying was that she had to marry him, and then she could spend the rest of her life with people like Tessa harassing her son when no one could protect him. The gossips would say she'd trapped his father. She hated being such a wimp but she couldn't help it.

Cameron could grow up in the non-judgmental environment of the valley and she would help out as the second midwife. Maybe her mother would come with her. She shuddered to think what Vivienne was going to say about this mess.

The phone rang and she glared towards the stairs. If that was Sinclair she didn't want to talk to him.

'Scarlet?' Her mother's voice floated up the stairs. 'It's Leah. She says she's in labour.'

Scarlet dropped the brush she was punishing her hair with and sprinted down the stairs to take the phone from her mother. 'Leah. How're you going?'

'Hello. Scarlet?' Leah's voice was tremulous. 'I started contractions during the night and I'm driving down the mountain this morning. Crystal said the baby is still breech.'

'That's really brave of you, Leah. I believe it's the best for your baby to be born down here if he's coming bottom first. You'll be able to go home after a few hours if all goes well.'

Leah started to cry. 'My boyfriend, Josh, doesn't want me to come down. He and Crystal are angry I'm not birthing here. I'm driving myself down.'

Scarlet frowned. 'Surely Crystal wouldn't let you do that?'

There was no answer from Leah.

'What about one of the other women? Surely someone can come with you and drive?'

Leah's voice was faint. 'There's a tummy bug go-ing around at the moment and everyone is either sick or busy.' She sniffed. 'I'll be fine. I'll ring you when I get up from the valley to the pass.'

'Do you want me to come up and get you? How strong are the contractions?'

'They're fine and I only get about three in half an hour. Could you meet me at the hospital when I get down from the mountain?'

'I'll be with you as soon as I can. Ring me from the pass and I'll come and pick you up. It only takes ten minutes to get down the mountain but those bends are hard to negotiate with a belly in the way. Prom-ise?'

Scarlet could hear the relief in Leah's voice. Scarlet fumed. How dare Crystal let Leah drive herself? She couldn't help the prickle of foreboding that gnawed in her stomach.

Crackling interference interrupted Leah's voice. 'I promise.'

'OK, I'll hear from you soon.' Scarlet put the phone down and went through to the kitchen to see her mother.

Vivienne looked up from the dough she was roll-ing. Flour hung in the air like fine mist.

'Mum, Leah is in labour and I'm meeting her up at the pass to drive her down. Her baby's still breech so she's coming in to Southside for the birth.'

Vivienne put down the rolling pin and brushed a strand of hair off her face. A white trail crossed her cheek. 'Will you leave Cameron here?'

'I'd like to, if that's OK. I'll feed him before I go, and if I get held up at the hospital there's a heap of frozen breast milk in bottles in the freezer. I'll worry about supplies for work when I get back.'

'That's sensible. The rain's stopped but there's another storm front coming, so be careful.'

Scarlet glanced out the window and noticed the thick, dark clouds moving their way.

'Just what we need. Why do babies like being born in storms?'

'It's nature. You were born in a storm.'

Scarlet tilted her head and looked at her calm and wonderful mother. 'I love you.'

Vivienne looked up in pleased surprise. 'Thank you, darling, and I love you.'

Scarlet shook her head. 'I never asked about my birth. When I come home I'd like to hear about it.' The distant sound of thunder rumbled along the valley. 'I'd better get Cameron fed and be on my way.'

She sprinted up the stairs and into the nursery. Cameron was asleep. 'Sorry, old mate. Have to wake you for this one.' She unwrapped him from his muslin sheet and checked his nappy. Cameron's eyes opened and he blinked owlishly at her. She dropped a kiss on his forehead and carried him across to the rocking chair.

It was then that she realised Sinclair was coming this morning. She wouldn't be home. Her absence left Cameron and her mother to face him. She sighed. There was nothing she could do about it but the timing couldn't have been worse.

Or better, if she wanted to avoid him. Her mother and Sinclair would probably think they had it all worked out by the time she came back. They'd realise their mistake.

By the time she was ready to leave, fat raindrops

were flicking against the window of the kitchen again.
As she kissed her mother goodbye, the phone rang
again. It was Leah and her fear was thick in her voice.

'Scarlet.' Leah sniffed and Scarlet could tell she
was trying to pull her voice under control. 'The pains
are down to three-minutely and I can't sit in the car
any more. It's raining so hard and I'm scared.'

'It's all right, Leah. I'm on my way. Where are
you?'

'I'm outside the Lookout Motor Inn in a phone box.
The water is rushing down the road in the storm and
I'm starting to get pressure.'

Scarlet winced. 'Stay in the car and I'll be there.'
She slammed the phone back on the hook, grabbed
her tote and her keys and tore out the door. Straight
into Sinclair.

CHAPTER EIGHT

SINCLAIR grasped Scarlet's upper arms to stop her falling. 'Not so fast. I'm here to see you.'

She shook his hands off. 'Let me go.' Scarlet flicked her hair out of her eyes and stared wildly up at him. 'Follow me in your car. Leah's on the mountain and she's almost in second stage with a breech birth. I could do with your help. If you're coming, let's go!'

She didn't know if he followed but she didn't have the time to convince him if that's what he needed. But as she reversed out the driveway in her four-wheel-drive she saw his sporty car swing in a U-turn and wait at the gutter for her to go first.

That was the good news. She would have the best back-up person she could wish for at the delivery.

She peered through the foggy windscreen. How tragic that in the interests of safety she'd placed Leah in more danger than if she'd had her baby in the community with Crystal. If anything happened to Leah or the baby, Scarlet would never forgive herself.

She glanced back over her shoulder to the floor beside the rear seat. Her delivery set was there beside where she'd thrown her tote bag. She'd been caught without delivery equipment once before, and now it stayed in the back just in case.

Sinclair had opted for headlights behind her and she switched her own on. The windscreen-wipers were working as fast as they could but visibility was down to a few feet. She hoped Sinclair knew the road as well as she did.

It was a tense drive around the bends and already the waterfalls had started at the side of the road. The gutters were full and overflowing onto the tarmac, narrowing the road even more.

There was no traffic in front of her so it only took fifteen minutes. It probably should have taken twenty-five in the conditions and she'd lost sight of Sinclair a few bends back. Scarlet ground the big car to a halt beside the telephone booth and she saw the shape of Leah still shut in the booth.

Scarlet grabbed her bag and when she opened the car door she was drenched before she'd crossed the few feet to the booth. The fear in Leah's eyes as she opened the door was a sight Scarlet would never forget.

Leah fired herself into her friend's arms and sobbed into her shoulder. 'I had to stand up. I couldn't sit in the car.'

'Good girl. You and baby will be fine.' The head-lights of Sinclair's car appeared around the final bend and Scarlet heaved a sigh of relief. 'Look. I've even brought Dr McPherson to help.'

'Here comes another one.' Leah grunted and swayed in Scarlet's arms. Sinclair got out of his car with an umbrella and splashed through the water to-wards them.

Later she would remember that picture of him, calm, dry and unflappable.

'She's in second stage. I don't think she'll make it far and we need to get somewhere dry.'

'Get her in my car and we'll book into the motel.' He opened the back door and held the umbrella over

Leah with one hand and pulled his mobile phone out with the other. He pointed to the sign advertising the motel, complete with phone number. 'I'd say every minute counts.' He spoke briefly into the phone as Scarlet helped Leah across into the back of the car.

By the time they'd pulled up at the office a woman with her own umbrella was signalling them towards a room.

'I'm Marie Peters. Call me Mrs P. This way.'

A man hurried towards them with an electric kettle and Scarlet had to swallow the bubble of slightly hysterical laughter as she realised what he was doing. Everybody had seen the movies and knew you needed boiling water to have a baby. She met Sinclair's eyes and a brief amused look passed between them as they helped Leah out.

By the time they were in the room, Mrs P. had whipped off the quilt and thrown a large plastic sheet over the bed and covered it with towels.

'I'm not lying down!' Leah shook her head and Scarlet squeezed her hand.

'That's fine, Leah. How about you squat up here and we'll put two chairs either side of the bed for you to hold onto? That way we can see how far baby's come down.'

Leah nodded, reefed off her sarong and her underpants and grunted and groaned as she crawled up onto the bed to heave herself into a squat. In that position, between Leah's legs could be seen a tiny bulge of baby's bottom and a tiny swinging scrotum. Mrs P. took one look, snatched the boiling water off her husband and ushered him to the door.

'Out,' she said. She turned back to Sinclair. 'What do you need?'

He looked at Scarlet.

Scarlet was calm now. The worst hadn't happened and she needed to salvage this moment for Leah. 'Some facecloths and hand towels would be great, thanks.'

Mrs P. opened the door, fired an order and shut it again. Then she moved up to stand beside Leah's shoulder for support. 'Squeeze my hand, sweetie, if you need to.'

Someone knocked on the door and the woman hurried over, took the hand towels and shut the door again before standing back beside Leah.

Sinclair threw his jacket on the dresser, rolled up his sleeves and went to stand on Leah's other side. 'Well, Leah. Of all the breech positions, frank breech is my favourite. Baby has his legs up around his neck and he's going to come out beautifully. Would you rather Scarlet helped him into the world?'

Scarlet flashed a look at him, unable to believe he wasn't going to insist on doing the delivery himself. It seemed like hours since she'd pulled up at the phonebox, fearing Leah would have her baby in the rain.

Leah nodded and Scarlet wasn't going to let the opportunity slip by. She'd only delivered half a dozen breeches, but the concept was the same. Let the mother and baby do the work, and beware of the head delivering too fast.

She undid the knot on her delivery pack and the sheeting rolled out to reveal a tiny plastic mouth sucker, a dish for the placenta, two cord clamps and a pair of scissors. She moved another tied roll aside for use later if needed.

Sinclair was ever practical. 'Do you have gloves in

that bundle of tricks on the table? Perhaps you'd better get them on.'

She wasn't touching anything until the last moment so Scarlet ignored him. 'How're you doing, Leah? You're pushing beautifully. Did we mention this child is a teapot with a spout? This is the only time we get to see what it is before we see who it is.'

Leah smiled up at Scarlet. 'So he's a boy.'

'Yep. No doubt about that. Why don't you have a feel?'

Leah snaked her hand down and tentatively felt between her legs. 'Oh wow. Two little cheeks and some boy parts.' Her eyes widened. 'Here comes another contraction.' She bore down steadily.

Scarlet slipped her gloves on and watched the buttocks elongate to include the tops of the baby's legs, then the knees on either side of baby's trunk. She didn't need to do anything yet and watched the buttocks and trunk deliver onto the bed. Once the legs were clear, the two little feet flopped down to hang in their intended position.

'Just arms and head to go. Leah, you're doing so well. I'll just catch his little arms so that they're born before his head.' Scarlet slipped her finger in beside the baby's chest, hooked one elbow down and out and then the other so that the entire baby had been born except for the head.

She allowed the weight of the baby to encourage its own birth until baby's neck was clearly in view. Then she supported the baby's body on the palm of her hand and the inner surface of her arm to ensure delivery of the head was slow and steady.

'It's really stinging,' Leah panted.

Scarlet looked up at Mrs P. whose eyes were like two dinner plates. Scarlet flashed a grin at her.

'I know. You're nearly there. Baby's head is the tough part. Little breaths and let gravity do most of it. We like to see baby's head born nice and slow for this part because he's had a quick trip through the pelvis and hasn't had a chance to change shape for the journey.'

Baby's chin showed first and then nose, eyes and forehead. Scarlet concentrated on preventing the back of the head from coming out too fast. 'Little panting breaths now, Leah,' she murmured.

Finally the entire baby was lying on the bed below his mother. Leah reached down and stroked his arms and chest before she lifted him carefully to nestle him against her skin. He cried briefly before shoving his fist back in his mouth.

'Congratulations, Leah.' Sinclair's voice was deep with emotion and his eyes met Scarlet's across the bed. He nodded and she inclined her head at his approval. The warmth in his eyes heated her own cheeks.

The next half-hour saw Leah and baby Edward settled down for a well-earned rest. Scarlet cleaned and repacked her equipment for later sterilising. She shouldn't have been surprised when Sinclair offered to hold Edward.

She caught him tickling the baby's cheek to try and make him smile and the sting of tears made her blink. Edward turned his cheek and latched onto Sinclair's finger and he looked up at Scarlet and grinned.

He'd missed that with his own son, she admitted to herself. And she had been the one who'd decided that. Scarlet bit her lip and turned away to watch

Mrs P. bustle around as if she were the proud grand-mother. At least Leah seemed to welcome the cos-seting.

Sinclair left soon after to see about rooms for him-self and Scarlet and the rain continued to fall in sheets from the leaden sky. News had come through that the pass was closed for the night because of the risk of landslides.

Again Sinclair surprised her by being more philo-sophical than Scarlet had thought he would be.

'I'm happy not to move Leah and baby in this weather anyway,' he said. 'We'll just have to find something to do to kill the time.' Scarlet shot him a look from under her lashes and what she saw in his expression made the heat creep up her cheeks.

Sinclair handed Scarlet a key and some dry resort clothes from the motel supplies, and she uncon-sciously clutched them to her chest.

'On the house, I'm told.' He grinned at Mrs P.

'Thank you,' Scarlet said, but the proprietress dis-missed the favour.

'You three have made my day,' she said, and smiled fondly down at baby Edward.

She shooed Scarlet and Sinclair out. 'If you two are happy with Leah medically, do you want to shower and change? There will be lunch on up at the restaurant soon. I'll get a tray myself for our little mother.'

Scarlet turned to Leah. 'Are you right with that?' Leah nodded without moving her eyes from her new son. Scarlet suppressed a sigh. There goes that excuse, she thought. She crouched down beside the bed. 'If you have any questions, you can phone me on my room number or the restaurant.' She checked her key. 'It's room nineteen, next door to you.'

'That's fine. Thank you for everything, and you, too, Dr McPherson.' Leah flashed a brief smile up at Scarlet and then returned to her new favourite pastime. She looked lovingly down at her baby.

'It certainly was stimulating. I'm glad we can all relax now.' Sinclair's smile was genuine as he looked at the doting mother. 'Let's go, Scarlet. Leave Leah and Edward in our landlady's capable hands.'

Half an hour later, Scarlet was showered and dressed in shorts and a motel T-shirt. She'd tipped out the contents of her tote bag for toiletries and the red dress lay scrunched beside the rest.

She glared at it. Was it a good omen or bad luck following her around?

She combed her hair and damp tendrils curled around her face. Now that her hair was short, it curled at the ends in rainy weather. It was certainly easier than long hair.

She looked longingly at the bed and wished she'd said she was too tired to eat. Last night's sleeplessness was catching up with her and the thought of lunching with Sinclair was becoming less attractive by the minute. Especially when she knew she had to tell him she was going back to the valley community.

In the end, lunch wasn't the ordeal she'd thought it would be. Sinclair must have decided to leave the serious discussion until later. They talked about Edward's birth, the road closure and the torrential rain and devoured delicious bowls of home-made tomato soup and crusty rolls. Within an hour they were standing outside Leah's room after looking in on the patient—both mother and baby were asleep.

It was Sinclair who suggested that an afternoon rest wouldn't go astray. Then he looked up, an arrested expression on his face. 'Will Cameron be all right? What about feeds?'

'I've stockpiled plenty in the freezer. I rang Mum before lunch and she doesn't expect me until tomorrow. He'll be more comfortable than I will,' Scarlet said.

Sinclair winced as he looked at her straining T-shirt. 'I'd forgotten about that. How will you manage?'

Scarlet laughed. 'Our trusty landlady has helped me there. Her daughter is a counsellor with Nursing Mothers and she left me some equipment.'

'The woman's a marvel.'

'I don't think she's had such an exciting day in her life.'

'Well, I could live without it,' he said dryly. 'I've booked the restaurant for dinner at six. We need to have that talk.'

Scarlet resisted the urge to make a rude gesture with her tongue but 'Oh goody' slipped out. Sinclair just looked at her from under his brows. There goes my chance of sleeping, she moaned silently.

To her surprise, though, she slept for two hours after going back to her room, and felt better for it once she shook off the sleepiness. After a prolonged visit to Leah and Edward, she still made it back to her own room with half an hour to spare until dinner.

Scarlet sighed. She and Sinclair did need to talk. Sinclair's response when he'd discovered Cameron was his son hadn't suggested lack of interest. She smiled grimly at the memory of Sinclair's face. It was time for her to face the fact that he did have some claim. But claim on her son—not on her. She could be doing Cameron more harm than good if she excluded his father from his life. And herself more harm than good if she didn't keep him at arm's length.

That was the rub. Sinclair would be a good father and that was something she'd never had. She had no right to deny Cameron his.

Which brought it back to her reasons for putting a wall up between Sinclair and herself. Was it fear of him taking over or fear of her welcoming that state of affairs? She sighed. He only had to touch her and she'd lose the plot.

Again her lips twitched. If she knew Sinclair and his effect on her, she wouldn't have any choice. The least she could do was listen to how he wanted to approach his involvement with Cameron.

Which brought her back to whether to iron the red dress or not. She'd been putting off the decision all afternoon.

The mist and torrential rain seemed to have settled to stay here on top of the mountain and it felt like they were marooned in a cloud. It wasn't the warmest dress but neither were the shorts and T-shirt. When she looked out of the bedroom windows, visibility was down to less than twenty feet where an impenetrable wall of mist and rain blocked out the magnificent vista she knew was there.

The feeling of isolation was dreamlike, as was the slither of the red dress over her shoulders as she dressed.

Good or bad omen, there was no denying the dress

was with her and looked better than the other choice for dinner.

Besides, she didn't have a white flag to wear.

The thought made her eyes flash. She wasn't surrendering, just reassessing the boundaries of their relationship, and she was going to do it from a position of strength. She remembered saying after Carrie and Jim's bathroom delivery, 'If I was trying to make you notice me you wouldn't have to ask me. You'd notice.'

When Sinclair knocked at Scarlet's door he didn't expect to be greeted by the woman of his dreams. But there she was.

Her short copper hair curled around her face and her long neck seemed to float, swanlike, out of the plunging red neckline. He almost gulped. He cleared his throat and dragged his eyes out of the deep valley between her straining breasts to meet her eyes.

'Wow.' He couldn't actually think of anything else to say at that precise moment until he saw the amused glint in her eye. He held up his hands. 'I admit I'm a sucker for that dress.'

'And I thought it was me you fancied.'

He shook his head. 'No. It's the dress.' But he bet she could tell he was lying. He couldn't believe that she was in a playful mood and he felt the first glimmer of hope that everything would turn out right. He'd spent the afternoon trying to decide on his approach to a subject she wouldn't discuss. But maybe she was ready? He hoped so. Enough time had been wasted.

He crooked his elbow and she tucked her arm

through his. 'So the rain slowed down for a change,' she said.

He enjoyed the feel of her walking next to him and faint drifts of soap and some exotic perfume that he wouldn't have associated with her teased his nose. She really was delicious.

He realised he hadn't answered as they covered the distance from the rooms to the restaurant. 'The council is worried about landslides on the Waterfall Way and the road's still out, at least until tomorrow.'

She shot him a sideways look under her lashes. 'Afraid I'll run away, Sinclair?'

He shrugged ruefully. 'It's happened to me before.'

Scarlet had to give him that. 'It seemed like the right thing to do at the time.'

Sinclair didn't comment, just squeezed her hand and opened the door of the restaurant for her to precede him.

The manager came up to them and immediately ushered them to their table opposite the crackling fire. Once drinks and menus were brought, silence fell between them.

The moment had arrived. Scarlet drew a deep breath, lifted her head and met his eyes. She'd done enough running and hiding.

'So, what is your side of the story, Sinclair?' She put her drink down on the tablecloth but her fingers tightened around the stem of the glass.

'My side?' A small humourless smile crooked at the side of his mouth. 'Well, I suppose I met this vision one night.' He smiled down at her. 'And she looked very much like you do tonight, except for a cloud of copper hair around her shoulders.'

Scarlet couldn't help touching the hair that curled

around her ears and her face warmed more from his obvious appreciation than the roaring fire in front of them.

'Anyway, it turned out I knew this woman but had never really seen her until that night. What transpired holds a very special place in my memory.'

The sincerity in his voice couldn't be denied and she blinked back the sting of tears in her eyes. If only they'd had a chance to talk and her damned inferiority complex had allowed her to be there when he'd woken the next day. But she'd done what she'd needed to do at the time and she still wasn't sure it hadn't been the right thing to do.

Almost as if reading her thoughts, he continued. 'But then I lost her the next day.'

He picked up his drink and finished what was in the glass. His voice hardened at the memory.

'Nine months later she turned up married and in labour. Something she said…' he met and held her eyes '…made me wonder if there was any way the baby could be mine. But then I assumed that if that was the case surely she would have told me.' He looked away. 'You didn't want to see me, which was understandable to me as you were a married woman, but there was definitely something fishy going on.' He looked back at her.

Scarlet winced, and he saw it.

'Exactly.' She saw him watch her grip tighten on the stem of her glass. 'Now we both know that Cameron is mine as well as yours and we both need to decide what's best in this situation. Don't you agree?'

Sinclair obviously planned to have a say in Cameron's future. She nodded. 'I agree.'

'Whatever we decide to do, I'd like there to be no more hiding or fabrication between us.' He reached out and put his fingers over hers on the glass. 'Do you think we could do that, Scarlet?'

His fingers were sending signals up her arm and she tried to shut the feeling out to keep her mind clear. 'We could try, for Cameron's sake.'

Sinclair took his fingers away, sat back and sighed. 'I'd hoped it would be for all our sakes, Scarlet.'

She rubbed her hand gently across the tablecloth. 'Look, I'm sorry. This is hard for me, too. In my defence, I've spent most of my life ensuring that I didn't make the same mistakes my mother made. One night with you and all that caution went out the window. Even you said you'd never *really* seen me before that night. How did I know if it would take another five years for you to notice me again?'

His gaze travelled over what he could see above the tablecloth and one eyebrow lifted in amusement. 'I would have noticed you.'

She tossed her head impatiently. 'I needed time to sort myself out. Especially when the person I worked so hard to be was no better than the original version. So why have I been kidding myself for so many years? I needed to live in my real skin and feel comfortable. And guess what? I like the Scarlet I am.'

He captured her fingers in his and stroked her palm. 'I like her, too. Very much. What do I have to do to make you realise that?'

The sensation from her hand held in his clouded her eyes with indecision. 'That's the part I'm having problems with. I'm not used to seeing myself as something positive in someone else's eyes. Even if that is because I've had a baby with them.'

He squeezed her hand as if to deny her comment. 'Scarlet.' His voice was stern now. 'If you hadn't had Cameron, I would still be trying to have this conversation with you.' He ran his other hand through his hair until a spike stood up crazily at his crown. She resisted the urge to straighten it. The silence lengthened and she sneaked a look at his expression to find that he was waiting for her attention again.

Her voice was more tentative than she'd intended. 'What about the gossip?'

He shrugged his shoulder impatiently. 'What about it? So the doctor and the midwife are human. Big deal. They'll see I'm besotted with you.' His eyes were warm and he continued to stroke her hand.

She looked up. 'Say that again.'

'What? That I'm besotted? I go to sleep at night and you're the last thought I have in my head. I dream about you. I wake up in the morning and my first thought is of you. The idea of you beside me when I go to sleep and wake up for the rest of my life is one hell of a thought—and that's where I'm heading with this.'

His beautiful eyes met hers and the love in them finally left her in no doubt of his feelings. 'I love you and I want you as my wife.'

She couldn't believe he'd said that. His whole argument backed up his statement and she felt like crying again.

Here was more than she had ever dreamed of, but the lost child within her refused to believe it. 'You love me and want to marry me?'

His voice was dry at her paltry response. 'Rather than an echo, I was hoping for something like you loved me and want to marry me.'

She sat back. 'Technically you haven't asked me.'

'Technicality is your strong point, young lady.' He took her hands in his and their eyes met.

He held her gaze. 'Will you marry me, Scarlet?'

She was so close to saying yes. But she couldn't do it. Look what had happened the last time she'd rushed into something with him. 'Let me think about it.' She watched disappointment cloud his eyes and almost wished the words back. But it was all too pat. He'd found out Cameron was his child and wanted to marry her the next day.

Scarlet felt like a parachutist sitting on the edge of her first jump. Sinclair was the parachute she had to trust or miss out on what could be an exhilarating ride through life. But the downside was that she'd die if the parachute failed her. She temporised. 'I know I'm alive when you're around. I've never been the same since that incredible night we had together but I need some time to get used to the idea you want to marry me.'

He narrowed his eyes for a moment and she wished she could read his mind. Suddenly he pushed aside the menu and rose to his feet. 'Come with me now and let me show you what you have to get used to.'

Before she knew it she'd placed the napkin from her lap carefully on the table and had stood up. 'Where are we going?'

He leant down and whispered in her ear. 'For a night of sin.' Scarlet closed her eyes briefly and fought with her conscience. His breath on her ear won. She needed another night to remember.

CHAPTER NINE

SINCLAIR slid his arm around Scarlet's shoulder as they walked the length of the long verandah back towards their rooms and she savoured his possessiveness. The lights glowed fuzzily yellow under the verandah roof then disappeared ahead and behind into the mist. Scarlet felt as if she were cocooned with Sinclair in their own world. She'd always associate the smell of fog and rain with this night.

He opened the door to his room without taking his arm from her shoulders.

'Did you think I might escape?' He only raised one eyebrow and she admitted to herself the unlikeliness of it. She was where she wanted to be at this moment. She looked around and her eyes widened. 'This room is huge.'

'And the bedroom is separate.' He grinned wryly. 'This is the honeymoon suite.'

She laughed at the irony. The curtains were shut and a comfy lounge and stereo filled one side of the room. She draped herself across one corner of the lounge in a vampish pose. 'You were very sure of yourself.' She could feel the heat from his gaze.

'No. It was wishful thinking. Now, come here.'

She felt his desire like a real thing and when she looked into his eyes she marvelled at the softness she saw in his face. Softness for her. A chill ran down her spine and she shivered. It was too good to be true.

Suddenly frightened of losing the moment, she

158

moved towards him with a new intensity. This time was too precious to waste. She circled him, feeling the power of the woman course through her the way only he could make it flow. With her red dress swirling out, she shifted seductively in front of him.

When he caught her in his arms and brushed her lips with his, in that first touch she melted and sighed. The memories and incandescent feelings came flooding back. The taste and scent and pressure of Sinclair had been missing from her life as if she had been living in monochrome and only Sinclair could turn on the colour.

His lips grazed her cheek, the corner of her chin and that soft spot on her neck beneath the jaw. The goose-flesh rose along her arms at the tender warmth of his breath on her skin. They were together at last.

'I adore you, Scarlet Robin, mother of my son.' She tried not to stiffen in his arms. It was as if he had to again stake his claim on Cameron and her. To remind her of the plans he'd made.

She was frightened again for a moment of how much she had to lose until the new, stronger Scarlet reached up with her arms to pull his face down to hers, push aside her doubts and kiss him back. She would have memories to take with her.

All the time they'd wasted suddenly exploded into a volcanic need. His hands slid up her thighs and down again with a controlled urgency. Her need to feel him in her was so great and, combined with that eerie premonition, she whispered, 'I'll die if you don't take me here and now.' Unashamed, she pulled away from him to kick off her pants.

When she went to step out of the dress, he shook

his head and whispered 'Please, leave it for the moment.'

In a frantic shuffle of clothing beneath a scorching melding of their mouths there was no barrier between them except for the red dress and his shirt.

Suddenly he swept her into his arms and her feet left the ground as he twirled her once so that the ceiling spun above her. 'I can't believe I finally have you back in my arms. You taste beautiful, you look beautiful.' He bent his head to brush her neck and the valley between her breasts with his nose as he breathed in her scent. 'And it's been too long.' He hugged her and the sudden deepening in his voice sent quivers of anticipation flushing across her skin.

Scarlet's dress bunched around his strong forearms as he lifted the hem of it to bare her back and she felt the rush of warmth of her own readiness to welcome him. He cupped her buttocks firmly in his hands.

With hungry lips and anxious hands they poured the fears and frustrations of the time they'd lost into the communication of their bodies until he lifted her with intent and she answered his need by twining her legs around his body.

She felt his muscular thighs bunch against hers as he carried her like a limpet the few steps to the wall opposite and the cool surface of the plaster against her bare bottom only accentuated the heat and maleness that pressed against her belly. His chest and arms and flat stomach were hard against her as he lifted her one last time.

When he entered her she met his lips with hers and he muffled her cry with his mouth as they ground together in a mad, primitive coupling that went on and on and welded them in a hot, fiery place that seemed to shimmer so brightly it was almost too much.

Slowly the world returned to a calmer place and his hands gently massaged her buttocks as she quivered in his grasp. He brushed his lips down her cheeks and kissed her hair as they both struggled for breath.

He searched her face in sudden concern. 'I'm sorry,' Sinclair said. 'That was more unrestrained than I intended. You drive me insane. Did I hurt you?'

'No, no.' She soothed him back and uncurled her toes as the last shudders flowed like molten lava through her body. Scarlet felt like all the bones in her body had melted away.

He smiled. 'Let's not leave it so long next time.'

They leant quietly against the wall for a moment to catch their breath.

'My bottom is getting cold!' Scarlet whispered, and they both smiled, slightly embarrassed, and shook their heads at such wild abandon.

He carried her through to the bedroom as if she were very precious, and she snuggled against him.

'I love you,' she mouthed silently into the darkness so that he couldn't hear.

The bedroom curtains were closed and a small lamp glowed in the corner to welcome them. The room was dim and warm and the noise of the rain outside made it even more private.

Sinclair stood her gently beside the huge colonial bed and they both smiled at the mirrors on the ceiling.

He shucked his shirt off. 'You still have way too many clothes on.' His voice fanned in her ear as he slid the rest of her dress down her body. Scarlet shivered at the feathery sensation. She remembered that other time.

Scarlet lifted her hands to lay them above his heart and feel the pounding beneath his skin. She buried her nose in his chest. The tang of the distinctive aftershave she would always associate with him teased her memory. Tiny whirls of springy hair tickled her nose and she couldn't resist a tiny taste with the tip of her tongue. He shuddered. Delighted, Scarlet slid her tongue across his chest from one side to the other, nibbling and sucking until he held her head still and firm against his chest as he shuddered to control himself.

'You drive me crazy. Did I say that?' His voice was gravelly with desire and she lifted her head to meet his lips.

'Yes, but I'm glad.' She opened her mouth and merged with his warm breath, lips gliding and meeting and duelling with his tongue in erotic mindlessness for long intimate tastings.

When they moved apart, their breathing was audible even over the noise of the rain outside and they both laughed gently. It was as if they were suspended in time.

Suddenly, Sinclair moved to cup her buttocks again and he pulled her hard against his naked lower body once as if to reassure himself she was still there. His strong hands slid up to massage her shoulders in slow strokes that made her arch her back towards him. 'Your skin feels beautiful,' he murmured, and bent his head to capture one aching nipple in his mouth.

She moaned at the pleasurable pain and he soothed her with gentleness before reaching behind himself to flip back the frilly quilt so that he could sit her on his lap, facing him. With infinite care he caressed her other breast before returning to her lips.

From that point on their joining flowed like mercury, a ball of silver longings, rolling together and seamless in forming one molten entity that swept them away again and again until even their murmuring stopped and they fell asleep in each other's arms.

When Sinclair woke after midnight, Scarlet was gone.

His stomach dropped and he tightened his hand on the bedhead. He couldn't believe she would do it again. He slid from beneath the sheets and checked the bathroom and lounge room. Both rooms were empty.

Where could she go?

Then, in the distance, he heard a baby cry and he realised she would be with Leah.

He sighed. Today he would find out about the shortest length of time it took to get legally married and start leaning on her for a decision. He couldn't take the strain of wondering if she would disappear again.

He sat back on the bed and picked up her pillow. When he inhaled her scent from where her head had lain, he smiled. He'd wait for her to come back.

In the morning, the rain had cleared and they shared their first sunrise together. Sinclair filled the spa with hot water and bubbles and carried her, laughing and kicking, into the water. Scarlet found that washing him was a delightful occupation.

'There's something special about a bath big enough for two people,' Sinclair murmured afterwards, and Scarlet grinned.

'We should get one for the maternity ward. This would be ideal for our water births, you know.'

He groaned. 'Get me the protocol first. I can see a

lot of changes in the next year. I think we should have another baby to give me some rest at work.'

Scarlet stiffened and wouldn't meet his eyes. She slid from the water and wrapped herself in a towel. 'I have to see how Leah is doing. Crystal is coming for her at eight.' She tried for lightness. 'I'm starving. Why do you think that is, Dr McPherson?'

Sinclair rolled over in the water. 'Come here and I'll feed your hunger.'

'Is that what you're going to do every time I don't instantly agree to your plans? Drag me off to bed?'

'Give me a break.' He reached over and tried to grab her ankle. 'I've been celibate since November.'

Scarlet narrowed her eyes. That reminded her. There was something else she'd have to clear up. 'What about the delectable Tessa? I hear you went out with her a few times and that she even considers you secretly engaged?'

Sinclair grinned, rolled back onto his back and put his arms behind his head. 'Jealous?'

'Should I be?' She watched him in the bathroom mirror and felt sick as she waited for the answer.

'No. I only ever dated Tessa a few times and nothing ever happened. We're certainly not engaged, secretly or otherwise.' The conviction in his voice made her shoulders sag in relief. She leant over and kissed him. 'Thank you for a wonderful night and morning.'

He ran his finger down her leg. 'Let's go home. I need an answer from you and I can't wait to see our son.'

Later that morning, after a phone call from Scarlet, Leah's repentent boyfriend had arrived with Crystal to take his family home.

'He's still in the sin bin,' Sinclair remarked as the youth's tentative apology was ignored by Leah.

Scarlet smiled at the term for football discipline. 'So he should be. But she'll allow herself to be worn down with some spoiling. They do love each other. Apparently his friends are partially responsible for his attitude—but he's a father now. His first loyalty is to Leah and Edward. She'll make sure he gets the point.'

'And if you say yes, do you think you'll train me, too, Scarlet Robin?' Sinclair's arm was strong around her shoulders and she stored another memory.

He was pushing and she was finding it harder to resist the urge to throw caution to the winds. He wasn't playing fair. Her voice was quiet. 'No matter what we decide, I'm sure we've both got some learning to do.'

As the two cars disappeared, Sinclair turned her to face him. 'Drive carefully. I nearly had a heart attack, following you up the mountain. You drove like a maniac.'

Scarlet planted her hands on her hips. 'How can I drive like maniac when I drive an old Landcruiser? We plod along.'

'Well, if that's plodding, stick to a crawl. I'm going first so I know where you are.' His voice was dry.

'You're not earning yourself any brownie points by being dictatorial, you know!' She still had her hands on her hips.

He stepped forward and slid her hands down her waist with his own. 'It's only when I get scared I might lose you.'

She nearly said, You be careful, too.

Fifteen minutes later, as they started down the

treacherous mountain, she wished she had. The road had been open for an hour and freshly bulldozed landslides were heaped at the cliff side of the road. The road was full of slush and mud and Sinclair's car wasn't as happy wallowing in it as Scarlet's heavy Landcruiser was.

Water cascaded off the banks and every few feet small rocks bounced off the mountain. Scarlet had never seen it so wet or unstable. The Landcruiser ground down the hill steadily but Sinclair's car ahead slithered and slipped.

His driving was impeccable and showed a skill far greater than Scarlet's, but there was nothing he could do to avoid the sudden giving way of the cutting to his right. His red taillights flashed on as he braked and Scarlet's heart thumped in her chest.

For a moment she thought he might have stopped in time to avoid being sucked across the road by the rubble. But more bank gave way behind the first and a wave of mud and sticks and great tree trunks all came tumbling across the road in an inexorable wave that plucked up Sinclair's car like a toy and rolled it over the edge of the left bank towards the cliff edge.

Scarlet screamed and slammed on her own brakes and the Landcruiser stalled.

She didn't dare blink as she followed the flashes of Sinclair's car as it was rolled in the mud and huge branches until finally the mud monster sighed in one final heave and settled. The rear of Sinclair's car poked into the air about six feet from the edge of the cliff. The front half was submerged, and she tried to remember if the windows were up on his car. Apart from the risk of him suffocating, she knew that any shift of the earth again and the whole car was over the edge for sure.

With teeth chattering in shock, she inched her big car as close as she could get to the edge of the soil from the slide and pulled over. She jumped from the car only to end up ankle deep in thick mud and rubble, but she didn't feel the cuts to her feet as it scratched and tore off her thin sandals. She heard another car pull up behind her but ignored it as she fought to unhook her winch from the front of her bull bar. It was stiff and dry and needed maintenance it hadn't received since Cameron's birth.

She tore at it with her nails almost weeping with frustration.

The slosh and slurp of mud announced the arrival of others. She didn't turn around. 'There's a man buried in that car. We have to pull his car out before he dies.'

'Let me help, lady.' The big man behind her slid burly arms past her shoulder, worked the hook free and gave it to her. She ducked under his arm as he started to uncoil the winch line to give her slack. Scarlet slipped and slid with the line in her hand as she dragged it towards Sinclair's car.

She had shut down all thought except that if she hooked Sinclair's car to hers at least he couldn't go over the cliff. When she reached the car she wanted to drop the line and claw at the windows, but there was sanity in securing the line around the strongest point she could find. With that done, she turned to find the burly man at her shoulder.

'We'll try the rear door but gently goes, missus.'

Scarlet wiped a distracted hand muddily across her cheek and nodded. The car was sticking out of the mud like a thrown javelin; evidence of it having been rolled in the mud obscured any view inside.

The burly man heaved on the rear door and it creaked open a little until it jammed on a mound of mud. Scarlet fell to her knees beside the obstruction and clawed to make a dent deep enough to allow the door to open. Finally they could open it enough to see in.

All the windows were shut and no water or mud was in the car. Sinclair flopped against the restraining seat belt as he hung forward, unconscious, against the belt. Blood dripped slowly down his face. But he was breathing!

A sound of sirens came closer and the man pulled her back gently but firmly as Scarlet went to climb in.

'Just wait, lady.' She tugged against him but he wouldn't budge. 'They know how to move people without doing more damage.'

She sagged back, suddenly weary and frightened of doing more harm than good. 'You're right.' She could hear more people squelch closer through the mud and she stepped back out of the way.

She retreated to the edge of the mound and leant her back against a wet tree. Rivulets of water trickled down her back but she didn't feel them. She felt locked in a solitary nightmare as a group of yellow-coated emergency workers converged on Sinclair's car. They talked amongst themselves and discussed the best way to get Sinclair out, and she felt as if she were listening to a serial on the radio. Except that it was about someone she was terrified of losing.

'Good idea, the winch. But it could've pulled both cars over, I reckon,' one said.

'He's lucky it didn't fill up with water,' said another. 'Where's the ambulance guys?'

'Just pulling up now. I don't want to move the car until they've been in for a look.'

'We'll start digging this out and maybe it will sink back this way.'

Scarlet's teeth started to chatter again and she wrapped her arms around her stomach to stop the nausea that threatened to overwhelm her.

The burly man came up to her with an army blanket and pulled her away from the tree to throw it around her shoulders.

'You might be better in your car now it's getting busy around here.'

She gazed up at him as if to gain some idea of whether Sinclair would survive but, of course, he couldn't know. She looked down and allowed herself to be led back to her car.

'Thank you for your help.'

He squeezed her shoulder. 'You know him, don't you?'

She swallowed the lump in her throat. 'He asked me to marry him last night.'

The burly man opened her car door for her. 'Well, I hope you said yes.' Her eyes filled with tears.

The next hour dragged past and Scarlet felt a hundred years old by the time the ambulance pulled slowly away from the scene. They would transport Sinclair to the mountaintop and a helicopter would fly him to Northern Rivers Hospital. He hadn't regained consciousness and his face was the colour of white marble and just as still.

The burly man had vouched for her and she'd been

allowed to squeeze Sinclair's hand once and kiss him on a part of his face not covered by the oxygen mask. But the concern of his attendants hadn't encouraged her to hold them up long and soon he was gone.

It was then that a sense of urgency set in. She had to get home to Cameron and they needed to be at Sinclair's side. She had this awful fear that if she wasn't there to encourage him he might never wake up.

The road to the valley below would be blocked for days, and that meant she'd have to go back up the mountain and further north to get down by a different pass. She swung herself back into her car and reversed out of the quagmire and back onto the wet road.

By the time she pulled into her mother's driveway the tears were streaming, unchecked, down her cheeks. Her mother was standing beside the car by the time she opened her door.

'Thank goodness, you're safe. They said one person critically injured on the mountain and I rang the motel. They said you'd left hours ago.'

Scarlet stepped wearily from the car into her mother's arms. 'It's Sinclair. His car was caught in a landslide and he's unconscious. I thought he was dead. Where's Cameron?'

'Come inside and sit down.' Her mother looked her up and down. 'On second thoughts, come in and have a shower. You're saturated and covered in mud.' She frowned at the streaks of blood on her daughter's feet and the wild look in her eyes. 'I want to see your feet after your shower, too.'

'I can't stay long. I've come to get Cameron and I'm going to sit with Sinclair until he wakes up.'

Vivienne's voice was firm. 'You'll be no use to Sinclair if you're a physical wreck. I'll ring to check he's there safely, and I'll come with you and help with Cameron. Jump in the shower and I'll get some things together.'

By the time Scarlet came downstairs from her shower, Vivienne had packed a picnic basket of food and a large overnight case for the three of them. A plate of scrambled eggs sat on the table and Vivienne was sipping tea as she jiggled a solemn Cameron on her knee.

When he saw his mother his tiny face screwed up and he let out a loud wail as if to ask why she'd left him.

Scarlet scooped him up and buried his face against her neck and sniffed his sweet baby smell. 'Poor baby. Mummy's here.' She unbuttoned her shirt as she sat down and whistled at the bitter-sweet agony of overfilled breasts and Cameron's eagerness.

When she had her breath back, her eyes searched her mother's face. 'Is Sinclair all right? What did they say?'

'Not much. That he was in Intensive Care and still critical but stable at the moment. Eat your eggs and we'll go as soon as you finish Cameron's feed.'

Scarlet looked across at her mother. 'I love him, Mum. He asked me to marry him.'

Vivienne squeezed her daughter's hand. 'I hope you said yes.'

Scarlet shook her head and her heart ached for all the things she hadn't said. Having seen Sinclair lying there, so still and white as they'd taken him away from her, she realised what she might have lost because she'd been too weak to take a risk. She wished she could block out the idea that she might never have a chance to tell Sinclair all the things she wanted to, and tried to concentrate on normal things. 'How did you go with Cameron?'

'He was an angel. A little sad at times but took his bottles once he realised his favourite way of drinking wasn't going to happen. How did you cope with your poor breasts?'

'I managed. Which reminds me, the cold bag is in the car and I have to freeze the milk in there.' Her thoughts returned to Sinclair. 'Does his father know?'

'Yes. Poor Frank. Sinclair is all he's got.' Vivienne stood up as if she had to do something. 'I'll pack the car and lock the house.'

CHAPTER TEN

WHEN they arrived at the hospital Scarlet felt like an intruder in an alien world. The corridors were unfamiliar and the faces unknown, and she felt invisible in her fear that Sinclair wouldn't recover. It smelt like a hospital and that was something she never noticed when she went to work at Southside.

Vivienne pushed the pram while Scarlet scanned the corridor for signs to the intensive care unit. Her rubber soles squeaked on the linoleum. When they finally found the right ward, the thick frosted-glass doors were shut.

She pressed the bell for entry and it seemed hours before anyone came.

'Can I help you?' The tall blonde sister looked strained.

'I want to see Sinclair McPherson, a patient.'

'Are you immediate family?'

Scarlet felt like screaming, He's the father of my child, but what if Sinclair died? She couldn't do that to old Dr McPherson. Sinclair had an unblemished reputation.

'We're very good friends.' But she knew that wouldn't be good enough.

'I'm sorry. His condition remains critical and the specialist is with him at the moment. Perhaps you could take a seat out here. His father is with him. We'll let you know if there are any changes.'

Scarlet put her hand on the woman's arm as she

173

went to close the door. 'Is he conscious?' When the sister shook her head, Scarlet closed her eyes. She heard her mother's voice asking if they'd let Sinclair's father know that they were here, but it seemed to come from a long way away.

Scarlet sank down on the hard vinyl seat beside the door and felt like crying with frustration.

The sister was still talking to her mother but trying to edge away. 'Look, I'll try, but he's talking to the neurosurgeon and it's very busy in there.' Her smile was distracted and then she closed the door. They could see her shadow shrinking through the glass as she hurried back to what she'd been doing.

Scarlet felt her mother sit down beside her. 'She said a neurosurgeon. That doesn't sound good.'

'Sitting out here, with suppositions and scraps of information, is no good. So don't go imagining what you have no idea about,' Vivienne soothed. 'Where is Frank?'

As the words left her mouth the glass doors opened and Sinclair's father came out. He looked even older than usual. 'I'm here, Vivienne, and thank God you are, too.' He opened his arms and Vivienne went into them as if she belonged there. She hugged him and then stepped back.

She looked down at her daughter and grandson. 'They wouldn't let us in.'

He leant over and squeezed Scarlet's shoulder. 'Well, did he pop the question?'

Scarlet's eyes widened. 'You knew?'

'That Sinclair loves you and wanted Cameron to be his son more than anything in the world.' He smiled sadly. 'I hope you said yes.'

She bit her lip and then looked away. 'I will if I

get the chance.' He sat down beside her and slid his arm around her shoulder.

'Then you'd better get inside and tell him. Talk some sense into him. The longer he remains unconscious the bleaker it looks. There really is only room for one at a time in there. I'll stay with your mother and Cameron out here.' He rang the bell and the tall sister appeared again.

'This young woman is my son's fiancée. Please, give her some time with him.'

The walk from the glass doors to Sinclair's bed was the most frightening thing Scarlet had ever done. What if nothing she said or did could help Sinclair? She had to try for herself, for Cameron but mostly for the wonderful man that was Sinclair.

She thought of the power of the human mind—and all the births that had awed her because of the mental power of the women. As she came closer to the room she closed her eyes for a moment and drew a deep breath. If she could reach Sinclair's mind, who knew what they could accomplish? Hearing was thought to be the last sense to shut down in unconsciousness and if Sinclair could hear her then there was hope.

She eased into the room and looked down at the man she could finally admit she loved with all her heart. Now, when it was almost too late. Tessa and gossips and illegitimacy were all mere flyspecks on the window of life. The thought of losing Sinclair finally freed her from the fishbowl she'd swum around in for too long. Other people looking at her only mattered if she cared. What she cared about now was Sinclair and the life they should have had together.

'Oh, Sinclair,' she whispered. 'I'm sorry.'

The heart monitor leads criss-crossed across his chest like gaudy jewellery and his arms lay limply by his sides with intravenous fluids trickling into him in measured doses. The hiss of the ventilator had always made her uncomfortable but in this instance she acknowledged her relief that it helped Sinclair as it breathed for him.

There seemed so much extra equipment standing by in case it was needed.

She sank down in the chair beside him and wrapped all her fingers around his right hand. Where did she start?

'Sinclair. It's Scarlet here. I don't like to see you lying so still and quiet. You've always been larger than life to me.'

She leant over and stroked his face. There was a vivid graze across his right cheek and a purple bruise shadowed under one eye.

She thought back over the changes to her life in the last year since she'd come to love him.

'You know it was you and my response to you that I hid from all those years.' She sighed.

'It was a scary thing for me to realise that I could totally lose myself in you. But I've finally come to realise that really I grow when I'm with you and you grow with me. We're part of the same tree, Sinclair. A family tree that we've broadened to include Cameron.

'But I'm not afraid of that love I have for you now. It's a powerful love and I want to harness that power and use it to make you come back to me, Sinclair. I love you with all my heart and I need you to know that. You can't leave Cameron or me. We both need you. So wake up, my darling Sinclair. Wake up and smile at me.' She rested her forehead on his hand.

Scarlet heard the sister come in. She sent Scarlet a brief apologetic smile and busied herself with a round of observations that made Scarlet think of Toby in the crib the other day.

She searched Sinclair's face for any changes but his beautiful eyes remained hidden from her by his long lashes and his mouth was still.

Constrained by the other woman's presence, she found herself doing gentle reflexology massage on his palm and fingers, and it soothed her to go through the relaxation hand massage she'd learnt to give women in labour.

Once she thought she detected the smallest squeeze back from him but when she froze her movements there was no movement from the hand in hers. The excitement died in her chest and she sighed as she lifted his hand to slide it across her own cheek. The reserve she felt in the other woman's presence faded until she didn't notice her. All she could think of was that the man she loved was slipping away.

'We'll buy a strong, safe, family car. None of these little sporty numbers you like so much. Look how useless it was to protect you. I can see you in a big shiny silver Volvo sedan, Sunday driving with Cameron and I and maybe a little brother or sister for him in the back as well.'

She closed her eyes and laid her head down on the bed over his hand. 'But I need you in that picture, Sinclair. Wake up, my darling.'

But he didn't wake. Not that day or the next. The brain activity scan was inconclusive and there was some discussion on transferring Sinclair to Sydney to a more long-term facility.

Scarlet spent three nights snatching sleep in the sick relatives' section of the nurses' home, with Cameron sleeping in the pram in the room.

Cameron fretted more than normal as his baby antennae picked up the tension and fear from his mother and grandmother, and he'd cried the one time she'd sneaked him into the child-free zone of Intensive Care to see his father. Now, each time she visited, she booked him into the crèche. Her mother was busy enough looking after Sinclair's father.

She couldn't go home, had to be close to Sinclair in case he woke—but he didn't.

On the fifth day they would transfer him and she'd follow to Sydney. Scarlet stared blindly around the small, bare relative's room with the few comforts her mother had brought to soften her solitude and the bag of disposable nappies they'd resorted to using. She didn't even have a photo of Sinclair to put on the metal dresser.

She dashed away the weak tears and put the earphones of her portable CD player in her ears. In ten minutes she could go back again and sit with Sinclair. Maybe tonight…

Later as she followed the sister through the door of Intensive Care she bit her lip. Either she was getting paranoid or the doctors and nursing staff were avoiding her eyes. Dread sat like a vulture on her shoulder. Sinclair's father was in the room with Vivienne and they both stood to wait outside to allow her to take their place. Frank had aged more each day and even her mother was starting to look despairing of a miracle.

'Did you sleep, darling?' her mother asked.

'I closed my eyes. How is he?' She stood aside as they moved past her towards the door.

'No change.' Frank's voice was gruff and Scarlet saw her mother squeeze his shoulder in comfort. In his creased face, his eyes were suspiciously bright. Scarlet felt the tears prick in her own throat.

She watched them walk away before moving into the room to smile woodenly at the sister who'd just finished recording Sinclair's observations. The nurse smiled at a point just over Scarlet's left shoulder as she left the room.

Scarlet felt as if she were living in a lonely wind tunnel that was sucking the life out of her—and Sinclair. There had to be something she could do.

The chair felt warm where her mother had been sitting and she was grateful for that small comfort. She picked up Sinclair's hand and squeezed his fingers. His hands were limp beneath hers.

'What can I do to make you wake up, darling?' She stroked his fingers with her other hand and thought of the first night they'd been together.

That moment at the bar, when the drunk had grabbed her shoulder and Sinclair had appeared out of the crowd like a magnificent mirage. His gorgeous smile as he'd looked down at her had gone straight to her heart and had stayed there ever since. All the nerves she'd felt about playing for the audience had been nothing compared to her nervous response to Sinclair—her rescuer. She'd loved him for so long, and had hidden it from herself behind her façade of meekness. Tragically, there was so much they still didn't know about each other. There were so many things they had yet to share.

She thought of her saxophone, tucked away in its case at home. The tears started again when she realised that she might never be able to play just for Sinclair. She wiped her eyes and leant across to stroke his brow.

'I wish I could have played for you. I haven't played since just before Cameron was born. If anything happens to you I don't think I'll ever play again.' His eyes remained closed and her mind couldn't help bargaining with God and with Sinclair.

'If you wake up, we could sit on your verandah and I'd pour all the love I feel for you into the music. I'd play so that the notes would soar into the air and up and down the river until they found a home in the mountains or the sea.' She pictured them sitting there, on a summer evening, Cameron in Sinclair's arms as she played. She could almost feel the warm summer breeze on her face. 'I want to share that with you, my darling, as your wife. If only I hadn't been so scared. I should have said yes when you asked me. Please, give me another chance.'

The tears ran down her face and she dashed them away with a sniff. She wouldn't give up. When she rummaged in her bag for a tissue, she clucked impatiently as it became tangled in the headphone cord. The portable CD player her mother had brought and her own CD was in there. She unravelled the cord and drew it from her bag. He could hear that at least.

Scarlet looked up at the sister as she entered the room again. 'Is it all right if I put headphones on Sinclair to listen to some music?'

The sister looked surprised but agreed. 'It can't do any harm.'

Scarlet pulled out the Discman and set the controls—checking it wasn't too loud—before she slipped the headphone plugs into his ears. She watched his face carefully for any signs. There was no response, but what had she expected? At least she could play for him.

She sat back and took his hands again to start the gentle reflexology she had performed each day as he'd lain unconscious.

She would never give up. One day he would wake.

The first time his fingers moved in hers she froze and cautioned herself against false hope. The movement wasn't repeated and she rested her face against his hand. She must have imagined it.

The second time she felt Sinclair's finger move she knew it wasn't a dream. His knuckle had rubbed her cheek and she could feel the movement vibrate through her.

She lifted her head slowly and looked into his face. His eyes were open!

The world suddenly shone with more brightness than she knew how to cope with. The sister dropped her chart as she glanced across and saw his open eyes. She leant towards the door and called to other medical staff and suddenly the room was filled with people.

Her heart thumping, Scarlet slid out of the door and leant her back against the wall. Dry sobs of relief welled up in her throat and she ground her knuckles into her mouth. She pushed herself off the wall. She had to find Sinclair's father and her mother to break the news.

The next hours passed with aching slowness as they waited in the corridor for Sinclair to be disconnected from the ventilator and have exhaustive checks run on him. But he had crested the hill of recovery and all the news was good.

When they were allowed back into his room his eyes were closed again. But he must have heard their voices because he stirred and smiled at Scarlet.

'Did I dream you said you'd marry me?'

She rested her head on his chest. 'It wasn't a dream. I can't wait.' She kissed him gently on the lips and stepped back.

Sinclair smiled tiredly at his father. 'Hi, Dad.' He turned his eyes towards Scarlet. 'Have you met your new daughter-in-law-to-be?'

'And my new grandson. About time, too. Now, you get better soon, and I'll have a few more fine fellows like Cameron, thank you.'

Vivienne leant across and kissed Sinclair's brow. 'I'm just staying long enough to welcome you to the family. Take it easy, Sinclair, no new grandchildren yet,' she said, and stepped back.

Sinclair smiled up at her. 'And when do I get to welcome you into the family?'

Vivienne just smiled and said, 'We'll see.' The older couple slipped out.

Scarlet leant across and kissed his lips again. 'Thank you for coming back to us. We all love you. But I'm in love with you so don't go away again. Promise?'

'I promise,' he said, and his eyes closed.

EPILOGUE

THE bride wore a pale ivory gown that rustled as she walked and spring flowers nestled like a crown in her bright copper hair.

The marquee poles were satin-bowed and trailed with tiny white baby's breath that disappeared into the canopy. Most of the town seemed to have driven up the mountain for the ceremony and gaily dressed children played under the trees.

Frank McPherson stood tall and straight, his face creased with lines of happiness as he gave Scarlet away to his son. His eyes softened as he winked at the new woman in his own life and Vivienne, as matron of honour, smiled wickedly back at the man she'd been in love with all those years ago. The joy and love on the raised platform overflowed onto the gathered guests.

When the lone saxophonist played 'Ave Maria' the notes floated gloriously across the rolling green grass of the lookout and over the edge of the mountain. The vista below them stretched gloriously all the way to the sea as vows were taken and lives joined together for ever.

Cameron was perched in his old-fashioned pram, dressed in a miniature suit to match his father and grandfather. He clutched a satin pillow in front of him. As best man at his parents' wedding, he had a very important job to do.

Sinclair, tall and straight in his black suit, reached

across and untied one of the rings from the pillow. He dropped a kiss on his son's head before turning to his bride. Her eyes met his and for both of them the sun seemed to shine a beam right at them. He slid the ring onto Scarlet's finger and his voice carried strongly across the lawn.

'With this ring, I thee wed...'

THE MIDWIFE BRIDE

by

Janet Ferguson

Janet Ferguson was born at Newmarket, Suffolk, and during her going-out-to-work days was a medical secretary working in hospitals both in London and the provinces. It was when she moved to Saltdean in Sussex that she settled down to writing general fiction novels, then moved on to medical romance. She says 'as to where I get my ideas for plots (writers are always asked that), they come when I'm walking my dog on the Downs; the wind whispers them into my ear... do this... do that... say this... say that... go home and write it *now*. With the elements to inspire me, not to mention two nurses in my family, I aim to keep writing medical romance, and to 'plot till I drop'.

CHAPTER ONE

'Now that you're meeting a galaxy of new people you may fall in love again,' Kate observed, watching her twin sister, Ella, step out of her uniform dress and get into loose cotton trousers and overshirt.

'Midwives only see already-spoken-for men,' Ella pointed out, bending to the dressing-table mirror to loosen her buttercup hair down from its workaday bun.

'Still, on your days off you can get out and about,' Kate said, persisting with her find-a-husband-for-Ella campaign. The fact that she, Kate, was separated from her husband, and had endured a miserable marriage, seemed not to deter her from plugging a new marital state for her sister. Ella had been widowed for three years and, to Kate's way of thinking, she was exactly the type to make a good second marriage and have at least two more kids. At present she just had Hannah, who was six and precocious. She needed siblings to straighten her out.

'Mummy.' Hannah's voice was echoing up the stairs now. 'Merlin's ready, I've put his lead on, we're going to be late!'

'I'm coming.' Pulling a face at her sister, Ella made her way down to the hall, where Hannah and her little black dog—a mixture of Peke and pug—were dancing in duo by the open front door.

'We shan't be long, Kate—hope not, at any rate.' Waving goodbye, they started the short walk to the veterinary surgery, crossing the road to the cliff-top.

5

It was the first week in June, and a warm evening. Hannah's hair, the same shade as her mother's, gleamed in the westering sun. Merlin's appointment—for his booster vaccination and general check-up—was for five-thirty. It was now twenty past, and Hannah insisted on hurrying. 'We don't want to miss our turn.'

'We shan't miss it.' Ella sighed a little. Truth to tell, she could have done without this little trip after a long day of postnatal visits and a meeting afterwards. Still, it was Friday, thank goodness, and being free until Monday meant that she could give Hannah the best weekend possible.

Her love for her child was absolute. After all, she is part of Tom, and if I spoil her, as Kate says I do, then so be it, she thought, gazing down at the yellow-haired sprite in her blue and white school dress. She was tugging at the skirt of it, pulling it away from her legs. 'I wanted to wear my shorts, but Kate said I must ask you first,' she grizzled rebelliously, squinting into the sun.

'You can wear them tomorrow when we go down to the beach,' her mother promised, glancing at her watch, noting with a little dart of alarm that it was very nearly five-thirty. They really *were* running late. 'Let's jog, shall we?' she suggested, and they quickened their pace over the tussocky cliff grass, Merlin jerking on his lead.

On their left, some two hundred feet below, the sea was dawdling in on an ebb tide, leaving the shingle washed and jewel-bright. There were few people down there at this time of day, most having gone home to tea. It would be another month before the true holidaymakers crowded Easthaven beach. Many preferred Charding—a livelier resort—a mile along the coast. The Regent County Hospital was there, and Ella could see the rise of its tower block as she and Hannah hurried along. On the right of the cliff-top was the main coast road, with a tide of a different kind—that of traffic, traffic and still more traffic, hurtling up from the lights.

Descending to the pavement alongside it now, Ella, daughter and dog were instantly engulfed in its noise and clamour and rush. The lights were against them, and they had to wait to cross. 'We'll be late, we'll be late!' Hannah's anxiety was mounting to panic point.

Cursing herself for not having allowed more time, Ella grabbed her tightly as the green man showed, then over the road they streaked, past the chemist's on the corner where the high street began, to the Ark Surgery next door.

There was no one in the waiting room but Miss Remer, the receptionist. 'You're a little late, Mrs Fairfax.' She gave Ella a tight little smile. 'Our five forty-five client has gone in in your place. He had a difficult evening in front of him, he said, so didn't want to wait.'

'I see,' Ella said, sitting down on the nearest chair. 'Surely he must have been early, it's only a quarter to six now.'

'Well, yes, he was,' Miss Remer conceded, 'but hope-fully he won't be long.' A murmur of voices could be heard from behind the closed consulting-room door.

Hannah fidgeted, ten minutes passed, the conversation drone went on. 'They're taking *ages*, Mummy!' she complained, just as the door moved inwards to emit a tall, fair-haired man in his thirties, formally dressed in a suit, carrying a bemused-looking Border terrier under his arm. He was attractive…striking… A flicker of excite-ment made Ella catch her breath. Behind him, several inches lower, Mr Savers was smiling at her, but it was the man who riveted her attention, and for a second the two of them stared, or glared, at one another—she who'd been late, and he who'd had the cheek—and, yes, it *had* been a cheek—to go in in her place.

'You went in on my appointment!' She was annoyed to hear her voice sounding quavery-weak.

'You were late!' He inclined a little towards her, *his* voice smooth as milk.

'Not by much!' She cleared her throat.

'Even so, you weren't on time, so I feel I was justified.' He smiled then, and Ella felt furious, as well as weak at the knees. Men like him thought charm could justify every move they made. She had no time to say any more, though, before he was turning from her to say goodnight to Andrew Savers, after which he crossed the floor, waved, and went out. With conflicting feelings, most of them angry, Ella watched the stranger pass the window, then, aware that Andrew was waiting for her, entered the consulting room, Merlin dragging his feet on the vinyl as though he were on skids.

Andrew said nothing about the switched appointments, being of the firm belief that minor discords between clients didn't matter so long as the patients weren't affected. With a smile for both mother and daughter, both of whom he knew, he proceeded to give Merlin his check-up, beginning with sounding his heart. The big pulse in his flank was felt, his eyes and ears were examined, then came the injection which, due to Hannah's forethought in producing a biscuit at exactly the right moment, was scarcely noticed by Merlin who thought a flea had got him again.

'That was helpful, Hannah.' Andrew smiled at her, making her pink with pleasure. The little girl liked him because he liked Merlin—it was as simple as that. As for Andrew himself, he was attracted to her mother and meant to do something about it. His parents had the house next to Longmead where she was now living permanently. This could make things easier all round, make them evolve naturally. He wasn't, however, the type to rush, he liked to take his time. Seeing her to the street door and saying goodbye to Hannah, he invited a man with a greyhound into his sanctum, and remarked on the weather again.

Back on the cliff-top, but facing home this time, Ella's thoughts returned to that haughty, attractive stranger in the grey suit. Fancy wearing a suit to visit the vet. Most people dressed down for that. She was trying to put him in the wrong, if only through his choice of clothes. He'd suited the suit, though, he'd been tall with long legs. She could see him now, walking over to the door, moving with easy grace. He was the kind of man who would never be clumsy. Ella's thoughts rioted, and at this point, feeling uncomfortably warm, she dismissed him from her mind.

She began to dwell instead on the way she had altered her life by coming to live in Sussex. It was great being with Kate, of course, but had she really been wise to leave Seftonbridge, Cambridgeshire, where she'd felt so close to Tom? It had been well-meaning relatives and friends who'd kept advising her to get a life. Her retired parents had been worried about her ever since Tom had died. 'You can't cling to the past for ever, Ella, you have to move on. You're only twenty-eight with your whole life in front of you. It doesn't do to look back.' As for Kate, well, Kate's voice had been the loudest of all. She, separated from her husband Paul, had been living at Longmead, Easthaven, with their parents for nearly a year before they'd retired. When they'd 'emigrated' to Scotland Kate had remained there, which suited both her and them as they had no wish to sell the property—at least, not for the time being.

Left on her own in the roomy, five-bedroomed house, Kate had suggested that Ella should join her, had pressed for this to happen. 'We're twins, for heaven's sake, we ought to be together, and the house is big enough. You'd get a midder post down here in no time. And as I work from home, there'd be no problem about Hannah. I could do the school run and everything. Please, Ellie, give it some thought. Apart from anything else we'd have *fun!*'

Ella had thought it over for a long time, for she wasn't impulsive like Kate and she was attached to Seftonbridge. She knew it like the back of her hand. She had trained there, worked there, married and had Hannah there. She got on well with her team midwives, all of whom were friends. Still, she had reasoned, thinking mainly of Hannah, perhaps she should join Kate. And perhaps fate had been on her side, too, for a few weeks later she'd seen an advertisement for a replacement midwife to join a team of three, based at Easthaven, and she'd applied straight away. She'd been shortlisted, had attended an interview, been awarded the post, and at the end of April, with the skies weeping tears for the life she was leaving behind, Ella had come to Sussex and joined her sister at Longmead.

The best thing of all to come out of this change was that Hannah had settled well. To be living at the seaside in Granny and Grandpa's house was the child's idea of bliss. She was a tough, adaptable little girl, thank heaven, Ella thought as they re-crossed the road, climbed a short, steep hill and came within sight of home.

Longmead stood between two similar houses, each with modest grounds and a view of the sea. The house on its eastern boundary, called Drummers, had been empty for months. According to Kate, it had had loads of people to view it, and around six weeks ago, during the week Ella had come, a SOLD notice had been slipped over the FOR SALE one, so any day now, the two women supposed, the new owners would be moving in. The garden was a wilderness, which upset Ella each time she had trespassed over there to retrieve one of Hannah's balls. There were some healthy shrubs—hydrangeas and roses—under a forest of weeds. She longed to take spade and trowel to dig one or two up for herself, but managed to resist the temptation, for what self-respecting mother would allow herself to thieve?

'You're garden barmy,' Kate told her. 'Good job one of us is.'

Kate was a proofreader for a publishing firm in London and worked from home. She did her share of the housework, but didn't like what she called 'mucking about with soil', so Ella was surprised to see her in the front garden as she and Hannah came up the drive. She was weeding, too, much to Ella's amazement, but she sprang up when she saw them, tossing back her russet hair.

'Ellie, what do you think? Someone's come next door—they must be moving in. You can just see the car roof.' She nodded to the left. 'I saw a woman get out with a little boy. They arrived just after you'd gone.'

'Oh, good, a proper family!' Looking up at the house, Ella could see opened windows, hear the faint beat of music…the place was coming to life. No sooner had she thought this than a removal van of vast proportions swayed into the drive, followed at a safe distance by a sleek cream car.

'Come on.' Kate grabbed Ella's arm. 'Up to the land-

ing we go. We can watch operations from there, behind
Mum's old nets!'

'You can, I've got Hannah to see to.' Looking round
for her daughter, Ella found her in the kitchen up on a
stool in front of the line of cupboards, reaching for
Merlin's biscuits. Opening the packet and handing it to
her, Ella succumbed to curiosity and joined Kate upstairs.

'A man's come,' she was told. 'Youngish, attractive.
He's gone into the house with a dog. He'll be out again
in a minute, I expect. Don't miss a treat. Oh, there he
is, look... Can you see him, over by that cabinet thing?'

Ella could see, and drew in her breath with something
like a gasp, for the man in Drummers's drive, partially
concealed by items of furniture being borne into the
house, was the stealer of appointments, the man she'd
encountered at the vet's. True, he'd taken his jacket off
and had rolled up his sleeves. True, his fawn hair was
ruffled and he was laughing with the men. But it was
him all right. There was no mistaking that long, male
shape, that easy way of moving, as he helped shift tea-
chests down from the van.

When at last Ella found her voice it came out in a
raspy croak. 'Actually, Kate, I've just met him,' she said,
'down at the vet's. He went in on my appointment, we
were a few minutes late. We didn't talk for long, but it
is the same man.'

'Well, I'm blowed!' Kate's nose pressed against the
net curtain, 'He's gorgeous, sexy!'

'Yes, I noticed that.'

'So who is he?'

'I've no idea...I mean, how would I?'

'You could have asked the punctilious Andrew.'

'Well, I didn't,' Ella all but snapped. 'Actually, I

thought he was rude, making his point with such… precision, putting me in the wrong!'

'He was probably on edge about moving.' Kate looked at her sister in some surprise. Ella was thinking about the woman and little boy Kate had mentioned…were they his wife and child?

'And we *were* late,' Hannah chirped from behind, having made her way up the stairs. Remembering her flair for picking up on adults' conversation, Ella looked warningly at Kate as they made their way downstairs.

'Of course,' Kate observed when the child was in bed, and the van had trundled away, 'I can find out who next door are from Letty Hobbs. I'm meeting her tomorrow for coffee at The Creamery—she'll fill me in.'

'Is she likely to give out classified info?' Ella asked. Letty Hobbs was a secretary at the estate agents' Office in Easthaven high street.

'I doubt if it's all that classified by now,' Kate said, stretching out full length on the settee. 'Once we're filled in we can go round and make ourselves known to them, which is what Mum and Dad would have done if they'd still been here.'

'They'd have been round there now, whoever they were, offering help,' Ella said, then quickly added, 'All the same, there's no need for us to rush. The man didn't look all that approachable to me. His wife may be different, of course. Let's just wait a bit and see.'

At lunchtime next day, arriving back at Longmead after a morning on the beach with Hannah, Ella learned from her sister, who she joined on the patio, that the new owner of Drummers was Patrick Weston, Gynae-Obstetrician Consultant Surgeon at the Regent Hospital. 'Now, how about that for an item of news? Not that it surprised me too much.' Kate strained forward on the garden chair, watching Ella drop into hers. 'I mean, he looks eminent, doesn't he? He looks like someone of note.'

'You were saying yesterday that he looks sexy.'

'Well, that, too, of course.' Kate grinned, then babbled on, 'Apparently Letty's sister has been seeing him in Outpatients—something wrong with her tubes. She said how kind he was—gentle and everything.'

'I'm so glad,' Ella said sweetly, and Kate gave her a sharp look.

'You look boiled, Ella. I hope you haven't been in the sun too long. You ought to have taken your hat to the beach. You know you have to cover up.'

'I'm perfectly all right, just hot.'

Kate nodded absently, her mind still on Patrick Weston. 'I'm just surprised,' she said, 'that you haven't run into him when you've been at the hospital, visiting your new mums. Are you sure you haven't seen him?'

'Quite sure.' Ella nodded emphatically. 'I expect he's in Theatre most of the time, or doing his round of the gynae ward. He's unlikely to be in Maternity unless there's a crisis. You know that as well as I do,' she added impatiently.

Kate did know for, along with Ella, ten years ago she had begun an academic course in nursing at St Saviour's, Seftonbridge, but whereas Ella had stayed the course and qualified, Kate had married during her final year and had turned her back on nursing for good. 'All the same,' she said, 'it's an amazing coincidence, and I think we ought to compound it by making ourselves known to him and his wife. If we leave it much longer we'll be like those sad folk who believe in keeping themselves to themselves.'

'Right now I could be one of them.' Ella laughed,

feeling though still reluctant, a sense of challenge like an urgent pushing hand. The challenge had a voice, too, it rang in her ears like a dare—go on, do it, get round there, look the man in the eye! 'All right, you're on,' she agreed. 'We'll introduce ourselves now. I'll just put a dress on and tidy Hannah, then over the way we'll go.' Springing up from her chair, lithe in shorts and a blue cropped top, she looked around for her daughter, then stiffened, for coming through the wicket gate at the bottom of the garden was a tall man with fawnish hair, looking about him with interest. Even clad as he was in jeans and checked shirt, Ella knew him instantly. At his side, similarly attired, walked a small, fair haired boy.

'Kate, he's here!' she hissed, but her sister who had seen them, too, was running down the steps, followed by Merlin who was yapping and darting, all but tripping her up. Hannah, hearing the din, appeared from inside the house to stand by her mother in a paroxysm of shyness completely foreign to her.

Up the patio steps they came—Patrick Weston and son—escorted by Kate, who was jabbering introductions. 'Meet my sister, Ella, she's my twin. And no, we're not alike, everyone says that! Ellie, this is Mr Weston and Robin from next door!'

'Oh, Patrick, please.' His hand clasped Ella's and as their eyes met he said at once, bland-faced and smiling, 'You and I have met before.'

More clashed than met, Ella was tempted to say, but resisted and substituted, 'We met at the vet's yesterday. We swapped appointments.' There was a tiny silence. 'I was late,' she added, wanting to start off on the right foot.

But all he did was stare some more and utter a flat 'yes', followed by the comment that he was sure they'd met somewhere other than at the vet's. 'I seldom forget a face.'

'Not many people do forget Ella's,' Kate interrupted, ranging herself alongside her sister, who was bending down to Hannah.

'Darling, this is Mr Weston's little boy.' Ella was trying to steady her voice.

'I know him, he goes to my school, but he's not in my class.' Hannah looked up at her mother, whose hand felt slippery wet.

'Robin is probably older than you.'

'I'm seven,' he burst out, speaking for the first time.

'We've been in the area since the beginning of December,' Patrick supplied, 'living in rented accommodation while I looked for a property to buy. I felt Drummers had the look of a solid family home, which is what I was after. It's a little farther from the hospital than where we were before, but not too far to matter, and it's nearer Rob's school, which is important.'

He was moving down the lawn a little to survey the three houses in one single sweep. 'I would imagine they're the same size,' he commented, 'although the elevations differ.'

'They're all five-bedroomed, two reception,' Kate supplied. 'Ella and I have been in yours, and the one on the other side. Our parents bought Longmead ten years ago. We were away from home then but, of course, we came here for holidays. Yours has been empty for yonks, you know, it had an artist in it once. The one on this side…she flapped a hand to the right '…belongs to the Savers—Andrew Savers's parents.'

'And Andrew lives over his surgery.'

Patrick's eyes met Ella's for a skimming second, jerking her into saying, very nearly accusingly, 'Your garden's a shocking mess.'

'I know, and the house is that way, too, which is why—' He broke off as a young woman in dungarees burst through the party hedge. She had long dark hair tied back in a band, a small-boned, suntanned face and white teeth, very slightly buck. Enter the wife, Ella thought, wiping her hands down the back of her shorts.

'Valerie, for heaven's sake.' Patrick was helping her over a border.

'Sorry to arrive by the forestry route!'

'Couldn't you have used the gate?'

'Too far, too lazy!' She was looking over at Ella and Kate a little coolly.

Patrick introduced her as 'my fiancée, Valerie Trentham, who's helping me in the house'.

'Doing most of the work, too,' she supplied, linking arms with him.

Fiancée, not wife, Ella was thinking, but was she Robin's mother? It looked very much like it, they looked like a unit standing there in a group. Maybe they'd lived together for years, but were now tying the knot for reasons of their own. It was usual enough these days, goodness knew. People did it all the time. She came out of her reverie to hear Kate suggesting that they go into the house for a drink.

Valerie looked all set to agree but, without glancing in Patrick's direction, Ella knew he was going to turn the invitation down, which he very adroitly did. 'That's really kind but, as you can guess, we've a hundred and one things to do.'

Valerie nodded, supporting him. 'And what I came for,' she said, 'was to ask if you had any mint in your garden. Believe it or not, in our jungle plot I can't find one little sprig. Lamb chops without mint sauce are like boiled eggs without salt.'

'We've got loads,' Kate said at once. 'Come with me and take your pick. We've even got two varieties—how's that for efficiency?'

They went off together, Hannah and Merlin with them, leaving Ella on the patio with Patrick and his son. 'How's your dog today?' she asked the child.

'She's resting in the house.' He looked at her shyly, twisting a strand of his fringe.

'Lucy's getting an old lady now, so she needs lots of sleep,' Patrick said, as he and Ella sat down.

'She has vitamin pills from Mr Savers to build her up,' Robin expanded, feeling braver away from Hannah's sceptical eye.

'I expect they make her feel young again.' It was easier, Ella found, to talk to the child than to his father, although why she should feel so gauche in his presence she had no idea. Of course, it would have been better if she'd had a skirt on. As it was, she felt over-exposed.

'Been on the beach this morning?' he asked, and she felt he'd homed in on her thoughts.

'With Hannah, yes.' She met his eyes over the space between their two chairs. His lashes were light brown, darker than his hair, his brows the same shade, the eyes themselves a deep sea blue. 'It's not all that often…' she cleared her throat '…that I get a whole weekend off.'

'What work do you do?'

'I'm a midwife…community.'

'So *that's* where…' His fist thumped his palm. 'That's where I've seen you before! At the vet's yesterday I was flummoxed…couldn't place you. I've seen you at the hospital, in the parking lot, getting into your car!'

'I'm there most mornings, visiting mothers who've

given birth on our patch.' She hadn't seen him, though, had she? If she had she wouldn't have forgotten. 'The birth rate is pretty high in Sussex, there's plenty for us to do.'

'Which GP practices do you cover?'

'The two at The Moorings Medical Centre, here in Easthaven. It's our base, actually. There are four of us, plus a team leader.'

'The hospital midwives are the ones I see most of. I have a gynae-obstetrics post there, but perhaps you know that?' His voice lifted a little in query, as did one of his thick, level brows.

'Yes, I did know. I heard just recently.' She could feel herself colouring and, furious because of it, she went on to say, 'I expect you take the view that all babies should be born in hospital.'

He looked challenged, and a little amused. 'I think some GPs do,' he said.

'But what is *your* view?'

'If a woman's pregnancy has proceeded normally, and she wants a home birth, then I'm all for the community midwife doing her stuff!' His face was perfectly straight as he said this. Even so, Ella had the distinct impression that he'd somehow spiked her guns.

'What I mean to do eventually,' she told him, 'is practise independently—set up on my own.'

'An ambitious project.' He eyed her keenly.

'It's what I want to do.'

'Then go for it,' he said easily, as though he didn't much care, then asked her if she was a single mother.

She bucked a little at that. 'I am now. My husband died three years ago.' Not giving him a chance to comment, she went on, 'Kate looks after Hannah when I'm on duty—she works from home. Once I'm established with my own practice, I'll be able to see more of her.'

'It's not easy, balancing a job and a child.' Patrick's eyes slewed to his son, who was sitting on the steps, watching a ladybird running over the back of his hand. 'I've had a live-in housekeeper ever since my wife died. With a hospital post and the possibility of being called out at night, it was the only option. I was lucky enough to get a retired nurse with no family ties. She's clearing up at our rented place in Charding this weekend, but will be here on Sunday night.'

'Oh, I see.' Ella was taking in the amazing even startling fact that he was a widower. Somehow or other she hadn't thought that, and to hide her surprise and slight confusion she went on to say, 'You must have succeeded Mr Easter at The Regent. He operated on my mother about seven years back. I remember going to see him during her time in hospital.'

'Simon Easter and his family emigrated to Australia just before Christmas. I succeeded him, yes.' Patrick's look was quizzical, perhaps wondering what she was going to say next.

'I can't imagine *not* working, not having a caring job,' she stated.

'Ella's a born nurse.' To her relief, Kate's voice cut in as she emerged from the side of the house with Valerie, whom she'd been taking on a guided tour. 'Me, now, I gave up in my final year, but, then, I'm not a stickler like she is. I'm all for variety.'

'And I'm all for getting back to grill our chops.' Valerie waved her posy of mint, looking over at Ella and Patrick.

'Yes, we ought to be going. Good to have met you both, and you, too, Hannah.' Patrick leant down to the child's level. 'Perhaps you and Robin will become friends now that he's living next door.'

Ella held her breath, for Hannah wasn't given to making flowery responses, so she was taken aback to hear her say, 'Yes, we might play cricket. I've got a proper bat and a set of stumps.'

'A great idea!' Patrick straightened up. 'We'll have to arrange a match.' Robin said nothing, neither did he evince any interest. He was already down on the lawn, walking close to Valerie who was making for the hedge again.

'Not this time you don't!' Patrick's arm snaked about his fiancée's waist. 'A little civilized behaviour is called for, and that means using the gate.'

'Whatever you say, sir.' Valerie leaned back against him, smiling over at Ella and Kate. But it was a smile that didn't quite reach her eyes. 'Thanks for this, just the job.' She held the mint aloft again. Then with Robin walking soberly behind them, they made their way to the gate.

'Good. Now we've got 'em taped,' Kate said when they'd gone. 'She's a bit nosy, wanted to know all about us—how we came to be living here, what we did for a living.'

'Did you fill her in?'

'More or less. After all, we've nothing to hide. Anyway, how did you get on with *him*?' Kate's glance was curious.

'Oh, you know—back and forth. All right, I think. I got in that we knew who he was, without saying how. I told him I was a community midwife, and about wanting to go it alone. He, by the way, is a widower.'

'Yes, he lost his wife two years ago, and that fiancée of his was his wife's cousin,' Kate supplied.

Ella was all attention. 'Oh, was she?' It came out on a note of surprise.

'When she, the wife, was killed in a road accident, Valiant Val stepped into the breach to help him *and* the kid sort themselves out. She's a chartered physio, with her own rooms and practice out at Gaunt's Hill. She'll be down here at weekends, she says, till they marry some time this year. Obviously they're lovers, well, it would be funny if they weren't. My betting is that once they're married she'll shift her practice to next door.'

'Hmm,' Ella muttered. She felt chilly and shivered as a brisk little wind blew up. She also felt bleak without quite knowing why.

'Interesting, isn't it?' Kate persisted. 'Happy families and all that. She's fond of the kid, you could see that, not to mention the gorgeous Patrick, whom she must have known for yonks, being kind of related—cousins by marriage. Probably fancied him for ever as well!'

'Perhaps she did.' Ella shivered again, rubbing goose-pimpled arms.

'And as everyone knows,' Kate said, as the two of them went indoors, 'stepping into the breach as she did, can sometimes pay just rewards.'

CHAPTER TWO

ON MONDAY Ella decided to leave the two mothers who had given birth over the weekend until last on her morning list of postnatal visits. Usually she started at the hospital end as this suited the latter's routine, but she knew the staff well there now and no one would mind if she got to the unit when feeding time—either of infant or mum—was in hand.

'You have to work things out so that every mother is done and dusted and happy by the end of the day,' one of her fellow midwives had told her when she'd first joined their charmed circle. Not that it *was* a charmed circle, more a happy one, all four young women working and fitting in well with one another.

Having arranged the order of her visits, Ella set off for Kempton Road to see Claire Purton and her three-day-old baby boy. Claire was just home from hospital, and her mother-in-law answered the door—a big, confident lady who had reared three children, each of them bottle-fed.

'And I tell Claire that's what she should be doing,' she declared as she led Ella upstairs. 'Her nipples are sore, but will she take any notice of me? She will not. With the variety of baby milk about these days, it would be a simple matter to change. She's feeding Chris now—you can see for yourself what he's putting her through.'

Ella did see and, after tactfully persuading Jean Purton to leave her alone with Claire, she sat down with mother and baby and watched Christopher tucking into his breakfast with eye-popping greed.

'Well, he certainly loves your milk, Claire, there's no doubt about that.' She laughed. 'But I think I can see why he's making you so sore. You need to latch him farther on, get the areola as well as the nipple into his mouth. As he's positioned now he'll be rubbing you with his tongue every time he sucks.'

'They told me that at the hospital,' Claire admitted, 'but I was afraid he'd suffocate, that his nose would get in the way.'

Ella shook her head, 'No chance. Breast-feeding is a skill, remember, even though it's a natural process.' She watched Claire as she adjusted her baby's position, pressing him close. 'That's it, that's right, he's still getting what he wants, and you'll soon be more comfortable and enjoy feeding times. How are you managing with bathing and changing him?'

'Bathing's still a bit scary.' Claire looked up from her busily sucking infant. 'Especially with Jean hanging over me, giving advice. When Bob's here he tells her off, but he's having to work this week up until Thursday, then he'll take the leave due to him.'

Ella nodded sympathetically. 'You could always,' she said, 'bath Chris in the evening if it suits you better, then just top and tail him first thing.'

'Yes, the hospital told me that, too—they even said it might help him sleep better—but Jean said she'd never heard of such a thing. ''Babies are always bathed in the morning.''' Claire mimicked Jean Purtons's authoritative tone, giggling as she did so. At least she's not letting things get on top of her, Ella noted as, with the baby sated and winded, she popped him onto the scales.

'He'll soon make up his birth weight—he's a fine healthy lad.' With the child held against her shoulder, Ella smiled over at Claire, who, with the bleary appearance of most young mothers, was trying to clear some of the baby paraphernalia from around her feet. 'Now, I'll just…' she put the baby in his carrying basket '…take a peep at those stitches of yours, and then I'll leave you in peace.'

'Will you be here this evening?' Claire climbed onto the bed.

'No, tonight you'll have Rosa, but it'll be me again tomorrow morning. On Wednesday you'll have Shirley, as I'm on call that day, which means I do no routine visits, just ones I'm especially called out for.'

'I think you've all been—all *are*—brilliant,' Claire said when Ella had finished. 'The hospital midwives were great, too, but I know you outside ones better.'

'You make us sound like hardy perennials,' Claire teased, and the two of them laughed together, making Mrs Purton wonder why, as she brought in two steaming cups.

'Chocolate for you, dear.' She gave the tall one to Claire. 'And coffee for you, Nurse, that is if you can spare the time.' Ella couldn't, not really, but as being sociable was part of her job, she nodded her thanks and took rapid sips as she listened to Jean Purton's description of *her* last confinement and all she'd gone through. 'That was with Bob, Claire's husband, you know. He's always been difficult.'

Escaping at last and back in her car, which was like an oven, Ella drove to one of the new bungalows in the next street to visit Jane Rackham with her week-old baby girl. Here her ring was answered by Jane's husband so quickly that she felt he must have been looking out for her.

'She's got a lump down here.' He made graphic signs, his pink youth's face creased into old man's lines.

'It's probably nothing, Eric. Sometimes odd things happen after a birth. But we'll soon see, won't we?'

Ella went through into the sitting room where Jane, looking far calmer than her husband, was changing baby Eve. As the child was awake, Ella examined her first, looking to see if the cord was drying up, popping her onto the scales, assuring Jane that she was thriving. 'And beautiful with it, an absolute poppet, in fact. Now it's your turn for the check-up stakes. Perhaps Eric would like to nurse his daughter whilst we go through into the bedroom.'

Eric emerged from the kitchen, still looking worried. With the baby, however, he was adept and confident, moving her head into the hollow of his shoulder, uttering soothing words.

'He adores her,' said Jane, through in the bedroom, climbing out of loose jeans, 'but he worries about me to the point when I could send him packing.'

'Now, you know you don't mean that,' Ella said after she'd completed her examination and was stripping off her gloves. 'This little lump, which is more of a ruck, has been caused by your stitches. It'll disappear completely in time, but you can help it on its way if you like by rubbing in a little oil. Actually, you're looking very good down there, you've nothing to worry about.'

'I wasn't all that worried, to tell you the truth.' Jane moved off the bed. 'But you'd better tell the good news to Eric before he goes berserk!'

'What are you saying about me?' Eric appeared in the doorway. He'd been lurking again, Ella could tell, but she explained all the same, making a broad grin crease his boyish face. 'Great!' he said, looking over at his wife, 'but I heard what you said, and for that you can take this smelly little bundle. I'm off to the shops!' As he handed the baby over to Jane the look the young couple exchanged caused a jolt of envy to assail Ella. Did they know how lucky they were?

Three more calls in the same vicinity were made after that, and it was half past twelve before she reached the hospital. The lunch trolleys had only just been wheeled out of the postnatal ward. Out of the dozen or so mothers and babies settling down for their quiet hour, Ella quickly picked out the two relating to her team.

Alison, the first one she went to, was touchingly pleased to see her. 'I've been dying to tell you all about it.' She was sitting on the side of the bed, the better to view her day-old son, fast asleep in his cot.

'He looks great, Alison, and big, too,' Ella was quick to praise.

'Eight pounds. I thought I'd never get him out, I thought I was going to split. Well, I did, I've got stitches in, I didn't *enjoy* the birth, but once I held him…well, *you* know!' Her smile was weary, but happy and relieved. Ella smiled back at her, for she had heard this said so many times and had experienced it herself as well.

Kathleen Treves, three beds down, had had an easy birth. 'I was ever so quick, only eight hours from start to finish!' She scooped her baby girl out of the cot, anxious to give Ella the best possible view of her—a round little mite with an upstanding shock of bright red hair.

'She's blissful.' Ella looked down at the tiny folded hands.

'We're going to call her Geraldine. I'm dying to get her home, then the fun will start, I dare say.'

'Sure will.' Ella laughed. 'But you'll get plenty of help, you know—a twice-daily visit from us midwives for the first three days, then daily for a week, then once a week or whenever you call us. Help, if you need it, will always be close at hand.'

Leaving the unit at last, and wanting her own lunch, Ella stopped off at the hospital shop to buy a packet of sandwiches and an apple. She could have had, if she'd liked, a cooked lunch up in the canteen with the ward midwives but, feeling in need of some fresh air, she decided to picnic on the seafront.

Sitting on one of the long planked seats on the upper promenade, she was able to appreciate the weather which, being sunny and warm, was bringing out workers from nearby offices. Coaches were setting down day-trippers at the Palace Pier and Sea Life Centre. People milled past in a continuous stream, some making for the beach, some leaning over the promenade rail, looking at the sea.

Munching her sandwiches, feeling screened and unnoticed among so many moving forms, Ella's thoughts—probably because she was still only a hand's throw from the hospital—turned to Patrick Weston. What was he doing now? Her mind played out various scenarios—he might still be in Theatre, turning from the table, leaving his registrar to tidy and close up a wound. On the other hand, he might be in the doctors' dining room, having a hot lunch to set him up for the afternoon.

It was at this point, or very soon after, that the cavalcade of strollers in front of her thinned out into a straggle, and she sighted him some fifty yards away, coming towards her, not seeing anyone, simply walking along—straight, and tall, and fair of head, face lifted to the sun.

In an instant she was aware of her quickened heartbeats, of the piece of tuna sandwich she'd had in her mouth going down in a painful lump. Damn! She hoped he wouldn't see her. She wasn't in the mood for polite conversation, not with a carton of fishy-smelling sandwiches leering up from her lap. But he did see her, and came to sit down beside her.

'Enjoying the sun?' he asked.

'Oh, hello… Yes, I am.' Ella feigned surprise, even though with half an eye and all of her senses she had seen him veer to the seat. Conscious of the remains of her sandwich still in full view, she tried to shroud it with paper and cover it under her hand.

'Don't let me stop you having your lunch. You're probably pressed for time.'

'No more than usual, but I expect you are—pressed for time, I mean.' She began eating again, taking self-conscious bites, listening to him telling her that he'd had the usual Monday morning in Theatre, followed by lunch with his registrar. 'Then there's a ward round this afternoon, but you'll know the routine, I'm sure.'

'I can remember my time on the wards,' she said, 'although no doubt there've been changes since then. I've been community-based for the past five years.'

'And soon to be your own boss,' he teased her lightly, and good-humouredly, making her laugh.

'I wouldn't say soon.' She swallowed the last of her sandwich, thankful to have it gone. 'But it may happen in two or three years' time. By then I shall have got to know the area like the back of my hand, although it's not exactly strange to me now as I was often down here on visits to my parents.'

'With your husband?'

His question caught her off guard. 'With Tom and Hannah, yes,' she said, 'until Tom became too ill to want to move very far. He had a brain tumour,' she added dismissively, not wanting to go into details sitting on a promenade seat.

'What appalling luck.'

'Yes.' She was grateful to him for not going on and on, for not affecting a sadness that he couldn't possibly have felt. Ending the tiny silence that followed, she asked him about Drummers. 'How are you getting on over the hedge? I expect it's all systems go?'

'Well, as to that...' he uncrossed his legs, trying to get more comfortable on the rock-hard seat '...I'm afraid it still resembles a squat with things all over the place. Still, Barbara, my housekeeper, arrived last night, and two young bloods from Groundwork Services began on the garden this morning.'

'It'll soon be shipshape, house *and* garden,' Ella said encouragingly.

He nodded. 'And when it is I want to give a party, most likely a barbecue. It'll have to be at a weekend when Valerie will be down, but not too far ahead as we'll want to take advantage of the warm summer evenings.'

'It'll be summer for ages yet, we're only just on the brink of it.' Ella was picturing him and Valerie on newly manicured lawns, moving amongst their guests like the married couple they were soon to become. When were they getting married? she wondered.

Then she heard him say, 'Naturally you and your sister will be invited, bringing a friend each, if you like.'

'Great, thanks,' Ella said brightly, forcing a polite smile.

Two elderly ladies in sunhats and glasses joined them on the seat. Patrick moved up to give them more room, coming close enough to Ella for his upper arm to brush her shoulder, close enough for her to be able to study his hands as they rested in his lap. They were good hands, well shaped with long, strong fingers—a surgeon's hands, a lover's hands, too. Awareness of him peaked, making it difficult for Ella to breathe. Surely her heart had stopped. The sun blazed into her face as she forced herself to speak.

'Kate and I love Longmead, you know.' She could hear the gush in her voice. 'We really, really love it…the spaciousness and everything!'

'Isn't it rather *too* spacious for two ladies on their own?' he queried, looking down at a gull pecking at crumbs around their feet.

'Hannah lives there, too,' she reminded him, 'and our parents are likely to visit us from time to time. Anyway, Drummers is of like size, so the same applies to you.'

'For the moment, yes, I agree,' he said, staring in front of him, 'but once Val and I are respectably married—' he gave a small half-smile '—we hope to have a child, or children. Be good for Robin, too.'

'Oh, yes, of course.' Ella had the feeling that she'd walked right into that one. 'She seems very fond of Robin,' she commented quietly.

'They're fond of one another.' Patrick got up to deposit Ella's sandwich container into a nearby bin. Reseating himself, he went on to say, 'After Evelyn, my wife, was killed, Val was right there for Robin and me. She helped us when we were *in extremis*… It's not the kind of thing one forgets.'

'No, of course not.' Further words seemed to stick in

Ella's throat. She was amazed at her thoughts, too, one of them being how lucky Valerie was to have been *able* to help them like that.

'You'll remarry too, bound to, it's the natural order of things,' Patrick said in the following small silence, and Ella jerked in her seat.

'You've taken the words right out of my sister's mouth.' She laughed. Not that she felt like laughing, for his remark had been carelessly couched, very nearly tossed at her, just been something to say. 'And now I must go.' She slid the strap of her shoulder-bag into place. 'I've got a booking-in history to take at half one, during my client's lunch-break, so I mustn't hold her up.'

'I notice you say "client" and not "patient".'

They rose and stood by the seat. Ella could feel its hard arm prodding into her thigh.

'Well, they aren't patients, are they?' she was quick to say, 'not until they get into hospital, when they're all dubbed the same!'

'True, very true!' He cupped her elbow, guiding her to the kerb. She was aware of his touch like nothing else—a warm hand against her bare flesh, sending little quivers of feeling up to her shoulder and neck. 'Where have you left your car?' he shouted against the traffic din.

'At the hospital.'

'Perks of the job?'

'Absolutely!' She laughed, glad…thankful…that her car was there, for now he'd walk up with her.

But that wasn't going to happen. His hand was leaving her arm. 'Watch how you cross,' he was saying. 'Use the bollard, don't traffic-dodge.' He was stepping back with a little salute and returning to the seat.

How can he be so ungallant? She fumed, crossing the road without incident. Walking up the hill to the hospital between the rows of terraced houses, she could hardly believe he had cut himself off from her with that little flick of his hand. But before she got to the hospital precinct common sense reasserted itself. Whatever had she been thinking about? Why should he put himself out? She hardly knew him, or he her—she was being ridiculous. Even so, she couldn't resist a glance back down the hill before she turned the corner. She could see him quite plainly, not on the seat but standing at the promenade rail—straight, tall and fawn of head, gazing out to sea.

Her lunchtime visit, the booking-in one, was to a Miss Carla Lane. Mentally Ella prepared herself for it as she set off in her car. First visits could be tricky, with two strangers meeting, and with so many questions of the personal kind having to be addressed. She knew from Carla's GP that she was a thirty-year-old into the tenth week of her pregnancy, and that she had an executive post in PR with a company in West Charding. Her address was number five Marine Mansions—a modern block of flats midway between Charding and Easthaven, near the famous girls' boarding school.

Less than five minutes brought Ella turning into its parking lot. Reaching for her midder bag, she walked up the steps into the palatial entrance hall, with its fountain and potted plants.

She found flat number five without difficulty, her ring being answered by Miss Lane herself, sylph-slim in a cream skirt and dark red blouse. Her manner was distant at first, but to Ella's relief she relaxed and leveled with her once the visit got under way. Not unexpectedly, she was very precise, knowing exactly what she wanted, which was shared care between her GP and midwife, delivery in hospital, then home with her partner as soon as practicable.

'You *could* settle for a domino delivery.' Ella, wreathed in smoke, felt she should outline all the possibilities, whilst trying not to cough. Carla had lit up almost as soon as Ella had entered the room, and by infinitely tactful means she would have to be advised to stop or at least cut down. Ella's eyes watered as she tried to write in her notes.

'What on earth is a domino delivery?' Carla got up to open a window and stub out her cigarette.

Relieved and encouraged by this, Ella went on to tell her that a domino delivery—short for domiciliary in and out—meant that the community midwife would stay at home with the woman until labour was well advanced, when she would take her into hospital, deliver the baby there, then bring them back home again to recover in home surroundings, with twice daily visits from the group midwives to check that all was well. 'The advantage of a domino,' Ella concluded, 'is that the woman is delivered by a midwife whom she knows.'

Carla looked undecided, then shook her head, 'No, I don't think so,' she said. 'Not for me. I'm quite happy to have the hospital midwife, whoever she may be. I'm told that these days newly delivered women are discharged pretty smartly anyway, which will suit me just fine.' Her hand reached out to her cigarettes again, but she didn't light up this time.

'Right, well, that's fine,' Ella said. 'It's just a case of making a choice. We'll be more than happy to look after you, both before and after the birth. By "we" I mean myself and my three colleagues. I'll leave you with our details.' She handed over a printed sheet with a photograph of each midwife at the top and a potted biography underneath. 'You'll soon get to know us, and these...' she passed over more documented details '...are the dates when the antenatal classes are held at The Moorings Centre.'

Carla sighed and took them, laying them down on a small low table. 'My partner, Rodney, will want to attend the parentcraft classes,' she pointed out, just as Ella was about to leave. 'I mean to return to my job as soon as I can after the baby's born. Rod was made redundant at Christmas, and he's anxious to be the one to look after our child. He's unlikely to get another decent post as he's over fifty. *I'm* well paid—' she made this clear '—so my salary will cover us all.'

'Oh, great,' Ella said, smiling back at the self-possessed mother-to-be, who wasn't much older than her. The domestic arrangement she'd outlined was by no means uncommon. Even so, not many fifty-year-old men took on baby care.

'He's looking forward to it,' Carla emphasised, perhaps reading more into Ella's remark, and reaction, than the latter had realized. 'He's far more maternal than I...very caring in every way. He'd have been here today to meet you, but he's taking a friend of ours to London for an appointment at Guy's. And before you ask...' she got to her feet, adjusting her skirt '...we didn't plan this child. It was a shock when it happened, but now that we're getting used to the prospect, we're both very pleased.'

But she'd not spoken with very much conviction, Ella was thinking as she left the flats. Maybe it was the fifty-year-old Rodney who was pleased, as he'd have a role to play. She found herself curious to meet him at one of the parentcraft classes.

Each of her following four visits brought her nearer to home, the final one being to Catherine Dewar who was due any day. At forty weeks, enormous, and feeling the heat, she looked tired and drained, her fair hair hanging round her thin, perspiring face. She was booked for a domino delivery—the kind Carla Lane had disdained. It was her first baby, too, and she was understandably nervous. 'Will it be you with me?' she asked Ella, easing herself onto a chair.

'Well, I'm on call from eight on Wednesday morning till eight next day for imminent births or emergencies, so if you start your pains then, yes.' Ella smiled reassuringly. 'If not, it'll be either Rosa, June or Shirley, but you know us all more or less equally now—one of us will see you through.'

As Catherine was seeing her GP that evening, Ella's call was more of a social one than anything else. She was there to be confided in, to hear any last-minute worries, even to suffer bear-like hugs, for pregnant women near the end of their waiting were inclined to be emotional. She knew that Catherine's husband, Jim, intended to be at the birth, just as Tom had been at Hannah's birth, six whole years ago. She had been a squalling scrap of humanity, weighing exactly three kilograms.

That same scrap, no longer squalling but jumping up and down with excitement, greeted Ella when she drove through Longmead's gates just after six. 'Merlin keeps going through the hedge, Mummy, to play with Lucy. I went to get him, and a lady in an orange dress asked me who I was. She's all thin and pointed. I think she's a witch!'

'She's Patrick's housekeeper,' Kate said, as in the cool of the little room they called the breakfast room she poured them both a drink. 'I went round to apologise about Merlin. Actually, she's very nice. She was making tea for the men who've been beavering in the garden, cutting the grass and shrubs and taking that tatty old shed away.'

'Sounds a hive of industry!'

'It's that all right.' Kate took a long swig at her drink. 'It feels really weird after all this time, having someone next door.'

'I saw him—Patrick—at lunchtime on the seafront, quite by chance. I was having my lunch there,' Ella volunteered, looking down at her glass. 'We chatted a bit...'

'Well, go on, then, you can't stop there!' Kate was all but out of her seat.

'They're giving a party, he and Valerie Trentham, and we're to be invited.'

'When?' Kate's eyes sparkled.

'Some time during the summer, when the house and everything's finished. I don't know why you're so excited, Kate, it's no big deal. I mean, he could hardly *not* ask us, being next door. I dare say the Savers will be asked as well, and there'll be people from the hospital.'

'You may meet someone nice, Ellie.' Kate was quieter now.

'So may you.'

'I'm not looking for anyone. I'm married, aren't I?'

'Yes.' That was all Ella said, going into the kitchen to give Hannah her supper of macaroni cheese beautifully cooked by her aunt.

Later, sitting in the bathroom whilst the little girl had her bath, Ella's thoughts returned to Kate and her marriage state. Why she didn't divorce that philandering husband of hers, she couldn't imagine. So, OK, marriage was for life, but Paul Delaney had no respect for it, or for vows, breaking them time and again, always coming back to Kate, always being sorry, till at last even she had ceased to believe him and had left him to cope on his own.

He hadn't, of course, been on his own for long, but even now—even now after two whole years—Ella knew, she just knew, that Kate fantasised about him turning up at Longmead, all contrition and promises, begging her to come home. The thing was, as she was still in love with him, she might do exactly that, Ella thought worriedly, grabbing a towel as Hannah got out of the bath.

As she dried her daughter, or helped to do so, she was told how one of the dinner ladies had tried to make her choose salad for lunch. 'I told her I didn't like the look of it.' Hannah pulled a disgusted face. 'Only Trudie Green had it, and she's too wet to say no.'

'But you like salad at home, darling.'

'It's not the same.' Hannah's rosy, bath-heated face emerged through the neck of her nightie. 'At home it's not bad, but at school it's yucky, with brown bits on the stalks.'

'Oh, dear,' Ella sympathized as they went through to the bedroom, where Hannah, scrambling under her duvet, asked for the next part of her favourite book to be read aloud to her. She was well able to read herself, but at bedtime she liked the cosy, safe feeling of her mother doing it, sitting on her bed. 'I'm up to the part where he and his friends got into the flying car.'

CHAPTER THREE

AFTER reading to Hannah and having supper with Kate, Ella decided to stretch her legs and take Merlin for a walk. Kate wanted to watch a documentary so, leaving her to it, she set off along the cliff-top with the little dog on his lead. It was too risky to let him off, for the sketchy wire rails, which prevented humankind from falling down the cliff-face, were no barrier to a small dog intent on chasing gulls.

As they neared the part where the cliff sloped down to The Gap, which was the start of Easthaven high street, Ella saw Andrew Savers crossing the road with his Labrador, Beth. Now this, she thought as he spotted her and came up the slope to join her, is plainly my day for meeting men. She also knew she was pleased to see him, pleased to have company. Brown-haired, brown-bearded, looking good in khaki shorts and a brilliant white T-shirt, he was no less pleased to see her.

'Lovely evening,' he greeted her conventionally, bending down to give Merlin a pat.

'Too good for staying indoors.'

'I couldn't agree more. I'm on my way to see my parents—you going into the town?'

Ella was wearing a cool linen dress and her gold hair was fastened on top of her head. She could, he thought, be going anywhere, but as she had the dog...perhaps...

'No, I'm not. I was just about to turn around when I saw you coming,' she said.

'Splendid, then we can walk together.'

She smiled assent and, with the dogs deciding to suffer one another and the sun at their backs casting long shadows, they moved off together.

Ella liked Andrew, what she knew of him—not that that amounted to much. They had only ever met at brief intervals, when she and Tom had been down for weekends, or holidays, at Longmead. She could recall one occasion when, hugely pregnant with Hannah, she'd stumbled and fallen in Easthaven high street. He'd seen her and helped her up, taking her into his surgery till she'd got her breath back again. His parents were nice, too. Only last week they'd said how glad they were she was home for good ''to be with your sister, Ella…lovely for you both.'' Now Andrew was asking her how she was liking living on the coast.

'Well…' Ella strained to be honest. 'I miss the Seftonbridge crowd. Tom and I made a lot of friends there, and I miss our home. It was such a wrench to sell it, like dragging myself up by my roots to be transplanted, not to an unknown place but to one that I'd outgrown. I'm still at the stage when I keep taking little glimpses over my shoulder.'

'Beginnings are tricky,' Andrew observed with a swift glance at Ella's face. 'They're a bit like a climb—until you get a firm hold you're apt to slip back. Longmead must seem strange without your parents.'

'In a way, yes, it does, but if they were still here, with Kate, I don't suppose I would have come,' Ella pointed out with a flicker of impatience, then changed the subject by asking Andrew what sort of day he'd had.

'Oh, action-packed!' He let out his breath in an exaggerated sigh. 'Being single-handed means there's scant time for socialising. Since Dad retired from the practice it's been a constant struggle. He still takes the occasional clinic, and I have cover for some weekends, but I need a full-time assistant, with a view to him, or her, coming in as a partner in time. I want to talk to Dad about it this evening, discuss what will be entailed.'

'There are so many more people living down here now it's a popular retirement area,' Ella remarked, leashing Merlin in to let a man with a Dobermann pass.

'That's true, and retired people are apt to go in for pets—not that I'm complaining, far from it,' Andrew was quick to add. 'Even so, I don't want to be wedded to my job.'

They had reached the part of the cliff where it was time to descend to the road and begin the walk to the three houses standing on their hill. They had all but reached them when Patrick's cream car passed, tooting its horn. Andrew waved energetically, Ella lifted her arm. 'There goes another workaholic…just finished his day. You're lucky to have him as your other neighbour, Ella.'

'I met him at the weekend. He came over with his little boy.' Ella was watching the vehicle's sleek chassis disappearing into Drummers's drive.

'I play squash with him—that is, when we can both make the time. He's a ferocious player. I've not beaten him yet, but still live in hopes.'

'And squash is the absolute ultimate in energetic sports,' Ella said thoughtfully, looking at her watch. It was nearly nine o'clock.

She was about to take her leave of Andrew when Kate hailed them from Longmead's front garden and came out to speak to him. She knew him rather better than Ella did, having been in the area longer. She thought him attractive and 'dead reliable—a bit like,' she'd once remarked to her parents, 'a tad like Ella's Tom'. She was smiling at him now and he at her, he saying that seeing the two sisters together had given him an idea. 'I've been given two tickets for *Marriner's Folly* for this coming Friday. I wonder if you two would like to have them. Melinda Harrison is playing the lead, and I'm told it's very good.'

Ella's face lit up. She loved the theatre, and the reviews of *Marriner's Folly* on its trial run to the West End had very nearly fired her to try for tickets, but somewhere along the line, as was often the case these days, her enthusiasm had waned, and nothing had been done.

But now...now here was a chance handed out on a plate.

She was just about to voice her thanks and accept when Kate cut in, 'Oh, dear, sorry, Andrew, but no can do. Ellie and I can't go out together unless we can get a sitter for Hannah, and Friday is too short notice to get anyone reliable.'

Ella gasped, very nearly audibly, for Kate was talking nonsense. Getting a sitter for Hannah simply wasn't a problem. Either Rosa or Shirley—her colleague midwives—would undertake that chore. They had children themselves, plus husbands, and they had told Ella when she'd first joined the group that they would always help out. Kate knew this, and knew it well, so what was she playing at? Ella was soon to find out, for her sister was still in conversational spate.

'But there's no reason why Ellie shouldn't go.' She was talking directly to Andrew. 'And if you haven't seen the play, why don't you go together? I mean, it seems such a pity—' She broke off as the phone rang inside the house. 'Oh, sorry, sorry, but I'll have to answer it, I'm expecting a call!'

In the aftermath of her departure Ella turned a flushed

face to Andrew. 'I don't know what Kate was thinking about, Andrew. I feel really embarrassed!'

'There's no need to be, believe me, there isn't. You see, I'd like us to go together,' he was quick to say, and Ella felt cross.

'You've been dragooned into saying that!'

'Absolute nonsense!' His tone was firm, and she looked at him in surprise. 'I don't allow myself to be manipulated unless I like where it takes me. As a matter of fact, when I was handed the tickets you came into my mind. I wanted to ask you, but my courage failed me. I felt it might be too soon. Then, seeing Kate gave me tonight's idea—that you might like to go together. I confess I'd forgotten the problem of Hannah.'

Unwilling to expose Kate's excuse for the white lie it was, Ella said how good she was with Hannah. 'She pretends not to like children much, but in her heart she does.'

'I'm sure she does.' Andrew was looking at Ella, all thoughts of Kate having fled. 'So, do we go together, having an evening out? I can get Dad to take any out-of-clinic calls, so if you're not on late duty…'

'I'm not and, thanks, Andrew, I'd like to come.' Ella was doing her best to sound pleased and enthusiastic. Oh, how *could* Kate have landed her with this?

Andrew smiled, making his beard move outwards. His teeth were the kind she liked. Being a dentist's daughter, she always noticed teeth, and now she was noticing *him*. She was remembering how he'd been when she'd come to Easthaven just after Tom had died. He'd been really nice in an unmawkish way, and sweet with Hannah, taking her to the surgery to see a litter of puppies, bringing her back in his car. He'd been going out with his receptionist then, not Miss Remer, but a rather uppish and snooty kind of girl with glossy hair and glasses. Mr Savers, who had still been in the practice then, had said she was a cool customer, whatever that might mean. So really she had known Andrew on and off for years. It would be like going out with a friend.

Even so, she told Kate off when, a few minutes later, she went into the house. 'Don't you *ever*,' she said, running her to ground in the kitchen, 'do anything... anything remotely like that to me, ever again.'

'Oh, come on, Ellie, wise up...as they say! Those tickets were never given to Andrew. I bet you any money you like that he bought them with the idea of taking you out—all my vibes tell me so!' Kate practically bounced her words out, astonishing Ella yet again.

'I think your vibes are way off track.' Her voice shook a little. 'If he bought the tickets—and I do say "if"— why didn't he just invite me along? Why go all the way round the houses, offering them to us?'

'Oh, I don't know, don't ask me how the male mind works! I expect he had an attack of cold feet, or something of that kind. He's a lovely man, I've always thought so, but he thinks things over a lot. Anyway, are you going with him? Don't tell me that after all that, you've turned the poor chap down!'

'No, I haven't. I'm going.' Ella helped herself to an apple from the dresser.

'Jumping catfish, then it's all been worth it!' Kate flopped down onto a chair. 'It's time you started going out with someone other than me.' Swivelling round, she treated Ella to one of her all-seeing looks. 'You won't suddenly backpedal and decide you're on duty, I hope?'

'I shan't let him down, if that's what you mean. My on-call duty is from eight a.m. Wednesday through to breakfast-time the next day, and I'm not on late duty till the following week.'

'Great! No holds barred, then!' Kate grinned, watching her sister's long slender back disappearing up the stairs.

Ella's first telephone call on Wednesday came through at precisely eight, the voice at the other end sounding excited and alarmed.

'Oh, Ella, it's Polly Spender, I think I've started! I've been having pains every ten minutes since half past five. My waters haven't broken, but do you think I ought to ring the hospital?'

It was a first baby and not due for another fortnight, Ella remembered. 'Are the pains getting worse each time they come?' she questioned carefully.

'No, I don't think so.' Polly sounded uncertain. 'But they're very uncomfortable.'

'This could be a false alarm, Polly—our old friend Braxton-Hicks. I'll come along now, though, then we'll see how you're doing.'

'You won't be long, will you?'

'No, I'm setting off now. Make yourself a cup of tea, and I'll be with you before you've drunk it!'

Polly, who lived half a mile away, was married to an army corporal stationed in Northern Ireland. She was thirty-eight weeks gone, and ideally she needed to have someone living with her during this anxious time. Usually a relative or friend helped out, but in Polly's case there appeared to be no one. At least, Ella thought, she knows she's got us at the end of the phone, and surely her husband will get leave once the baby is born.

Deciding whether Polly was in true labour or not didn't prove difficult. Internal examination showed no dilatation, and during the half-hour Ella spent at the house her pains eased and tailed off.

'I'm so sorry, Ella, I'm so *sorry*, but I really did think…' She was apologetic, very embarrassed and perhaps just a little relieved.

'You've nothing to be sorry for.' Ella was repacking her bag. 'False alarms, at the stage you're at, are almost the norm. Now, ring if you're worried, don't let this put you off doing so. I'm on call until breakfast-time tomorrow, and if I'm engaged with someone else when you ring, either June or Shirley will come.'

Even as she spoke her mobile rang. After reassuring Polly yet again, she drove off to see Catherine Dewar—the girl who'd been feeling the heat so badly on Monday afternoon. Catherine's husband, Jim, answered the door. 'She's well advanced,' he said. 'Wouldn't let me ring before…wanted it to be you who'd come.'

Catherine was walking about in the bedroom, wearing a loose shirt. She greeted Ella with a grin which changed to a grimace as a powerful contraction took hold. When it had passed, Ella palpated her abdomen and listened to the foetal heart—not an easy exercise as the baby was pitched for birth.

'Everything is exactly as it should be,' she said, 'but it'll be some time yet before you're ready to go to hospital, so the three of us will be keeping one another company for a time!'

'Me, I'm poor company.' Catherine heaved herself off the bed.

'You're the star turn.' Ella was watching how she coped with another contraction. Once it had eased she suggested that they all go downstairs, where there would be more room for Catherine to walk about if she chose.

She did choose. She prowled constantly, sometimes

on all fours, much to Jim's distress, till Ella assured him that it was perfectly normal. Some two hours later she said she wanted to lie in a warm bath, and this, too, was applauded by Ella. 'It'll help you relax and the water will be soothing.' She ran the bath for Catherine, Jim helped her in and sat with her, topping up the water occasionally, which gave him something to do.

At one point Catherine said she wished she could stay where she was and have the baby at home, not have to be transferred. Ella, however, assured her that it really wouldn't be all that different in hospital. 'Not with Jim and I there to look after you…it won't be so different from here.'

But it *was* different for institutions could never be quite like home. Yet the delivery room into which they were shown just before one p.m. was well equipped, light and airy, and had a birthing chair in addition to the bed. Best of all, it had a door that shut, and *stayed* shut. Often enough in the past Ella had had experience of delivery rooms resembling railway stations, with various members of staff popping in to get something out of a cupboard or fetch something they'd forgotten. There was nothing of this at the Regent. Apart from the muted sounds of hospital life going on in the corridor, they had privacy and quiet, and Catherine had space in which to move around.

Between checking her at regular intervals and monitoring the foetus, Ella carried on with writing up her notes. At first Catherine wanted to be talked to, but after a while she reached the stage when she needed to sink deep into herself and have no distractions at all. Jim had been massaging her lower back, but soon she didn't want to be touched. Nearing the end of the first stage and asking for pain relief, she began gulping in gas and air until finally at four o'clock she was overwhelmed with an urge to push, and forty minutes later her son, James William, made his way into the world.

'He's *gorgeous*!' Cutting the cord, Ella handed him up to his parents, looking a mess, as newborns did, screwing up his face in a scowl. They thought he was beautiful, of course. He weighed all of eight pounds, and when washed and dressed, but still yelling his head off, he undoubtedly had a look of his dad.

Whilst Catherine rested in a small room leading off the ward corridor, Ella cleared up in the delivery room, completed her documentation, rang The Moorings Surgery to let Catherine's doctor know about the birth, then, at the invitation of one of the staff midwives, went with her up to the canteen for tea and a bun.

'Was it your first domino?' May asked, passing her the sugar.

'My first one here.' Ella was parched and the tea went down in gulps. 'I've only,' she added, 'been here six weeks.'

May's brows shot up. 'Oh, well, then, you won't have met Patrick Weston, our consultant. He's an absolute dish, knows how to make a woman feel good about herself—much needed on Gynae where the patients, poor dears, often feel depressed. As for the obstetric side, he's not Caesarean-prone, as some surgeons are. He delivered twins by the vaginal route last week, and the second one was breech. The encouragement and strength he gave to the mother was something I'll never forget.'

'He lives next door to me,' Ella said mildly, buttering her bun.

'Next door...does he?' Once again May's brows were in the ascendant.

'He moved in last weekend.'

'You must live in a very large house.'

'Meaning *he* couldn't live in less than a mansion?' Ella had to laugh.

'Well, no, but...'

'Actually, we do live in a large house. My sister and I share it. I have a little girl.' Briefly she explained the details to May, who took them in, open-mouthed. The two young women warmed to one another as they chatted on. May was off duty and Ella appreciated being taken under her wing when Ella could have been on her way home. Presently, though, Ella looked at her watch and said she ought to be going. 'I think Sister would like me and my entourage out by seven.'

Catherine was awake when Ella went down, and was anxious to get home. Jim, who had been telephoning the good news round to relatives and friends, fetched a wheelchair from the end of the corridor and wheeled his wife to the lifts. Ella followed, carrying the baby, now fast asleep.

Once back at the house, Catherine was settled into bed, James junior in his crib at her side. 'Now if he wakes you in the night, which he assuredly will...' Ella smiled '...don't be nervous of handling him. Feed him on demand at this stage. He likes your milk, he's already demonstrated that, and with Jim to help you on the nappy front, you'll manage beautifully. Now, I've been in touch with Shirley and she'll be here at breakfast-time, then it'll be me again in the evening. No, don't come down with me, Jim, I can let myself out. After today I know these stairs quite well!'

Ella was bushed, too, and starving when she got home half an hour later. After greeting Kate, who was watching television, she went straight upstairs to check on Hannah, finding her fast asleep, flat on her back, arms

flung up on either side of her head. She looked innocent
and angelic, although the latter wasn't always apparent
during waking hours. 'My little horror,' she murmured.
'The best little horror in the world!'

Ella had rung Kate earlier, so supper had been kept
back. The lamb casserole and dumplings might have
been winter fare, but they tasted ambrosial to a famished
midwife who'd been existing on snacks all day. 'Well,
there's one thing—I'll be at full strength again if I get
a call in the small hours!' She laughed, reaching for a
hefty banana, just to round the meal off.

At twilight she went into the garden to close the
greenhouse vents. On her way there, walking along by
the boundary hedge, she halted by the thin part and
peered into Drummers's garden. The house and its lights
were far enough back for her to be reasonably sure that
neither Patrick nor his housekeeper would spot her doing
her little snoop. In the dusk which was gathering more
quickly by the minute, she could just make out scythed
grass looking pale and stubbly, the outline of a lopped
tree and a patch of scoured earth where the old shed had
been. The summerhouse, or gazebo, was still in place,
but it looked pretty shoddy. She strained to get a better
view of the shrubs, becoming so absorbed that she didn't
hear the rustle of a walker on the other side of the hedge
till she found her view blocked by Drummers's new
owner, barely a handsbreadth away.

'Good evening, Mrs Fairfax!' He sounded amused,
but there was a question, too, in his voice.

All but startled speechless, she explained herself, ig-
noring his greeting. 'You've caught me having a snoop!'
She laughed and moved back, but her belt caught on a
twig.

'Here…let me!' He freed her easily, then held the

hedge apart. 'If you're interested, why not come through and have a proper look round?'

She demurred at once. 'It's getting dark!'

'There's light enough to see!' The amusement was back in Patrick's voice. Perhaps he liked catching people out. 'If you're coming,' he continued, 'hurry up, or I'll ruin the hedge for ever, manhandling it like this.'

'Sorry!' She stepped through, misjudging the distance and almost landing on top of his feet. 'I feel,' she said jerkily, breathless again, 'incredibly foolish.'

'Oh, don't worry, it'll pass.' He helped her over the border on to the grass. 'I saw you,' he explained, 'from Robin's window. Barbara is out tonight, so I'm in charge. I came down for a chat, not to catch you out. I felt like company.'

'That makes me feel a little less guilty.' Ella wished he'd kept hold of her arm. He walked close beside her, but there was space between them. He warned her to watch her step.

'The terrain is dangerous!' He infused a little high drama into his voice.

'No concealed wells, I trust!' She matched her mood to his.

'If there were I think the gardeners and builders would have fallen down them by now!'

They began to tour the whole of the garden, starting from the top end, where streamers of light spilling out from the house showed up the cleared flower borders and edges of the lawn. They passed through an arch into the herb garden, the mingled scent of trampled lavender and rosemary making Ella exclaim and sniff it in appreciatively. 'Good for a sound night's sleep,' she said.

'Herbs are big business these days—alternative medicine and all that…' Patrick said, laughing at Ella as she sniffed again, declaring that she could smell mint. 'You can. I don't think Valerie made a very thorough search last weekend.'

'Is she keen on gardening?' Ella felt she ought to try to keep her in their conversation.

'She is, and doesn't mind dirtying her hands. Val is a good all-rounder. She won't be coming down this weekend, though, not until Sunday morning. Her mother, my late wife's aunt, is ill, and Valerie's driving to Ackminster to see her and staying over.'

'A long drive.'

'I don't think she minds,' he said absently. His voice sharpened and he shouted a warning as a deepish trench loomed up.

'I can see it,' Ella retorted, jumping it easily. 'I have cat's eyes. Most midwives have—it's one of their attributes!'

He chuckled. She heard him out of the darkness, for now it really *was* getting dark. By the time they reached the down-at-heel summerhouse, which he seemed determined to show her, she could only see it in derelict outline. 'What a mess!' was all she said.

'It won't be when I've done with it.' He lifted the door away, and they peered inside, breathing in mouldy damp, looking up at the drooping roof. 'The base is all right, solid cement—uncracked, unworn. The rest will have to be taken away, but on the base, emerging like a phoenix from the ashes, will be a log cabin type of gazebo for Rob to use as a den. It'll be his own place to do as he likes in. Boys love dens, or hideaways, or whatever they call them. Don't you think it's a good idea?'

Ella nodded, catching his enthusiasm. Already she could see, in her mind's eye, the little rustic building that was to be Robin's own domain. 'I think it's a brilliant idea,' she said simply.

'He can have other kids in, if he likes. It'll give him something to boast about, he needs to feel special. Rob's happiness nosedived when his mother was killed. He's recovering—*has* recovered—but he's not the boy he was.' Ella watched him lift the door back in place and wedge it with a brick. She had moved back a little to give him room, but they were still fairly close as Patrick straightened and turned, his voice coming softly out of the darkness. 'We have single parentage in common, don't we? A small, very important person to keep happy and safe.'

'I know.' Her voice shook with emotion, for he'd mirrored her own thoughts about Hannah. A kind of empathy flowed between them, and it seemed entirely natural for him to reach out and take her into his arms, not crushingly, not passionately close, but close enough for her to savour his nearness and maleness, feel his breathing warmth.

It had its effect. Her body awoke and she was fighting a different emotion now, one that was making her long to slide her arms around his back and hold him tightly against her, lay her head on his chest. But common sense, although running out fast, hadn't quite deserted her. 'We love our kids, Patrick, they're all that matters,' she said, drawing away from him. 'And now I must go, or Kate will think I've fallen down that mythical well!'

He still had her hands, and held them fast, but as she tugged he let them go. 'Which exit—hedge or gate?' She heard the rasp in his voice.

'I think gate, as we're practically on top of it.'

'Right, then, out you go.' He opened it for her, and she passed into the lane that gave access to the three houses, but there was no sound of the gate closing. Without turning round, she knew that the way was still open for her to walk back into his arms. She wanted to do so…really she *wanted* to do so…but by not turning her head she managed to keep her feet moving forward, give him a backwards wave, even call out goodnight in a jaunty way, and reach her own garden gate.

CHAPTER FOUR

ELLA slept in snatches only that night, and not because she was still on call. The scene in Drummers's garden kept replaying itself in her mind. Patrick should have had the sense to keep his distance, she seethed, wanting to cast blame. If he had I wouldn't have reacted as I did, giving the game away. He knew how I was feeling, he knew I wanted him…as he did me, just for a fraught second or two. He had no business to behave like that…he had no right! He was hardly being very fair, was he? What about Valerie? Ella jerked and kicked out under the duvet. There she was, casting blame again.

I'd been wanting him to touch me, she admitted to herself, the second I set foot through that hedge. It's called sexual attraction and no one, but no one, should underestimate its power. Bodily needs, as she knew full well, didn't lie down and never come up again when one's nearest and dearest died. Oh, they might for a time, *had* done for a time so far as she was concerned, but she was passionate, and loving, her nature was warm. And exactly two years after Tom's passing she'd had an affair. It had brought what she could only describe as thin happiness. It had brought bodily relief, but little else, and had lasted only weeks.

Afterwards, appalled at herself, she had declared never again, not unless she loved the man in question, not unless he loved her and was free to do so. She wanted nothing underhand. She liked Patrick, she reasoned, but not all that much. He was just an attractive

55

man who was engaged to be married, which put him out of bounds.

By breakfast-time, the end of her on-call shift, Ella was up and dressed, feeling better, ready to take Hannah to school. This could only ever happen when she was on late duty, which didn't begin until one. 'We'll walk there,' she told the child. 'We've got plenty of time.'

'And take Merlin?' Hannah scraped the last soggy cornflake out of her dish.

'Yes, and take Merlin. Now, go and brush your teeth.' Ella watched her run upstairs.

Kate, who didn't start work until half nine, was putting the breakfast things into the sink. 'Leave those, I'll do them when I get back,' Ella told her, hooking an ecstatic Merlin onto his lead.

Shortly afterwards goodbyes were said, and she and Hannah set off, not along the cliff but farther up the hill, turning left through the network of crescents and avenues and closes that made up the main route to the local primary school.

They walked amid hubbub and noise and clamour, for schooltime meant just that. Cars passed them, loaded with children, pedestrian mums plodded along with their offspring, some pushing buggies with pre-school toddlers strapped in securely. There were one or two babies in arms, some carried in slings. Lunchboxes, clean socks and clean faces were all part of the scene. At the school gates and all along the railings the crowd was six deep in chattering mothers all watching their offspring line up in the playground, waiting for whistle-blow-time.

Arriving there with five minutes to spare, Hannah spotted Robin being decanted from a blue Renault by a woman in a shirtwaister dress. 'There's Robin with Barbara,' she shouted, pushing her way towards them before Ella could tell her off for using the housekeeper's first name. Maybe I should introduce myself, she thought, so, dragging Merlin away from the ravaging nose of a springer spaniel, she edged her way to the kerb.

Barbara was bending down, tying up Robin's laces, so Ella addressed the back of her head as she shouted above the din, 'I don't think we've met. I'm Ella Fairfax from Longmead, next door.'

As she rose to her feet Ella saw how tall she was—angular too, with jutting bones—but witchlike she was not. How on earth had her inventive child likened her to that?

'No, we haven't met.' She looked directly at Ella from under a fringe of salt-and-pepper hair. 'I'm Barbara Manders,' she supplied, her eyes on Robin as he and Hannah raced into the playground to join their peers.

When the whistle had been piercingly blown, and they were all safely in, Miss Manders, seeing Ella about to walk on, offered her a lift. 'Presumably we're going in the same direction?' She half turned towards her car.

Ella hesitated. She would rather have walked, but on the other hand it seemed churlish to turn down the offer. Also, and she was a little ashamed of this, she might learn a little more about the ménage nextdoor.

'Thanks,' she said, 'a lift would be great—that is, if you can put up with Merlin in the car.'

'If you keep him on your lap I don't mind at all,' Barbara said briskly, and smilingly held open the passenger door.

Wondering if their talk would be sticky, Ella was pleasantly surprised. Initially they talked about the children, Barbara commenting on what a robust child Hannah was. 'An outgoing type, I would imagine, the reverse of little Robin. Of course…' she broke off to negotiate an enormous refuse truck '…losing his mother at five years old didn't help.'

'I'm sure not.'

'Are you a widow?'

'Yes, of three years standing. I'm also a midwife,' Ella said stiltedly, bracketing the two states without in the least meaning to.

'I was in nursing all my life.' Barbara threw her a lightning glance. 'That's how I met Mr Weston and his wife. I was a theatre sister before I retired. When Mrs Weston was killed he came to see me, and I've worked for him ever since.'

'It must have been a relief to him to get someone caring—someone he knew,' Ella said carefully, wondering why this rather proud woman should feel the need to explain herself.

'I just happened to be free.' Barbara Manders cornered sharply, making Merlin tip onto the floor. 'Miss Trentham—now Mr Weston's fiancé—was a splendid back-up help. She's very like the late Mrs Weston in looks—being cousins, I suppose that's not surprising.'

'No, I suppose not.' Ella digested this then, in the silence that elapsed, took to wondering whether Miss Manders's services would be required once Patrick and Valerie were wed. They might only need a daily cleaner then, and somehow or other she couldn't quite fit the professional Barbara into that worthwhile but lowly niche.

Coming out of her reverie, she saw that they were home and it was time to get out. Over in Drummers's garden the men were already at work. The whine of a chainsaw split the air, and a bonfire had been lit, its smoke spiraling joyously upwards, its flames cracking like whips.

'Yes, and before I know it they'll be wanting what they call their "brew",' Barbara Manders said, but she looked decidedly cheerful at the prospect.

Ella wondered, as she entered her own driveway, if Barbara might be lonely. She was on her own all day till school was out, and Easthaven—even Charding—was a far cry from London. Being retired didn't necessarily mean one wanted a quiet life—sometimes, at least in the beginning, the reverse was the case.

During the four hours before she was officially on duty Ella tackled her own and Hannah's washing, cleaned their two bedrooms, ate a pitta-bread sandwich filled with cheese and got into her uniform. She had a parentcraft meeting that afternoon down at the health centre. She'd got out a brief agenda for it, and flipped through it before she set off. ''Introduce any new-comers...ask about worst fears...discuss analgesia... take them through breathing and meditation proces-ses...home with baby...lactation...how to cope with broken nights.''

The value of parentcraft meetings, as Ella well knew, differed from the monthly antenatal clinics in that they provided more opportunity for the women to get to know one another, to discuss with the midwife every aspect of giving birth and to learn the craft of parenting, not to mention how to prepare for and cope with the vast change in lifestyle that having a baby brought about.

Twelve mothers-to-be came very soon after Ella arrived. It was a good number for integrating as a group. Ella made sure they all knew one another, and started off with a relaxation and meditation session that some of the mothers would be familiar with from antenatal classes. When they were all arranged in two neat rows, she asked them to think about their babies.

'Each of you imagine what life must be like for him cuddled up inside you, not knowing what it is like to be separate from you, but able to hear your heart beating and the sound of your voice when you speak. Remember, too, that when he's pushed out on the traumatic day of his birth, he'll recognize your voice...he'll know you're his mum.'

Silence reigned for a minute or two, broken only by sounds infiltrating from the street and the tapping of the blind against a window. Finally Ella suggested that they all move to the chairs which were arranged in a group. She invited questions and they very soon came, the first from a woman in her third trimester who wanted to know if labour and giving birth was as painful as shown on TV.

'You see women yelling their heads off...is it really as bad as that, and if it is why can't more be done to relieve it, for goodness' sake?'

This prompted a discussion on analgesia, which Ella led. 'And remember,' she told them, 'that everyone's pain is different. And making a noise sometimes helps.'

'Are stitches inevitable?' another girl asked. 'I've never met anyone yet who hasn't had them.'

Ella assured her that not everyone had to have them.

A question on episiotomy followed, together with several on how they would look ''down there'' after the birth, and how soon intercourse could be resumed, and would it be all right?

By the time they were onto breastfeeding, and bathing, and getting enough rest, it was time for tea, and high time for most of the women to visit the loo. 'Let no one tell me that having a kid is romantic!' one woman said, joining Ella in the small kitchen and offering to carry the tray. 'I've got a shelf to rest it on, you haven't!' she said wryly, when Ella protested.

After the meeting—probably feeling more exhausted than the mothers-to-be—she drove to the hospital to visit three mothers who'd recently given birth. After that she had five home visits, all postnatal ones, the last being to her domino delivery of the evening before.

It was just after eight when she got to their house in Clement Road. Baby James had been put down and was fast asleep, looking pink and composed. Catherine was in bed with Jim lying beside her, fully clothed.

'We thought we'd get what rest we could,' he said, 'before James wakes again. He does more crying than anything else—do you think that's right?'

'I don't think there's anything wrong, if that's what you mean,' Ella said. 'Babies do cry a lot, it's the only way they've got of complaining and getting what they want. James is missing the cosiness of being tucked up inside his mum, of having food on tap through his umbilicus, of being cuddled all the time. He's not used to the real world yet, but he'll adjust and so will you.'

She read Catherine's notes, which Shirley had left at the house at breakfast-time, took her temperature and blood pressure, checked that the discharge of lochia was normal. Yes, Catherine was fine, and her weariness was normal. Even so, Ella was glad to learn that her mother would be arriving next day for a two-week stay.

'She'll see to the cooking and shopping and Jim will see to the house, leaving me free to devote myself entirely to James. I may even…' Catherine spoke through a yawn '…have time to wash my hair.'

Ella had time to wash and blow-dry hers when she got home at teatime on Friday—the day of her theatre date. At least, Kate kept calling it a date—Ella insisted otherwise. 'It's an outing with a friend,' she corrected, slipping on a cotton wrapper whilst she sat in the kitchen with Hannah, who was eating a boiled egg.

'I expect Mr Savers would like me to come, too,' she said hopefully, her wide blue eyes engaging her mother's.

'Oh, no, he wouldn't,' Kate answered for Ella. 'This is a special evening for your mother, so hurry up and finish your supper, then she can go and get dressed.'

It was a coolish, windy evening, and a little rain was falling when Andrew's green estate car turned into the driveway at seven. Ella, in a floral silk and organza dress, buttercup hair twisted on top of her head, came down the stairs on high heels, a light jacket over her arm. Andrew, with an umbrella already unfurled, was standing in the porch, an unfamiliar figure in a suit that was a shade too tight for him.

'My, we *are* smart!' Ella teased as he helped her into the car. 'I'm used to the man in the white coat!'

'Which suits me better, I think,' he answered agreeably, getting in on his side. 'And while we're on the subject of appearances, you look fantastic. I'm a proud man tonight.'

It was an old-fashioned compliment and he meant it, his lingering glance told her that. 'The vet and the midwife set off for the evening!' she jested, trying to keep things light. She wanted nothing but friendship with Andrew. He simply wasn't her type in any other sense, good-looking though he was.

Fifteen minutes or so later, when they were shown into their front row circle seats, she turned to him with a small gasp. 'That client of yours must have been megagrateful to hand over tickets like these!'

'Not so much grateful as too lazy to hand them back

to the box office. He bought them for himself and his wife, then his elderly father was taken ill and they had to go rushing up north.'

So much for Kate's conviction that Andrew himself had bought the tickets with the intention of taking me out, Ella thought with wry amusement. So much for Kate's vibes! 'Parents,' she said, 'are a grave responsibility.' For some reason, at that point Valerie popped into her mind—the mint-acquiring, dark-haired one, motoring to Wiltshire this evening to visit *her* sickly mum.

'I'd be lost without mine,' Andrew said quietly, just as the curtain went up.

The play was as good as the first-night critics had said. Melinda Harrison gave the performance of her life. There was applause and a collective buzz of approval when the curtain fell at the interval. Neither Ella nor Andrew wanted to leave their seats and join the scrum in the bar. Instead they were content to sit and talk, and occasionally look over the balcony ledge into the auditorium below.

Ella was interested in what the women were wearing. Most people in the front stalls were in evening dress. One woman especially caught her eye. She was wearing a scarlet dress with an immense rose—probably made of the same material—perched on the top of her head. The man with her was very attentive—in fact, he was all over her. How embarrassing in a theatre *and* in the front stalls. I would loathe it, Ella thought, just as the footlights flicked up to full strength, just as the curtain rose, just as she saw with a shock that the woman was *Valerie Trentham*!

She sat back in her seat, shaking her head when Andrew asked, 'Seen someone you know?'

For one thing, she couldn't explain, because the play

was in full swing again. And for another, she felt she
could have been mistaken, *had* to have been mistaken,
for according to what Patrick had told her on Wednesday
night Valerie was bound for the West Country right now,
not sitting in the Arts Theatre, Charding, being pawed
by a man with long arms.

When the play ended the cast were called back to the
stage no less than five times. Some people stood up to
applaud them. Ella and Andrew did, so did Valerie and
her escort, for, yes, it *was* her. She had turned her head
to her companion and in the full glare of the lights there
was no mistaking those small even features, that tumble
of dark hair and tight, slight little figure outlined in the
scarlet dress.

Ella mentioned nothing to Andrew as they drove
home. She didn't quite know why, but for some reason
she felt it was best to keep quiet. She told Kate, though,
for after all, Kate was her twin. She was just about bursting to tell someone and it all came out in a rush.

'Are you *sure*!' Kate's eyes were round.

'Yes, absolutely sure.'

'And you say Patrick told you she was going to
Wiltshire? You didn't mention that before.'

'He told me when I saw him out in the garden the
other evening,' Ella explained, but she felt caught out,
and her colour rose, which wasn't missed by Kate.

'Well, it could be something and nothing, couldn't it?
The bloke could have been anyone—a client, probably—
and her poorly mum could have got better suddenly, so
she didn't have to go. Quite possibly, any minute
now…' Kate drew down the kitchen blind '…her car
will be arriving next door.'

'Mmm,' Ella said doubtfully, eating the sandwiches
her sister had made her. Kate had been shocked to learn

that Andrew hadn't taken her out to supper after the theatre. Ella had explained that it had been late and she'd wanted to get home, but now her sister wanted a blow-by-blow account of the evening.

'Are you seeing him again? Did he kiss you good-night?' she probed.

'I'm meeting him on the beach tomorrow afternoon, taking Hannah, and you're invited, too. I hope you'll come. It'll make it more fun, we can swim and everything.'

'Yeah, all right, I'll think about it.' Kate looked pleased. 'But you still haven't told me if he kissed you goodnight!'

'Yes, he did, if you *must* know!' Ella laughed.

'And?'

'If by that you mean, what variety of kiss—closed, no tongues!'

'A true gentleman!' Kate grinned, dodging the cushion Ella threw at her.

The beach outing next afternoon was a great success. They all enjoyed it, especially Hannah who, thrilled to be piggybacked out beyond the breakers by Andrew, swam with a good deal of splashing from him to Ella and back again, lengthening the distance each time. Hannah wasn't very proficient as yet, but determination got her through. 'We'll have you swimming the Channel in no time,' Andrew teased, and the little girl adored it *and* him, making no secret of the fact.

'Men are nice, aren't they, Mummy?' she said that night, when Ella was getting her ready for bed.

'*Some* men,' Ella qualified.

'Oh, I know all about the nasty ones, who give little girls sweets, but nice men are nice.'

'Yes, of course they are, poppet,' Ella agreed, watching her hop into bed.

'She wants a male figure in her life, the kid wants a dad,' Kate said bluntly when Ella relayed all this at suppertime. 'You could do worse than set your cap at Andrew, it wouldn't take much. He's not dead romantic, but he's the faithful type—anyone can see that.'

'For someone who was so anxious for me to come and live with you down here, you seem very anxious to push me out,' Ella said, a trifle tartly. 'What's it all about?'

'I'm not anxious to get rid of you.' Kate looked shocked. 'I'd be upset if you went, but I don't suppose we'll be living here together for ever. You're bound to remarry, or get the chance to. You attract men, you know you do. And as for me—' Kate's back was to Ella as she opened the fridge door '—one day Paul might want me back again.'

'I can't believe I'm hearing this,' it was Ella's turn for shock. 'You *can't*,' she went on, 'want him back after the way he's gone on!'

'When I left him,' Kate went on as though her sister had never spoken, 'I felt I hated him…I *did* hate him…I never wanted to see him again. Now, after two years, I know I still care for him.'

'Oh, Kate, I wish you didn't!' Ella had never liked Paul Delaney.

'Well, I'm not going to divorce him!' Kate said vehemently, and Ella wisely said no more.

It was just after midday next day, Sunday, when they heard Valerie arriving at Drummers. They were sitting in the sideway to catch the breeze, so they saw her car slide into the drive.

Robin was calling out to his father, 'Valerie's here

again, Daddy!' He sounded, Ella thought, not especially pleased, even disconsolate. Maybe he had been enjoying having his father to himself.

Kate, who'd been reading the *Telegraph*, peered round it at Ella. 'So, the prodigal's come home to roost.' She grinned. 'But from where we do not know!'

CHAPTER FIVE

OVER the following three weeks, almost certainly due to Robin's den being up and running, Hannah stopped referring to him as "that boy" and became more friendly towards him. Kate and Barbara also gravitated towards each other, taking it in turns to do the school run, swapping recipes. Often, when Ella got home in the evening, she would find Kate and Barbara having tea on the patio whilst the children played in whichever garden was the favourite for that day.

There were signs and sounds of Patrick, of course, mostly at weekends, in the garden with Robin or Valerie, sometimes with both. Ella hadn't seen him to speak to, though, since the evening he'd invited her through into the garden and she'd felt so close to him.

As for Andrew and herself, they had been out together several times. To the County Agricultural Show at Bewlis which was always held in July, to the beach, sometimes taking Hannah, sometimes on their own. And once they'd donned boots and walked on the Downs, breathing in the scent of salty air flavoured with grass and thyme.

All this should have added up to romance, but it didn't, not for Ella. She liked Andrew, really liked him, and looked forward to their outings, but she didn't want things to change between them. She wanted them to stay as they were, which she knew wasn't fair, not to Andrew who was beginning to want more. His embraces, although restrained, told a story of their own.

I ought to stop seeing him, she thought. He thinks I'm holding back now because I need time to adjust after Tom, and that really isn't—she brought Patrick to mind—the case at all. I'm as bad as Hannah, wanting what I can't have.

Things were going well for her at work—in fact, couldn't have been better. She was well liked by all her pregnant mums, even asked for especially, which she felt augured well for the time when she would be practising independently. She had so far, since coming to Sussex, not run into any special crises, until one Sunday at tea-time, finishing her shift after a weekend on duty and driving back to base, her mobile rang. It was Polly Spender, the young woman who was married to a corporal stationed in Northern Ireland.

'Oh, Ella…' Polly sounded scared. 'My waters have broken, so it must be the real thing this time! Shall I ring the hospital and go in now, or do you think it's too soon?'

Ella pulled onto the verge and stopped the car, the better to talk to her, asking how long since it had happened and whether she was having contractions. She knew Polly was booked in for a hospital delivery, but to go in now, especially as Polly told her she wasn't having painful contractions, was plainly premature. Waiting for hours in an antenatal ward, hearing other women in extremes of labour, hearing babies crying in the distance and longing for your own labour to get going, would have been an unnecessary ordeal, and not one that she wanted Polly to go through. On the other hand, the girl was alone… Making up her mind, she told her she would be with her in a matter of minutes. 'I'm on my way home so I'm practically passing your door,' she said.

Arriving at the house in Ralston Road, she found

Polly in the sitting-room, looking out for her. 'Will everything soon start properly?' she asked, almost before Ella had got in the door.

'I don't know, but I'll take a look at you and see how things are faring.' She smiled.

Polly lay on the couch whilst Ella opened her bag and got out her surgical gloves. Kneeling on the floor beside her, she performed a gentle internal. At first puzzlement struck her, for what on earth was she feeling against her fingers—something firm, yet springy, something pulsating? Then horror filled her. She was feeling the cord, which had prolapsed and could become compressed against the foetal head, reducing, even stopping, its oxygen supply. It was a grave obstetric emergency and she knew she had to act fast...try to reassure Polly and get her to lie in a left lateral position before the ambulance came.

It wasn't the easiest thing in the world to explain to a frightened woman that she has got to go into hospital at the double or her baby might die, nor to explain why, but Ella managed this between contacting the hospital and positioning Polly, asking her to dip her head onto her chest and pull her knees up as high as she could.

'Yes, that's right, curl up for me as much as you can, I know it's difficult because of your bump—I'll put these cushions under your knees. All this will help to keep the cord away from baby's head!' And please, please, she prayed to herself, let that be true!

'Will I have to have a Ceasarean?' Polly's voice sounded far away.

'Yes, probably, and I know you didn't want that, but it'll all be over very quickly. You won't know anything about it, and your baby will be safe.' Ella crossed her fingers, and began to pray again.

The ambulance came quickly, its team so efficient and so cogent of the situation that within seconds Polly was being rushed out of the house, humped up on a stretcher, still maintaining her strange position, a blanket over her for dignity's sake. She wanted Ella with her and said so, but one of the doctors shook his head. 'No room in the ambulance,' he shouted to Ella. 'Follow us if you like, and go straight up to Maternity Theatres!'

Ella nodded, the ambulance doors were closed and the vehicle sped away, its siren blaring, to the interest of several of Polly's neighbours who wanted to know if she was due. Fending them off, Ella locked up the house and drove swiftly away, losing the ambulance several times in the crush of Sunday traffic on the main coast road. Once at the hospital, and in Maternity, one of the midwives whom she knew bore her off to Theatres where a gown and cap were found for her. Donning them quickly, she was just in time to get to the anaesthetic room as Polly was being given an epidural injection.

She had expected the operation to be performed by the senior registrar, but the anaesthetist, who was already summoning the porter to wheel Polly through, told her Patrick Weston would be doing it. 'By luck he's in the building.'

Even worried as she was about Polly, Ella felt an anticipatory glow at the thought of seeing Patrick in action. She had been a theatre midwife for a time before she'd gone over to the community side so the scene that met her eyes as she walked in alongside the trolley was familiar. There was the team—the scrub nurse, runner, paediatrician, a nurse by the resuscitaire, and over all, standing straight and tall in his blue theatre outfit, eyes intent over his mask, was Patrick, attuned to the task in front of him, and anxious to get on with it. In spite of this he allowed himself a brief word with the patient, for a 'patient' Polly had now become, Ella thought ruefully.

'This will be over in a matter of minutes, Mrs Spender, and you'll have your baby.' He spoke quietly to her as she was transferred to the table. 'You'll feel nothing, you understand…nothing at all. You and your birthing partner—' he glanced at Ella as he straightened up '—will be able to have a little chat if you like, or even have a nap!'

As he spoke a screen was being erected over the table, blocking Polly's view of what would be happening on the other side of it. Other things were getting under way, too—the scrub midwife was pushing the instrument trolley up to her side of the table, a second midwife was standing with a towel over her arms ready to take the baby the instant it was born, drapes were placed above and below where the incision would be made.

Ella, sitting up by Polly's head, could see little of what was going on because of the high screen, but in her mind's eye she could follow every move Patrick was making—cutting through the layers of muscle and fat, snipping the peritoneum, taking up a scalpel to incise the uterus. At this point she got to her feet, for she wanted to recount to Polly the precise moment the baby would be lifted out. Patrick's hand was down, he was feeling for the head, then out the infant came in a matter of seconds, and almost at once piercing yells rent the air. There were cries of relief from the team.

Polly was shouting, 'Let me see!'

And there was Patrick saying, above it all, as he clamped and cut the cord, 'You have a splendid baby boy, Mrs Spender. Congratulations!'

The baby was handed to Polly, wrapped in the towel.

Not having had to battle through the vaginal tunnel, he was unsquashed, not bloodied, but covered in vernix. Everyone admired him, and when he was weighed he turned the scales at seven pounds and had an Apgar score of nine.

Patrick, having removed the placenta by cord traction, began closing the wound, inserting a tube for drainage, its end running into a bottle placed on the trolley where Polly now lay. As she was wheeled out she thanked him.

'Thank you all,' she said, 'and Ella for acting so quickly, but not for scaring me stiff!'

'Alas, I'm afraid there are times when the truth can't be concealed,' Patrick said seriously. He didn't add that had it not been for Ella the baby might have died.

With Ella walking alongside the trolley again, Polly was wheeled into a room off the main ward. She was welcomed into it by Sister, who told her that her baby would join her once he'd been washed and dressed. She undertook to ring Corporal Spender's regiment in Ireland. 'He'll come, he'll get leave, he'll be here to-morrow!' Polly was still on a high, declaring she felt well enough to go home, but this wouldn't, as Ella knew, continue for long. Once the effect of the epidural had worn off, she would need strong analgesia for a day or two. A surgical incision wasn't the most comfortable thing to have.

Saying goodbye to her, promising that she would visit her in the morning, Ella went to get out of her theatre garb. Stripping off gown and cap and overshoes, she became aware of the feeling of anticlimax which so often followed a time of great moment and triumph. She was tired but unsettled and home, for once, didn't seem to be beckoning. Even so, that's where I must go, she thought, glancing at her watch, noting with astonishment that it wasn't yet six o'clock! Good Lord, had all that really happened in under two hours? She must ring Shirley, whose shift it was. She must also ring Kate to tell her she was on her way home, although she might just add that she was going up to the canteen first for, there was no doubt about it, she needed the company of other nurses at the moment, she needed their brand of chitchat.

'Oh, that's all right, do that,' Kate said when she explained. 'Hannah is over with Robin, and probably hasn't given you a thought. Supper is cold and two hours off. Go and give yourself a break.'

Replacing the receiver—she was using a payphone in Casualty—Ella felt a light hand on her shoulder. Turning round, she saw Patrick looking down at her. 'I hoped I'd catch you,' he said. 'I'm dying for tea, and I feel like company, so what about joining me?'

She pretended to think about it, for there was no need to jump for joy. She meant to accept, well, of course she did, but before she could do so he asked her, rather more anxiously, if she was at the end of her shift.

'More than that.' She pulled a face. 'I've been on overtime since half four, and I'm absolutely parched!'

'Right, then what are we waiting for?' He shrugged into his jacket. 'We'll get out of here and go over the road, shake the hospital dust off our feet.'

They moved down the long casualty hall, out into the sunlit brightness of the yard, then crossed the road to Tuckers Teas, which sold pastries and cakes and served them with tea in china pots in the garden behind.

'We're lucky to get afternoon tea so late,' Ella said, once they were seated at a round, rather rocky table with their spoils in front of them.

'They stay open till seven in the summer, so I'm told.

Probably pays them to do so,' Patrick said, glancing at the other dozen or so tables, which were all occupied. 'It's a popular place, I've been here before. I like the garden atmosphere.' Ella nodded, for so did she, when he was part of it. She could hardly believe she was with him, that it was him sitting there, waiting for his tea to be poured.

'How have things been with you lately?' he asked, watching her absorbed, careful expression as she lifted the pot.

'Not bad, not bad at all, really.' She passed him his cup, grateful for the steadiness of her hand and arm. 'Everything,' she went on, 'was normal until today. I was really shocked when I examined Polly Spender, and telling her the truth wasn't easy either. I don't like frightening people.'

'Good thing you acted quickly. A cord prolapse is fairly unusual, but can be fatal for the foetus.' There was a hint of lordliness in his manner as he said this, and she gave him a straight look, which he interpreted quickly and immediately apologised.

'I was putting on the high and mighty, wasn't I?'

'Just a bit.' She let him off lightly.

'Sometimes,' he went on, 'I find it difficult to remember your years of experience.'

'You'll be telling me next that I look young for my age.'

'I don't know what your age is.'

'Twenty-eight.'

'Then you do, but I expect you've been told that before.'

'Many times.'

He looked at her carefully. 'We're not quarrelling, are we?'

She shrugged. 'Just sparring,' she said. He laughed and she joined in, much of her initial awe of him melting. She was beginning to enjoy herself.

They went on to speak of the children, Ella telling him how much Hannah liked playing with Robin in his den. 'I hope she isn't a nuisance, always slipping through that hedge. She tells me she never ventures unless Barbara invites her, but I can't help wondering if, when I'm not there, she takes advantage.'

'If she does, what of it?' Patrick queried. 'She's good for Rob, sorts him out, and they seem to get on all right. At this moment, I might tell you, the den is a shop—a supermarket, of course—with stacked-up boxes for shelves and a biscuit tin for a till.'

'I hear about it most nights.' Ella laughed, pouring Patrick a second cup of tea. 'She's got a birthday, her seventh, coming up on the twenty-first of this month. She wants a party, which is fair enough. The trouble is, she wants it to go on into a sleep-over, which I'm not having at any price!'

'I don't blame you. Talking of parties, Drummers's house-warming one will have to be held later than I'd hoped. Mrs Trentham, Valerie's mother, is still very unwell. She had a slight stroke—a TIA—a couple of weeks ago. She's at home with nurses going in, but Valerie wants to go down there for a few weeks till she's stronger and more able to cope.'

'I can understand that.' So her mother, Ella was thinking, really *was* ill.

'She's down there now.'

'You must miss her,' she said, her thoughts taking wing again. What would he say if she told him about that Friday night, the night of her theatre outing with Andrew, when Valerie was supposed to have been on her errand of mercy but instead had been enjoying herself with Long Arms?

'You have a look,' he said, making her jump, 'of a lady who's hatching a plot.'

She reddened, she could feel herself doing so. 'No plot.' She laughed then, really for something quick to say, she told him that she and Andrew had been to see *Marriner's Folly*. 'It was very good, every bit as good as the critics said.'

'I heard you'd been. Andrew told me, he thought it was pretty good, too. Valerie was keen to see it, but it's not always easy for me to plan in advance, and it was only here a week.'

Ella kept her head well down. Don't worry, she's seen it, she thought, then paid attention when she heard him say, 'I suppose you knew Andrew Savers before you came back here to work?'

'Oh, yes, we go back a long way.' What a relief to have the subject changed. 'I knew Andrew when he and old Mr Savers were in practice together.'

'Nice chap.'

'Yes, very.'

'He's a brilliant squash player.'

'Actually, he told me *you* were!'

'I like to keep fit, and that's a good way of doing so.' Patrick's tone was brusque, making Ella wonder if he wanted to go or needed his cup refilled.

'More tea?' she asked. 'There's heaps left.' He shook his head, and she set the pot down again, feeling a little rebuffed. 'Well, in that case—' she began, but got no further. She had a split-second glimpse of a bounding dog before it cannoned into their table, sending teapot and milk jug flying into her lap.

Her shout and Patrick's rang out together. As she

jumped to her feet, hot stewed tea dripped from her dress, down her legs to her feet, leaving little gobs and blobs of its leaves clinging to her front.

Patrick, on his knees, had snatched her dress away from her legs. 'Are you scalded, Ella?' Horror sat on his face, stiffening his features. She shook her head, stepping back from him. 'I'm not hurt at all. You can let go…I'm all right!' And so she was, she realised. 'Tea well off the boil,' she managed to add just as Mr Tucker, the proprietor, came running out of the shop.

'Are you all right?' He'd brought a towel just in case. 'I'm so sorry about what happened. The dog is my brother's—he had no business letting it loose!'

Over his shoulder—he was a small, tubby man—Ella could see the dog, a red setter, straining on a leash, its tail wagging joyously. She could also see people at the other tables turning to stare at her. Clammily cold now, she tugged at Patrick's arm. 'Let's go, let's get out of here.'

Having satisfied himself that she was all right, he picked up her bag, looped it over her shoulder and paid Mr Tucker for their tea. Taking her hand and walking a little in front of her to hide the disaster zone, he towed her across the road to the hospital parking lot and over to her car.

She slid inside, grateful and thankful to be decently out of sight. He bent to the open window. 'Are you fit to drive?'

'Of course I am.' She laughed, now seeing the funny side. That dog, and everything flying off the table—what a sight it must have been!

Patrick's face was grave. 'You scared me, you know. If that tea had been as hot as when it was served, you could have ended up in Casualty!'

'Well, it wasn't.' She looked back at him. His face was very near—a lean, seamed, handsome face, with eyes as blue as the sea. She swallowed convulsively. 'Were you really scared?' she asked. She shouldn't have asked, she knew that, she knew why she had as well, and so did he... He leaned farther into the car.

'My heart stopped,' he said hoarsely, then, cupping her face between his hands, he kissed her on the mouth.

CHAPTER SIX

'JUMPING catfish, what happened to you?' Kate exclaimed when Ella got home. 'Don't tell me someone's waters broke all over you!'

'It's tea. I'll tell you about it later.' Ella ran upstairs to change, not escaping Hannah's sharp eye as she passed her door.

'Your dress is wet, Mummy!' She picked at it carefully as Ella bent to kiss her goodnight.

'Some tea got spilled on it.'

'Does it feel yucky?'

'Yes, it does, which is why I'm going to take it off.'

Questions, questions, the joys of returning to a family, Ella was thinking as in her own bedroom she stripped off the offending dress, together with cold, clinging tights and pants. A few minutes later, showered and comfortable in shirt and trousers, she looked at herself in the mirror, placing her hands on either side of her face and reliving Patrick's kiss. It had lasted seconds only, for they'd been in a public place, but it hadn't been a casual coming together. She had sensed the hunger in him, the reined-in passion and the longing, and felt her own needs flare in response.

Stepping back from the car afterwards, he had looked as he always did—slightly head-in-the-air, a little grave, totally in control. It had been she who had had to concentrate like crazy to start the car and drive down the hill into the main traffic stream, when the absolute necessity to keep her mind on what she was doing had got her safely home.

Over supper she gave Kate an account of her day, or rather of her afternoon, starting with Polly Spender's call, her fright about the cord, and going into Theatre with her, watching Patrick perform the Caesarean.

'So you watched him do his stuff, did you?' Kate was very interested. She was even more interested to hear about the tea episode. Ella praised Patrick's efficiency and concern for her, but left out the kiss...not even to her twin could she relate that, not when it still felt so new.

Kate had a gift for sussing things out, though, and her glance at her sister was shrewd. 'He must like you to seek you out like that. He wasn't all that friendly at first, or you weren't with him.'

'The children have helped, given us common ground.'

'Hmm.' Kate considered this, taking their plates out into the kitchen, then coming back to say, 'He probably fancies you rotten, Ellie, but I hope you don't feel the same way about him. I mean, even if he took you to bed he'd still marry Valerie. Those two are too entrenched to break up now. She was there for him when he needed help most, he won't be forgetting that, and there's the kid who already looks on her as his mother—they're entangled tight as a knot. Even if they're not crazy about one another, they're still a good match. And sometimes—' she looked wistful suddenly '—those are the marriages that last—no spin, just real affection and getting on with things.'

'Thanks for the sermon. I love being preached at!' But what Kate had said had held grains of truth and Ella knew it. The thing to do, of course, was avoid being alone with Patrick, for she didn't trust herself.

* * *

She had four postnatal patients to visit at the hospital next day, and after a brief word with Sister she made her way into the side ward to visit Polly, who was pleased to see her but said she felt grim.

'A Ceasar is a major abdominal operation,' Ella told her. 'You're bound to feel sore and groggy on your first post-op day.'

'Bryan will be here by lunchtime, he's got a week's leave.' Polly winced as she moved to look at the baby in his cot. 'He looks like Bryan, which is just as well. If it weren't for that, I'd have a job to believe he's really ours. Not giving birth to him properly, not having to work for him, leaves me feeling that I got him through the post!' Her eyes filled as she said this. Ella, who had heard other Ceasar mothers say something similar, was quick to emphasise that but for Patrick's swift intervention Baby William would almost certainly have died.

'I know, and I'm grateful.' Polly took a tissue from the pack Ella held out to her. 'I didn't feel like this yesterday. Now I just seem to be down in the dumps.'

'It's baby blues, and they're horrid,' Ella consoled, 'but you'll feel better tomorrow, even better the next day. In the meantime, concentrate on how well you're feeding William. You're a natural, it's not every new mum who's successful straight off.'

In the main ward, where Ella went next, there was a good deal going on. Babies were being weighed after feeds—some quiet, some not. Recently delivered mothers were dragging themselves to the loo, certain that their insides were falling out, walking like snails. The house obstetrician was doing his round, accompanied by a student who looked scared out of her wits. Ella's four mums, all of whom were to be discharged that day, said they'd be glad to get out of it all…away from the bang-ing doors! Even so, they'd had good care and they knew it. It was simply that home was best.

Having her lunch-break with Shirley at the medical centre, Ella learned the sad news that Carla Lane, the young high-flying executive, had had a miscarriage, and was in hospital in the gynae ward after a D and C operation.

'I got a call from her partner soon after I took over from you last night.' Shirley, eating a double-decker sandwich, spoke through a mouthful of crumbs. 'She was, as you know, just on thirteen weeks. When I got to the house she was bleeding badly and having pains, poor girl. She actually aborted in the ambulance.'

'Oh, dear, I'm sorry to hear it,' Ella said. She had visited Carla three times so far, and had been impressed with the way she had given up smoking and been ready to take advice. 'If I can, I'll go back to the hospital later on this afternoon,' she said, consulting her afternoon list, working out how to manage it.

It was five o'clock when she actually got there, parking her car in its usual slot and taking the lift up to Egremont, the gynae ward—Patrick's territory. Monday was its main operating day and most of the patients were comatose, there was an air of quietness broken only by faint sounds out in the corridor, and the subdued tones of two nurses talking up at the central ward desk.

Carla Lane, who was sitting up in bed, greeted Ella coolly, but pressed her to stay a while. 'I want to know *why* it happened,' she said. 'No one has really explained. Do you think it was something I did, or didn't do? I don't like failing.'

'No, I don't think that, not for one moment, and it may surprise you to know that miscarrying during the first twelve or thirteen weeks is quite common, Carla.

Often no specific cause can be found…as in your case…' Ella had glanced at her notes.

'It was painful.'

'I know. I've heard other women who have had a miscarriage and then go on to have a full-time healthy baby later on say that the miscarriage was more painful than the successful birth.'

'We mean to try again.'

'Oh, do you?' Ella exclaimed, surprised.

'Yes, Rodney and I talked it over during visiting earlier on. The first one wasn't planned…well, I told you that…but the next one will be, which might make all the difference. I mean, maybe the last one felt he got planted by mistake!'

Again Ella was hard put to it not to show surprise, for whimsical thoughts were the last thing she would have expected from Carla.

'I just don't like failing,' Carla repeated. Now, this Ella *could* believe, and she was just about to advise her not to be in too much of a hurry when the registrar entered the ward.

Ella half expected to see Patrick as well, but there was no sign of him, then ten minutes later, down in the car park, she ran straight into him. 'Hello, there…you OK?' he asked her, but barely stopped.

Before she could get out a solitary word he was halfway to his car. She stared at his back view, at his striding legs, and a little bubble of annoyance at being brushed off like a brown paper bag made her run and catch up with him on her way to her own car.

'There's no need to speed away from me, Patrick. I'm not expecting you to treat me to another tea.' She laughed, as though she couldn't care less.

He was halfway into his car, but leaned out to say,

'Sorry, no offence, but I've a long drive ahead of me. I'm going down to see Valerie and her mother, and I want to get there before dark.' And with that he fastened his seat belt, switched on the engine and with a final swift glance at Ella closed the door and set off.

It was like a small rebuff in itself—not the driving off, but where he was going, Ella thought on the way home. Perhaps he was feeling guilty about yesterday and wanted to redress the balance.

'Barbara's been round, told me Patrick made a sudden decision to nip down and see Valerie and her mother for a couple of days,' Kate told her when she got in. 'I suppose Valerie's mum is his aunt-in-law, soon to become his mother-in-law, so fully merits a visit and a bunch of purple grapes.'

'True.' Ella lifted Merlin onto her lap, but he was soon dislodged by Hannah who took his place.

'Kate's going out tonight, Mummy, so it'll just be you and me,' she said in dulcet tones, winding her thin, little arms around her mother's neck.

'Yes, Barbara has asked me next door to supper. You don't mind, do you?' Kate looked across at her sister.

'No, of course I don't,' Ella said at once, and knew she spoke the truth. She felt like an evening on her own. She had some thinking to do, and she wanted to do it away from Kate's all-seeing gaze.

Private time was denied her, though, for soon after Hannah was in bed and fast asleep, Andrew, who'd been discussing business with his father, came over from next door.

Brown-haired, brown-bearded, spruce, he stood smiling on the doorstep. 'I thought we might go for a stroll, Ella, perhaps finish up at The White Horse for a drink. I've left the car at home.'

'Oh, dear.' Ella shook her head. 'No can do, I'm afraid. Kate's out this evening, and I need to stay with Hannah.'

'Of course, yes.' He looked disappointed. 'I've got some news to tell you, too.'

'Well, tell it to me here. Stay for a bit…I could do with some company,' she told him, not entirely truthfully. But she did want to hear his news, which was probably, she thought with genuine interest, about the practice.

It was, and he was clearly excited as he told her he'd appointed an assistant vet, who would start at the end of August. 'She's thirty, with another practice in Kent at present. Dad rang them and they speak very highly of her. They don't want to lose her, but they can't—in the foreseeable future—offer her a partnership, which is what she's after. She has no ties, wants to live down here, has a friend who will put her up for a time, so no problem there.' He paused for breath, and Ella fetched glasses and a bottle from the sideboard.

'This calls for a celebratory drink. It's only supermarket plonk, but it'll mark the occasion.' With their glasses filled, she raised hers and said, 'To Noah's Ark, and all who sail in her! I couldn't be more pleased, Andrew. Now you won't be so rushed off your feet.'

'No, and by the end of the summer I hope we can see more of one another,' he said solemnly, bending sideways to fondle Merlin's ears.

The sun slanting in through the open patio doors painted a pink slash across his shirt, and as he straightened and looked across at her, clearly waiting for some sort of comment from her, Ella knew that this was the moment to tell him how she felt.

'Andrew, I love coming out with you, I've enjoyed

every single time,' she began carefully, hearing the nervous wobble in her voice.

'But?' he prompted. 'Because I know there is one—it's rising out of your head in one of those balloon things that cartoonists go in for!' This was said with a smile, which encouraged her to continue yet at the same time made it no easier to get to the point. As she sought for words he found them for her. 'I think what you're trying to tell me…' he set his glass back on the tray '…is that you don't want our friendship to turn into something else.'

'No, I don't,' she said bluntly, realising that this was her chance to clear the air. 'I really like you, Andrew, I've always liked you, but I don't want to get in any deeper…not with anyone…not for years. I'm happy as I am with Hannah, and my job, and living here with Kate.'

Now, this wasn't—and she was thinking of Patrick and the joy she felt in his presence—entirely true, and she knew it, but she didn't want to dent Andrew's pride harder than she need to. 'I'm really sorry,' she finished up.

Andrew's mouth primmed a little and he avoided her eyes. 'It's all right,' he said at last. 'I guessed anyway. I do have *some* sensitivity, you know. Still…' He looked up and smiled at her, his old, easygoing expression in place. 'We can still see one another occasionally, surely? Friendship's a pretty good thing to have. Meanwhile—' and now he was grinning broadly '—there's no reason why I shouldn't keep my eye open for some gorgeous female who's dying to ravish me!'

Ella laughed, he'd surprised her. 'Perhaps,' she said, 'you'll fall in love with your new assistant vet.'

'I can't see that happening.' He was solemn again,

looking down at Merlin, busy chewing a paw. 'I didn't feel any pinpricks of longing at the time of her interview. She has a good face and a pleasant voice, patients and clients alike will take to her.' He went on then to tell her about Miss Remer, who had asked for the following Saturday off. 'She's booked herself on a coach trip to London—going on the Eye. I would have thought that at her age she'd have preferred to stick closer to the ground.'

'That's mean!'

'I know.' He looked ashamed. 'But it puts me in a spot. Saturday morning surgery is the busiest of the week, with kids bringing their pets in, queuing half-down the street. There's no appointments list on Saturdays—it's first come, first served.'

Ella was quiet for a moment, digesting this. Perhaps she could help him out. It was time she did, for all she had done was take from him so far. Telling just now that she felt only friendship for him had been the right thing to do. Even so, she felt badly about it. Perhaps, she thought, I can salve my conscience by offering to do a good deed.

'Andrew,' she began, 'I'm free on Saturday. I could help out, if you liked. I'm sure I could manage reception duties—answer the phone and all that. The only thing is, I'd have to bring Hannah. I can't leave her with Kate on a Saturday, it wouldn't be fair.'

'Good Lord…am I hearing aright?' Andrew's jaw went slack. 'Did you actually say—?'

'Yes, I did and I meant it. But, please, say if you don't like the idea.' She was beginning to regret it already.

'Not like it? I think it's brilliant and, of course, bring Hannah. She can play out the back—there's an enclosed yard with a bit of grass, room for her to run about. I'll take you both out to lunch afterwards.'

Ella discovered, on Saturday, that Andrew's remarks hadn't been exaggerated. From eight to noon, patients arrived in a positive flood—rabbits, guinea pigs, gerbils, an assortment of dogs and cats, not to mention a tortoise with an eye infection and a budgie with an overgrown beak. Ella couldn't imagine how Andrew was coping through in his consulting room, or how he managed to look so unfazed when his face came round the door. It was all she could do to keep her head in the midst of all this mêlée and ripe animal smells.

However, by twelve-fifteen, only one small boy with a chinchilla rabbit remained to be seen. He went in when an elderly woman came out with a Pekingese. As she paid her account at the desk, she stared hard at Ella. 'You're like one of the nurses,' she said, 'who visited my neighbour when she had her baby.'

'I'm a midwife, so I expect that *was* me,' Ella said with a laugh. And I'd rather do my proper job any day than the one I'm struggling with now, she thought as she showed the woman out. She returned to the desk just in time to take the small boy's money as he and his boxed-up rabbit came out of the consulting room.

Once he'd gone, Andrew appeared, unbuttoning his surgical coat. 'Right, that's it, now we can pull up the drawbridge. We're very unlikely—' he started to say, just as a shadow appeared on the other side of the street door, which opened to admit, first, a terrier on a lead and then a man in jeans and a cream sweater, whose gaze went straight to Ella at the desk who, wearing her 'welcome to clients' smile, stared back at him.

'Patrick! Unusual to see you here on a Saturday!' This was Andrew, bending down to give Lucy a pat. Miss

Remer's gallivanting this morning, so Ella's helping me out,' he said, quite likely with the intention of breaking the tension in the room.

'Of course, I *could* be moonlighting, nurses' pay being what it is!' Ella joked, turning to Hannah, who had just come in from the back.

Hannah, too, bent over Lucy. 'Is she ill?' she asked.

'I hope not.' Patrick looked towards the consulting-room door. 'May we?' he said to Andrew.

'Of course.' In they went, the door clicking to behind them, shutting Ella and Hannah out.

'I want to know what's wrong with Lucy,' Hannah grizzled. And not without cause—she'd had a boring morning.

'Patrick will probably tell us, but if he doesn't you musn't ask,' Ella said, pushing wisps of hair off her hot, flushed face.

He was with Andrew some time and, fed up with waiting, Hannah went back into the yard where she thumped her ball against the wall, wishing that either Robin or Merlin were there to keep her company. She was still outside when the two men came out of the consulting room, so she missed the verdict on Lucy—that she was four weeks pregnant.

'Oh, *dear*!' Ella said involuntarily, for this couldn't be welcome news, not at Lucy's age, not when… Then her mouth dried up at the challenging—no *accusing*—expression on Patrick's face. She knew the reason for it, too. 'You think it was Merlin, don't you?' she burst out. 'You think he mated with her.'

'I do, don't you? After all, your hedge is no kind of barrier.' There was the faintest emphasis on the word 'your', which Ella picked up at once for that particular hedge *was* Longmead's responsibility to maintain. Kate and she should have seen to it. Even so, she was damned if she was going to take the blame for Lucy's condition.

'If you'd warned us she was in season,' she said jerkily, 'we'd have seen Merlin didn't stray. It's up to the owner to see that his bitch is kept shut up at those times! And, anyway…' She stopped there, seeing the slightest but telling change come over Patrick's features. 'You didn't know she *was* on heat, did you? And you a gynae man… Lucy may be old but dogs don't have a menopause. Surely you knew that!'

'I have other things to concern myself with, of *course* I—' Patrick began, but was interrupted by Andrew who, anxious to keep the peace, made the observation that at Lucy's age she would have had a very small show. 'It would have been easy to miss it.' He smiled at them both, massaging his beard.

'I had hoped,' Patrick said, still looking at Ella, 'that Andrew would agree to abort.'

'Which I don't advise,' Andrew emphasised. 'It would be far more dangerous for her to be anaesthetised and aborted than going on with the pregnancy.'

Patrick swung round to Andrew. 'Your advice is what I came for and, naturally, I'll take it. I don't want to lose the dog. Robin would never forgive me, and I'd never forgive myself.'

'Is Lucy ill?' a small voice enquired. Hannah had come in from the back.

'No, sweetheart, she's just come to be checked.' Andrew stooped and picked her up. Almost at eye level with Patrick now, she proceeded to tell him that they were all going out to lunch at *the hotel*!

'Uncle Andrew's taking us, and I can have a pizza, if I like, because I've been good all morning, haven't I?'

she turned her head to her mother who, getting over the shock of her calling Andrew 'uncle', managed to nod.

'Then I'd better leave you to it, hadn't I? Send me your bill, Andrew! Bye, Ella, bye, Hannah!' Clearly making an effort to be pleasant, Patrick and Lucy—the latter with an almost imperceptible swagger—made their way to the door.

'Trouble in paradise!' Ella tried to shake off the remains of her guilt, then as promptly indulged it. 'Kate and I should have stopped all that traffic through the hedge, Patrick clearly thinks so, too.'

'He's worried.' Andrew set Hannah down as she asked to go to the loo. Watching her run off, he added, 'Lucy was his late wife's dog, so she's especially dear to him.'

'Will she be all right?'

'I don't know. She may or she may not.'

'Oh, dear, you're making me feel worse than ever.'

'Merlin may not be the sire. When a bitch is on heat dogs come from far and wide. They've been known to tunnel under fences, even a full hedge would pose no problem. It will be a blessing if Merlin *is* the culprit— at least then the pups will be small. Both Patrick and I think there are two but time, as they say, will tell.'

'When is Lucy due?'

'During the third week in August.' Andrew, in the small back cloakroom, was sluicing his face. Emerging from the towel, he smiled at Hannah who'd come jigging back. 'Come on, you two, let's forget about work, and go out and enjoy ourselves.'

Later that evening Ella made an inspection of the hedge, or rather of the infamous gap, wondering how best to fill it. There was a piece of trellis in the greenhouse, she remembered. Perhaps that would do. She went to fetch it and was standing it upright, wondering how to secure it, when Patrick called out to her and came striding down from the house.

'What are you doing?' His question came sharply and she answered in like vein.

'What does it look like?'

'You can't put that up.' He peered at the trellis in distaste.

'I've got nothing else.'

'Then leave it as it is, unless *you* want it filled. I certainly don't.'

'But I thought you said… This morning you said…' She let the trellis crash to the ground.

'I probably said a good deal too much, and for that I apologise.' He was smiling at her through the wicker-work of twigs, not looking in the least contrite, but concerned, as though he was anxious to set matters right. 'What you *could* do in the course of time—no rush, of course—is plant one or two cuttings there and let grow in naturally.'

'That'll take ages!'

'I don't mind if you don't. Shame to spoil the kids' right of way.'

Ella was surprised but tried not to show it. She was also relieved. She wanted to say she was sorry about Lucy, but before she could get the words out, Patrick asked her if she'd enjoyed her lunch.

'Yes, we all did, it's a nice hotel.'

'I must try it sometime.' He swiped at a wasp that was circling his head.

'How's Mrs Trentham?' Ella asked.

'Oh, doing very well, almost back to normal now. With a modicum of luck Valerie will be able to come down next weekend. We've fixed the date of the house-

warming party for August the sixth. We're inviting about
thirty people, so there'll be quite a crowd.'

'You'll have a crush in your garden, and what about
parking—cars, I mean?'

'A crush again!' Patrick laughed, lifting his hands in
mock horror.

'You're welcome to use our drive and forecourt to
take the overspill.' The thought of the party depressed
Ella. Patrick's and Valerie's party, rubber-stamping their
relationship, making them even more of a couple—an
engaged-to-be-married couple. What could be more telling than that?

'That's helpful,' Patrick was saying in response to her
offer. Afterwards silence fell between them, thickening
with every second, a loaded silence of locked-up words,
a silence that hurt the ears.

'I must go in and see to the supper,' Ella managed to
say at last. 'Kate, like Andrew's Miss Remer, has been
in London all day and is feeling zonked out.'

'Lucky Kate to have an administering sister. Come to
that, lucky Andrew to have a stand-in receptionist on
tap,' Patrick said, raising a hand in farewell before lop-
ing back to the house.

Kate had still got her feet up when Ella went indoors.
Hannah was in bed and, hopefully, asleep, Merlin was
lying by the kitchen door, trying to catch a draught. It
was eight o'clock and still very warm. Ella drank a tum-
blerful of water as she stood by the sink.

'I expect it was baking in Town,' she shouted through
to Kate. She seemed, Ella thought, very far away, not
her usual bubbly self. She hadn't, for instance, wanted
to know what she and Patrick had been talking about
just now in the garden. Neither had she exclaimed over-
much about Merlin's fruitful interlude with Lucy. Even

more, she hadn't enlarged on her shopping trip, or meeting up with Sandra Cross, her one-time neighbour and friend from Ranstead, Surrey.

'Yes, it was hot.' Kate roused herself to shout back to Ella in the kitchen. 'And Oxford Street was chock-a-block as usual.'

'Where did you have your lunch?'

'Selfriges.'

'And how was Sandra?' Ella persisted, setting the potatoes on to boil.

'Oh, fine…you know Sandra. But she misses me, she says, even after two years—there's loyalty for you! She told me, by the way, that Paul and his live-in girlfriend have parted company. She doesn't know who left who, but Paul is on his own now, has been for a couple of months. Sandra says she hasn't seen anyone else around, he's keeping himself to himself.'

'Knowing him, he's probably just resting before shacking up again.' Ella gave an extra vicious bang to the steaks before putting them under the grill.

'Yes, that's what I thought.' There was the sound of a swift movement from the sitting-room as Kate got to her feet. She was looking in the mirror over the mantelshelf when Ella went in, bearing gin and tonic in long cool glasses with lemon floating on top. Something about her reflected face, something about the way her eyes didn't meet Ella's in the mirror, filled the latter with foreboding. Surely she wasn't…surely she couldn't possibly be…

'Kate…' Her voice was shrill. 'Kate, you're not even *thinking* about getting in touch with him, are you?'

'I wouldn't be that much of a fool!'

'Good!' Ella passed her her drink.

'Even so,' Kate said, after two or three sips, 'he's not

all that bad, you know. He still pays money into my bank account every quarter. I've never acknowledged it, I don't want it, I've never ever touched it. Even so, he puts it there.'

'A man is supposed to keep his wife,' Ella snorted. 'It probably eases his conscience.'

'As I say, he's not all bad,' Kate persisted, and wisely, although she longed to argue, Ella let her have the last word.

CHAPTER SEVEN

DURING her morning visits on Monday Ella caught sight of Claire Purton wheeling her baby son in the direction of the high street. Ella no longer went to the house but, interested to see how he'd progressed, she slowed down and stopped.

'He looks fine, Claire,' she exclaimed, leaning out to look under the fringed canopy at the sleeping infant.

'Yes, they're pleased with him at the clinic.' Claire wheeled him closer, tilting the pram to give Ella the best possible view of him. 'I just wish he'd do a bit more sleeping at night. It's not so bad for me, I can nap during the day, but it's tough on Bob who has to go to work. Not that he complains. He adores Chris, but there's no doubt about it—he's an exhausting lad!'

'It'll get better,' Ella said, then wondered, as she drove off, if that had been a false promise. Certainly it would get better in time, but it might be another six weeks and then some more before the young Purtons had an unbroken night.

She turned into the high street, which was awash with holidaymakers, managed to park in a side road and made her way to Barkers, the shoe shop, to visit Doris Jones, who was in her tenth week of pregnancy. Doris was an assistant in the shop, which her husband, John, managed. She was serving a teenager when Ella went in, but her husband took over whilst the two of them went upstairs.

Doris's main complaint was of nausea and vomiting.

'I'm a dead loss in the shop,' she said. 'Feet aren't the thing to be dealing with when you want to throw up!'

'You'll feel much better when you're in your second trimester,' Ella told her. 'In the meantime, there are things you can do to help things along. You could, for instance, try eating root ginger. Lots of women find this helps…just sliver a pellet off with a sharp knife and chew on it like gum. Even ginger ale helps some women, so do fizzy drinks.'

'Believe you me, I'll try anything,' Doris sighed.

'Your blood pressure's fine.' Ella unwrapped her arm. 'Now, don't forget, your next clinic date is Thursday week.'

'I won't, I've got it written down. Will I see you there?' she asked as they went back downstairs.

Ella nodded. 'You will, actually. Shirley and I are taking that one together.'

There were three customers waiting in the shop— business seemed to be brisk. Poor Doris, Ella thought, stepping out into the street.

Her next visit, farther up the road where she'd left her car, gave her cause for concern. Eileen Fern, hugely pregnant at thirty-nine weeks, came to the door. She was fully dressed and gave Ella her usual smiling greeting, but confessed, on being questioned, that she felt 'a bit funny'.

'In what way funny?' Through in the sitting-room Eileen, puffing slightly, slithered sideways onto a chair.

'Muzzy, a bit dizzy and sickish.'

'Any pain?'

'No, but I don't want to eat, and look at my ankles— they're more swollen than ever this morning!'

Ella had already noticed this, and her anxiety mounted as she took Eileen's blood pressure and found it to be raised. The distolic was still less than 100, however, so she could just be showing signs of pre-eclampsia, but only a mild form. Would it be safe to leave her until this evening, when Shirley was calling? She didn't want to alarm her and have her blood pressure rising still more. On the other hand, Eileen was a newcomer to Easthaven, and her circumstances were unusual, even dreadful—her husband was serving time in prison for embezzlement from his firm. She had alienated herself from her neighbours because of this so had no one to turn to, apart from the community nurses. Her mother lived up North.

Making up her mind, and trying to sound as reassuring as possible, Ella told her that she felt her GP should be informed. 'I'd like him to take a look at you, Eileen. Not that I think there's much wrong, but better be safe than sorry. The baby's fine, so no problem there.' She had listened to the foetal heart after taking the blood-pressure reading.

She called the medical centre from the phone in the hall, having closed the sitting-room door, but was told that all four doctors were out on their calls. 'If it's urgent we can contact Dr Mason, he's nearest to where you are now, but it could take—'

'It's all right, leave it!' Making up her mind, Ella got straight through to Maternity at the hospital and asked to speak to the registrar.

'Bill Corby's on leave, Ella.' Sister Martin came on the line. 'But you're lucky. I've got Mr Weston in the office with me now.'

'Oh, thank goodness!' Ella expelled a breath of relief. Seconds later Patrick's calm voice was asking her what was wrong. She explained, neither exaggerating nor making light of Eileen's symptoms.

'Mild re-eclampsia without a doubt,' he said, 'which could worsen, of course.'

'Well, yes, that's what I thought, and as she's on her own...'

'Is she booked for a hospital delivery?'

'Yes.'

'Right, then, we'll play it safe and get her in now. Hang on, will you?' You bet I will, Ella was thinking, hearing him talking in an aside to Sister. She caught the words 'Yes, I agree, a side-ward would be better' then he was back with her. 'There's a bed available, so she can come in at once. We'd better play this one by ear. I'll arrange transport...'

'Mr Weston, I can bring Eileen in, it'll alarm her less. She can lie on the back seat of my car.' It was amazing, Ella thought, how the formal term 'Mr Weston' came out perfectly naturally. They were both on duty, which made a world of difference. She could hardly arrive on the maternity floor and address the consultant as Patrick.

She had no idea how much Eileen had overheard when she went back into the sitting-room. Not wanting her blood pressure to climb any higher, Ella explained what had happened, and what was going to happen, as casually as she could.

'Will I have to stay in? I don't mind if I do as I'm so near my time.' Eileen's hand went up to shade her eyes as though the light hurt them.

'I don't know. It all depends on what Mr Weston thinks.'

'I've got a case packed, so I'll take that, shall I?'

'Clever girl!' Ella praised, going upstairs to get it, telling Eileen to stay where she was.

Five minutes later they were on the coast road, heading for the hospital. Once there Eileen, with Ella beside her, was wheeled up to Maternity and into the side-ward, whilst Patrick was bleeped. He came very quickly and silently. He was a quiet-moving man, deft and friendly whilst never ever attempting to cross the doctor-patient divide. 'Not feeling too clever, Mrs Fern?'

Eileen shook her head and immediately winced. Sister helped her on the bed whilst Ella made herself scarce, her role now that Eileen was in hospital being more or less over. Even so, she intended to hang about so she went along to the postnatal ward to visit two of her new mums. When she returned to the corridor half an hour later, Sister called her into her office.

'Mr Weston wants to keep Mrs Fern here till her baby is born,' she explained. 'As she's so near term and is unwell, he feels this to be wise. The last thing we want is for her to go into a state of fulminating pre-eclampsia. And, no, I don't think he intends to perform a Caesarean section or induce her at this stage,' she added, answering Ella's unspoken question. 'It's more a case of giving her total rest prior to the birth.'

'Well, yes, especially as she's placed.'

'Exactly. He's read the notes you brought in with her, so knows her history, poor love. Anyway, go in and see her if you've got a moment—she was asking if you'd be back.'

Already Eileen had the appearance of an inpatient—pillows banked up high, a covered jug of water on her locker, charts at the end of her bed. All she needed were some flowers and get-well cards to complete the picture. Ella asked her if there was anyone she would like her to contact, but she shook her head.

'I think not, at the moment. If I let Robert know he'll only worry, and he can't do anything about it. I can't see them letting him out to visit.' She gave a small

twisted smile. 'His letters to me will come to the house.'
She began to look troubled again, whereupon Ella promised to pick up her post for her.

'I'll call every other day.' She could, she felt, do this
small thing for Eileen. 'And I'll post anything you want
to write back,' she added, realising that to ask a stranger
to post a letter to an inmate to one of Her Majesty's
prisons would be an embarrassment. Some people had
to know her circumstances, but not the entire obstetric
unit. The poor girl had her pride.

'As for my mother, I'll write to her when the baby's
here,' she said just as Ella was leaving the room. 'Not
that she's likely to be all that thrilled—quite the reverse,
in fact.'

Wondering about this as she crossed the landing, Ella
saw Patrick at the lifts. With him was a shorter, slightly
overweight man with black, slicked-back hair.

'Ah, Ella!' Patrick turned and made way for her.
'Meet Professor Moden from Haematology…Anthony,
this is Sister Fairfax, community midwife.'

'Hello, Sister Fairfax!' That the Professor was
American was plain from his drawl. That he was fascinated by Ella's English rose looks was even more apparent.

Smooth blighter, Ella thought as he all but bowed over
her hand, holding onto it whilst his dark eyes roamed
the length of her. 'Delighted to meet you, Ella.' He had
picked up on her first name.

Trying in vain to free her hand, she uttered a staid
'Good morning' and wished that the lift would arrive.

'I'd be happy to be having a baby if you were the one
to be in attendance,' he said, very nearly in a whisper,
close to her ear.

'I don't think so, Professor.' Ella got her hand back
at last. 'The population would dwindle alarmingly if men

had to give birth. I'm sure you've heard that said before but, believe you me, it's true.'

'Still, we males have our uses, don't we?' He moved in close behind her as the lift arrived at last.

Ella made no reply, she thought this wisest, and much to her relief he got out on the next but one floor, touching her shoulder as he went and nodding goodbye to Patrick who had watched the little charade with amusement. 'You made a hit there,' he commented as, getting out on the ground floor, they walked through A and E along to the exit doors. 'Our friend was well and truly smitten,' he added teasingly.

'Somehow or other I don't think it takes much to smite the professor.' Ella laughed, but there was a tartness to her voice, and she heard Patrick's chuckle as she left him to cross to her car.

He wasn't making for the car park, she noticed, but was walking off the precinct, striding down the hill and turning right at the bottom. He was probably meeting someone and lunching in the town. Oh, well. She switched on the ignition and adjusted her mirror. What he did and who he did it with was nothing to do with her. With no more calls to make in Charding she could lunch back at home before starting on the rest of her Easthaven postnatals—two with breastfeeding problems.

The remainder of the week passed uneventfully— Eileen Fern improving in hospital, Polly Spender recovering from her Caesarean at home with her soldier husband. There was the antenatal clinic shared with Shirley, the midwives' meeting at the centre, three first visits to be made and two call-outs to false alarms. It was a normal week's work, all part of the job. Even so, Ella wasn't sorry when Saturday came round and it was her free weekend.

Hannah, however, wasn't in the best of moods right from waking up. She didn't want to go to the supermarket with her mother and aunt. 'I don't like it in there, it's boring!'

'Well, you're coming and that's that,' Kate told her, losing patience. 'We can't leave you at home on your own.'

'I can go over to Robin's.'

'You can't, not this morning, he's got his Aunt Valerie there. I expect they're going out somewhere, probably to the shops, like us.' Both Kate and Ella had seen her car arrive at Drummers last night.

'Valerie will be pleased to see me.'

'No, she won't, not right at this moment,' Ella said in the kind of voice that quelled further argument. 'We're going to the shops, and when we've finished we'll have an ice cream.'

'As I've said before, you spoil that child,' Kate muttered in an aside to Ella as they crossed to the garage.

'And you antagonise her. There's no point in that.' Ella was quick to defend herself *and* her child. 'Kids have moods as well as adults, you know!'

Kate sniffed and said nothing, and Ella found herself praying that Hannah would be all sweetness and light for the rest of the morning. She was, and there were no more grumbles, no more sulky looks. There were one or two 'can I haves' as they traipsed the supermarket aisles, but no fretful demands, and her butter-wouldn't-melt-in-her mouth demeanour, as she ate her ice cream, attracted a good deal of admiring comment, and Ella was proud of her.

After a light lunch at home the two of them went down to the beach, where they were meeting Andrew Savers. He had been as good as his word in maintaining a friendly relationship between them. They could see him at the water's edge, standing in his blue trunks, the waves curling over his toes. Hannah ran to him and he lifted her up, pretending to drop her, fully clothed, into the incoming breakers. She loved every scary moment, and when he set her down it took her less than a minute to pull off her shorts and T-shirt and dance around in her scarlet swimsuit, clamouring for a piggyback. Whilst this was in progress Ella performed her own strip, emerging in an emerald green one-piece cut high in the leg. She was a serious swimmer, so forswore bikinis, which easily came adrift.

She and Andrew spent several minutes, as they usually did, encouraging Hannah to swim from one to the other of them, praising her each time. She *was* improving, Ella could see that, but she was still inclined to splash too much. She hadn't yet got the confidence to lie in the water and let it do much of the work.

When they returned to the beach Andrew looked after Hannah whilst Ella had her swim—a steady, rhythmic crawl, cleaving away from the shore. She loved the feeling of isolation, of having nothing in front of her but the glittering water and the beckoning horizon.

She didn't hear anyone coming up behind her until he was alongside.

'You're too far out,' he said.

Swivelling her face sideways out of the water, she encountered Patrick's streaming countenance and plastered-down, waterlogged hair.

'Good Lord, King Canute!' She laughed, treading water.

'You're too far out,' he repeated.

'By the same token, so are you!' She felt weightless, happy, deliriously so…all this and Patrick, too!

'Turn back with me…you're too far from shore.' He wasn't laughing. He was deadly serious, very nearly stern.

'I heard you the first time!' Obediently she turned, and they swam breaststroke side by side silently back to shore. Well before they reached it Ella spotted Valerie in a sundress, sitting on the pebbles, talking to Andrew. The children—for Robin was there, too—were tossing a beach ball to and fro.

'Back to reality,' she said, before she could stop herself.

She expected him to agree with her, but he made no reply, or if he did she didn't hear him for the children were rushing to them, creating their usual din.

'We thought you were making for the Normandy coast,' Valerie said to her, smiling but with a slight edge to her voice. She was wearing a sunhat—a big white straw one—which was immensely becoming against her tanned skin and black hair. Ella supposed that was why she was wearing it. 'Aren't you going in?' she asked.

Valerie shook her head, nearly dislodging the hat. 'No, I'm no mermaid. I prefer to do my swimming and sunbathing at a lido. Patrick's the one who favours the sea.'

'It's more invigorating, no chlorine.' He was letting himself down beside her as she spoke, making a rattle on the shingle. Ella, on the other side of Valerie, tried not to stare, but allowed herself one or two glances as she dried the ends of her hair. Stripped off, he looked tanned and fit…muscled and strong, his lean, long body tapering down into black swimming trunks. His legs—and surely she could feast her eyes on those—were stretched in front of him, lean and long like the rest of him, his feet high-arched and strong.

Andrew, a couple of yards away, was playing with the children, but Robin soon returned to his father, asking to go into the water. Patrick hoisted himself up. 'No rest for the exhausted! Come on, tiger, race you to the edge!'

Robin was clearly at home in the water. Once out beyond the breakers he swam side by side with his father parallel with the shore.

'He can swim better than me,' Hannah observed, frowning and not looking pleased.

'Robin is older than you,' Ella said swiftly, fearing a scene.

'I taught him to swim almost as soon as he could walk,' Valerie said, watching Andrew lift Hannah into his lap. She had met him before at the leisure centre and once at his surgery premises. Wondering what his relationship with Ella was, she remarked, a little coquettishly, on how different people, especially males, looked on the beach.

'It's because they don't have clothes on.' Hannah clasped Andrew to her, rubbing her face against the curling dark hair on his chest.

'And you, little madam, are too sharp by half.' Valerie managed to laugh.

'It's a case of ask a silly question, isn't it?' Ella defended her daughter.

Kate appeared at that moment, clashing over the shingle, bearing picnic bags.

'Oh, good.' Her eyes took in Valerie, then Patrick and Robin who were emerging from the sea. 'The numbers have swollen. I thought I was going to be a gooseberry when I set out. Now I needn't worry. I've brought scones, cake, chocolate and a Thermos of tea. The food will go round, but the tea won't.' She looked expectantly at Andrew who said he'd bring a tray of tea down from the beach café and some cola for the children.

Both he and Patrick pulled shirts on and set off, together with the children, who were demanding ice creams. There was the faintest element of strain between the three women after they'd left, broken by Ella apologising for not having asked Valerie about her mother. 'I do hope she's better.'

'Well, she is or I couldn't have come this weekend.' Valerie watched her climb into her shorts. 'The trouble with these mini-strokes,' she continued, 'is that they so often preface others.'

'Not always,' Ella replied, in an attempt to be reassuring.

'Well, anyway, our house-warming party has been fixed for a fortnight next Friday, but perhaps Patrick has already told you?'

'Yes, he has.'

'And next Wednesday we've got Hannah's birthday party, her seventh,' Kate supplied, intent on unpacking her picnic bags as the men were on their way back. Patrick had bought sticky buns and chocolate wafer biscuits from the café. 'It's a good job we've all had our swim, or we'd sink to the bottom,' he said.

Talk was sporadic whilst everyone was eating. It wasn't until everything had been consumed, and the children were playing ball, that any real conversation got under way. This started off with a discussion on late night television and the compulsive viewing of 'soaps'. One thing led to another—television to cinema—cinema to live theatre, culminating with Valerie saying that she and Patrick were seeing a play at the Haymarket in London at the end of the month. 'It's *Marriner's Folly*, with Melinda Harrison. It had its pre-run here.'

Ella jerked a little at Andrew's side, then heard him

say, 'Yes, Ella and I—' But almost immediately he was interrupted by Kate.

'What a pity you didn't see it when it was on here, Valerie!' Her smile was open and bland.

'That, I'm afraid, was my fault.' Patrick stirred at Valerie's side. 'I left it too late to get tickets. I was remiss, in other words!'

'Andrew took Ella.' Kate was still smiling. 'They had front circle seats, if you please!'

Ella's neck began to go stiff. Shut up, Kate, she prayed. Please, please, leave it, don't say a single word more.

'The tickets came my way by chance, actually.' Andrew was being honest. 'And I'm not surprised that Patrick was unlucky. The box office was taking bookings ten days in advance.'

'What night did you go?' Valerie asked Ella.

'Friday, the last performance.'

'Yes, and she raved about it.' Kate was off again. 'And circle seats are so interesting, aren't they? Such fun to be able to look down into the auditorium and see what's going on there, especially in the stalls where people dress up in all their finery.'

Valerie's face under the becoming hat, which she'd tipped a little forward, didn't move a muscle as she looked back at her tormentor. 'Funny you should say that,' she said sweetly. 'The stalls are my favourite seats. If I can, I always plump for them, and that is where…' she put her hand on Patrick's leg '…we'll be sitting when we see the play in Town.'

'At the Haymarket, too. That'll cost you!' Andrew joked, wondering why Ella was looking so tense, wondering, too, why a three-pronged uncomfortable atmosphere was well in evidence. If Patrick was aware of it, he was showing no sign, merely saying that he'd had to redeem himself somehow or Valerie would have given him his marching orders.

Soon after that the party split up. Ella reminded Kate that their parents would be ringing up at five. Andrew said that his father was expecting him. Hannah meekly agreed to be taken home...providing she was given a piggyback.

'How *could* you, Kate?' Ella accused her sister, once the Hannah-burdened Andrew was ahead and out of earshot. 'How could you? She knew you were baiting her. Now she knows I saw her that night, she knows I told you about it, and she probably thinks Andrew and I chewed it over. She must hate the lot of us!'

'What if she does? If I've made her uneasy, I'm glad. Serve her right for telling porkies to Patrick—he deserves better than that!'

'You've made an enemy of her.'

'Don't be so dramatic...what can she do to me?' Kate ran a few paces to catch up with Andrew, who was setting Hannah down.

Ella sighed. As Kate had said, what could Valerie do? Nothing, of course, absolutely nothing. Kate held all the cards. Even so...even so...a little seed of worry took root in her mind. Valerie Trentham, rubbed up the wrong way, could be the paying-out kind.

CHAPTER EIGHT

As Kate fitted the key in the front-door lock, they could hear the phone ringing inside the house. 'That'll be Mum.' She ran in to answer it. Andrew by then had left them and gone next door to his parents'. Hannah had had to be restrained from going with him.

"They'll be pleased to see me," she'd said.

Ella told her, "No way." And prised her away from him.

As she bustled the little girl upstairs for her bath it was obvious that Kate wasn't speaking to their mother. Ella caught remarks like, "It's a surprise…you can't expect" and "No, of course I can't stop you." After that there was a long listening silence from her sister and, once in the bathroom with the taps running, further eavesdropping was out.

'Was Kate speaking to Granny?' Hannah asked, as she stepped into the bath.

'No.'

'Who was it, then?'

'A friend of hers, I expect.' And it was then, at that point exactly, that Ella felt she knew who it was. Kate had looked rigid there by the phone, and her voice had been odd. It had been Paul, her husband. Why was he ringing, and what was it that Kate couldn't stop him doing? Alarmed, and worried, fearing for her sister, Ella couldn't wait to find out.

But when she went back downstairs with Hannah, who was clamouring for her supper, Kate was on the phone yet again, and this time it *was* their mother. Ella had a brief word with her, so did Hannah, during the course of which they were pleased to hear that Mum and Dad, alias Granny and Grandpa, were coming to stay for three weeks from the middle of August.

After this had been talked over and Hannah had gone to bed, Kate, without any prompting from Ella, told her that the first phone call *had* been from Paul. 'I felt as thought I'd been shot, Ellie.' She turned a white face to her sister. 'It's over a year since we spoke, and that was on the phone, about the cash he was paying in for me, when I told him I didn't want it.'

'What did he want...this time, I mean?'

'To come down here...to see me. I told him you and Hannah were with me now, but that didn't put him off—'

'Pity!' Ella said, before she could bite it back.

'He suggested Wednesday.'

'But that's...'

'I know—Hannah's birthday. I told him that, and that we were having a party and that it wouldn't be a good time.'

'Did he tell you he was on his own now?' Ella pulled a chair out from under the kitchen table, and sat down with a bump.

'Yes, he told me that first of all.'

'Cleared the decks, in other words!'

'He's coming, Ella, I couldn't stop him. He'll have his lunch out, and then come on here afterwards. He's driving down, of course.'

'Plainly he wants you to go back to him, start all over again.' Ella wished Kate would turn round and face her, but she was busying herself at the cooker, lifting saucepan lids up.

'I couldn't stop him,' was all she said, and Ella groaned inside.

'Oh, well, look on the bright side—Hannah will be pleased to see him, especially if he brings her a present. He may even—' she tried the effect of a joke '—help with the party—pin the tail on the donkey, organize musical chairs and all that!'

Kate tried to laugh, but didn't quite manage it. Ella could see how disturbed she was. She was very quiet all evening, and neither of them was sorry when bedtime came and they could be alone, free to indulge their own thoughts.

There was a strong possibility that Kate would go back to Paul, Ella realised that. She had never actually said she still loved him, but that she did was plain enough. I want her to be happy, Ella mused, but can she be happy with *him*? He had been so blatantly unfaithful in the past, had all but flaunted his conquests. Surely Kate wouldn't risk that kind of humiliation again. Of course, he might have changed, people sometimes did. The saying about leopards never changing their spots didn't always apply.

More selfish thoughts followed, relating to her own position. How, for instance, would she manage if Kate went back to Ranstead to live with Paul? How would she be able to do her job with Hannah to look after as well? She sat up in bed to consider this, switching the light on as though to see the answer on the wall. She would have to use the services of a minder again—someone who would see Hannah to school and see her home. This had worked well at Seftonbridge, but it still wasn't ideal, and down here she had more on-call shifts when she could be called out at night. The best thing would be to engage a housekeeper, exactly as Patrick had done, but with one essential, important difference. He could afford that luxury, she, Ella, could not.

She fell asleep, still worrying, but when morning came, her confidence and optimism were back in place. She would work something out, if and when it happened. Meantime, it was Sunday and her turn to make the tea.

After two routine home visits on Monday, she drove to the hospital to visit Eileen Fern who had given birth on Sunday night to a seven-pound baby girl. Eileen looked exhausted but happy, and she wanted to talk.

'She came quite quickly, Ella, in just under eight hours. I wasn't induced or anything. I feel quite proud of myself!'

'And so you should be.' Ella looked at the baby, lying in her cot, wide awake, tiny hands folded. 'What are you going to call her?'

'Roberta, after my husband, Robert.' Eileen's face clouded a little. 'He doesn't know she's arrived yet, which seems terrible, doesn't it? The prison he's in is Bewlis, which isn't far from here. I've got a phone number, and I could ring, but I don't want to do it in here, not in the ward, it's a bit public. Do you think...' she looked worriedly at Ella '...you could wheel me out to a phone in the corridor?'

'I should think so, yes...I mean, I don't see why not,' Ella was saying when the bed curtain was twitched to one side and Patrick, unaccompanied, stood there looking down at them, and especially at the baby.

'Couldn't wait to see this one,' he said. 'You've done a great job, Mrs Fern, and with no medical intervention, *and* you're looking well.' He looked at her charts, then at Ella. 'Now, did I hear someone saying something about a telephone?'

'Yes, Eileen would prefer to use the phone outside the

ward—the one in the corridor. I could wheel her out there, I was about to ask Sister,' Ella said firmly, wondering if he knew Eileen's circumstances.

'Sister's not around at the moment. What I suggest is that you take Mrs Fern to the interview room. There's a phone in there, and less disturbance, and certainly less noise.'

Ella looked at Eileen, who nodded. 'That would be even better.'

'Splendid. I'll leave you to it!' With another smile for Eileen and her baby he was off up the ward to talk to a young mother whose baby was in Intensive Care.

He caught up with Ella again when she returned to the ward after wheeling Eileen to the interview room and leaving her there to phone. Beckoning her into the office and shutting the door, he perched on a corner of the desk and said, 'I suppose Mrs Fern is ringing the prison?'

'Oh, you know about it?'

'As her next of kin her husband's name, number and present address appear on her notes.'

'I'm so sorry for her.'

He shrugged. 'She seems happy at the moment. The worst thing about it, from her point of view, is that it makes her isolate herself.'

'She avoids her neighbours, I know that, which is why I was so worried about her before she came in here.'

'She'll have a job to avoid them once she's home and wheeling her baby around. There's nothing like a baby for attracting attention…amongst womenfolk, that is.'

'I'll keep an eye on her. I and the other three midwives all like her and know her circumstances. I can go round as a friend once or twice when I'm off duty.'

Expecting approval of this, expecting him to say that it was kind of her and just like her, expecting a beaming smile, all she got was another shrug and a penetrative look. 'Doesn't do to get too involved...detachment is all.'

'Not get involved, be detached!' Ella was outraged. 'That's your prerogative. Surgeons *can* remain detached. Not so a midwife, they can't and never are. Becoming involved with a patient is the name of the game. We almost become part of the family for a time, that's what community midwifery is all about!'

'Yes, I can see the difference,' he conceded, looking faintly amused, which didn't endear him to her, especially when he said, 'I noticed you used the word "patient" just now, which you told me was a taboo word when applied to pregnancy.'

She had no time to reply for Sister swept in, probably wondering what they were doing in her office and why there seemed to be an atmosphere prevailing, and why Ella looked so cross. 'No problems, I hope?' She looked at Patrick.

'No, Sister, not one,' he replied smoothly as Ella went out to collect Eileen.

With her phone call done, Eileen was all ready to be wheeled back to the ward. 'They told me,' she said, all shiny-eyed, that a message would be given to Robert within a matter of minutes. The man I spoke to was really nice, congratulated me and everything! Perhaps prisons aren't as bad as they used to be. Robert works in the library, you know. He's not a proper...he's not a proper...' And then she burst into tears.

'Baby blues...they all get it!' one of the hospital midwives said as, in the ward, Eileen was helped into bed. But saying goodbye to her, Ella wasn't too worried, or told herself she wasn't, though it was a very sad situation. How old, for instance, would Eileen's little Roberta be before she and her father met?

'She'll take her in to see him on visiting days,' Kate said that evening. 'I mean, the baby won't know where it is, will it, so it won't be affected.' In short, Kate wasn't all that interested. She had other things on her mind—like Paul's visit the day after next.

Picking tomatoes in the greenhouse after supper, Ella reflected on her brother-in-law's visit, trying to work out ways and means. Kate would need to have time alone with him, which wouldn't be easy to achieve in the hours running up to Hannah's party. She, Ella, had swapped shifts with Rosa so as to be free that day, mainly to get ready for the birthday tea, with all that entailed. When he gets here, she thought, I'll have to make myself scarce—blow up balloons in the garden, keep out of the sitting-room, stay in the kitchen, buttering things, with the door firmly closed. Fancy him choosing to come on Wednesday. It really was too bad.

She went on picking, the overripe fruit all but bursting in her hand. From the garden next door she could hear the sound of a cricket ball being thwacked and the shouts of the players—Robin's piping voice, Barbara's deeper tones. Hannah wasn't with them because her bedtime was earlier than Robin's. She wondered if Patrick was playing, making one person to bat, one to bowl and a third to field. If she looked through the hedge she would be able to see them—they seemed to be playing near it. Picking up her basket, she walked down the greenhouse. She had very nearly reached the door when the cricket ball, spinning over the hedge, burst through the roof like a bomb, sending shards of glass showering onto the floor, one of them spearing Ella's arm.

She cried out with shock and pain, stumbling out onto

the grass, blood running from elbow to wrist and covering the back of her hand. Instinctively she held her arm upright, but by then she was surrounded by people—Patrick, Barbara and Robin who'd burst through the hedge, Kate who'd come running from the house. Patrick was sitting her down on the grass. She felt his hair brush against her face, heard him call her 'darling', then more crisply add, 'It's not too bad, a small cut, but deep. We'll have to get you to Casualty.'

'Oh, surely not. Can't *you* do it?' Feeling steadier by the second, Ella stared into the concerned face so close to her own.

'I'm afraid not.' He shook his head. 'For one thing, I haven't got the wherewithal at home, and even if I had, I wouldn't attempt to suture that wound until it's been examined for splinters of glass.'

Kate's face was white. 'Oh, *Ellie!*' Barbara Manders was surprisingly mute. Robin, Ella noticed, looked very pale and automatically she said, 'Robin, don't worry... You didn't mean it...I mean, balls have a habit...'

'I was batting, it was me.' Barbara spoke at last.

Patrick looked impatient. 'Never mind that. Get Rob indoors. Kate, fetch a clean white towel and wind it round Ella's arm—not too tightly, she's not bleeding to death—then bring her through the house and I'll get the car up to your front door.'

'For heaven's sake, I've got the use of my legs, I can walk all right.' Ella, helped to her feet by Patrick, went into the house with Kate. A towel was fetched and held in place, by which time Patrick's car was at the front door and he was helping her inside.

'Is it painful?' he asked as they turned out into the

road, Kate watching till they were out of sight, wishing she could go as well.

'It throbs, but it's bearable.'

His hand came down on her knee for a second. 'Dear one, I'm so sorry!' He looked very tense, the line of his jaw taut.

'It was an accident.'

'Yes, and it happened because I was showing off.'

'What on earth do you mean?'

'I was bowling to Barbara, trying to spin the ball. It caught the side of her bat and over it went…over that bloody hedge!' he growled deep in his throat. Despite her throbbing arm, Ella wanted to laugh. It was unlike him to be contrite. 'Naturally,' he went on, 'I'll pay for the repair to the greenhouse, and when we get home I'll clear up the mess.'

Privately Ella thought that Kate was probably clearing it up already, but all she said was "Thank you. Please, don't worry about it." Then, more to the point, she asked if they were likely to have to wait half the night in Casualty.

'Not if I can help it.' They left Easthaven behind, and set off along the coast road. 'This is one of the occasions…' Patrick passed a bus '…when I intend to pull rank.'

Ten minutes later in A and E he seemed to have done just that. Ella was seen shortly after eight p.m. by the registrar in charge. Her inch-long wound was probed and pronounced clear of glass. 'We'll clean it up, insert a couple of stitches. Are your tetanus jabs up to date?' The young registrar, who wore half-moon spectacles, gazed at her over the top of them.

'I had a booster six months ago,' Ella told him, wondering where Patrick was. He hadn't come into the cubicle with her. He appeared immediately she was finished, though, so he must have been within earshot. 'I thought you'd deserted me!'

'Never that.' His eyes searched her face.

'How are you feeling?'

'All right.'

He took her good arm in his, 'Well, in that case we'll totter over the road to the Swan and Goose, where I'll ply you with a stiff drink.'

'There's no need, Patrick, there's no need to feel—'

'Not because I feel guilty, which I do—that's not the reason. I'm quite simply wanting your company for just a little while longer, *if* you feel up to it.'

'I do.' Ella was charmed by the compliment, but tried not to show it too much. The prospect of a drink was welcome, too, for she was feeling really parched. Maybe suffering an accident, however mild, had a dehydrating effect.

'You'll take tomorrow off, of course,' he said, as they crossed the road.

'I certainly will *not*!' Ella replied with heat. 'All I've got is a modest cut, it's not going to get in the way. I'm not a vet, you know, I don't have to use long-arm tactics, my clients aren't cows!'

He laughed. 'Even so…'

'Even nothing. I shall be on the job tomorrow unless I have a relapse in the night! The next day, yes, I *am* having off, because of Hannah's birthday.'

Patrick's further comment was lost to Ella, as an ambulance sped past, its siren blaring, and once it had gone there they were in front of the Swan and Goose. Even situated as it was in the heart of the town, it had a rustic ambience, with its dark oak tables set well back from the bar, its beams and brasses and coconut matting. Even the old English sheepdog, admitting all comers with tail-wagging indolence, added to the atmosphere. The cheerful bartender, who plainly knew Patrick, addressing him as 'Doctor, sir', brought the drinks to their table, handing the tomato juice to Ella, the brandy and soda to Patrick. Swiftly Patrick switched them over as soon as his back was turned.

'Drink up,' he said, raising his glass. 'You'll feel a new girl afterwards. Mind you.' He looked ruefully at his glass. 'This won't do a lot for me!'

Ella sipped from her glass and choked a little, 'Heavens, it's strong!'

'There's nothing like brandy for making one feel bucked-up, comfortable and relaxed.'

And it did all three things, Ella discovered. Most of all it made her feel easy and relaxed with *him*. Nothing was an effort, everything flowed…Why had she never drunk brandy before? She told him about her parents who were coming to stay in August. 'Kate and I will have to have a blitz on the house, wipe off some of the dust!'

'Where exactly in Scotland are they living?' Patrick asked, his professional eye noting with satisfaction that Ella's colour was coming back.

'Inveray, on the west coast. They love it there. Mother is Scottish, you see. It was always understood that they would retire there—I don't think Dad had very much say!'

'My folks retired to Aldeburgh on the Suffolk coast. They, too, have settled well. Sea, golf and music, they say…what more could a couple want?'

'Was your father a surgeon?'

'Both parents were. Dad was a consultant ortho surgeon at The Walbrook in London, Ma a paediatrician at the same hospital. I haven't encouraged them to visit yet, not till the house is in better nick.'

'I expect they'll come for your wedding,' Ella remarked, knowing full well that she was putting out a feeler and realising, as soon as the words left her lips, that Patrick knew it, too.

'Of course,' he replied, equally enough, but said nothing more. In fact, he turned the tables on her, asking if she and Andrew were heading for matrimony.

'It's not on my agenda, in spite of everyone I know writing me up for it. Anyway, Andrew and I aren't on that kind of wavelength,' she added honestly.

'Even so, he'll be harbouring hopes.'

'Oh, you know that, do you?' She was startled and showed it.

'I know people, and Andrew's not hard to read. You look like a family unit already—you, he and Hannah.'

'Yes, Hannah likes him.'

'Which counts for something, surely?'

Ella set down her glass and sighed. Patrick's persistence was beginning to irritate her. 'Well, of course it does,' she said, 'but having your child fond of someone isn't good enough reason to marry them. That's putting the cart before the horse!'

'You're speaking from a woman's viewpoint.'

'Well, I can hardly speak from a man's, and we're getting into one of our spats, aren't we? Shall we talk about something else—like gardens, for instance, *your* garden?' She made herself smile at him.

Patrick laughed then. There was one thing about him—he didn't mind losing an argument, he didn't fight to have the last word. He was a nice man...lovable...decent. Hard on the heels of this thought came others, came feelings strong to bursting point. His hand on the tabletop tempted hers to reach out and touch it, but she didn't move. She simply wasn't brave enough 'Shall we,' he said, and now *his* hand had made the journey across the table, 'agree to keep on safe subjects in future?'

'I'll drink to that!' Her free hand drained what was left in her glass, but the rest of her was electrified. As his fingers interlaced with hers, desire—hot, strong and sweet—coursed through her with pulsing throbs, whilst the look in his eyes held her fast.

'I think,' she said shakily, 'that we ought to be going.'

'Undoubtedly we had.'

As his hand left hers she almost grabbed it back. Instead she reached for her bag, wincing a little as the movement hurt her arm.

'Here, let me.' He retrieved the bag for her, sliding it onto her shoulder. He seemed as anxious as she was to go, although his expression told her nothing, making her feel—and not for the first time—that he'd closed a door in her face.

The sun was dipping itself into the sea as they emerged into the street, a big red-orange globe turning everything pink—the sea, the shore, the promenade, the road. Even the roofs of the houses climbing the hill were bathed in its light. Patrick's arm lay about Ella's shoulders, but he didn't draw her close. 'Once the sun disappears so the magic fades,' he said, steering her towards the car.

Ella nodded, but said nothing, wondering if his remark was in the nature of a *double entendre*…if he was referring to more than the setting sun…if he was trying to tell her that flashes of passion had no real substance, were as ephemeral as the light.

As though anxious to avoid a silence, he asked her

about Hannah's birthday. 'If you want extra help with the party I'm sure Barbara would assist, although I dare say you and Kate have got everything planned out.'

'We have, yes, or rather we had till we heard that Kate's husband will be coming down. It's two years since she and he met, and she's more than a little upset.'

'Is she hoping for a reconciliation?' Patrick asked with his eyes on the road.

'In her heart, yes, I think she is. Kate belongs to that band of stalwarts who think marriage is for life.'

'Not a bad principle. Where is he living now?'

'In the marital home in Surrey.' It wasn't necessary, she felt, to divulge more—to tell him what a louse Paul was, and how he'd betrayed Kate time and again. He didn't ask for details and she was thankful. Once again she thought how decent he was, and sighed deep inside herself.

'I suppose,' he enquired after he'd successfully passed a coachload of trippers, 'if they decided to join forces again, Kate would go back to Surrey.'

'Almost certainly, I should think.' She was surprised to find he was slowing and stopping the car, drawing onto the verge and turning to face her as though this was an important issue at stake. 'I always knew,' she went on, 'that we were unlikely to be living together for years and years, but somehow or other I never envisaged Kate going back to Paul, although once I was actually down here I suspected she still had feelings for him.'

A tendril of gold hair broken loose from her bun, caressed the side of her face. 'What would you do,' he asked hoarsely, 'if you were left here on your own?'

'Well, I can't go back to Seftonbridge, so I'd carry on as I am. And I'm not on my own, I have Hannah.' She heard the defensiveness in her voice. 'I shall manage, I always have. I shall work something out. All I hope and pray is that Kate will make the right decision for herself.'

'If you moved out of Longmead I'd be…I'd miss you.' He restarted the car, aware of the arousal of his body and what it might tempt him to say.

'As I live there rent-free,' she told him crisply, 'I'm unlikely to move out. I'm far more likely to move some-one in, as a lodger or paying guest!' It was necessary to take this tone, to seem hard and businesslike, other-wise—she stared out of the window, averting her face from his—she might find herself asking him to stop again. Then she'd launch herself into his arms, and to hell with everyone, especially Valerie, who was a liar and a cheat.

CHAPTER NINE

PAUL DELANEY'S green BMW turned into Longmead's drive just before midday on Wednesday, Hannah's birthday, and she rushed out to meet him. She had been only four when she'd last seen him, but in no way had she forgotten that he was a "fun" uncle, who gave her presents, and she was hoping for one today.

He came into the house through the open front door, tugged along by Hannah, looking, Ella noticed, much as he always had—well dressed and personable, his hair a shade too long. His eyes, flickering slightly, went straight to Kate. He's nervous and so he should be, Ella thought, receiving his kiss on the cheek.

Hannah, tearing the wrapping off her present—an expensive doll—turned not a hair when he told her that he couldn't come to her party. 'I'm taking Kate out,' he said, 'and we shan't be back until it's all over.'

'Paul, I have to be here! I mean, twelve kids take a bit of handling. I can't leave Ella...' Kate protested, but Ella could see she wanted to fall in with his plans.

'I can manage. Don't worry, Barbara's coming over—you go,' she said, and waved them off a few minutes later, mentally grinding her teeth. 'Plausible beggar,' she muttered, getting some salad out of the fridge.

There was a surprise in store for her, though, for when three-thirty came, and the garden was full of excited, noisy children, it was Patrick, not Barbara, who offered himself up as a helper.

'Dad had to take Barbara to the dentist. Her face is

all puffed up, and it hurt, too. We felt sorry for her,'
Robin explained.

'Abscess,' Patrick explained more briefly, 'so I
thought I'd come in her stead, that is, unless Kate and
you would rather...'

'Kate's gone out with her husband.' Ella tried not to
jump for joy for the sheer pleasure of seeing him there
in the kitchen. 'I couldn't,' she said, 'be more pleased
to see anyone!'

'Now, that is the nicest thing anyone has said to me
for a very long time!'

'Oh, rubbish,' she said, not daring to look at him. 'If
you really want to help, go outside and blow a whistle
and get the rabble in for tea!'

He did, and he sat down with them, too, and tucked
into the fare of pizza, chicken nuggets, crisps and sau-
sage rolls, ice cream and red jelly, and a generous slice
of birthday cake which Ella cut for him once the candles
had been blown out by Hannah, who was charmed to
have him there.

Afterwards he and Ella made an arch for Oranges and
Lemons, a ring was formed for the Pass the Parcel and
lines of chairs set up for Musical Chairs. And when a
fight broke out between two little boys, 'you pushed
me...its not fair!' Patrick sorted them out.

Kate appeared just as the party bags were being given
out, Paul having dropped her off and driven back home.
Pretty soon after that the first of the collecting cars
turned up the drive. Patrick, with an exhausted Robin,
left for next door before Ella had had a chance to thank
him properly, with so much going on.

By half past seven all the children had gone—all, that
was, but one little boy called Darren Parks, who stood
in the middle of the sitting-room looking rather forlorn.

'I expect your mummy's car has broken down,' Hannah suggested helpfully, dripping orange juice down her front.

'She's too big to drive. We walked here. I expect she's got her feet up.' Darren looked at Ella. 'Our house isn't very far, Mrs Fairfax, I could go home by myself.'

Ella shook her head. 'We'll wait a few more minutes, Darren, then if Mum's not come, we'll walk along to your home together. I know where it is. Now...' She took the orange juice from Hannah and set it on the table. 'Why don't you two go into the garden whilst I clear up here?'

They went off, neither of them very willingly, and Ella started to shift pieces of furniture back into their rightful places and pick papers up off the floor. The house, bereft of children, had a hushed, deserted air, the chink of crockery, as Kate loaded the dishwasher, the only sound to be heard.

Outside in the garden Hannah and Darren were half-heartedly tossing a ball. Looking at them, and especially at Darren, Ella frowned. She had known what the child had meant when he'd said his mother was too big to drive. At thirty-eight weeks pregnant, Tessa Parks was well out in front, making it a virtual impossibility for her to get behind a wheel. She had been walking to relieve her cramps, she'd said when she'd brought Darren earlier, but she had looked—and Ella was re-calling this now with a stab of anxiety—drained and haggard, not her usual beaming self. With so many chil-dren arriving *en masse*, there had been no real chance to ask her how she was. She was, strictly speaking, on Shirley's list, but Ella had visited her from time to time and had seen her at classes. Her husband, she knew, commuted to London each day, but surely he'd be at home by now.

The children gave up the ball game and sat forlornly on the grass. They were both tired, Hannah especially. Making up her mind to delay no longer, Ella was opening the casement to call Darren in when the doorbell shrilled, followed by a frenzied thumping and the sound of urgent cries.

'Who on earth…?' Kate, in the kitchen, set down a pile of plates with a crash.

Certain she knew, Ella flew to answer the door. Tessa Parks all but fell into the hall. 'The baby…it's coming…it's coming *now*!' Her groans changed to a volley of shouts as one contraction merged into another. Kate came running and Ella helped Tessa into a squatting position with her back against the wall, having snatched off her pants, telling Kate to fetch newspapers, sheets, towels, 'and my bag up in my room.'

The baby's head had crowned and was clearly visible before Ella could don her gloves, then it eased back as the contraction ceased, giving her time to spread the newspapers and sheets, comfort Tessa who said she felt sick and tell Kate to take the children next door.

Another contraction mounted and gripped, Tessa shrieked and pushed, then stopped pushing and was shouted at by Ella. 'Go on…go on… Don't stop, keep it going… Go on… Push that pain right out!' Then out it came, the small dark head—brow, eyes, nose and, with a little help from Ella, the chin.

'Clever girl, clever girl… The worst is over now!' It was at this point—with Tessa looking down at herself, astounded at what she was seeing—that Ella was aware of someone entering the hall from the back. She could see shoes and legs, men's legs, but had no time to look up for with the next and final contraction the rest of the baby was born and shot into Ella's lap, the yellowish blue and white umbilical cord piling on top of it.

'You have a little girl, Tessa.' Ella handed the child to her, slippery and yelling, blood-streaked but perfect. Tessa cried all over her.

'Thank you for what you did... Thank you for what you did!' Mother and daughter gazed blearily at one another, the baby flailing her arms.

Ella took her, clamped and cut the cord and wrapped her in a towel, after making sure that her airways were clear. It was at this point that the owner of the legs she'd glimpsed earlier appeared from Kate's workroom. It was Patrick. He squatted down to Tessa's level. 'Well done, Mrs Parks! Now, that's what we call a no-fuss delivery. That's a fine little girl you've got there!'

Ella introduced him. Tessa merely nodded, which was just about all she could do. As for Ella, the mere sight of him, and the fact that he'd come to her rescue again, caused a rush of happiness to flood her being, and just for a second or two the three of them—or four, with the baby—were joined in a ring of content.

There was clearing up to do, and Patrick did it whilst Ella saw to Tessa, helping her latch the infant to her breast, knowing that this might, with a bit of luck, get the afterbirth to manifest itself. Once it had done so, she and Patrick helped her to the downstairs cloakroom, where she was washed and made comfortable. She wanted her husband. Through in Kate's study, wrapped in a dressing-gown and half lying on a couch, she looked meaningfully at the telephone, cradling the baby in her arms.

Ella dialled the number for her, and both she and Patrick left the room whilst she spoke to her husband,

Jon. Even so, they couldn't help overhearing what she said. 'Yes, I'm fine, so is Megan—we said we'd have that name, didn't we? Yes, terribly quick, I very nearly didn't get here. I simply didn't realise... I thought I'd got hours, you know, like when Darren was born... Yes, he's next door, yes, being looked after... Jonnie, come and collect us now. I shan't need to go to hospital after all, so come right now, then we can all go home together!'

It was when she said this that Patrick's eye caught Ella's. 'With a fast birth,' he said, 'it's usually best for the mother to have a few hours in hospital, preferably one night.'

'Well, you go and tell her, then,' Ella said more briskly than she'd intended. 'While you're doing so I'll go and get Kate and Darren.'

As it turned out, Tessa proved remarkably compliant about spending a night in hospital. Her husband was in agreement—in fact, he was probably relieved. He'd had the presence of mind to bring with him the overnight bag which Tessa had kept packed and ready over the past two weeks. The case, as well as her night things and toilet articles, contained the baby's clothes, so Megan was able to be properly dressed before they all set off—Tessa half sitting half lying in the back of the car. Darren for once, and to his infinite joy, joined his father in the front.

'Stay and have a drink with us,' Kate said to Patrick once it was established that the family could make it to hospital on their own. 'I should think we all need one.'

'Ella does, I was an onlooker only.' Patrick smiled. 'I'd love a drink, but on second thoughts, why don't you both come over to Drummers? Hannah, too, of course. Barbara's getting a cold supper. There'll be plenty for the lot of us. It won't hurt the kids to be up late for once…being school holidays.'

'Now, that's the best suggestion I've heard for ages,' Kate said, looking at Ella as though daring her to disagree. Not that she had any intention of doing so…

'Just give me five minutes,' she said with a smile, 'to freshen up. And you, too, young lady.' She picked Hannah up and gave her a hug. Hannah had been very quiet since she'd seen the Parkses' baby, which she didn't think was lovely at all, although everyone kept saying it was.

Hannah's understanding of the facts of life was rudimentary. She knew her mother helped to get babies born, and that they came out of tummies. So far she had never enquired how they got in there in the first place, but by the look of her this evening Ella couldn't help wondering if Darren and Robin had extended her knowledge. Patrick, she was sure, would have given chapter and verse to Robin long ago. All this was passing through Ella's mind as she pulled off her party shirt and trousers and reached for a clean cotton dress.

The cold supper over at Drummers was enjoyed by them all. Even Barbara managed to sip a little wine, and eat very cautiously on the unswollen side of her face. The children were tired, though, especially Hannah who'd had a long day. 'I think I should get her home,' Ella said when they'd finished. Not that she wanted to go…not that she wanted to make any move that would wrest her from Patrick's side. She was pleased, therefore, when Kate got up.

'I'll take her,' she said. 'I have to get back anyway. Paul said he'd ring, he should just about be home by now.' She flashed a smile round at them all.

Shortly afterwards Barbara shooed Robin upstairs and,

refusing Ella's offer to help her clear up, replenished the coffee pot and left her to talk to Patrick.

'How about taking this into the garden?' Patrick lifted the tray. 'It's as warm as black velvet out there, and we can both do with some air.'

'Sounds a good idea.' Ella's heart began to beat in uneven jerks. 'I expect,' she said, trying to keep her feet firmly on the ground, 'that you're hoping for this kind of weather for your party.'

'I haven't really given it much thought, to be honest.' He sidestepped Lucy who, well into her pregnancy, was slow on her feet.

It was nine-thirty and the twilight was thickening. Assuming they were going to sit near the house, Ella was startled when Patrick carried the tray down to a seat outside Robin's den. 'Just in case,' he observed as he set it down on an old upturned box, 'You're thinking that I've brought you down here for nefarious purposes, I'll put your mind at rest by telling you that I often bring my coffee down here. I like looking up the garden at the house and relishing that it's mine—like a kid with a new toy maybe, but it gives me a buzz.'

Ella gulped at the coffee he'd passed her, half scalding the back of her throat. Deciding to ignore the first part of his explanation, she concentrated on the rest. 'I know what you mean. I'd love to own Longmead, but my parents don't want to sell it, and even if they did I'd need a very large mortgage, which would put it out of bounds.'

Patrick grunted a reply which she didn't catch. He was pouring his own coffee now, leaning forward, his fair head bent, his long legs flexed. Ella could hear the faint sound of the liquid going into the cup. All his movements pleased her. Even his back view thrilled. She

wished he hadn't assured her that she had nothing to
fear from him, wished he hadn't made a point of it,
wished he'd allowed her just a vestige of 'will he, won't
he', not killed it off at a stroke.

Even so, even with nil anticipation, it was good to sit
with him like this in the silent gloaming, drinking their
coffee, chatting about this and that. The three houses
looked down on them from their elevated positions. At
Elmhurst the lights were subdued and on in the ground-
floor rooms only. In the other two houses lights fairly
blazed, upstairs and down.

'Where there are children,' Ella said, 'there are always
more lights. It's the natural order of things.'

'Until Robin was five,' Patrick replied, draining his
cup, 'he wouldn't go to sleep without a night-light. After
Evelyn died he refused it, just like that. It was as though
he felt it was time to grow up, or it was the result of so
many folk telling him he'd got to be brave because his
mother would have wanted it.'

'Poor little boy!'

'Yes, poor little kid. It was a shocking time, both father and son were pretty needy then. Still, one moves
on, as they say. Now, let me replenish your cup.' He put
a hand out for it, and she caught her breath as his fingers
grazed hers.

'I ought to be going.' She was actually panicking, not
distrusting him but herself.

'Not quite yet.' He was already pouring, turned away
from her again. 'I want to tell you, at the risk of stating
the obvious, that I thought you did a splendid job on
Mrs Parks earlier on.'

'She did most of it herself, *and* at the double.' Ella
settled down again. 'But I like a bit of praise. I mean,

who doesn't? What I especially liked was that when I
was in the throes of it all, you didn't interfere.'

'Of course not.' He sounded shocked. '*You* were the
one in charge. We have a golden rule in hospital about
that—the midwife assisting a woman to deliver is left to
do just that. There may be others present—very often
are—but whoever they are, of whatever rank, they're
subordinate to her at that time. It would be demoralising
for the labouring woman to have more than one person
shouting at them.'

'Did I shout at Mrs Parks?'

He smiled. 'Just a bit, but you had to, to make yourself
heard above her shrieks!'

'Try having a baby yourself!'

'Nature hasn't fashioned me for that!'

'No,' Ella replied, but thinking how he *was* fashioned...right at that moment...made her whole body go
weak. She must go, she had to go. She started to get up,
but he was quicker, blocking her way, reaching out for
her, folding her close to him. She sighed deeply. His
long warm length against hers was exactly what she
wanted. She sighed again, raising her arms, and as his
mouth closed over hers, the grass, the trees, the whole
garden spun away, leaving just the two of them in a
limbo of touch, and feeling, and joy, flying off into space
where nothing mattered but staying close to him.

Coming back was a small agony, tempered only by
Patrick's voice telling her that she was lovely, so lovely,
whilst his hands moved them apart. Her body cooled
without his, helping her gain control. 'So much for good
resolutions!' She even managed to laugh.

'Yours or mine?' His voice sounded thick.

'Both, I suppose.'

'Mine started off firm, yet were easily toppled.' She

heard him clearing his throat. 'You're enticing, Ella, a sweet temptress. Your name should have been Eve.'

Ella stared up at him, trying to make out his expression in the darkness. What he'd said should have sounded like a compliment, yet somehow it did not. It made her feel like a tease, made her feel to blame, made her feel the guilty one. 'Oh, for goodness' sake.' Her voice rose. 'It was only a kiss. We got carried away. So what? It happens all the time!'

'As you say, only a kiss.' He turned and picked up the tray, then faced her again, holding it aloft, making—or so it seemed to the over-sensitised Ella—yet another barrier between them.

'Do you want to go out by the wicket gate?' He inclined his head towards it. 'Much quicker,' he added, as though speeding her departure.

She gave him a withering look, which she knew he couldn't see but hoped he felt. 'No, thanks, I'll come up to the house with you and go out the front. I want to say goodnight to Barbara.'

'All right.' He made to lead the way, but she caught up and walked at his side, stumbling along in the darkness, reflecting miserably that less than an hour ago they'd walked down this same lawn as a couple who were in tune with one another, who enjoyed one another's company, but now...now they were walking back up it as separate people. And all because of Valerie. Ella ground her teeth. All because we feel guilty. What I'd like to do is tell him she's not worth it, tell him what I saw, tell him she lied to him. But of course, I never will for if I did he'd hate me for it.

So she felt angry and frustrated, as well as miserable. It didn't help either that when she got home Kate was waiting for her and wanted to talk about Paul. 'He rang me as soon as he got in, said he had a decent run back, and he's coming down again at the weekend, staying at the hotel.' She was flushed and excited, and Ella's heart sank to an even lower level.

'He sounds keen.'

'Yes, I know. Oh, Ellie, he still…he still *fascinates* me. The feeling I have for him is the same as when we first met. He makes me feel young again!'

'You *are* young, we both are!'

'Since we split up I've felt ancient.'

'Well, you haven't looked it. You've been looking great, better than when you were with him!'

'I expect you think I'd be a fool to go back to him.'

'Yes, I do. But it's what *you* think that matters. It's your decision and only you can make it. All I ask is that you don't rush things. Give yourself time to imagine what it would be like if you went back to him, put your trust in him and then got let down for your pains. He's charming and plausible, and women will always want him. He may stray again.'

'He says he's changed.' Kate sounded deflated.

'Oh, sweetie, he may have, I may be quite wrong!' Ella went over and hugged her tight. 'You must know him better than I do. All I'm doing is preaching. Just give yourself time, though. Make him sweat a bit.'

Kate laughed then, hugging her back. 'What a tough cookie you are,' she said.

CHAPTER TEN

ELLA was shocked to run full tilt into Valerie in the maternity corridor next day—a very professional-looking Valerie in a trim white surgical coat, her dark hair swept back in combs. By her expression she was as taken aback as Ella. 'I thought you were community-based,' she exclaimed unsmilingly.

'I am, but I'm here most days, visiting newly delivered mothers. Don't tell me you've come to give them physio. We midwives are the prime instigators of pelvic-floor exercises!' Ella joked deliberately in a bid to ease her own awkwardness. But she was curious, too. What was Valerie doing here, looking so efficient and, as usual, so pleased with herself?

'I'm not stealing your thunder, no.' Her mouth moved in a little smile. 'I'm here for a few mornings in Physio while Tim Dyer's on leave. Patrick suggested I should put myself forward so, of course, I did. I like to do *some* NHS work, and it's not all that far to travel. I have to get back to my own patients in the afternoons, otherwise I'd stay at Drummers.'

Ella nodded, taking all this in. Tim Dyer, as she well knew, was one of the physio team.

'I'm surprised Patrick didn't tell you,' Valerie added, 'but perhaps you've not seen him lately.'

Ella stiffened. 'I have, but he didn't,' she said perfectly truthfully.

'Well, why I'm here now is to look for him.' Valerie

peered into the ward. 'We're supposed to be lunching together before I go back to Gaunt's Hill. I've already been into Gynae and they said he'd be here.'

'I think,' Ella said, for she was the one facing up the corridor, 'that this is him now, just coming through the landing doors.'

'Brilliant!' Valerie swung round, and set off to meet him, whilst Ella made a quick dive back into the ward, having no wish to see the couple converge and walk away together. Shifting round the big luncheon trolley which was being trundled out, she caught the eye of May Walker, who asked if she was having lunch in the canteen. 'If so, hang on for me, I won't be two shakes.' May was stripping down Tessa Parks's vacated bed. Tessa and her baby girl had gone home half an hour ago, full of thanks for all Ella had done.

'Did you know,' May asked a few minutes later when they were queuing up for toad-in-the-hole, 'that Patrick Weston's fiancée is doing a stint in Physio?'

'Yes, I did. I've just seen her—she was in Maternity looking for him!'

'Apparently…' May reached for a roll…'she's very efficient—"a little cracker" was how Jim Marsten described her. She's OK with all the equipment, too, and good with the patients. I bet Patrick loves having her under the hospital roof.'

'I expect so.'

They sat down with their food, May still full of chat. 'No doubt you've heard,' she said, busy salting her food, 'that they're giving a party in August. Bill Owen and his wife are going.'

'So are my sister and I,' Ella told her.

'Good Lord, *are* you? Lucky you!' May exclaimed.

'Only heads of departments are going from here. Sister is, of course, and her husband—no one below that rank.'

'Well, as Kate and I are neighbours,' Ella said carefully, 'I suppose he'd feel bound to ask us.'

'Are you going with anyone?' May was curious.

'Yes, with Andrew—he's the vet at Easthaven. I think Patrick…Mr Weston…has asked several of the locals.'

'You'll have to let me know all about it in *detail*— store it up in the old memory box.'

'I'll programme it for you,' Ella said, playing up to her whilst trying to rid herself of a feeling of dread where the party was concerned. Still, it wasn't for another two weeks, and in the meantime the ordinary, mundane things of life had to be attended to.

She was working over the weekend so she didn't see Paul when he arrived on Saturday, but when she got home in the evening there he was in the sitting-room with Kate, watching television. He rose to his feet, greeting her warmly as though *she* were the guest, saying something to the effect that the bad penny had turned up again.

Yes, and a very bright and confident bad penny, Ella was thinking as she went into the kitchen to get Hannah's supper. He looked as though he was back in the fold already, sitting there on the settee with Kate. She could see the two of them, see the backs of their heads as she stood at one of the worktops, cutting toast into strips. They were going to the hotel for dinner, so she and Hannah would be on their own.

The little girl was tired and made no protest later when Kate told her it was time for bed. 'I had a lovely time today,' she said watching the green BMW ease out of the drive. 'In the morning Uncle Paul played flock golf with me on the lawn.'

'Clock golf,' Ella corrected. It had been Kate's and her birthday present to Hannah.

'And in the afternoon we went on the undercliff and I took my scooter, and we had an ice cream in the café, and we saw Robin go by.'

'On his own?'

'No, with Patrick and Valerie. They were going swimming. We could see them going into the sea. Valerie's bottom looked fat.'

'Did they see you?' Ella decided to ignore her comment on Valerie's back view.

'No.' The little girl was reaching for her teddy—a sure sign that she was tired. 'Mummy, now that I'm seven I'm as old as Robin, aren't I?' she asked.

'Well, you're both seven,' Ella conceded.

'Yes, that's what I told him, so now I'll tell him again,' she said with emphasis, kissing her mother goodnight.

Ella was thinking of Valerie as she went downstairs. So, she was here this weekend, was she? And next weekend she and Patrick would be going to Town to see *Marriner's Folly*. 'Well, let's hope she enjoys it the second time round, and doesn't give herself away,' she muttered to Merlin, who was wagging his tail in the hall. Maybe they'd go on to a club and spend the night in Town. With all her heart she wished that the other night in the garden hadn't happened. All it had done had been to unsettle her, make her want him more and feel helpless and miserable when she thought of him with Valerie, living next door. If Kate does go back to Paul, maybe I *will* move out and find something on the other side of Easthaven just for Hannah and me.

She was in bed when Kate got home a little after eleven. Kate was in a thoughtful mood and didn't, when she came in to say goodnight, seem to want to talk. She did say, however, that she'd asked Paul to Sunday lunch next day. 'Couldn't you manage to get home for it?' she asked, knowing Ella would be on duty.

'Shouldn't think so, no. I've got a caseload as long as my arm, plus a long session at the hospital, so count me out.'

Just for a minute Kate seemed to hover, as though about to say something else, but in the end she blew her sister a kiss and went quietly to her own room.

It didn't help that Sunday, from start to finish, was a day of tumultuous rain. This made driving difficult, especially along the exposed coast road, where wind was a hazard as well. Ella decided to make the hospital her first call. There had been four babies born in the night, all of them to 'her' mothers.

Sundays on the ward quite often meant fewer midwives on duty, so she knew there would be plenty to do, teaching new young mothers breastfeeding skills, weighing their infants, reassuring them that they wouldn't always feel like geriatrics when they walked along to the loo.

Not all mothers took to their babies on sight, and Ann Harrison hadn't. Ella had seen her on home visits and at the antenatal clinic over the past six weeks. She and her partner, Clive, had seemed happy about the pregnancy, and according to the record of birth, which Ella read in the ward, her labour had been normal and the baby boy healthy with an Apgar score of eight. She greeted Ella apathetically, yet roused herself to talk. 'Honestly, Ella, when he came out I couldn't believe how awful he looked. I couldn't believe he was mine. I still can't, and I wish he hadn't happened. I'd like things to be as they were before, just me and Clive!'

She was crying in earnest, and Ella, who'd been cradling the baby, put him back in his cot and gave Ann all her attention. In no way was she shocked by her outbursts, for she'd met this reaction before.

'He's a lovely boy, Ann.' She spoke quietly but firmly, sitting on the side of the bed. 'And when you're not feeling so ragged and tired, and when you get home in familiar surroundings, with Clive fussing over you, you'll feel entirely different. Plenty of mums feel like you do at first. It *is* a shock when you first see your baby, when you realise he'd actually come—a yelling, screwed-up little stranger who's put you through so much.'

Ann looked doubtful, and Ella encouraged her to take a good look at her son. 'See, he's waking up. Lift him out, get used to the feel of him, hold him to you, cuddle him. That's right, he knows you're his mum! Now, how can you say he's ugly? I've never seen such blue eyes!'

'He's got Clive's jug ears.' Ann refused to enthuse, but she didn't, Ella noticed, put him down, and she was still holding him and looking at him when Ella crossed the ward to visit the other three new mothers, all dying to tell her how they had fared and to show her their babies.

The rain was still coming down in sheets when she left the hospital and drove back into Easthaven to do her afternoon house calls. It didn't help that because of the rain she arrived on every doorstep dripping water from the waxed coat and sou'wester she always kept in the car. The Parkses' house was her last call, that being the nearest to home. It was half past four when she got there, and Darren opened the door, looking fed up because of the weather, which meant he couldn't play outside. He was pretty bored with the baby, too, and told Ella so whilst she stood in the hall and shook her mack outside, trying not to drip over the floor. 'She's always crying, even in the night. It's all different since she's come.'

'Tiny babies *do* cry, I'm afraid, Darren,' Ella was saying when Tessa came out of the sitting-room with four-day-old Megan in her arms. Unlike her son, she was all bright and blooming.

'He resents the baby a bit,' she confided to Ella when the little boy was out of range. 'He's not so bad when his father's at home, but he's gone to the hospital this afternoon to see Peggy, his mother. She's having an operation tomorrow—a hysterectomy. Mr Weston's doing it. She's been on the waiting list for absolute yonks—before he even came here. Anyway, with luck—' she crossed her fingers '—it'll all be over this time tomorrow. They say he's very good. He was certainly wonderfully kind to me when I gave birth in your hall!'

'He's an obstetrician as well as a gynaecologist,' Ella said in neutral tones, weighing baby Megan with her back half-turned.

'You never forget the people who are with you at times like that,' Tessa continued, unaware of the turmoil assailing her favourite midwife. 'I shall never forget you, for instance. And if…*if* I ever have another child, I'll book in for a home birth, choosing my own home instead of yours!' She laughed happily as she took the baby back into her arms, although it did cross her mind that Ella looked pale, as though she were sickening for a cold.

Paul had gone when Ella got home just after five. By then the rain was abating a little and a glittering sun was coming through, forming an almost perfect rainbow, much to Hannah's delight. 'Where does it start from, Mummy, and where does it go? Will it last until tomorrow, and where will it go at night?'

'Your mother is exhausted,' Kate said briskly. 'She's been answering questions all day. I'll tell you all about the rainbow when we've had our tea.'

Later, over supper, she told Ella that she was going to Town on Wednesday. 'I've got to call in at Atchinsons anyway, so I'll meet Paul for lunch.'

'Sounds all right.'

'He's taking me to the Gay Hussar.'

'Even more all right.'

'You did say it was your day off, so you'll be here for Hannah?' she asked.

'Yes, I did.' The beef sandwich Ella was eating, liberally spread with horseradish horse, was having a tonic effect. 'You going to give Paul a favourable answer over a boozy lunch?' She eyed her sister carefully, and watched a blush come up.

'Probably not. At the moment,' she said, 'I'm enjoying being wooed. He's coming down here again the weekend after next, so he'll come to the party as my partner, which will do wonders for my self-esteem.'

'I can see that.' Ella smiled, but felt a prick of misgiving, very nearly strong enough to be called foreboding, which she told herself was absurd.

During the early afternoon of Monday, Ella who had been taking a booking history from a woman in Marlborough Road, was surprised to see Patrick's cream car parked at the opposite kerb. He was probably, she thought, paying a domiciliary visit on a patient too ill to get to his clinic. As she was getting into her own car he emerged from the house—let out by an elderly man whose hand he shook. Ella dawdled deliberately, employed slow-motion tactics, not that she needed to for as soon as the elderly man had gone in and closed his door Patrick, who had seen her, made his way over to her.

'A quick word only,' he said as she let down her window, 'to remind you to get those stitches of yours out on Wednesday.'

'I shan't forget.' When she smiled her face felt stiff, but she persevered relentlessly, for she would *not* let him see how his presence affected her. He was bending down low to see into the car. She could see the grain of his skin, the wide mouth, slightly smiling, showing the tips of his teeth. 'I had remembered.' Her jaw stiffened, but she went on speaking and smiling as well. 'The practice nurse at the centre will oblige, I shan't need to come up to Casualty. I'm amazed that *you* remembered.' Her hand went out to turn the key in the ignition.

'As I was responsible for the injury I'd hardly forget,' he said, flattening himself against the side of the car to let a van go past. When it had gone he took his leave of her, striding back to his own car, which was pointing in the direction of Charding, the opposite way to hers. When they each drew off, the distance between them yawned as wide as a gorge, which just about, Ella thought sadly, summed up the way things were between them—glimpses only, chance encounters and, just occasionally, a stolen moment, whetting her appetite for more.

It wasn't like that on Wednesday, though. The tide ran in her favour. It was her day off, and in the morning she had her stitches removed—flicked out disdainfully, in a matter of seconds, by the centre's efficient nurse. Barbara had looked after Hannah all morning, Kate having gone up to Town, so, with the idea of offering to have Robin for the afternoon, Ella went over to Drummers, noticing with a small dart of pleasure that

Patrick's car was in the drive. She remembered then, that if he possibly could, he snatched an afternoon off midweek, depending on the state of his list. She hesitated, wondering whether to ring the doorbell or not. Clearly Robin would rather spend the afternoon with his father so, restraining Hannah who was all for leaping up the front steps, she was just about to turn away when the door opened and there they both were—father and son, the latter clutching a kite, the former a large plastic bag.

'Hello. You looking for Barbara?' Patrick joined them on the path, tall, all male, cool in cream chinos and short-sleeved blue shirt.

'Well, I was going to ask her if she would like me to take Rob out for the afternoon—down to the beach, perhaps, with Hannah—but now that you're at home…'

'We're going on the Downs to fly my new kite.' Robin held it out for Hannah to see.

'Oh, can't we go with them? Can't we, Mummy? We can go on the beach any day,' Hannah entreated, before Ella could stop her.

'Please, come with us, we'd both like you to,' Patrick broke in. '*I'd* love you to.' He was looking directly at Ella. 'Barbara has packed a picnic tea.' He swung the plastic bag. 'There's far too much for Rob and me. Besides, you haven't told me how your arm is.' And somehow this was said as though his invitation had already been accepted, for he was handing her into the car!

'Now, that,' she said, happily settling herself, 'was a very slick manoeuvre!'

'Practically sleight of hand—do you mind?' He was sliding in beside her.

'Maybe not.' She was catching his mood, 'I mean, if I haven't anything better to do, why not fly a kite?'

'I adore you!' he said, and she exulted, then wondered if she'd heard aright. The children were making such a din in the back, perhaps she'd heard what she'd wanted to, but when she glanced at him he winked at her...*wickedly* winked at her.

'A little time free from care—' he grinned '—is what we're having this afternoon!'

A few minutes later, with the car parked in a rutted lane at the foot of a slope, they all began to climb the gentle incline known as Beacon Hill. It was a favourite spot for walkers, but this afternoon it was all theirs—the green slopes, the rim of the sea blue as the peerless sky, faint sounds reaching them airborne, traffic down on the road, the shouts of golfers on the miniature course and, nearer at hand, the mewing of the kittiwakes wheeling overhead.

Happiness filled Ella. Perhaps it came in with the air. When Patrick reached for her hand as they got nearer the top, she felt her cup was full. I love him, she thought, I really love him! Why, I love him even more, or perhaps I mean differently from the way I loved my dear Tom. And I don't believe he loves Valerie. I just *don't*, or he wouldn't be like this with me!

The children's voices, high-pitched, blew back to them. 'Daddy bought me the kite,' Robin was saying, 'but I haven't been able to fly it yet because the weather hasn't been right.'

'Well, it will be today.' Patrick and Ella caught up with them. 'There's this brisk little wind to help us. We'll have lift-off in no time at all.'

And this was the case, after one or two tries, Patrick instructing his son. 'Remember, the higher it flies, the greater tug it exerts, so let the tether out v-e-r-y gradually and concentrate all the time. Kite-flying is a science, Rob, and has to be learned.'

And he, Ella thought—meaning Patrick—is having the time of his life. The red and blue kite with its bunting tail dipped and dived and soared, straining on its tether, soaring even higher. Robin was speechless with delight, but when the tether was fully extended, when there was no more to be wound out, Patrick stood behind his son, taking the handle as well. 'Because we don't want it hang-gliding you over the Downs to the sea!'

He was brilliant with the child, Ella observed, and the child with him. There was tremendous rapport between them—father and son at their best. Ella's hand strayed to Hannah standing close by her side, her golden head flung back, her mouth wide open as she stared up at the sky. 'You'll have the kite drop right down your throat if you don't watch out,' she teased.

When the kite-flying was over, they sat down to eat a short distance down the hill, Patrick unpacking the sandwiches and cake Barbara had packed. 'It's nice here, better'n the beach,' Hannah declared, smiling winningly at Patrick with her mouth full of egg and cress.

'I like both,' Robin said stoutly, brushing crumbs off his jeans. They were the same blue as his father's, their hair the same fawnish fair. They look good enough to paint. The thought passed through Ella's mind, just as an elderly couple came into sight on one of the upper paths. They were looking their way, they were stopping, then the woman called out to them. 'I was just saying to my husband what a lovely family picture you make, picnicking in the sun. Children love it, don't they? So good for them out in the air. Make the most of them while they're little—they grow up so quickly these days!'

'Kind of you to notice us. We certainly treasure our kids!' Patrick got up to wave to the couple as they proceeded along the narrow bridle path, walking carefully with sticks.

'Should you have said that?' Ella's hand shook slightly as she poured tea from the Thermos jug.

'Don't see why not.' He helped himself to cake. 'It did no harm, it was easier than going into explanations. Besides...' he chewed reflectively on a nut '...a chap can dream.'

Ella blushed and was furious with herself for doing so, and furious with him for playing silly games. He was watching her like a hawk. 'I wonder what it's like to be old,' she said, looking past his head at the elderly couple in the near distance stopping to admire the view.

'Hopefully we shall find out one day.' Patrick was sipping his tea, his gaze transferred to his cup.

'Grandpa's *very* old,' Hannah remarked, in the same breath asking if she and Robin could go and play ball 'down on that smooth bit—we don't want to eat any more'.

Separate parental consent being given, off they went, two little figures, one taller than the other, one blue-jeaned, one pink-frocked. Ella's eyes strayed to the man at her side. She hadn't quite got over the shock, or thrill, at having been taken for his wife!

'Want to join them?' he asked, still watching the children.

'Not really.'

'That's good.' He moved closer to her, slipping his arm within hers, turning it to look at her scar. 'A tiny blemish on smooth-as-silk skin.' He raised her hand to his face, laying the back of it against his cheek, kissing the knuckles one by one. She melted with love for him, waited for more, waited for him to hold her, to bring his mouth down on hers. 'Dear one, I daren't!' He could read her so easily, he was looking straight into her eyes. 'If I kiss you I'll never be able to stop!' And with that he jerked to his feet, putting space between them, not even looking at her till he stooped and helped her up. 'Best not to.' He was smiling again, but his face was very white.

'I couldn't agree more.' She hadn't quite recovered. She found her sunglasses and put them on. 'I think a good rousing ball game with the children would be a good idea,' she said, 'and after that I'd like to get home. Kate will be back from London at six. I want to be there when she comes in.'

In the car going home there was silence in the front and a hullabaloo in the back. Robin and Hannah were squabbling, tired and overwrought. Patrick had to concentrate on the traffic which was heavy at that time of evening. Ella spoke now and then, but mostly to the children, trying to shut them up.

Kate was getting out of a taxi as they turned into Drummers's drive, so goodbyes were necessarily brief. Robin and Hannah parted as good friends again, the latter rushing over to Kate, who was bursting to tell Ella her news—that she was going back to Paul.

The details of her day were all revealed later once Hannah was in bed. 'We went down to Surrey and saw the house, it was as though I'd never left. You *are* pleased, aren't you, Ellie? Say you're pleased for me!' She got up and hugged her twin. Ella hugged her back.

'Of course I'm glad, of course I am, if it's what you want.' Her voice faltered just a little as she added, 'I know you've always loved Paul.'

Kate went on to tell her that he would be away on

business over the following ten days, 'but he'll come down here on the night of the party, he's booking us in at the hotel for the three weekend nights'.

'Why the hotel? What's wrong with here? You don't have to be bashful,' Ella teased.

'No, but the hotel will be like being on honeymoon. I shan't be joining Paul permanently until the following Saturday.'

'When the parents come down.'

'Oh, I'll see them before I go, and it'll help *you*, won't it, them being here for a bit? I mean, thinking about Hannah and when you'll be at work…they'll be tickled to death to be able to help out.'

'Temporarily, yes.' Ella felt as though a rug were being tugged from under her feet. The thought of what lay ahead appalled her, but she tried not to let it show. 'I'll have to start making long-term arrangements even so— find a minder and all that. Still, I've done it before and I can again. Now, how about two large drinks to celebrate your good news?'

CHAPTER ELEVEN

APART from fleeting glimpses, Ella didn't see Patrick until noon on the day of his party. She was just leaving the ward after visiting three mothers who'd given birth during the night. Thinking about lunch and crossing to the line of lifts, she saw him there with Valerie and a crowd of other people, including Professor Moden from haematology. Because of Valerie, and also because of the professor, she hung back. She'd get the next lift down. But Patrick spotted her, so she joined them—she could hardly do anything else, particularly as he was looking pleased to see her. She went forward, eager now, scarcely seeing anyone else.

As for the professor, he was ogling Valerie, one of his hands hovering about her trim person, as though dying to land. 'You know, my dear,' he was saying in his best treacly voice, 'I'm certain I've seen you somewhere before—not here in the hospital, but somewhere outside. I never forget a beautiful face!'

Patrick looked amused, Valerie laughed, the professor continued to gaze, then burst out with, 'Of course, of course, I remember where it was—the Arts Theatre, *Marriner's Folly*. You were sitting in the stalls with your escort! My wife and I had a box. It was her birthday, so I remember the date—the ninth of June!

Just for a second, and Ella was watching her closely, Valerie looked disconcerted, then she said, again with a little laugh, 'Perhaps I have a double, Professor, for it certainly wasn't me. I was in the West Country that

153

night, visiting my mother. I *have* seen the play, but in London. Patrick took me last weekend.'

The professor's mouth opened and shut, but he had the sense not to say any more. Fortunately, at that point the lift arrived and they all got in. Squeezing to the back, Ella could see him staring at Valerie with a thoughtful expression on his face. He's rumbled her, she thought. He knows what he saw, but will he leave it at that, or do a little spiteful stirring, just for the sake of it?

'I hope he does,' Kate said, when told about the episode later. She and Ella were getting ready for the party a little before seven o'clock. Paul had walked in at teatime, but was getting dressed at the hotel. The babysitter for Hannah had arrived, and at Drummers two caterers' vans stood in the drive, whilst out in the back garden tables and chairs were being set out, extra lights being rigged. Now and again Patrick could be seen, directing operations, sometimes with Barbara in tow, sometimes not. There was no sign of Valerie.

'I bet he's dumped her...finally!' Kate was zipping herself into an emerald green slimly cut dress, perfect with her russet hair. Ella, already dressed so that Hannah could look her over, was in midnight blue flared silk trousers with a fringed tunic top. Her hair was down and drawn forward over her shoulders, to lie in silken yellow swathes over the swell of her breasts. 'You look good enough to eat,' Andrew told her, the look in his eyes suggesting his feelings weren't as purely friendly as he'd been pretending these last few weeks. Ella felt a twinge of guilt.

Paul, who had walked up from the hotel to save car space at the houses, arrived at Longmead soon after Andrew. Each remembered the other from visits in the past, before the crack in Kate's and Paul's marriage had widened to danger point. Tonight both men were dark-suited—Paul tall and suave, Andrew more stocky. They had a sherry apiece—a pre-party drink—but when they saw Andrew's parents passing the house *en route* for Drummers, off they went, arriving at the precise moment that Valerie's car turned into the drive.

'For the hostess, she's cut it a bit fine,' Kate whispered to Ella, and this was certainly the case, for eight or nine guests had already arrived. It was Patrick who was welcoming them in, shepherding them through the house into the sunlit garden. He was putting his all into it, too, persuading them to mingle, seeing that they were comfortably placed and supplied with drinks. He was delighted to meet Paul, or so he said, there was a kiss for both Kate and Ella. 'The most glamorous neighbours a man could wish for,' he joked, and everyone laughed.

Half the guests—about twenty-strong—had arrived before Valerie appeared. She was all apologies, blaming the traffic— 'a hold-up on the bypass!' She redeemed herself, though, going round to talk to all the seated people, and to the strollers, and to the newcomers, and guests who were still coming in. She came to Longmead's table last. 'Oh, great, people I know…' she began, then looked at Paul, open interest in her eyes.

'This is my husband, Paul.' Kate's introduction rang with pride and a hint of triumph as she watched the two shake hands.

Valerie's guests from Gaunt's Hill arrived at this point and Patrick was introduced as 'my cousin-in-law', not 'my fiancé' or even 'my partner'. Ella picked this up at once. What could it mean? Had there been a split? She looked at Kate, who gave a small grimace, although Andrew, downing his second drink, didn't appear to have noticed. Paul saw and noticed everyone, he was a party man to the core. Liking the look of the whole scenario, he prepared to enjoy himself. So also did Valerie. Flamboyant in a rustling jade and cream dress, she flitted through the crowd of forty or so guests like a chattering tropical bird. 'A flaming parrot,' Ella whispered to Kate, who giggled and agreed.

Parrot or not, she was out to charm Paul and made no secret of it. It was astonishing how often she found her way back to the Longmead table, chatting politely to all six of them but with her eye and attention mainly on Paul and a hand on his arm as she looked to him for confirmation of what she was saying. ''Now, *you*, Paul, I'm quite sure, will know exactly what I mean.'' Plainly he didn't mind the attention but, and Ella was watching him closely, he in no way invited it or sought to further it. But Kate's face wore an anxious look.

Supper was served inside the house, which meant that Valerie joined up with Patrick in seeing that each guest was served from the long buffet table, which had been set up in the hall, as the main sitting-room had been cleared for dancing later. The Longmead group, with four people from the hospital, carried their trays out onto the terrace. Dusk was falling, the sun, long set, had brought out the scents of the garden.

'I think it's wonderful what Patrick has done with it in such a short time,' Sister Martin of Gynae enthused.

'You must give me some credit for the garden.' Valerie was back again. 'It's the herb section that's so aromatic. When supper's over—' and once again she was looking straight at Paul '—you must take a stroll down there—it's well worth a visit.'

'So it may be, but it's not exactly Highgrove.' Patrick arrived to stand at her side, giving Ella a chance to look her fill at him for the first time that evening.

In his softly tailored dark jacket and light trousers, he was more comfortably dressed than many of the male guests, yet there was a tenseness about him, not lost on Ella. There was also a feeling of distance between himself and Valerie. Had the two of them reached some kind of crossroads?

The polished wood floor of the sitting-room was perfect for dancing, and after supper, with the beat of the music thrumming through her ears, Ella began to enjoy herself. She danced with Andrew first, then with Paul, three doctors from the hospital, then with the elderly Mr Savers, who ruefully admitted that he preferred the kind of dancing where he could hold onto his partner.

This, thought Ella, is a really good party. Patrick has planned it well. She wondered where he was, then saw him partnering Mrs Savers, smiling at something she was saying. Valerie was nowhere to be seen and neither—Ella glanced round the room—was Paul. Was this significant or not? She prayed it wasn't, and was about to look out on the terrace when Patrick asked her to dance. She went willingly, oh, so willingly, into his arms, forgetting all else.

'How do you think it's going?' he asked, holding her loosely, no more closely than if she'd been Mrs Savers.

'Relax!' Her hands slid down his shoulders. 'It's positively humming. Everyone's having a great time, and you're the perfect host!' She hoped to make him smile, and he did so, but stiffly. His eyes were everywhere but on her, and she felt affronted. Surely he didn't have to watch the state of play *all* the time.

'I'm sorry Valerie is making such a fool of herself with your brother-in-law,' he said so suddenly and unexpectedly that she trod on his foot.

'Oh, well…' Be careful, Ella told herself. 'It wouldn't

matter in the ordinary way, but their relationship is still at the being-mended stage, it's not well rooted yet.'

'I'll speak to Val.' And now he was being really distant, staring over the top of her head.

'Please, don't do that.' Ella felt irritated. 'You'll only make matters worse!' Speak to *me*, say something to *me*, to hell with everyone else! she screamed inside her head, but it didn't happen. He was courteous and pleasant, and this was all there was.

Andrew claimed her then, drawing her onto the terrace 'to chill out after the fray'.

'Where's Kate got to?' Ella asked him, looking back into the room, then at the couples on the terrace.

'She's gone home to change her shoes. One of the heels went wobbly when we were dancing,' he replied.

Ella laughed. She wasn't surprised. 'I think,' she said, 'that I'll slip home, just for a minute, to check if Hannah's all right.'

'I'll come with you.' Andrew jumped up.

'No, don't. You stay here. We can't all wander off.'

Deciding not to risk her silken trousers by pushing through the hedge, Ella made her way down to the wicket gate, and had passed through the screen of shrubs when she spotted Paul and Valerie on the seat outside Robin's den. Now, in no way could they be said to be entwined, but they *were* sitting close. Valerie's arm was through Paul's and they were curiously silent, their faces turned to one another, oblivious of Ella's approach. Dismay…and anger halted her steps. She was about to call out to them when Kate, who had seen them from the other side of the gate, snapped it open, reached them in seconds and stood in front of the seat.

'Admiring the view?' she enquired. 'What a good idea!' She sat down next to Paul. 'If you'll let go of his arm, Valerie, he'll feel more comfortable. Oh, look, here's Patrick, coming to find you.'

'Splendid!' Valerie slid her arm out from Paul's, very deliberately, making a show of it but staying where she was. By the time Patrick reached them, however, Paul was on his feet, jerking his cuffs down, standing next to Kate.

'Why are you all down at this end?' Patrick asked, for some reason addressing his question to Ella.

'I was on my way to check on Hannah—' she began, but was interrupted by Kate. 'And I was on my way back from slipping home to change my shoes, and then we both chanced on your fiancée about to swallow my husband whole!'

There was a terrible, breath-holding silence, broken by Paul, who, plainly deciding to ignore Kate's remark and looking the epitome of calm, said he felt it was time he and Kate were getting down to the hotel. 'It's been a terrific party—thank you for including me.' He held out his hand to Patrick, who took it.

Ella sighed with relief. And don't you dare say another word, Kate, she ordered inside her head. She managed to get the warning across, too, telepathy between them being strong.

Kate went off with Paul, silently exploding, and Patrick told Valerie that other guests were wanting to go. 'Please, come with me to see them off.' He waited for her to get up.

'Sure, why not? A hostess must host, and do her duty by all!' With a rustle of her skirt she got up from the seat, Patrick turned on his heel. 'You know,' she remarked to Ella as the three of them walked up to the house, 'your sister has a very unpleasant habit of making waves. I do hope you're not the same.'

'Very likely I am, being her twin,' Ella refused to be drawn. Patrick maintained a stony silence, which was probably just as well.

It was a shock to get home, some twenty minutes later, and find Kate slumped in a chair in the sitting-room. 'I told the babysitter she could go,' she said. 'Hannah hasn't stirred.'

'Where's Paul?' Ella asked sharply.

'At the hotel. I told him to go. There's no need to look like that, Ellie. You saw how he was tonight. Where women are concerned he can't be trusted. They've only got to look at him and he's all over them like a rash!'

'Well, he wasn't tonight. I thought he trod the very difficult path of having to be pleasant to Valerie as his hostess and fend her off as well.'

'That bloody woman.' Kate blew her nose with a vicious trumpeting sound. 'You warned me, didn't you, that day on the beach, about making an enemy of her?'

'Yes, she may have been paying you out for saying what you did. She may also have had a row with Patrick tonight and been getting her own back on *him*.'

'What do you think I should do?' She looked the picture of misery, and Ella's heart went out to her.

'Ring for a taxi, get your bag and go up to the hotel. I can't drive you, I've had too much to drink and so have you. Just go there and sort it out, one way or another. Come back here after, if you have to, of course, but give the man a chance.'

So off Kate went, when she didn't return Ella decided she'd done her good deed for the day and she climbed into her solitary bed. Her head still buzzed with the events of the evening, but just before sleep claimed her, she was thinking not of Kate and Paul but of Patrick and

Valerie. Had they had a row? *Had* they, and was it serious?

She was awakened just after seven next morning by Hannah, calling out and climbing all over her. 'Mummy, you've got to get up. Uncle Andrew's come, he's getting our breakfast!'

'At this hour?' Ella was still fogged with sleep. 'How did he get in?'

'He rang the bell and I let him in. I've been up hours and hours!' Hannah, in shorts and a T-shirt, her hair neatly brushed, was hopping first on one leg and then on the other, making her mother's head swim.

'Go and tell him,' Ella said, 'that I'll be down in five minutes.'

Going into the bathroom, she performed hasty ablutions then donned a skirt and sleeveless top. Fancy him coming at this hour. She dragged a brush through her hair then, trying to look as though she was pleased to see him, she made her way downstairs.

In the kitchen the table had been set, cereal poured into bowls. 'Three bowls like the three bears, Mummy, that's what Uncle Andrew said.' Bread had been sliced ready for toasting, whilst the coffee, freshly brewed, went at least part of the way to breaking Ella's grumpy mood.

'Shouldn't you be doing all this for your parents?' she asked, sitting down.

Andrew shook his head. 'They won't be up for hours. I've got to be because of surgery, but I thought we could eat together and perhaps plan something to do this afternoon.'

It was Saturday, of course. Ella shook herself mentally as she sipped her coffee. 'I thought,' Andrew continued, 'that we might go to the lido out at Heron's Point. We could have tea there at the café. You'd like that, wouldn't you, Hannah?'

The child beamed through a mouthful of toast. '*Can* we?' she asked her mother, who put down her cup and smiled.

'I don't see why not.' She looked across at Andrew. 'Yes, that would be nice,' she said. She had actually planned a day in the garden, doing calming things like weeding and loosening soil round roots, and perhaps catching sight of Patrick, finding out what, if anything, had happened overnight.

'It was a good party, wasn't it?' Andrew remarked, breaking into her thoughts. 'I enjoyed meeting Kate's husband again. I hope they make a go of it this time.'

'I hope so, too.' Ella's wish was heartfelt.

'Talking of which, I thought we might have heard some sort of announcement from Patrick about him and Valerie. Aren't they supposed to be getting spliced some time this autumn?' Andrew buttered his toast with a harsh scraping sound, setting Ella's teeth on edge.

'I've no idea,' she answered shortly.

'I would have thought the sooner the better, for Robin's sake.'

Ella was about to query this, to say that Robin seemed happy enough. He and Hannah, after a tricky beginning, had become best mates. They practically lived in that den of his, which had been everything under the sun from a supermarket, to a hospital, to a hut in the African jungle. It had also been an inspiration on Patrick's part, Ella thought with admiring warmth, just as a tap came on the door, the shadow on the frosted glass being clearly recognisable as Patrick's…she had virtually conjured him up.

'I'm unforgivably early, I know,' he began as soon as she opened the door, 'but I just came to ask—' Then he stopped in midsentence as his eye alighted on the breakfast table, and the sticky-mouthed Hannah, and Andrew getting up from his chair. 'Sorry, I didn't realise you had company.' He half backed to go out again.

'Oh, I'm just off.' Andrew started to clear away. 'Got a clinic starting at half-eight. No rest for the wicked, they say! Ella and I were just saying, Patrick, that it was a really good party.' He looked at Ella for confirmation, and she managed to nod, telling him to leave the washing-up 'or you'll make yourself late'.

'OK, will do!' He reached for his jacket. 'Pick you up at two. Your turn next.' He grinned at Patrick, brushing past him to the door.

'I didn't realise there was a queue!' Patrick's mouth moved in a smile that didn't ring true.

'There isn't,' Ella said shortly, stopping Hannah from dipping her finger into the sugar bowl. 'That's a dirty habit, I've told you before!' The child backed off, running out into the garden to talk to Robin through the hedge. 'Kids!' she made an expressive gesture, but Patrick didn't respond. She tried again. 'There's enough coffee left for two cups—would you like some?' she asked. 'We could take it out into the garden. It might help wake me up!'

'Plainly you've had an exhausting night!'

'That's a pretty cheap remark to make!' She turned a startled face to his—a stubborn face, too. She didn't intend to explain Andrew's early presence at Longmead, not when he jibed like that. 'Do you want coffee or not?' she snapped.

'Yes, if you please.'

'Good, well, take it, then.' She thrust the mug at him,

walked out of the door, round the corner of the house and onto the patio. He followed her and sat down.

'Is your sister all right this morning?'

'I've no idea. She isn't here. She spent the night at the hotel with Paul—they *are* husband and wife.'

'Of course, yes.' He gulped at his coffee, then began to question her. 'You saw Valerie and her boyfriend at the theatre, didn't you, that evening you went with Andrew?' The remark was more of an accusation than a question, making Ella put up her guard. She set her coffee mug down at the side of her chair, the movement allowing her to turn her face till she'd worked out what to say.

'I could have been mistaken,' she said carefully.

'As could the professor, I suppose?' Patrick leaned a little towards her over the wooden arm of the chair. 'You know you weren't mistaken, you *knew* it was her. You were so certain, so sure, that you went home and told your sister all about it, hence that extraordinary conversation she and Valerie had on the beach. I've no doubt you told Andrew, too, and pointed the couple out.'

Ella flinched. 'You're quite wrong. I said nothing to Andrew. So, all right, yes, I did tell Kate, but twins have a habit of confiding in one another. I'm...sorry you had to find out.'

'You didn't think to tell *me*, I suppose?'

'No, of course not!' she flashed.

'Not even when you knew I was in the process of booking seats for a play that Valerie had already sat through with someone else?'

'No, not even then, and if Professor Moden had kept his mouth shut you'd never have known.'

'And that makes it right, does it?'

'Well...no,' Ella floundered.

'What it does, what it did, is open my eyes to one or two unpalatable faces *and* make me look a bloody fool, taking a farcical trip up to Town, wasting valuable time!'

'Well, I'm sorry about that.' His anger was catching, and Ella's own temper flared. 'But it's nothing, *nothing* to do with me, and I won't take the blame. And how dare you come over and sit in my garden and hector me like this? If you want to pick a quarrel go and pick it with her…go and pick it with Valerie!'

'I already have!'

'Good, well, now perhaps you'll leave!'

He sprang up, his chair skittering back on the patio tiles—a tall, haughty man with a face like flint, his arms straight down at his sides. He stood facing her, facing the house, completely unmoving. It was Ella who saw Valerie come through the wicket gate, half walking, half running, calling Patrick's name. He wheeled round, stared for a second, then went to meet her.

'What is it? What's wrong? Is it Robin?' He reached her as she was hanging onto the greenhouse door.

'It's Mother. A phone call just now. She died an hour ago!'

Ella was just in time to hear her gasped words and Patrick's reply. 'Oh, my God!' He held Valerie, keeping her upright.

'I have to go down there…now, Pat!'

'Yes, yes, all right. I'll drive you. Now, come along.' He was taking her back through the gate, turning a worried face in Ella's direction when she said how sorry she was.

Half an hour later she saw them drive off, Patrick at the wheel of Valerie's car. Then Barbara came over, bringing two subdued children with her.

'I felt so sorry for Miss Trentham. Such a shock…just

when it seemed that her mother was going on well.'
Barbara's thin fingers raked through her fringe. 'It's terrible to lose your mother. I know how I felt when mine died.'

Secure in the knowledge that she still had both parents, and with her eye on the children who were half-heartedly playing clock golf, Ella agreed it was awful, and she *was* sorry for Valerie. Even so, the image that flicked in front of her eyes all day was of Patrick with his arms round Valerie, speaking softly to her, comforting her in a way that surely only a lover could. He was coming back from Wiltshire by rail on Sunday, Barbara had told her that. 'He'll be exhausted, poor man, then there's all his patients to see to on Monday!'

Barbara was in and out of Longmead all over the weekend. 'I can't settle,' she said. 'I have this horrible feeling that everything's going to change.'

Paul drove Kate home before breakfast on Monday. With the journey to Town ahead of him, he stayed only long enough to set her bag down in the hall and wave a greeting to Ella. Kate would be joining him for good on Saturday. With their parents arriving on Friday night, she would just have time to explain all to them before she set off.

Ella told her about Valerie's mother but, immersed as she was in her own happiness, she showed scant interest. 'Oh, well.' She shrugged. 'That's likely to result in two things—clip her wings for a bit and reconcile her with Patrick. How he stood her behaviour on Friday night, I'll never know! Of course...' And now a canny expression crossed her pretty face. 'Of course, she could have something *on* Patrick that we don't know about!'

'What on earth do you mean?' Ella stared at her.

'Well…' Kate straightened up from the fridge, a carton of juice in her hand. 'Have you ever considered that she could be Robin's mother?'

'*What?*'

'Think about it.'

'She's his *god*mother!' Ella lowered herself onto a chair.

'Yes, well, maybe, but *I* think she could be his natural mother. She and Patrick could be Mum and Dad!'

'How *can* they be?' Ella's head whirled.

'Usual way.' Kate grinned. 'Maybe she and Patrick had a little adulterous fling, with Robin as the result. Perhaps Patrick's wife couldn't have kids, perhaps they arranged to take the child over, bring it up. Perhaps they took him over right from birth.'

'I don't believe it… I don't believe it could happen… I don't believe any woman, any wife, would take on a child that her husband had made with someone else as the result of an affair!'

'She might. *I* couldn't but, then, everyone's different.' Kate swallowed a mouthful of juice. Ella, with the feeling that she'd been struck on the head, struggled to sort out her thoughts.

'I don't believe it,' she said again, yet perhaps a small part of her did. 'No, I don't…I don't believe it. You read too many novels, Kate!'

'Have to, for a living.' Kate smiled gently. 'Anyway…' She settled herself more comfortably, she was almost smug today. 'How about your news? How are things between you and the ever-faithful Andrew? I suppose he *did* spend the night with his parents, not nip over here in the small hours, plighting his troth?'

'I feel nothing for Andrew but friendship, and he knows it, and so do you!' Ella heard the snap in her voice. This morning, right now, wasn't the time for teasing, she couldn't cope with it. 'I'm in love with Patrick,' she said more softly, swallowing against a lump in her throat the size of a cricket ball.

Kate's mouth gaped. 'Oh, hell, Ellie, I was so afraid of this!' Her drink spilt and she looked really upset.

'Well, don't go on about it.'

'I won't... I wasn't going to.' She came round the table to give her sister a kiss. 'All I want is for you to be as happy as I am, and I can't see it happening with him—he's got too much baggage. But perhaps I shouldn't have said what I did about Valerie being Robin's mother. You know what I am about jumping to conclusions. I could easily be wrong.'

CHAPTER TWELVE

SHE'S wrong, she has to be, Ella was thinking as she drove to her first antenatal appointment of the day. Kate simply couldn't help adding two and two together and coming up with six. True, Patrick was a passionate man, but he was honourable, too. Once married he would never have cheated on his wife…*never*, she was sure of that. But supposing his marriage hadn't been happy…just suppose…but, no, she wouldn't, she wouldn't suppose anything! Whatever was she thinking about?

She saw him at the hospital on Tuesday, having a cup of coffee with Sister Martin in her office. It was eleven a.m. and Ella was on the point of leaving when Sister called out to her, 'Come and join us, dear, unless you're in a rush. Ella has been here since eight,' she told Patrick. 'We had four births in the night, one a breech. Bill Corby was called out at dawn.'

'Glad it wasn't me,' Patrick said, pulling out a chair for Ella.

'I was just asking Mr Weston…' Sister passed Ella's cup over '…how Miss Trentham was. It's a difficult time between a death and the funeral, I always think.' Ella agreed, Patrick nodded.

'She's still very shocked,' he said.

'I'm sure you didn't like leaving her.'

'No,' was Patrick's short answer, accompanied by a frown. Ella was aware of his every movement, even that of his coffee trying to get down his throat. 'How have things been with you?' he addressed Ella directly.

'Much as usual, thanks.' But how stilted she sounded. We might as well be strangers, she thought.

He excused himself and went off, and Ella was just about to follow suit when Sister told her that the funeral was on Friday. 'He's taking that little boy with him. I don't agree with that—a funeral and all that goes with it is no place for a child.'

'He must have a reason. Perhaps Val...Miss Trentham wants him there,' Ella said carefully, whilst the seed Kate had sewn about Robin's possible parentage struggled to take root.

'He said the child wants to go, and he wants him with him. They seem...' Sister took Ella's empty cup '...very close knit—the three of them, I mean. Nice to see it these days.'

'Yes, it is.' Ella wanted to escape, and did so by mentioning the list of antenatals she'd got to get through before lunch.

Her first port of call was midway between Charding and Easthaven, and was to a Miss Stephanie Biggs in her thirtieth week of pregnancy. Stephanie, although otherwise well, was suffering from early morning attacks of cramp.

'It grips my calves, it's agonising, and sometimes takes ages to shift. I get out of bed, and hang onto something, and try to make it move. Eventually it goes, but it seems to be happening most mornings now.'

'Yes, troublesome, and it's due to lack of calcium,' Ella explained. 'As the baby grows he's taking more and more calcium from you. You need to increase your intake in some way, either by taking a milk drink at bedtime, with extra skimmed milk whisked into it, or eating a little yoghurt or cottage cheese on a dry biscuit.'

'I don't like any of those.' Stephanie pulled a disgusted face. 'If I must, I'll try the milky drink. I mean, it's not for ever, is it?'

'No, but it's not very pleasant forcing yourself.' Ella smiled sympathetically. 'I think the best thing would be for you to see your GP. It's Dr Mason, isn't it?' She was looking at Stephanie's notes. 'Tell him what you've told me, and I'm pretty sure he'll write you up for some calcium tablets to take.'

'Oh, I think I'll do that.' The woman looked relieved.

'Meantime, I'll have a word with him when I'm at the centre,' Ella said.

After a hurried lunch at the centre, working through another set of visits, followed by a midwives' meeting, Ella was free to go home. Patrick's car passed her with a little toot on its horn along the coast road, and as she drove up the hill and swung the wheel to turn into Longmead's drive, he emerged from his driveway and waited for her to get out.

'I was hoping to catch you.' He pulled at his jacket which had blown back in the wind, a wind that was blowing his hair across his forehead, giving him a dishevelled look. He looked distraught, too, and worried. Ella's heart went out to him.

'Nothing wrong, I hope?' The words sounded offhand even to her ears, but she was wondering what she was about to hear and was unconsciously bracing herself.

'Something I'd like to put right, actually.' He halted a pace or two from her. 'I'd like to apologise for my rudeness on Saturday.'

'Oh, but, Patrick—' she was surprised and showed it '—that didn't matter in the least!'

'I blamed you for things,' he went on, 'that don't seem to matter now, but my rudeness still does, and I'm sorry. I had the manners of an oaf.'

'I'd forgotten all about it,' she said, not quite truthfully, but managing to smile at him.

He didn't smile back, and she felt she had probably made the wrong sort of response, and was searching her mind for a better way of putting it when he went on to ask how Kate was. 'Have things turned out as planned?'

'If you mean is she going back to Paul, yes, she leaves here for good on Saturday. Our parents are coming on Friday night for a stay of three weeks so it'll be all going and coming.' Her lips were sticking to her teeth. 'And you're going off again on Thursday, I think Sister Martin mentioned…'

'Ready for my aunt-in-law's funeral on Friday. Yes, I am. I'll be away and I'm taking Robin with me. Valerie will want to see him. We'll be home on Thursday evening, all being well.'

'I hope everything goes off all right, and have a safe journey,' Ella said, backing a little away from him to lift her garage door. She daren't stay near him, she daren't just stay there or she'd fling herself into his arms, or put hers right round him and tell him she loved him, no matter what.

'Thanks for everything,' she heard him say, then off he went, greeted at the bottom of his drive by Robin, who'd come running out.

'He sounded as though he was going away for ever,' Ella remarked to Kate later.

'He's got a lot on his mind, perhaps more than we realise.' Kate gave her a searching look. 'He'll be back and so will Madam…eventually, I suppose, although probably not for a week or two. When someone's died there's masses to do.'

Ella knew this only too well, and fleetingly her mind went back to those dreadful weeks just after Tom had died.

But *this* week, as she'd told Patrick it would be, really was a time of much coming and going.

Late on Friday the parents arrived, having taken it in turns to drive during the long journey from Inveray. At midday on Saturday Paul arrived to fetch Kate—they were each driving their own cars and would travel in convoy to Surrey. Ella felt very emotional when it was time to say goodbye.

'You'll take care of her, won't you?' she said to Paul, biting back the words 'this time'. Their mother, Iris Nevill was also sceptical about the possible outcome, but their father, Charles, after a good night's rest and a cooked breakfast inside him, was more cheerful than the others, although even he did a fair bit of nose-blowing as the cars set off.

During the days that followed Ella invited Barbara over to Longmead once or twice, for she must have felt strange being at Drummers on her own, with only a heavily pregnant Lucy for company. Ella's parents liked her, and always made her welcome. Mrs Nevill had taken over the running of the household as though it was still her own which, of course, as Ella realised, was technically the case.

'Your mother gives me the impression that she'd like to move back here,' Barbara said one evening when she'd been over to supper. Ella thought the same, and said so.

'Well, they only rent the house they're living in up in

Scotland,' Ella said, 'and as Dad and she still own Longmead, they could slot back in if they liked.'

'How would you feel if they did?'

Ella shrugged. 'I honestly don't know. I can't see myself, at twenty-eight, wanting to live with my parents. It wouldn't be good for Hannah either, not in the long term. Still, I'm not crossing any bridges yet. It may never happen, as Tom used to say.'

Things began to happen with Lucy on Thursday afternoon, and at six o'clock, soon after Ella got home, Barbara rang through to say that she thought the little dog had started to whelp. 'She keeps rubbing her back on the side of her box, and she's tearing papers up. I suppose—' Barbara sounded apologetic '—you couldn't come over, could you?'

'Yes, of course. I'll come now,' Ella said at once. Then with a word to her mother, who was making preparations for supper, she slipped through the hedge and round to Drummers's kitchen door.

There was no doubt at all that Lucy was having contractions, for she was panting and straining and giving little yelps. When she saw Ella she ran to her, then went quickly back into her box. Barbara, kneeling beside her, looked troubled. 'Do you think we should call Mr Savers…I mean, bearing in mind her age?'

'Animals usually cope on their own,' Ella said, 'and Andrew will be in the middle of evening surgery now.' On the other hand… She looked at Lucy. Supposing something went wrong? Being a 'human' midwife in this sort of situation might not help a dog. The birth process wasn't exactly the same, and how do I know that Lucy's heart will stand up to all the trauma? she thought. The little dog vomited suddenly, and that was it. Ella reached

for her mobile and punched out the surgery number.
Miss Remer answered and put her through to Andrew
straight away. 'Be with you in fifteen minutes,' he said.
'I'm just on my last patient.'

When he arrived he went straight to Lucy, assessing
her condition, speaking gently to her.

He looked at Barbara. 'I'll need a bowl of hot water,
soap, more paper, towels and a pair of sharp scissors—
a dustbin bag, too, if you've got one. Ah, here we go,
here comes the first pup in its membranous sac, which
Lucy tore off herself. Severing the cord, she licked her
baby, rough-housing it round the box till it squeaked.
Andrew examined it to make sure its airways was clear.

'A boy,' he announced, 'and, as you see, black...
undoubtedly Merlin's son!' It found its blind way to a
teat without trouble.

Lucy, looking dazed, stared at it sleepily, seemed to
nod off, then fifteen minutes later produced another with
far less effort, but left Andrew to tear off the sac.
Severing the cord with the scissors Ella held out, he gave
her the pup to dry. 'Rub it vigorously, then put your
finger into its mouth, and as soon as you feel it suck,
put it to a teat.'

Ella did so. She was beginning to enjoy herself—it
was a change from her ordinary work!

'This one's also male,' she said to Barbara, 'and fawn,
like his Mum!'

'Like Lucy, Robin will be pleased.' Barbara, also under Andrew's orders, was clearing the mess away, whilst
he, after sponging Lucy, slipped a square of old, worn
sheepskin under her and her pups. It was five minutes
later, when he was washing at the sink and preparing to
leave, that they heard the sound of a car in the drive.
'That will be Mr Weston and Robin!' Barbara looked

relieved. Out into the hall she strode to open wide the front door.

Standing in the kitchen, Ella and Andrew could hear Patrick's voice, then Robin's, then Barbara's...'Two lovely boy puppies, Robin—come and see!' There was no other voice, no sound of Valerie. Ella just had time to register this before they were in the kitchen. She seemed to see them through a kind of haze, the tall man in light trousers and sweater, the small boy in jeans— Patrick and Robin, Patrick and son—the latter now kneeling by the puppy-box, speechless and awestruck.

'Oh Dad,' he managed at last, 'come and look!'

Patrick did, squatting down on his haunches, giving Ella the chance to study his back view—the bent head, the broad sweep of shoulders, the neat male behind, and the litheness of him as he sprang up, facing them all again. 'I can see it was a case of all hands to the pump— two professional ladies and a full-blown veterinary surgeon!' He was smiling and looking at Ella.

'I called Ella, and she called Mr Savers, we thought it best,' Barbara said, just as the front doorbell pealed, making Lucy, weary though she was, give a little woof.

'I'll go,' Robin said, flying off into the hall. Seconds later he was back, showing Ella's mother, her attractive face flushed, into the crowded kitchen. Her eyes—brown hazel like Ella's—alighted on her daughter. 'I didn't know what to do about supper—' she began, but was interrupted by Ella, who introduced her to Patrick.

'Mummy, this is Mr Weston, and this is Robin.'

Her eyes widened. 'Oh, but of course, you've just got home, haven't you? I thought I saw you come! What a long journey you've had...so tiring, I always think! And hello, Robin.' She bent down, hands on her knees, to greet him.

'Would you like to see my puppies?' He moved aside to allow her to look down and see into the box.

'They look sweet!' she exclaimed dutifully, 'and so *newborn*. I expect you helped Andrew deliver them, Ella.' Pride was strong in her voice.

'Barbara and I were handmaidens only!' Ella flicked a glance at Patrick.

'Lucy was brilliant.' Andrew was edging doorwards. He wanted to be off, Ella could see that plainly enough, and when Robin yawned, leaning tiredly back against his father, it was the cue for them all to shift.

'So good to have met you, Mr Weston.' Iris beamed at him. 'You must come over and meet my husband whilst we're here.'

'Thank you, I'd like that.' In the dimness of the hall he passed her to open the front door.

'And bring Robin, of course. I believe he and my little granddaughter have become firm friends.'

'They have, and I'm glad,' Patrick said with conviction, watching Andrew making tracks for his car, watching Ella halfway down the drive, turning to wait for her mother.

'What a charming man!' Iris exclaimed when they were back in their own domain. 'And young, too. Somehow I expected a much older man.'

'He's thirty-eight.'

'As I said, young.' Iris turned the gas up under the potato saucepan, whilst Ella, unable to settle, stared out into the garden, her thoughts still next door. What had happened? What was happening? Would Valerie be back?

At the hospital next morning Ella learned that Patrick had arrived at eight o'clock and was, according to Bill

Corby, gowned up and in Theatre by half past nine. He didn't get home until nine in the evening either. Both Ella and her mother saw the car turn into the drive next door.

'I expect he's had a lot to catch up on,' Iris said, drawing the curtains now that there was nothing interesting to see.

Ella was quiet, dwelling on what Hannah had said at bedtime. She had told her mother that after all the thrill of seeing the puppies she and Robin had had their lunch in the den. 'Granny and Barbara brought it out to us, we pretended it was a hotel. Robin stayed at one when he was away, his daddy took him.'

Ella, alerted, stopped folding her clothes. 'That was nice for him,' she said, going on to ask if Valerie went as well, immediately hating herself for pumping her child.

'No.' Hannah slid under the duvet. 'She's going away. Robin says he won't see her for a long time, his daddy told him so.'

'Oh, poor Robin, that's sad for him.' A longing to know more seized Ella. What did all this mean?

'He didn't seem to mind... *I* would, though.' Hannah looked disturbed. Then she sat bolt upright, pulling at her mother's arm. 'Mummy, you wouldn't ever leave, would you...you wouldn't go away?'

'Sweetheart, never...never, *never*!' Ella snatched the child to her. 'I shall always be here for you,' she promised, '*always*, no matter what!'

Reassured, the little girl had settled down to sleep, but what Ella wondered as she joined her mother downstairs was what did it all mean about Valerie having gone away. Perhaps, tomorrow being Saturday, Patrick would come over to see her. Perhaps her mother would *ask* him over. Perhaps she could give her a broad hint. Unfortunately, as it turned out, everyone seemed to have made their own plans for the day.

Her mother and Barbara were taking the children to the Charding carnival during the afternoon. Her father was going to London to meet an erstwile dental colleague, and during the morning, when Robin came over to call for Hannah, he told Ella that Barbara and his father were busy upstairs…changing all the furniture around, getting ready for the painters. 'It looks all different, Ella, and Daddy's covered in dust.'

Hannah came running from the house at this point and the two of them squeezed through the hedge to play in the den. Iris was busy baking and, with no shopping or washing to do, Ella decided to cut the grass. As she walked up and down with the mower, she could see Patrick and Barbara working upstairs next door. The windows were wide open, which didn't surprise her in the least. It was a warm morning—a scorcher, in fact—and even the children looked hot and bothered when they came hurrying back through the hedge.

'You haven't been long.' She switched off the mower.

'Boys came—' Robin began.

'*Men* came,' Hannah interrupted. 'They had bows and arrows, like Robin Hood!'

'Oh, I see, those kind of men!' Ella smiled to herself. They were figments of their imagination, of course, she had heard it all before. Even so, when her mother called them in for a bun and orange squash, she took a quick look down the length of Drummers's garden, just to make sure nothing was amiss. Nothing was. The garden was empty, the door of the den was closed, there was no sign of Robin Hood!

Flopping down into an old deckchair she had found

in the garden shed, Ella continued to keep Patrick's upper windows in sight. Would he be working up there all the afternoon? Even if he didn't, there was no reason why he should come to see her. He was attracted to her, she knew that, she couldn't help knowing that after some of the things he'd said. Even if he and Valerie had split up for good, and she didn't know that for sure, he might not be attracted *enough* to want to get involved with her. Who am I kidding, for goodness' sake? she silently asked herself. But she still kept looking at those windows just the same—just to catch a glimpse of him.

When she first smelt burning she thought he and Barbara were getting rid of some rubbish. The smell grew stronger and there was the sound of crackling, like the sound of burning wood. Getting to her feet, she looked through the hedge. Her heart leapt into her mouth. The den was burning…the den was alight…its closed door was ringed with flames! Even as she looked…even as she stared…a billow of fire shot through its roof, and she was tearing through the hedge, shouting at the screaming children to stay where they were, just as Patrick dashed from the house, making…oh, God, no, no…making for the den, thinking the children were inside.

Ella had never moved quicker, never been so galvanised. With a yell she launched herself straight across the garden, straight in front of him. The impact when he hit her, when the two of them collided, when they crashed to the ground, stunned every thought in her head but the need to gasp that the children were safe. 'Not in there…not in there…don't go near!'

She didn't quite faint, but black curtains came creeping across her vision, blurring his face, blurring the garden and the fiercely burning den. She knew they were both on their feet, and that he was helping her into the house…that the children were there, secured by her mother, and that Patrick was easing her down on the couch in his sitting-room. His voice, his face, his breathing were close, everything else swam back. His lips were moving, she could see them.

'If you're asking if I'm all right, I don't know. What about you?' As she started to speak so did her strength return and everything became clear. Hannah climbed onto the couch with her, and she held her close. Iris, for some reason, was glaring at Patrick whilst Barbara, always one to be on the safe side, was dialling 999.

Remembering the children's story of men coming into the garden, Ella recounted this to Patrick. 'I should have checked more thoroughly, but I thought they were making things up.'

'So long as everyone's safe, nothing else matters a jot.' Ella's hand was fast in his.

'What I want to know is…' Iris turned a blaming face to his. 'How you came to fall over Ella. Couldn't you have looked where you were going?'

'Mum, for goodness' sake…' Ella started to say, but Patrick silenced her.

'Mrs Nevill, I saw the shed alight, I thought the children were inside it. I could hear them screaming, I thought they were in there, I was running at full pelt. I didn't even *see* Ella! What she did was deliberate. She was trying to trip me, she was trying to stop me from opening the den door and getting burnt to a chip!'

Ella gasped, her mother subsided, the fire engine arrived, jolting up the rutted lane that led to the wicket gate. Two able young men doused the small inferno in a matter of minutes. Two police officers—a man and a woman—spoke briefly to them, then came up to the house.

Questions were asked, and answered. Patrick apologised for having called them out for a simple thing like a shed. 'Shed or not, sir, arson is a serious crime,' the male officer said. He had children of his own, and had soon extracted from an awed Robin and Hannah the information that the garden intruders had been 'big boys with dirty hair'. 'We've had one or two complaints just lately about youths hanging around back gardens. But we're pretty sure we've identified the culprits. You won't have any more trouble.'

After he and his female colleague had gone, and the fire engine had reversed down the lane, they all—Patrick, Ella and the children, Iris and Barbara—went down to the bottom of the garden to see what was left of the den. It didn't amount to very much, just its concrete base and a few blackened stumps sticking up like teeth. The air was still full of woodsmoke, little tissue-papery flakes fluttered about the lawn. It was a truly depressing sight. Robin's face was suffused and brick red. He was trying not to cry, whilst Hannah was sobbing her heart out, hiding her face against her mother.

'I think Ella should rest,' Iris said, plucking at her daughter's arm—the one that wasn't tucked in Patrick's—then with a smile for Barbara, whose prompt action she thoroughly approved of, and shepherding Ella and Hannah before her, she went out by the wicket gate.

'Will Robin's daddy build another den for Robin?' Hannah asked at lunchtime.

'Perhaps…I don't know,' Ella answered absently, thinking about the way Patrick had been—so concerned for her. She could still feel not so much the awful jolt of the collision as the touch of his hand and arm afterwards, the reassuring warmth of his dear, near presence as he'd leaned over her on the couch. It was true she felt sore and shaken up, as though she'd been charged by a tank. She would have bruises by morning. But who cared? For all this meant…surely it meant that Patrick would come over to see her this afternoon.

When her mother announced that nothing would induce her to go to the carnival as planned, Ella practically pleaded with her not to let the children down. 'They need a treat after what happened this morning, and I know Barbara wants to go.'

'But you might faint again, here on your own. You've had a nasty shock.'

'I shan't faint. I'm quite all right. Please, Mummy, *go*!'

She agreed at last, and the four of them set off just after two. Barbara was taking them in her Renault. Ella saw them drive off from her bedroom window when she was changing her jeans and trainers for a sundress and sandals. She was just about to leave the bedroom when the sound of another car coming out of Drummers caught her attention. It was Patrick, he was turning into the road, *he was going out*! Sharp disappointment, disbelief, hit her in waves. She'd been so sure he would come…that he'd want to come over and see her.

Depressed, miserable, lonely even, she trailed out into the garden, dropping down into the ancient deckchair she'd sat in that morning. The grass was only half-mowed, she had never finished it. Unable to relax, she jumped up and switched on the mower. I'll do it now *and* trim the edges, and when I've done that I'll go round to the front and do the same there! She thought to herself. She was angry and uptight, and she was still angry when, half an hour later, Patrick in shorts and a blue and white T-shirt shouldered his way through the hedge.

'Oh, hello.' She feigned surprise. Well, she *was* surprised. With the clatter of the mower, and her angry absorption, she hadn't heard him coming.

'It's far too hot for that kind of job.' He frowned down at the mower.

'Yes, it is. I'll leave off, I think.' She could hardly believe he had come, she could hardly believe he was actually here, standing in front of her. He was wearing sunglasses so she couldn't see his eyes, but she thought his face looked strained.

They went to sit on the grass by the greenhouse, which gave a little shade. 'I saw you go out earlier,' she said, then stopped, feeling foolish. Now he'd think she'd been spying on him.

'Yes, I took the pups and Lucy down to be vetted. Andrew opened up the surgery especially for me.'

'Are they all right?'

'Splendid, and Andrew was amazed at Lucy. We're keeping the fawn pup, and I'm hoping to interest my parents in the black one. Anyway, that's enough about canines. I want to know how *you* are—you took quite a bang, you know.'

'So did you.'

'And I haven't even thanked you.' He turned to look at her, sitting bolt upright, his legs flexed, his arms about his knees. She stared at his legs, at his hands, at his arms, she longed to be touched by him.

'No need for thanks.' She sounded airy. 'You know what all rescuers say, "I acted on the spur of the moment, valour didn't come into it".'

He took off his glasses and laid them on the grass. He didn't laugh as she'd intended. He looked stern and anxious, and seemed to be searching for words. 'Look, Ella,' he began at last, 'I've come to tell you that Valerie and I are going our separate ways. She's going to the States to practise at a clinic there in partnership with an American who's been over here for six months. I met him at the funeral and it was fairly obvious they were more than would-be colleagues, I'm afraid. Valerie and I had been coming apart at the seams for quite some time. We finally split up for good on the day of the party.'

Ella knew she ought to say she was sorry, but the words stuck in her throat. 'But you must have loved her once, or…'

'Not enough,' he said. 'We became close through circumstances, and we knew one another well. When Rob was born Evelyn was ill for a very long time. Val pitched in and helped her *and* me—she was working in London then. When, five years later, Evelyn was killed, she was there for Rob and me.'

So she wasn't Robin's mother, Ella was thinking. I knew she couldn't be, I just *knew* it.

'Robin will have to see her sometimes, when she comes back to England on visits. When he's older, perhaps he can visit her in America. She's still his aunt.'

'Of course, yes.' A kind of constraint fell upon them then, and over the whole garden. Through the greenhouse door the smell of ripening tomatoes hung about like a pall. The silence became oppressive then, as though from some sort of signal, both of them began to speak at once.

'But why have you—?'

'What I want to know is—'

Their voices rang out as one, then with a single sweeping movement of his arm Patrick brought Ella close to him, pressing her head into the hollow of his shoulder, laying his face on her hair.

'I love you, Ella, that's what I've really come to say. I've loved you from the first moment I set eyes on you, and it's been driving me crazy ever since! I never thought I *could* fall in love again, I never thought it was possible!' He shifted a little, tilting her chin, making her look at him. 'I love you more than I've ever loved anyone. What do you feel for me?' His eyes were loving, searching and anxious.

'I adore you!' she cried, and remembered that he'd once said that to her, and she'd thought he'd been flirting, but now... Her heart filled... He really loved her. He was sitting here, telling her so. 'Dearest Patrick.' She touched his face. 'I've loved you since Hannah's birthday, when Mrs Parks gave birth in my hall!'

'Only since then?'

'Well, maybe before!'

He was laying her back on the grass. 'Sweet Ella.' He lay beside her, his face an inch from hers. His hands, skilful and warm, caressed her body, sending her into delight. She had known he would be skilful, she had known he would be gentle, she longed for him to go on but when he stopped for a second, his eyes questioning hers, she shook her head and sat up. 'I love you, I want you, but not here, not now.' She almost sobbed out the words.

'Dear one, it's all right... I know what you mean, it's not the right time or place.' He smoothed her hair from her face. 'Perhaps we could manage to wait a week, until next weekend, if we can both be free. We could go to Aldeburgh to see my parents, put up at a hotel and make love all night and all day if we liked.'

'Yes, oh, yes!'

'And when we come back, we'll get married as soon as we can, that is, of course…' he kissed her nose '…if you can manage to break your vow of not getting married for years.'

She said she thought she could, just for him, then with their arms about one another, they went into the cool of the house to wait for the family to come home.

After they married they lived at Drummers, which delighted Hannah. 'When Patrick makes another den it'll be mine as well,' she said.

Robin's comment was rather different and came some weeks afterwards. 'It feels like having a proper Mum, now you're here all the time,' he told Ella seriously.

During the next five years Ella and Patrick had two more children—a boy first, and then a girl. Barbara stayed on as housekeeper. Ella still worked, but part time only. It was a busy household, but with the parents next door—for they had moved back to Longmead—there was no shortage of babysitters, and things had worked out pretty well.

'Do you realise,' Patrick said, as they strolled in the garden one evening in late September, 'in two years' time we'll have been married seven years, and you know what they say about the seven-year itch!' He turned to grin at her.

'We won't even *think* about it,' Ella retorted.

And they never, ever did.

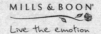

MILLS & BOON®

0606/01b

Live the emotion

Modern
romance™

THE MEDITERRANEAN MILLIONAIRE'S MISTRESS *by Maggie Cox*

When Lysander Rosakis meets beautiful Ianthe Dane on a Greek holiday, he neglects to tell her that he is a multi-millionaire. Is she in too deep? Not knowing that there is more to be revealed, Ianthe must decide whether to stay, or to turn and walk away...

BY ROYAL DEMAND *by Robyn Donald*

Gabe Considine, Grand Duke of Illyria, needs revenge. He believes his whirlwind fiancée, Sara Milton, stole a priceless heirloom from him and betrayed him with another man. Now Gabe wants his pride – and his property – back! If he has to seduce Sara into submission, he will...

IN THE VENETIAN'S BED *by Susan Stephens*

Nell is helpless to resist Luca Barbaro's brand of raw sexuality, but she can never forgive his brutality of years ago. Until they meet again in Venice, not as Luca and Nell, but as two masked strangers in the grip of pure, irresistible attraction...

A FORBIDDEN PASSION *by Carla Cassidy*

Talbot McCarthy was the only man who fired Elizabeth's passion. He was also her ex-husband's brother, so Elizabeth avoided him. But when Talbot offered his plane to bring her missing son home, and circumstances conspired against them, Elizabeth realised they had to hide their feelings – at all costs...

On sale 7th July 2006

Available at WHSmith, Tesco, ASDA, Borders, Eason, Sainsbury's and most bookshops

www.millsandboon.co.uk

THE HEIR'S CHOSEN BRIDE *by Marion Lennox*

As a widow and single mum, Susan is wary about meeting
Hamish Douglas, the man who has inherited the castle where
she and her small daughter live. Surely he'll want to sell up?
Hamish had planned to turn the castle into a luxury hotel
– until he met the beautiful Susie…

THE MILLIONAIRE'S CINDERELLA WIFE
by Lilian Darcy

Many women lust after millionaire Ty Garrett. Sierra has one
problem with that – he is her husband! Sierra wants a divorce
– but Ty has a suggestion. To deter all the lusting females
will Sierra stay for a while? Will she give their love a second
chance?

THEIR UNFINISHED BUSINESS *by Jackie Braun*

Even after ten years Ali Conlan's heart still beat strongly for
the man who had left her – and her body still responded to his
bad-boy confidence and winning smile. His visit to Trillium
was for business…but perhaps they could resolve their own
unfinished business?

THE TYCOON'S PROPOSAL *by Leigh Michaels*

When Lissa Morgan takes a two-week live-in job, she doesn't
realise that she will be in close proximity to Kurt Callahan
– the man who had broken her heart years before when she
discovered he had dated her for a bet! Can Lissa forgive and
forget…?

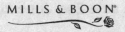

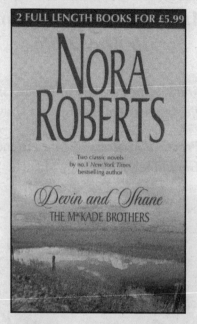

The child she loves…is his child.

And now he knows…

THE SEVEN YEAR SECRET BY ROZ DENNY FOX

Mallory Forester's daughter needs a transplant. But there's only one person left to turn to – Liddy's father. Mallory hasn't seen Connor in seven years, and now she has to tell him he's a father…with a chance to save his daughter's life!

HIS DADDY'S EYES BY DEBRA SALONEN

Judge Lawrence Bishop spent a weekend in the arms of a sexy stranger two years ago and he's been looking for her ever since. He discovers she's dead, but *her baby son* is living with his aunt, Sara Carsten. Ren does the maths and realises he's got to see pretty Sara, talk to her and go from there…

Look for more *Little Secrets* coming in August!

On sale 7th July 2006

www.millsandboon.co.uk

FROM *SUNDAY TIMES* BESTSELLING AUTHOR PENNY JORDAN

They had shattered her past.
Now she would destroy their futures.

Pepper Minesse exuded sexuality and power. She presented a challenge men wished they could master. But Pepper had paid dearly for her success. For ten years, her thirst for revenge had fuelled her ambition and made her rich.

Now it was time for the four men who had taken something infinitely precious from her to pay too – their futures for her shattered past.

On sale 7th July 2006

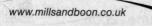

"I was fifteen when my mother finally told me the truth about my father. She didn't mean to. She meant to keep it a secret forever. If she'd succeeded it might have saved us all."

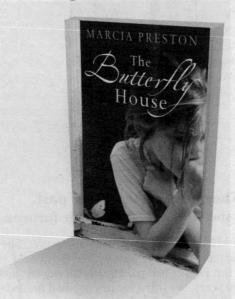

MARCIA PRESTON

The *Butterfly* House

When a hauntingly familiar stranger knocks on Roberta Dutreau's door, she is compelled to begin a journey of self-discovery leading back to her childhood. But is she ready to know the truth about what happened to her, her best friend Cynthia and their mothers that tragic night ten years ago?

16th June 2006

MIRA